Dear Reader,

Thanks to your overwhelming response, Harlequin Historicals is very proud to present our third holiday volume, *Historical Christmas Stories* 1991. This year, our three talented authors have ventured from Victorian England to the American Revolution and the days of the California boom towns to bring you their heartwarming tales.

Lynda Trent, Caryn Cameron and DeLoras Scott have each included one of their favorite holiday recipes and a personal remembrance of Christmas for you to enjoy.

At this time, all of us at Harlequin Historicals would like to offer you our best wishes for the new year, and our hope that your holiday season is one of miracles, great and small.

Sincerely,

Tracy Farrell
Senior Editor

Harlequin
HISTORICAL

CHRISTMAS

STORIES · 1991

LYNDA TRENT
CARYN CAMERON
DELORAS SCOTT

Harlequin Books

TORONTO • NEW YORK • LONDON
AMSTERDAM • PARIS • SYDNEY • HAMBURG
STOCKHOLM • ATHENS • TOKYO • MILAN

Harlequin Historicals first edition November 1991

ISBN 0-373-83225-7

Harlequin Historical Christmas Stories 1991
Copyright © 1991 by Harlequin Enterprises Limited.

The publisher acknowledges the copyright holders of
the individual work as follows:

Christmas Yet To Come
Copyright © 1991 by Dan and Lynda Trent

A Season of Joy
Copyright © 1991 by Caryn Cameron

Fortune's Gift
Copyright © 1991 by DeLoras Scott

Printed in U.S.A.

CONTENTS

CHRISTMAS YET TO COME

Lynda Trent

When it comes to Christmas dinner, we've done the baked turkey and dressing from time to time, but one year, it was medieval foods (which the kids hated), and last year, it was take-out barbecue (which the kids all raved over, though I secretly believe the praise was a ploy to keep me from cooking the medieval foods again). Christmas is always full of surprises around our house.

Several years ago, in my quest for a Christmas cookie with a difference, I came across the following traditional Russian recipe for peppernuts. Because my family and friends enjoy them, these cookies may become another Christmas tradition for us.

PEPPERNUTS

1½ cups sugar
1 cup margarine
1 egg
½ tsp vanilla (older recipes call for ½ tsp oil of anise)
2 tbsp light corn syrup
2 tsp baking soda
1 tsp cloves
1 tsp ginger
3½ cups flour

Cream margarine and sugar until fluffy. Add the egg. Add the liquids. Set aside.

Sift the dry ingredients together. Add half the mixture to the liquids, stir, mix in the remaining dry ingredients. Knead well. Place dough in tightly covered container and store in refrigerator at least overnight.

Roll dough into thin ropes and slice into pieces about the size of an acorn. Put the pieces on a greased cookie sheet and bake at 350° F for 7 to 10 minutes. Bake longer if you prefer crunchy cookies, less to make them more chewy. Remove cookies from pan while still hot and roll in mixture of cinnamon and sugar.

Chapter One

London, 1860

A glance at the mantel clock told Angelica Hamilton that she would be late again. Not that there was any special reason for being on time at Phoebe's house today, but her sister would no doubt tease her, and their mother would give her that where-did-I-go-wrong look.

Miss Ida Lunt, the spinster who was detaining Angelica, pressed her handkerchief once again to her beak of a nose. "It's this dreadful weather," she said in a congested voice. "It hasn't been above freezing since the beginning of November, and here it is nearly Christmas."

"It's the coldest year I can remember," Angelica agreed. "Now, about this room I have for rent..."

Miss Lunt shook her head mournfully. "As if you had seen many winters at your age. Just wait until you have as many years behind you as I have. As I was crossing London Bridge on my way here, I remarked to myself as how the Thames was frozen over earlier this year than ever. There will be many a river man without work for a spell." Rubbing the knuckles of her gloved hand, she added gloomily, "You can't imagine what it does to my rheumatism, and my poor chest is in a state."

"I could ask one of the Neville sisters to make you another cup of tea. Now, about the room—"

"No more tea for me, thank you, Mrs. Hamilton. I'll not be a bother."

"I think you will find my other boarders to be quite congenial," Angelica said. "You met the Neville sisters. My two male boarders live in the rooms toward the front of the house. As I mentioned, the room I showed you overlooks the back garden, and in the spring, it's quite lovely out there."

"The spring." Miss Lunt sighed. "The spring is to me what heaven must be to a sinner."

Angelica wasn't too sure how to answer this and, besides, she didn't want the conversation to take yet another turn away from the subject at hand as the clock was ticking the minutes away. "If the amount of rent is a problem, I could—"

"No, no. It's reasonable. Quite reasonable, really. Yes. Yes, I'll take it."

Angelica tried to hide the relief she felt—not only that the woman had at last made a decision, but that the room was finally rented. The room had been empty for a fortnight, and Angelica needed the extra income to keep the house running. Her money was scarce enough even when the house was full.

The house, a large one that had been built around the turn of the century by her deceased husband's grandparents, was beginning to show its age and, since Phillip's passing, the rough edge of genteel poverty as well. The gardens were no longer as well-kept as they once had been, and the shutters needed a coat of paint. Mr. Hart, the eldest of Angelica's boarders, now had the best room, the one she and Phillip had shared, overlooking the street. Her other male renter, Quinton Keyes, had the other large, upstairs front room. Both men had lived in her house for nearly three years. The Neville sisters occupied the back room across the hall from Mr. Keyes, and now, Ida Lunt would be in the smaller one between theirs and Angelica's.

The mantel clock pinged the half hour. Out of politeness, Angelica tried not to look at it or dwell on the fact that she was now an hour late.

"I presume I may move in at once?" Miss Lunt was saying. "Snow is threatening again, and I'm sure I'll have pneumonia if I have to be out in it."

"Of course you may." Angelica picked up two keys from the mantel and handed them to her. "The larger one is for your bedroom door. Most of us don't bother to lock our rooms, but the lock is there if you choose to use it."

"I certainly will use it. A woman alone can't be too careful. Especially not with male boarders under the same roof."

Angelica smiled. "You'll feel more at ease once you've met them. We're like a family here."

Miss Lunt didn't look convinced. "Nevertheless, my door will be locked at night, and so should yours be."

As graciously as she could, Angelica edged the woman from the front parlor into the foyer and at the front door, she handed Miss Lunt her woolen cloak and gloves from the hall tree.

"I'll have my things brought over this afternoon, if that's convenient?"

"That will be fine."

As if Miss Lunt were about to embark on an expedition into the Arctic, she took a deep breath of the warm air in the parlor and headed out the door. As soon as the woman was gone, Angelica lifted her skirts and ran to the kitchen. Peggy, the girl from the workhouse who Angelica had recently hired to work as cook and maid, looked up from stirring a pot of soup as Angelica breezed in, and Cecilia Neville paused in the act of pouring tea into her sister's teacup.

"Miss Lunt has taken the room!" Angelica announced.

"Thank heavens," Zenobia Neville said with relief.

"She seems pleasant enough," her sister said with a nod. "Doesn't she seem pleasant to you, Zenobia?"

Zenobia nodded, and her brown curls bounced in agreement. "Quite pleasant, Cecilia." To Angelica she added, "We've written Mother and Father and told them they must send the rent that's due you."

Cecilia nodded earnestly. "We were quite firm with them this time."

Angelica smiled at the sisters. They were new to London and neither was yet twenty. This was their first time away from home, and Angelica had concluded that their parents evidently adhered to the adage, "Out of sight, out of mind," because they rarely sent money for their daughters' support. Both girls worked at a nearby milliner's shop, but the pittance they earned didn't fully pay for the room they shared. Both had come to London anxiously seeking husbands, but so far, they had no prospects.

"You're not to worry about the rent money," Angelica told them. To Peggy she said, "Add another potato to the soup. I don't know if Miss Lunt will be here for supper or not, but it would be better to expect her and have too much than to run short of food. And this time, put in some salt and pepper."

Peggy, who rarely spoke, nodded her understanding.

Angelica added, "I took an extra quilt down for your bed. That basement can get so cold. If you're uncomfortable down there, you're to tell me. I can ask Mr. Hart and Quinton to bring your cot up here to the kitchen." After a moment, Peggy nodded again. The girl had been so painfully shy when she had come to work there that she had been in the house for two days before Angelica knew she could talk. Even now, the girl was still unusually quiet. Other than the fact that Peggy was Irish and might perhaps be as old as twelve, Angelica knew nothing about the girl. From among the girls at the workhouse, Angelica had chosen Peggy to be her maid because the girl had looked so pitifully thin, cold and miserable—and because the stern workhouse matron had advised against her.

"I have to hurry on to Phoebe's before she sends the carriage out to look for me," Angelica said. "Will you girls be able to get supper on the table?"

"Of course," Cecilia said. "You can depend on us." Zenobia's curls bobbed up and down again as she added her assent.

Angelica felt motherly toward the sisters as well as toward Peggy, even though she, herself, was barely five years older than Zenobia. For that matter, she felt protective toward all her boarders. Phoebe often teased her about being a mother hen to waifs of any age. Angelica could scarcely deny it.

"How do I look?" She ran her hands over her thick, auburn hair to be sure it was still neatly pinned into a bun.

"Your dress is beautiful," Zenobia said. "That shade of green is prefect for you."

"It doesn't make my hair look too red, does it?" After wearing the somber colors of mourning for so long, the dress seemed too bright, and this wasn't the first time she had been concerned about a green dress clashing with her hair color. But Phoebe had given her the material for the dress and the velvet to trim it, and Angelica wasn't about to let it go to waste.

"Zenobia is right," Cecilia echoed. "It's the perfect color for you. Wear the little brown hat trimmed in pheasant feathers. The one I made to go with your eyes."

"And brown gloves, of course," Zenobia put in.

"Of course." Cecilia smiled at her sister.

"All right. If the coal man comes, you'll find some money for him in the cracked sugar bowl in the pantry. Tell him I'll pay him the rest as soon as I get the rent from Miss Lunt. No, no, don't say that. He might think I won't be able to pay him. Just say he's to come by next week for the rest.'' Angelica smoothed her hands over her dress as the sisters nodded.

She hurried up the stairs to get her hat and gloves and to glance one last time in the cheval mirror. Maybe she should have overruled Phoebe and exchanged the bolt of green for a sensible brown. The green did look cheerful, however, and with Christmas right around the corner, it was time for a change.

At the hall tree in the foyer, Angelica paused, but only long enough to swirl her heavy, woolen cape around her shoulders and fasten the black frog braid at the neck. She glanced automatically at the landing where the grandfather clock had once stood. It was gone now—having been sold the year before to pay for the mending of the roof—but she had not yet broken the habit of looking for it to check the time as she was going out.

As she rushed out onto the porch, the frigid air stinging her lungs gave her a start. For an instant, she paused, exhaled a frosty breath, then carefully made her way down the steps, hurriedly pulling on her gloves. Snow blanketed the ground as it had for weeks now, and, as Miss Lunt had said, the sky was heavy with gray clouds. By dawn, there would be more snow. Quinton and Mr. Hart kept the steps and walks shoveled clear, but it was still slippery underfoot.

As Angelica didn't keep a horse and carriage these days, she walked quickly down Lady Slipper Lane and onto the more heavily traveled street that led to Phoebe's house. As she passed neighbors and shopkeepers she knew, she nodded greetings to them. Angelica didn't shop often anymore, but when she did, she paid as promptly as possible, and the shopkeepers liked that. She was well-known in the neighborhood and was generally well liked even if she had fallen on hard times, and even if her house was the only one on the short street in need of paint.

Phoebe and Geoffrey Addams lived only a few blocks away, but Angelica felt half-frozen by the time she got there. The Addamses house was as nice as her own had been in its heyday and, like her house, theirs was situated on a quiet little cul-de-sac that had no traffic to beat the snow off the street. It had the additional advantage of linking backyards with the house where Phoebe and Angelica's parents lived. Because of this, the elder couple visited Phoebe far more often than they visited Angelica, and Phoebe's house had become the family hub.

A maid in a black dress and white cap and apron let Angelica into the house and took her cloak, hat and gloves. Angelica breathed deeply of the scents of clove and cinnamon and baking bread that always filled Phoebe's house.

Before she could reach the front parlor, Phoebe came hurrying toward her down the hall. "Finally! Geoffrey and I had almost given you up."

"I'm sorry to be so late. A woman came by to look at my empty room and I couldn't get away any sooner. She decided to take it, so my house is full again."

Phoebe shook her head, but she smiled. "She isn't as peculiar as the one who left, is she?"

"Mrs. Dobbins wasn't peculiar," Angelica said loyally. "She was just...unique. I imagine there are a lot of people in London who collect stuffed birds and doorknobs."

"Come into the kitchen," Phoebe said, drawing Angelica away from the parlor. "The children are decorating gingerbread men, and I promised to bring you to them the moment you arrived." Phoebe stepped back and studied Angelica's dress. "It's perfect. I knew you had to have the cloth the minute I saw it. Perhaps we could loosen your hair just a bit, though—make it softer around your face."

Angelica laughed. "What difference does it make how I have my hair combed? And why did you want me to wear my new dress today? I had planned to save it for Christmas Day."

Phoebe smiled and a dimple appeared in both her round cheeks. When she smiled, she looked more like a child than a grown woman, even though she was already well into her third pregnancy. "It's a surprise."

Angelica knew Phoebe's surprises could mean anything at all and that it would do no good to press her for an answer. Silently, she followed her sister into the kitchen.

In addition to her housemaid, Phoebe employed a cook and a scullery maid, both of whom were scurrying about the kitchen, smeared with flour and dabs of colored icing in their efforts to help the three children at the table. The twins, Will and Tom, were laboriously spreading icing on two large gingerbread men. Their younger sister, Stella, was dotting bright yellow icing onto a gingerbread star. When they saw Angelica, all three blond heads pivoted to her and all three faces lit up with smiles. Stella clambered off the kitchen chair and ran to greet her aunt.

"Careful," Phoebe warned. "Don't get gingerbread and icing on Aunt Angelica's new dress."

Angelica knelt and kissed Stella's floury cheek, then let the child lead her to the table.

"I made a star," Stella announced. "A Christmas star, just like me."

Will and Tom gave exaggerated groans. At four years old, they thought they were far more mature than their sister.

"She's been saying that all day," Will informed Angelica.

"About being a Christmas star," Tom said.

"Just because she was born on Christmas Eve," Will concluded. They were not only physically identical but frequently finished sentences for each other.

"Well, I am!" Stella said with a frown for her brothers. "Mama said so."

"Don't put me in the middle of this," Phoebe said with a laugh.

"A star is nicer than gingerbread men," Stella said firmly. "*Everybody* knows that."

Phoebe hastily handed her daughter another star to decorate. "Why don't you ice this one for Aunt Angelica to take home with her?"

Stella took the star and, with the cook's help, began spreading icing on it.

"Why all the preparations, Phoebe?" Angelica asked as they went through the kitchen and into the dining room. "You aren't having a party, are you? You know I don't go to parties."

"You can't mourn forever," Phoebe said, "but no, I'm not having a party. Mother and Father are here and, well, a guest."

Angelica's voice dropped to a whisper so no one could overhear her. "Aunt Frederica isn't here, is she? You know how she insists that we sing hymns all evening, and last time she was here, she drank all the cooking sherry and became quite obnoxious."

"No, she's gone to her cousin's house for the holidays."

"Then who..." Anglelica's voice faded as they neared the parlor. She could hear a man speaking, and his voice was achingly familiar.

Before Angelica could retreat, Phoebe pushed open the door. "Look who finally got here, everybody!" She caught Angelica's hand and drew her sister into the warmer room.

Angelica tried to tell herself it was only because the dining room was so cold and the parlor was quite warm that a rush of heat was suddenly flowing through her. She tried to tell herself it was only because she hadn't seen him for so long that the unexpected sight of Matthew Thornton rendered her speechless.

Evidently, he was suffering the same amazement because his voice had trailed off in midsentence and he was staring at her. Time seemed to stand still as she let her senses drink in the sight of him. He was taller than she remembered, and more handsome. His dark hair was neatly combed even though he still avoided the use of pomade to keep it in place, and he was still unfashionably clean shaven. His eyes were as warm and as dark as she remembered, and by the expression on his face, she knew he hadn't been a party to this surprise.

Angelica recovered first. "Matthew," she murmured. Then because everyone was watching her, she added primly, "So good to see you." Even to herself the words sounded inane.

"And you... Mrs. Hamilton." With his utterance, his eyes became less friendly and his mouth took a set in the stubborn lines she remembered all too well.

Geoffrey stood and put his arm around Phoebe's shoulders. "Why so formal, Matthew? We don't stand on formality here."

Angelica felt her parents' eyes upon her. At one time, they had had strong feelings against Matthew. Had they been in on this? Impossible. "Phoebe, could I speak to you? Alone."

Phoebe stayed by Geoffrey. "Of course. Later."

Angelica could feel her blood beginning to boil, and it was only partly because she was in the same room with Matthew Thornton. Her family knew how she and Matthew felt about each other. Why had they dared to do this? With some considerable effort, she forced her feet to take her to a chair, and she sat down. "This is quite a surprise."

"Yes." Matthew hadn't taken his eyes from her and was glaring at her in the manner she remembered so well from five years before.

"Will you be in town long?" Her mind was pleading with him to say no. Surely he wouldn't be in town all through the Christmas holiday.

"I'm to leave on Boxing Day."

Angelica swallowed her groan. He *would* be in town during Christmas. A dreadful thought crept in. "Are you staying near here? With relatives, perhaps?"

"That's the best part of our surprise," Phoebe said with barely contained exuberance. "Matthew is staying right here. With us!"

Angelica heard her parents saying how nice that would be, but she was unable to make any response at all. She could only stare at Matthew and feel his eyes boring into hers.

At last, he looked away. To Geoffrey he said, "Perhaps it would be better if I cut my visit short. After all, it is Christmas and I don't want to be a burden on you."

"We won't hear of it," Phoebe said quickly. "Why, we specifically invited you here for the holidays. Not only that, but it's our fifth anniversary and little Stella's third birthday."

"I know which anniversary it is."

Phoebe finally had the grace to look embarrassed. Geoffrey went to Matthew and clapped him on the shoulder. "That was all a long time ago. Phoebe and I decided it was time our best friend and our only sister made up. You can't imagine how uncomfortable it's been to have you at odds."

"I assume you still live in York?" Angelica said in the silence that returned.

"Yes. Yes, I still live in York." Matthew's eyes turned back to hers and didn't waver.

"Matthew's father passed away this last spring," Geoffrey said. "Now that he's come into his inheritance, Phoebe and I are encouraging him to buy a town house here in London.''

''That's right,'' Phoebe said warmly. ''It would be so nice to see him more often. But if he's in town, we can't keep juggling your visits the way we have the past five years, so we decided that since it's Christmas, this would be the perfect time to let bygones be bygones.''

Angelica's mouth went dry. Matthew was moving to London? ''I wish you had discussed this with me,'' she finally said. ''I could have spared us all this embarrassment.''

''By staying home, you mean?'' Phoebe said. ''By missing out on Christmas?''

Their mother finally spoke up. ''Angelica! Where are your manners, making a guest feel ill at ease?''

Angelica tried to pull herself together. Her mother was right. She was behaving deplorably. ''Forgive me. Will you and your family be moving to town soon?'' she asked stiffly.

''I never married.''

Although his voice was level and his tone carefully controlled, she could sense the accusation behind his words. He hadn't married, but she had.

Phoebe went to the pianoforte and began ruffling through her sheet music. ''Let's sing some carols. That's a lovely way to break the ice.'' She selected one, and said, ''Come on, everyone. Gather round.''

As Phoebe began playing, Angelica eased closer to the door that led to the entryway and freedom. At the moment, she was so upset she could cheerfully ring Phoebe's neck as well as Geoffrey's. Matthew had evidently had the same idea because they found each other on the same side of the room.

Matthew glanced down at her green dress. "That's an unusual shade for mourning."

"Phillip died three years ago. I'm long out of mourning." This was only partially true. Because of her financial difficulties, Angelica hadn't been able to buy new clothes, so most of her wardrobe still consisted of brown, black and gray dresses.

At last Matthew said, "Please, pardon my misconception. Geoffrey never told me any particulars. I only recently learned you'd been widowed."

"Geoffrey's and Phoebe's minds don't seem to work like other people's. I had assumed you would be the first they told."

"I haven't encouraged them to talk about you."

Angelica looked back at the others. "I can't ruin their Christmas. Phoebe has talked for months about this anniversary, and this is the first year Stella has been old enough to understand what birthdays are all about."

"I agree. We'll just have to make the best of it. Fortunately, it will only be for two weeks."

She frowned up at him. "I suppose I can stand almost anything for two weeks."

"I didn't mean for that to sound so rude." Matthew looked as if he were barely able to hold himself in check.

"No? I did." Angelica lifted her chin and went to join the others. As she matched her voice with theirs, she tried not to scowl at Phoebe and Geoffrey.

* * *

Matthew sat in the comfortable guest room and stared at the coals on the small hearth. The house had long since grown quiet about him, but he was still fully dressed and not at all sleepy.

Angelica. Even her name was beautiful. The sound of it reminded him of carols and snowflakes and candles.

He had loved her all his life. Or at least all but the past five years, he amended. During those years, the thought of her had been a torment to him, a reminder that he had loved too well and had taken too much for granted.

Six years ago, he and Angelica had become engaged. Since Phoebe had promised herself to Geoffrey at about the same time and because they were all so close, they had planned a double wedding. It was to have been on Christmas Eve, and the sisters had made plans down to the last details. Lists had been drawn up, discarded and recreated for everything from guests and food for the reception to the contents of their bottom drawers.

Like Geoffrey, Matthew had suffered the usual bridegroom nerves. The nearer the date drew, the more nervous they had become. Unlike Geoffrey, who turned more talkative under pressure, Matthew had become withdrawn and silent. He had assumed Angelica would understand, but she had obviously believed he was having second thoughts. The quieter he became, the more upset she had grown, and finally, only days before the wedding, their tempers had exploded and a no-quarters-given argument had erupted.

By the time he and Angelica had vented all their pent-up nervousness, words had been said that couldn't be retracted. She had given back his ring—actually she had thrown it at him—and their engagement had been broken.

Matthew, in an agony of hurt feelings, had returned to his family home at York. Angelica had decamped to a cousin's house, where she stayed until time for Phoebe's wedding. A month later, Matthew had received a letter from Geoffrey telling him that Angelica had married Phillip Hamilton.

He had known Phillip. He and Phillip's young brother had been at Oxford together. Phillip himself had been perhaps ten years older, maybe a bit more. Matthew had never cared for Phillip before he married Angelica, and he had thoroughly disliked him in the years since. Now Phillip was dead.

As he stretched out his long legs toward the fire, Matthew wondered, not for the first time, how Phillip had died. He would have been rather young to have been taken by a disease, although such a thing could happen. More likely, he had fallen from a horse or been in a carriage accident. Had Angelica been brokenhearted? Was she still?

From his brief exchange of words with her earlier that day, Matthew knew she was still embittered toward him, but that didn't tell him anything about her feelings for Phillip. She wasn't still in mourning, but at twenty-five, Angelica would hardly be expected to wear black forever.

He didn't dare let himself dwell on those years when Angelica and Phillip had shared a home, a life, a bed.

Matthew rubbed his eyes and sighed. He shouldn't have come back at Christmas. He knew this was a time when families drew together—that he would be likely to see Angelica.

Maybe deep down, that was why he had come. To see Angelica.

He thought of how she had looked coming into the parlor; she had been smiling in the way that still haunted his dreams. Her hair was the same striking shade of auburn, and her eyes were sparkling with the dark fires he remembered. Phoebe, with her blond hair and blue eyes, might be considered more fashionably pretty by some, but Angelica was truly beautiful. Her hair had been pulled back in a way that wouldn't flatter many women, but on Angelica, it was perfect, accenting her high cheek bones and her delicately molded face.

Then he remembered the stunned way she had stared at him and how her words had borne out her displeasure at seeing him again. The ache in Matthew's heart expanded, and he wondered if he had been wrong to agree to stay.

Angelica sat on the window seat in her room, staring out at the night. A light snow was falling, and the tiny flakes made a nimbus around the gaslight down the street. Cold seeped through the window and into her body, but Angelica didn't care. Her heart was breaking.

Matthew had looked at her as if he hated her. Once the singing had started, they hadn't exchanged another word except for a terse good-night. She would have to see him again. It would be impossible to do otherwise. Seeing how easily he scorned her, Angelica knew she should be forever grateful that they hadn't married. Not that her own marriage had been pleasant.

Phillip had come on the scene soon after her fateful argument with Matthew. He had been older, more sure of himself, more settled in his ways. At the time, she had seen such traits as ideal. That, of course, was before she discovered Phillip's true nature.

They had married after a whirlwind courtship, and he had moved her into his house on Lady Slipper Lane, a street named for the flower and not because they were made there. No one on Lady Slipper Lane actually worked at a profession. They hired people to work for them. It was the sort of street she had been accustomed to as a girl.

Soon after their marriage, she got firsthand knowledge of Phillip's dark side. He drank, gambled and chased after women, all to excess. In two years, he had gone through his fortune and was drunk more often than he was sober. She had done her best to help him but Phillip was mean when he was drunk, and she had often been glad of long sleeves and high bodices that hid the bruises he inflicted on her. Phillip finally took up with the wife of a jealous man and was shot. The police called it a senseless killing, but they didn't know Phillip as well as Angelica did. To her, it made perfect sense.

A month after Phillip died, it became apparent to Angelica that her independence was threatened; bills were owed and she had no income. Rather than seek aid from either of their families, she began to take in boarders and found a shop that would sell her needle-work on consignment. Between the boarders and her skill with a needle and thread, she had no need to move in with her parents. She let them think she rented her rooms in order to have people around her for companionship. Her parents assumed that as Phillip's widow she would have no privations, and she let them continue to believe it. Phoebe and Geoffrey knew the truth, but Angelica had proved to them that she could make it on her own and had sworn them to secrecy. At times, she had wondered if her luck would hold, but it always had. She laughed at Phoebe and Geoffrey's fears and told them her success was due to the angel in her attic. They had to agree that Angelica did seem to lead a charmed life.

At least, she had thought her life was charmed—until she had entered Phoebe's parlor and saw Matthew standing there. Then all the old love she thought she had safely walled away had flowed over her, and now her heart was breaking over a man who had probably not thought of her in years. There was only one thing to do, and although she knew it wouldn't be easy to accomplish, she knew she had to do it. She had to keep Matthew from knowing she had never stopped loving him.

Chapter Two

Early the next morning, Angelica sent a note by her maid to Phoebe, asking Phoebe to exclude her from any daily festivities she had planned at which Matthew would be present. Her maid returned with a response written on Phoebe's pale blue stationery.

Angelica read the note and frowned. "I've been invited to go ice skating with the family. Did my sister say if Mr. Thornton is also going?"

"No, ma'am," Peggy said, not making eye contact. "I didn't know I was to ask."

"You did exactly right," Angelica said soothingly. Peggy was always so afraid of making a mistake that Angelica knew she was quite capable of worrying for the rest of the day over whether she had done wrong.

Although Peggy didn't look convinced as she went back toward the kitchen to resume her chores, Angelica wished she could do more to bolster the girl's confidence, but had no idea what else to do. And at the moment, she had other things to worry about.

As she looked back at Phoebe's message, Angelica realized it was foolish for her to be so concerned. Her note had plainly stated that she preferred to avoid

Matthew's company, and surely Phoebe would honor her wishes. The invitation undoubtedly meant that Matthew was otherwise engaged that afternoon. Moments later, another mountain of Miss Lunt's belongings arrived on the doorstep and Angelica put her concern about Matthew out of her mind. She offered her new boarder a hand at getting her things upstairs, but Miss Lunt waved her away, saying she preferred to handle such things by herself.

Angelica went to her own room to see to some mending and had barely gotten into her work when she was interrupted by a knock on her door. It was Quinton Keyes, and he was visibly upset. "I tell you, the new woman you let that room to is a menace," Quinton said in his rather effeminate way. "Yesterday, I tripped over a wicker basket she had left carelessly lying about in the hall, and she flew at me as if I had done it on purpose."

"Surely not," Angelica said as she patted his arm reassuringly.

"And just moments ago, she accused me of breaking her medicine bottles! As if I would do such a thing! I was merely trying to get over the box so I could get up the stairs. Is she ailing? I don't relish sharing my board with a sick woman, I can tell you."

Angelica suppressed a smile. "She seemes perfectly healthy."

He shook his head and pursed his lips. "Her color's not good. Not good at all. Too pasty." He took out his handkerchief and touched it to his nose. "I hope we aren't all being exposed to some disease."

"I'm sure she's quite all right. If you're concerned, perhaps you should take some of your elixir." She knew Quinton saw diseases lurking around every corner. Each spring, he tried to dose everyone in the house with his tonics.

"Perhaps I should," Quinton said thoughtfully. "After all, a person can't be too careful."

Angelica was no sooner alone again than Miss Lunt came bustling into the room. "I hate to be one to complain, goodness knows, but that man across the hall from my room is quite insufferable."

"Mr. Hart?" Angelica asked.

"No, no, the other. The little man with the sallow skin."

"That would be Quinton Keyes."

"That's the one. He kicked my medicine box and sent it sailing across the floor. Thank goodness nothing was broken, but it might well have been."

"Mr. Keyes has been here several years, and I can speak for his temperament. I'm positive he meant no harm. Perhaps he tripped over it." Angelica knew it wouldn't do to admit Quinton had already complained about Miss Lunt. "It was a medicine box, you say? Surely you aren't ill."

Miss Lunt looked at her as if she were offended. "I'm a lady of delicate constitution. I believe I can say I've never enjoyed good health such as a woman like yourself may know. It's the reason I've never married. Papa forbade it as being quite out of the question for a woman of my nature."

"I see." Angelica nodded in understanding. Having Quinton as a boarder had taught her not to try arguing a hypochondriac out of his or her maladies. "Is there any particular difficulty?"

"Melancholia is my curse," Miss Lunt said in a mournful voice. "That and the weather. The cold seems to seep right through me."

"How dreadful that must be. Mr. Keyes has a similar problem. I've found Peggy knows how to make an onion broth that has been entirely beneficial to him. Perhaps it would help you, as well."

Miss Lunt looked somewhat mollified. "An onion broth, you say? Not too spicy, I presume. My stomach is quite delicate."

"Peggy knows exactly how to make it. You go up and get some rest, and I'll have her bring a tray up to you when it's ready."

"It's so nice to meet a woman of your sensibilities and understanding. At my last place, I was never understood."

Angelica patted Miss Lunt's arm exactly as she had Quinton's. "Peggy will be up directly."

As Miss Lunt returned to her room, Angelica went into the kitchen. "Peggy, boil up some of your onion broth for Miss Lunt and take it up to her."

"The kind like I make for Mr. Keyes?"

"Yes, and go easy on the mustard this time."

"Law, Mrs. Hamilton, don't tell me there's another one here like Mr. Keyes!"

Angelica had to smile. This was as close as Peggy had ever come to complaining. "I know it's difficult, but she paid up front and that will satisfy the coal man. It's worth boiling an onion to have a fire in the grate."

"Yes, ma'am," Peggy said as she reached for an onion.

At noon, a letter came in the post for the Neville sisters, and Angelica was so hopeful that it might contain rent money, she took it to the girls at the milliner's shop where they worked. The letter turned out to be from an aunt, not their parents, and it contained news of a new baby cousin rather than money. Both girls assured Angelica that money would surely arrive soon, and Angelica tried to continue believing it. The sisters' embarrassment was obvious, and they were at least as upset over their parents' abandonment of them as was Angelica. She reassured them that she wouldn't put them out and that she harbored no ill will toward them. And it was the truth. Her anger was directed at the girls' parents, who could well-afford their daughters' upkeep and who ought to have known better. As she went back home, Angelica cast about in her mind for eligible husbands for the sisters, but she couldn't think of anyone who would be right for either of them.

The hours seemed to fly past. Miss Lunt and Quinton had instantly become rivals for Angelica's attention, as well as competitors in hypochondria. Peggy was out of breath from racing up and down stairs with bowls of broth and mustard cloths.

Angelica had all but forgotten about the planned skating party until she heard a knock at the door. Geoffrey stood on her step, his cheeks rosy from the cold and his breath making a wreath about his head. In the street behind him stood the Addamses' carriage. Phoebe lowered the glazed window and waved for Angelica to come join them, then quickly closed it again. "All ready to go skating?" Geoffrey asked cheerfully.

"Is it that late already?" she asked. She automatically raised her hand and smoothed at her hair as she let Geoffrey into the foyer. "Yes, let me run get my skates and a wrap." Angelica found herself looking forward to getting out of the house and away from the fledgling rivalry upstairs.

"Wrap up warmly. It's freezing out there."

Angelica left Geoffrey at the foot of the stairs while she dashed up to get her skates and wool cloak. At the top of the stairs, she could hear both Quinton's affected sneezes and Miss Lunt's melancholy moans. With amusement in her eyes, she gathered her things and in a short time, she returned to Geoffrey.

As he opened the door for her, Angelica called to tell Peggy where she was going and fastened her cape against the chill. Her excitement was growing as quickly as if she were a child again. The day was perfect for skating, even if it was too cold for comfort. A few turns around the pond would warm her up.

She let Geoffrey carry her skates and take her arm as she went down the porch steps. Icy snow crunched under her feet on the front walk as she hurried out to the carriage. Halfway there, she skidded on an icy patch and laughed as Geoffrey's grip tightened on her arm, preventing her from falling. When the carriage door swung open and she saw Matthew sitting with one of the twins by his side and with little Stella on his lap, her merriment vanished.

Angelica threw an accusing glare at Phoebe, but at this point, there was no polite way for her to refuse to go with them, especially with Geoffrey holding her skates and blocking her retreat to the house.

Begrudgingly, she climbed into the carriage and sat beside Will and opposite Phoebe. As Geoffrey stepped past his wife and Tom, Phoebe latched the carriage door shut behind them.

"Prop your feet on the brazier," Phoebe suggested to her sister. "That will warm you up."

"I'm warm enough already," Angelica pointedly replied. Phoebe pretended not to catch the double meaning to her sister's words.

"Aunt Angel'ca," Stella said, "Mr. Thorn has said he will teach me to skate."

"Mr. Thornton," Phoebe corrected with a smile at Matthew.

"I can't say that." Stella shook her head until her blond curls darted every which way.

"Then why don't you call me Uncle Matt?" Matthew said agreeably.

"Mr. Thorn is just fine," Angelica said to the child. "I thought I was to teach you."

Stella pondered, then brightened. "You can both teach me."

Angelica felt as if she had been trapped, and she wondered if the entire Addams family was determined to pair her off with Matthew.

"Me and Tom can do figure eights," Will said.

"Tom and I," his mother automatically corrected.

"We really can," Will said as he grinned up at Angelica. Tom nodded in agreement.

"I can hardly wait to see you," Angelica said to the boys. "That's wonderful."

"Uncle Matt told us how," Tom added.

Matthew laughed. "Looks as if I'm destined to be Uncle Matt. I never thought I would ever have anyone call me that."

Angelica wondered if that was meant as a barb for her.

"That's right," Geoffrey said. "You don't have any brothers or sisters to supply you with nieces or nephews."

"How sad," Phoebe said as the carriage turned left onto the more heavily traveled road. "I can't imagine what it would be like not to have a sister."

"Nor can I," Angelica said darkly. "Didn't you read the note I sent by Peggy?"

"You know, Angelica, I tried, but either your handwriting has become less legible or my eyesight is fading in my old age, because I just couldn't seem to make it out."

"Old age, indeed," Geoffrey said with a wink. "You have a few more good years ahead of you." Phoebe dimpled prettily and tucked her hand into his.

When they reached the pond, there were already a number of skaters on the ice. All three children fidgeted until the carriage rolled to a stop and the doors were opened. Stella was so excited, she jumped up and down. As soon as the adults were beside her, she grabbed Matthew's and Angelica's hands and said, "Put on my skates, Uncle Matt. Put on my skates."

They went to a park bench, and Stella scrambled up onto the seat. Her brothers and Geoffrey were already strapping on their skates.

Matthew knelt and slipped Stella's skates, formerly a pair belonging to one of the twins, onto her feet and buckled them into place.

"Now do Aunt Angel'ca's," Stella commanded.

"No, I don't think that's necessary," Angelica said.

"Why not?" Stella looked up at her with puzzlement.

To avoid making an issue of the matter, Angelica let Matthew help her. As he began fitting the first skate, she told herself that the tingle that raced through her was due to the cold and the children's excitement, not to Matthew's touch. She noticed he was having trouble belting the strap around her ankle, and she wondered if his difficulty might not be due to that same tingling excitement. However, the gruff expression on his face suggested that his fingers were clumsy out of his aversion to touching her.

As soon as Matthew's skates were on, Stella led them to the ice. Angelica held the child's hand firmly as she waited for a couple to glide past. Together, she and Matthew skated skillfully away from the snowy bank with Stella between them. Stella's feet, however, went in every direction, but her companions kept her upright.

"Slide your feet like this," Matthew said as he showed her how to shift her weight. "Look. See how Will and Tom are doing it?"

The twins had learned to skate the winter before and, while they weren't proficient, they were able to get around on the ice. Because of Phoebe's delicate condition, she couldn't skate, and once Geoffrey was sure the boys could manage, he had gone back to sit with her on the bench.

"Aunt Angel'ca, Uncle Matt," Stella was singing cheerfully. "Aunt Angel'ca, Uncle Matt."

Angelica realized that to strangers, they must look like a married couple teaching their child to skate, and the unsettling thought made her skitter to one side.

"Do you need to skate in the middle for a while?" Stella asked her.

"No, thank you. I just hit a rough spot on the ice."

Stella looked up at Matthew. "Miss 'Celia and Miss Zenie are making me a hat for Christmas."

"Who?" he asked.

"She means Cecilia and Zenobia Neville, two of my boarders. They are quite taken by Stella and have promised her a hat on Boxing Day."

"You keep boarders?"

"For company," Angelica said quickly. "I have such a large house and I get lonely."

Matthew was quiet for a minute. "Phillip's death must have been a blow to you."

"A grievous blow," she elaborated. "Indeed it was." She had no intention of ever telling anyone that it was also a relief and possibly a salvation.

"He was young to die. May I ask what happened?"

"It was an accident, the police said. A shooting accident. I really don't want to talk about it."

"No. No, of course not. Forgive me for asking."

Angelica held firmly to Stella's mittened hand as both of the child's feet flew out from under her. Stella's little face was serious as she concentrated on getting her feet beneath her again and learning to move her feet just as the adults did. Not for the first time, Angelica felt a pang of regret that she would never have a child of her own. To do that, she would have to remarry, and she was determined never to repeat that mistake. She glanced sideways at Matthew. If she had married him and not Phillip, would their marriage have been happy? She couldn't allow herself to dwell on that thought.

"Look, Aunt Angelica!" Will and Tom called out as they cast glances at her to be sure she was watching them execute shaky figure eights.

"Very good!" she called out. "I couldn't have done better myself."

"The children love you," Matthew observed.

"They know I love them. I'm the typical doting aunt, Phoebe says."

"I'm going to have a baby brother or sister," Stella confided.

"How do you know that?" Angelica asked in surprise. Such topics were never discussed with children.

"Will told me, and he says big brothers know everything."

Matthew and Angelica exchanged a smile over Stella's head. Both looked away quickly, and Angelica felt a sharp hurt, thinking he had turned from her because he couldn't bear to smile at her. This forced companionship must be as difficult on Matthew as it was for her—but for different reasons. While he clearly disliked being with her, she was having the opposite problem.

After a while, Stella had progressed to the point at which she could keep her feet under her with some consistency, although she was sliding her feet back and forth and going forward only with the help of Angelica and Matthew.

They took a few more turns around the pond, the twins trying to outdo each other as they vied for Matthew's attention. Phoebe apparently noted her children's pink noses and rosy cheeks and called them to her to say it was time for cocoa.

Angelica was glad to get back into the comparative warmth of the carriage. The driver had kept the brazier going, and she edged her feet closer to warm her toes. She tucked a lap robe over her knees and Stella's, and as Matthew did the same to Will, their hands brushed. Angelica didn't risk looking at him, instead pretending not to have noticed.

"I really ought to go home," Angelica said to Phoebe. "I have a new boarder and a civil war is threatening to erupt."

"All the more reason to stay with us for the evening," Geoffrey said.

"Besides," Phoebe added, "Mrs. Watson expects you and will have supper ready by now."

"But I never said I would—"

"Please, Aunt Angel'ca? Please?" Stella clutched her aunt's hand imploringly. "I want you to hear me sing. Mama taught me a song."

"And we have pictures we drew just for you," Will said. Tom nodded vigorously.

"All right," Angelica conceded. "But I can't stay long." She imagined that she could feel Matthew's relief at it being a short evening.

When they reached the Addamses' house, Stella drew Angelica to the piano and Phoebe played a simple melody to accompany the child's rendition of a carol. The boys ran up to their rooms and came tearing back with a drawing in each hand. As soon as Stella finished her song and she had been duly praised, the boys claimed Angelica's attention and told her what their drawings were all about.

Mrs. Watson put supper on the table as the children gave everyone a hug and headed upstairs under the care of their nanny to have their own meal in the nursery. The fare was simple, but Angelica noted it was a far cry from the toad-in-the-hole that Peggy was no doubt serving at her house on Lady Slipper Lane. Unlike Mrs. Watson, Peggy had no training as a cook and besides, Angelica frequently couldn't afford better meat than the sausage that Peggy was serving tonight.

After the meal, Angelica tried to slip away, but Phoebe sang out. "Let's play Forfeits!" Geoffrey was in quick agreement.

This game didn't require teams, but Angelica felt as if she had to stay or spoil everyone's fun. She reluctantly agreed.

"This wasn't my idea," she whispered to Matthew as they all went into the warm front parlor.

"Nor mine," he whispered back.

"You go first, Geoffrey," Phoebe prompted.

After a moment to think, he said, "I love my love with an almond because she's ample."

Phoebe laughed as she playfully swatted at him and arranged her shawl more discreetly over her rounding middle. "I love my love with a barrel because he's boisterous."

Matthew said, "I love my love with a comforter because she's cold."

Angelica frowned at him. "I love my love with a duck because he's a dunderhead."

Phoebe looked at them uneasily as she and Geoffrey took their turns.

"I love my love with a gourd because she's a guttersnipe," Matthew said when it was his turn again.

Angelica felt her temper rising. "I love my love with a flatiron because he's a fool."

"Perhaps we should play something else," Phoebe broke in. "How about How, When, Where?"

"I'm really not in the mood for games," Angelica told her sister. "I should go home."

"Shall I find you a cabriolet?" Matthew asked.

Angelica lifted her chin defiantly. Matthew was being too obvious in his haste to have her gone, and she decided not to give him the pleasure. "On the other hand, I suppose I could stay a bit longer."

"We could tell ghost stories," Geoffrey suggested. "It wouldn't be Christmas without a ghost story."

"Or we could sing," Phoebe interjected.

"Or play *rouge-et-noir*," Matthew said.

"We could play Blindman's Buff," Angelica proposed with a sharp glance at Matthew. "I wager Matthew wouldn't object to spending the rest of the evening with a blindfold over his head." Phoebe gave Angelica an admonishing shake of the head.

"I see maturity hasn't dulled your wit," Matthew said, then added, "Pity."

Phoebe hastily got to her feet. "Get out the magic lantern, Geoffrey. Neither Angelica nor Matthew have seen our new slides." She went about the room snuffing candles and turning down lamps.

Geoffrey hung a length of sheeting over two picture frames and positioned a porcelain box on a table Phoebe had cleared for him. He lit the oil lantern in the base of the contraption and pointed it at the sheet as Phoebe blew out the lamps around the room. Soon all was dark, except for the patch of light put out by the lantern.

"This is a series about Grace Darling," Geoffrey said as he slid the first plate into place. By means of levers, he sailed a ship over the sea and made it appear to sink. The Longstone lighthouse appeared, and Phoebe began to recite the familiar lines of the poem.

As Grace Darling rowed her boat out to rescue the shipwrecked crew, Angelica risked looking at Matthew. In the dim light, his features were shadowy and his black hair blended into the darkness of the room. Pale colors from the magic lantern rimmed the outline of his profile. He seemed completely preoccupied with the slide show.

Why did she still care, Angelica wondered. He had spoken to her only when necessary since they left the skating pond, and he had been obvious in his insults during Forfeits. Of course, she had been, too, she had to admit, but only after he implied she was cold. Did he see her that way? She had been the one to break their engagement, but she would hardly have described that occasion as cold. A niggling doubt crept into her mind. What if Matthew had meant nothing by what he had said and had only been trying to find words beginning with a *C?* If a player hesitated in his turn, he had to pay a forfeit. Perhaps Matthew had simply said the first thing that popped into his head because of the wintry weather outside.

If so, she had made a fool of herself.

Grace Darling completed her rescue just as Phoebe ended the poem. Geoffrey returned those slides to the box and took out another series. This set was made up of long, panoramic slides that were drawn slowly through the box, presenting a view of scenery as though the viewer were turning about in a foreign landscape.

As a caravan of camels, the pyramids and the Sphinx paraded across the sheet, Angelica thought she felt Matthew's eyes upon her, but she refused to look his way to see if she was right.

Geoffrey and Phoebe were marveling over the exotic sights as if they had never seen the slides before. Angelica knew she was being a miserable guest. They only wanted her to be as happy as they were.

She wondered how she would have felt if Matthew had shown the least bit of encouragement in this reunion. Would she still be as adamant in her decision never to forgive him?

She had dreamed the night before that he had been looking at her in that special way he had when their love was new, and they had laughed together while they walked hand in hand through a dream land-scape. She remembered little else about the dream; but above all, there had been a sense of rightness that she was walking along with her hand in Matthew's. In real life, that was as unlikely as the landscape had been. It was too good to be true.

Angelica's reverie drifted to thoughts of her future. She wouldn't be lonely—not with so many boarders about—but there was more to living than simply avoiding loneliness. She had learned what a risk marriage could be. What if she were wed again and found herself with another man cast to Phillip's mold? No, the prospect of being alone was better.

Matthew turned slightly and returned her gaze. She couldn't read his expression in the shadow. She sighed. It had always been like this with Matthew. He couldn't be read easily. Phillip had shown something of this same trait, and she had fancied it had meant Phillip was deep and mysterious and brooding. In Phillip, however, it only meant he was sullen and had no depth at all.

When she realized her eyes and Matthew's were still locked, she lowered hers. There was no point in long-ing for him. He no longer had any desire for her.

As silently as she could, Angelica stood and eased out of the parlor. In the entry, she put on her cape and tied her hat beneath her chin. She couldn't stay so close to Matthew without giving him even more of her heart to break.

She let herself out into the cold and glanced up and down the dark street. She had only a few blocks to go and she was unlikely to meet anyone who would wish to harm her, but the night was a dark one with no moon to light her steps.

As quickly as the ice and snow would permit, she made her way down the dark street to the main one with its gaslights that threw round puddles of light onto the snow. Moving quickly from one circle of light to the next, she tried not to dwell on the sounds she heard in the intervening darkness. Ahead of her, she saw two policemen and felt reassured, but the men soon rounded a corner onto a cross street, and again she was alone.

At last, she turned down Lady Slipper Lane with its air of calm and its graceful houses. As soon as she reached her door, she felt an overwhelming sense of relief. She never should have walked the dark streets alone, and she knew it. She looked back the way she had come and saw a solitary figure silhouetted in front of a gaslight. A rush of fear flooded through her, but then, the man turned and she recognized he was none other than Matthew Thornton.

He had come out into the cold to see her safely home, and he had been in such a rush to do so, he had left his hat behind.

As he walked back in the direction of the Adamses', Angelica let herself into her house. He had watched over her. Was it only what he would do for any woman, or had he followed her because of what they had been to each other in the past? Angelica didn't know the answer.

Chapter Three

Angelica awoke at dawn and stared up at the pale wallpaper on her ceiling as she waited for the sun to rise higher in the eastern sky. She hadn't dreamed about Matthew again as she had hoped she would, but that was because she'd hardly slept at all. She kept seeing him silhouetted in the gaslight, watching her safely and secretly home. Why had he done it?

She ran her hand over the emptiness of the other side of her bed. Alone in the dim light of her room, she let the pain she was feeling show on her face. At times, she was so lonely, she could cry. Not for companionship—her boarders provided more than enough of that—nor for Phillip. She didn't regret that he was out of her life. Her loneliness was for Matthew, and her regret was for the years they might have had together. Thinking back on the fateful argument, she couldn't recall who had spoken the first angry word or who had been first to speak against their upcoming marriage, but she had a sinking suspicion that she had been to blame.

She sat up in bed and wrapped her arms around her knees. Her thick, auburn hair fell about her shoulders and pooled behind her on the bed. Across the room, she could see her dim reflection in the dresser mirror. In that light, she might still pass for a girl of nineteen, just as she looked younger in her new green dress than in the black and gray ones she usually wore.

Did Matthew still find her attractive? Or did he merely see her as the widow of another man?

First light was being replaced by weak but persistent sunshine, so she got out of bed and ran across the cold floor to her washstand and splashed cold water on her face. She shivered as she dressed and considered whether her improved finances, with Miss Lunt as a boarder, would allow her to have a brazier of coals in her room. She pulled on a pewter-colored dress and began brushing her hair. Once she had her hair pinned in a heavy bun on the nape of her neck, she again studied her reflection. Both the dress and the hairstyle made her look older.

She unpinned her hair and bent at the waist in order to coil her hair high on her head. This way, the sides and back swept upward, making her brown eyes seem larger and more gentle. She hadn't worn her hair this way since the early days of her marriage. Out of habit, she picked up the mourning broach she always wore, then paused. With a finger, she traced the onyx willow design of the cover, then she opened the broach for a look at the tiny braid of Phillip's hair inside. Resolutely, she snapped it shut and put it away in the small drawer beneath the candle stand. In its stead, she pinned to her dress a cameo her mother had given her and went downstairs to start the day.

Mr. Hart, a man in his early sixties and a long-term boarder, came in at midmorning with a woman on his arm. "You know this young lady, I believe," he said to Angelica as he gestured at the woman.

"Of course," Angelica said with a smile. "How are you, Miss Blanche?"

The woman, who was every bit as old as her admirer, smiled and glanced coyly at Mr. Hart. "Quite well, thank you."

"I'll not beat about the rose bush," Mr. Hart began. "This lovely creature has long held a place in my estimation." Mr. Hart reared back with pride, and the buttons on his waistcoat strained.

Angelica smiled at Blanche, who was blushing like a schoolgirl. She and Mr. Hart had been keeping company for at least two decades by their own admission.

"This morning, this lovely girl made me the happiest of men," Mr. Hart continued with pride. "She consented to become my wife."

"Why, that's wonderful!" Angelica hugged them both. "When is the happy occasion to take place?"

"It already has. We've just come from there. May I present Mrs. Hart."

Blanche lowered her eyelashes. "He's so impetuous, you know."

Angelica's smiled broadened. A courtship of twenty years hardly seemed impetuous to her.

"I believe in striking while the flatiron's hot," Mr. Hart said with a smug smile. "No reason to waste time."

Blanche touched her iron-gray hair. "I never dreamed I would be a Christmas bride. Or almost, at any rate."

That reminded Angelica of her broken engagement with Matthew. If things had happened differently, she would have been a true Christmas bride married on Christmas Eve. Renewing her smile, Angelica said, "I'm so happy for you both. We must have a celebration! I'll help Peggy cook a ham and those currant muffins you both like."

"Goodness, don't go to such a fuss for my sake," Blanche said shyly. "I won't know what to do if everyone makes such a fuss." Except for Blanche's hair color and telltale wrinkles, she might have been a bride of tender years.

"Not go to any trouble over you?" Angelica said. "Why, I'll hear no such thing. All brides must be fussed over. And you, too, Mr. Hart. And to keep all this to yourselves!" She pretended to scold them but her laughing eyes belied her words.

"Mr. Hart is so impetuous," Blanche repeated as she tucked her hand beneath her new husband's arm. Mr. Hart looked so proud, Angelica thought his waistcoat buttons might fly off at any moment.

"Mrs. Blanche and I would like to continue at this residence," Mr. Hart said. "If it will be of no inconvenience."

"You'll find me very quiet and retiring, I'm sure," Blanche added. "I'll be no extra trouble."

"I wouldn't hear of you living anywhere else. Why, Mr. Hart was one of my first boarders. I can't imagine letting that room to anyone else."

"There, Mrs. Blanche. What did I tell you? Didn't I say Mrs. Hamilton was a peach?"

"This house has been too long without newlyweds," Angelica said. "You may have your things sent over as soon as you please, Mrs. Blanche."

"If you've no objections, Mrs. Hamilton," Mr. Hart said with a smile at Blanche, "I'd like to show my chamber to my lovely bride."

Blanche's face flushed bright red, and she appeared unable to lift her eyes above his watch fob. "Do stop, Mr. Hart. I'll die of embarrassment!"

Angelica hid the amusement she found in all this behind her fingertips as Mr. Hart led his half-swooning bride up the stairs.

"What's happening, Mrs. Hamilton?" Peggy tenuously asked as she poked her head out from the kitchen. "There ain't burglars in the house, are they?" She looked up to see Mr. Hart's trousers and a woman's skirt disappearing past the landing. "He's not takin' her upstairs!" Peggy's mouth dropped open.

"They've eloped," Angelica said with a laugh. "They were married this morning."

"Law, ma'am, I never expected it." For once, Peggy had forgotten to be afraid to speak her mind.

"Neither did I, to tell you the truth. We must have a grand dinner to celebrate. We'll have the smoked ham and that garlic sauce Mr. Hart fancies. Oh, and currant muffins. Do we still have any currants?"

"We have currants aplenty. You mean I should cook the ham you was holding back for Christmas dinner?"

"That's right. I'll find something else for Christmas. I have a week and a half. Maybe that lace shawl will sell, or the cut-work tablecloth. Love is very precious, Peggy, and a thing to be celebrated. Always remember that."

"Yes, ma'am."

"Love may be the most most important thing in all the world." Angelica felt perilously near tears, so she hurried toward the kitchen door. "I'll see if we have enough butter and flour."

The next day, even though Matthew expected Angelica to decline, he sent a card inviting her to accompany him to the band concert in Stonebrough Park that evening. When she accepted, he was not only surprised but pleased. Geoffrey and Phoebe were so elated by the news that they assured him they had no use for their carriage that evening and insisted that he was to use it as if it were his own.

That afternoon, he dressed with care and at the appointed hour, he parked the Addamses' rig out front of Angelica's house. A thin girl with strawberry hair opened the door and left him standing in the entry while she went up to get her mistress. Matthew turned his hat in his hands and tried not to shift about like a nervous boy, even if he did feel like one. Until he saw Angelica coming down the stairs carrying a cloak over her arm, he wasn't entirely sure she would actually go with him.

She was wearing the same holly green dress he had seen her in that first night at Geoffrey's house, and she looked radiant. Her beautiful hair piled atop her head glowed like dark fire, and the softer style was alluring, to say the least. Her bearing was one of confidence, but by the way her eyes studied his, he could see she was as nervous as he was.

"You're beautiful," he heard himself say.

Angelica paused on the stairs, then continued down. "Thank you."

When she reached the entry, she hesitated again. Matthew had forgotten through the intervening years how petite she was. The top of her head barely reached his chin, and her waist was small enough for his hands to span. He had tried so hard to forget, but her face and eyes and the sound of her voice –the memory of these had stayed with him for five years.

He took her cloak and wrapped it around her and for a moment, his hands rested on her shoulders. Angelica remained quiet and motionless, and he wondered if it was because his touch repelled her or if she, too, had felt something pass through the touch.

Abruptly, she turned to the girl who was coming down the stairs. "I don't know if I'll be late, Peggy, so you needn't wait up. I have my key."

The girl nodded but continued to stare at Matthew as if she had never seen his like before.

As Matthew escorted her to the carriage, Angelica let him steady her by tucking her hand beneath his arm. Matthew was amazed at the tenderness he felt for her. Her hand was so small, even in the padding of her glove. His fingers touched a thickness in the cloth of her glove where she had darned it, and he wondered, not for the first time, if Angelica was as financially secure as her family assumed.

He helped her into the carriage and saw to it that she was warmly wrapped in the lap robe before he tapped on the wall to signal the driver. The horses leaned into the harness and the carriage started rolling with a jolt.

"You have a fine house," Matthew said to break the silence. "I never noticed this street before, but I can see why you'd enjoy living here."

"I'm quite content with my house," she replied. "It's close enough to shops that I needn't keep a buggy or horse. I enjoy the convenience."

He nodded toward a house next door. "That's a grand place. Who lives there?"

"No one now. It belonged to two elderly sisters. One passed away and the other has gone to live with relatives. I hope it doesn't stand vacant too long. Houses need people in them to keep them alive."

Matthew was close enough to see the lace of her dark eyelashes and the rust-colored flecks in her eyes. "People need people, as well."

Angelica laughed and the sound warmed Matthew's heart. "I have plenty of people around me. I have a newlywed couple in the front room and two others who are trying to out-do each other with strange and imaginary illnesses, two sisters in need of husbands, and Peggy, who is afraid of her own shadow."

"I was thinking of myself," Matthew said. "As you know, I've come into my inheritance."

"Yes, I heard Phoebe say that. I'm sorry about your father. It must have been a blow to you."

"Yes, it was. Putting the estate in order took some time, but I have a good man to oversee it now."

"Is that why you're buying a house in London?"

"Partially. I considered going to America, but the political conflict between the states has some saying they may be headed for serious trouble, and I wanted no part of that. I missed London. Some of my happiest years were spent here."

Angelica made no reply.

"I assume since you're out of mourning that you have gentlemen callers," he said in an effort to see how matters lay.

"Actually, I don't. I've discouraged suitors. I have all I can do in running my house."

"A house is just a pile of bricks and mortar."

"No, it isn't. It's the people inside, as well. What would poor Quinton and Miss Lunt do without me to mediate between them? And there's Peggy—she'll go back to the workhouse if I don't take care of her. She's not skilled enough to hold another job. Anyone else might send the Neville sisters packing when they can't pay the rent, and then what would happen to them?"

"I see you've given this some thought."

Angelica snapped her mouth shut as if she had said too much. After a moment, she spoke again, "I don't intend to remarry, so there's no reason for me to encourage gentlemen callers."

"I see." Matthew told himself it was foolish to allow her words to hurt him. If she intended to remain a widow, it must mean she had loved Phillip too dearly to have another man in his place. He knew he ought to be happy for her having known such a love. But he wasn't happy about it at all.

They stepped from the carriage and approached the bandstand where the outdoor concert was to take place. Braziers had been placed around the area, but the gathering spectators still shivered with the cold, and when they laughed or spoke, a pale fog from their breath hung on the air. Smaller children darted about with youthful exuberance at the edge of the crowd, and the adults stood close together to collect their warmth.

"If you get too cold, you must tell me," Matthew said. "I don't want you to get a chill."

Angelica laughed. "Peggy filled me full of hot soup, liberally laced with pepper. I'm not likely to get cold." She studied the musicians who were warming up their instruments in preparation to play. With great casualness, she asked, "Are you calling on anyone else here in London?" Then she shook her head. "Never mind. It's really none of my business. I can't imagine why I even asked."

Matthew was standing slightly behind her, and he was able to study her profile without being obvious. It wasn't like Angelica to pry into another's private affairs for no reason. Did it mean she was interested, after all? Matthew never had been able to understand her, and five year's absence hadn't helped him gain insight.

The band began to play "Come Where My Love Lies Dreaming." The audience smiled and nodded their approval. A few even sang softly along with the band, although the elders in the group shot them glances of disapproval. Behind Angelica and Matthew, a group of boys was entrenching for a snowball fight.

The next tune was another favorite, "Lorena." Angelica's eyes sparkled, and Matthew was captivated by the pink flush on her usually pale cheek. Even though she was trying to remain decorous, he could see the rhythm was touching her as the band started on a lively tune from the Highlands.

"I'm so glad you suggested this," Angelica said.

"I remembered that you loved music."

"Did you?"

Her dark eyes sought his, and for Matthew, it was as if the quarrel and intervening years had never happened. "I remember a great deal about you."

She hastily looked away. "This afternoon seems so perfect. The music, the snow, all of it." She looked over at the playing children. "I love hearing their laughter and how that group of young people over there keep singing even though those dowagers are glaring at them. I love the way the trees look like white-and-black lace against the sky and how the birds plump their feathers until they're as round as balls with only their beaks and tails sticking out." She laughed. "I love being alive!"

"Yes," Matthew agreed with a smile. "I remember that about you, too."

Angelica seemed suddenly to recall to whom she was talking and she drew her exuberance back in. Matthew was amused at how hard she was trying to be decorous.

The band was talented and played a wide variety of music, and the crowd was growing larger by the minute as the music drew the attention of passersby. An errant snowball from the trenches behind Angelica and Matthew toppled a gentleman's beaver hat and the boys were obliged to take their game elsewhere.

The music lasted until sunset. Long, blue fingers of shadow stretched over the snow, and the trees reflected pink and gold from the sky. The crowd slowly dispersed, and as Angelica and Matthew made their way back toward their carriage, Angelica hummed, "We Three Kings of Orient."

"At times, especially at Christmas," Angelica confided as she walked by his side, "I feel as if there is magic in the air. Do you feel it?"

"I do at times."

"Maybe it's because Christmas seems to offer a new start. Everyone is friendlier and more forgiving. I love to see the plump turkeys in shop windows along with sugar plums and greenery. Geoffrey says he's going to put up a Christmas tree even if Mother and Father do think it's a silly idea."

"I like Christmas trees. It's one German custom I heartily endorse." Matthew handed Angelica into the carriage as the driver held open the door.

"Phoebe and I have been working on decorations for it. All the little candles must have holders to fasten them onto the branches and paper sleeves to catch the wax as it drips. I've cut snowflakes from white paper to hang on the branches. And we've made garlands of holly berries and cranberries."

"The children will be amazed at the sight of a tree full of candles and snowflakes in the house," Matthew offered.

"I know. It will be a lovely surprise for them. Perhaps we'll do this every year now that Geoffrey has decided to overrule Mother and Father this time."

"What about you? Will you have a Christmas tree?"

Angelica shook her head. "There are no children in my house, although Peggy is little more than one. No, I'll share Phoebe's tree."

"Is that all you want? To share the happiness of your sister's family?"

She gave him a sharp glance. "I think that's plenty. Phoebe and I have always been close, and Geoffrey is like a brother to me. I adore the children."

"You deserve more." Matthew had taken the seat opposite her and he could see the discomfort in her eyes. "You deserve happiness of your own."

"I'm perfectly happy, and I think it's churlish of you to say otherwise."

"I wasn't trying to make you angry. I only meant—"

"I know what you meant! Don't make matters worse by repeating it."

Matthew drew back so shadows would hide his face. She wasn't happy with her life, despite her insistence to the contrary, and it hurt him to acknowledge this. Angelica's happiness was too important to him. "I've always wondered," he said, "did your parents have any part in your decision to break our engagement?"

Angelica was silent for so long, he almost expected her not to answer at all. At last, she said, "Not in the breaking of it. All that came about because of our argument. I assume you recall that?"

"In every unpleasant detail."

She nodded and sighed. "We were so young. At times, I find it difficult to believe I was ever that young and that naive. Mother was never entirely pleased that Father gave you permission to court me in the first place."

"What did she have against me?"

"Nothing personally. It's only that your family home is in York and that's so faraway from London. Of course, the railways have changed that to some extent, but Mother always wanted Phoebe and me to be close by."

Matthew bit back his opinion of a mother who could be so selfish about her children's happiness.

"When I told them I had returned your ring, she convinced Father that it had been a bad match from the beginning. Mother is friends with the Hamilton family, and when Phillip began to show interest in me, she encouraged him."

"I wondered why my letter was never answered."

"Letter?" Angelica leaned forward. "What letter?"

Matthew frowned. "I wrote you after I returned to York. Didn't they give it to you?"

"It must have been lost. I never received a letter from you . . ." Her voice trailed off as if she were deep in thought.

"I assumed when you didn't answer that you wanted nothing more to do with me."

"And you only wrote me once?" she asked.

"When we parted, you said you never wanted to see me or hear from me again! For that matter, you could have written me if you had changed your mind."

"And wouldn't that have been a ladylike thing to do!" she said with marked sarcasm. "Mother would have taken to her fainting couch if she'd known I had ever so much as considered such a thing."

"Does that mean you did consider it?"

"I don't want to talk about it." She refused to meet his eyes.

This gave Matthew quite a bit to think about. He had never considered that she hadn't received his letter.

When they reached her house, Matthew walked Angelica to the door. She paused and said, "I'd like to ask you in, but with two new lodgers, the house is in a turmoil."

"I understand." Matthew hadn't noted any particular discord within her house when he'd come to pick her up, and he recognized her explanation for the excuse that it was.

For a moment, he gazed at her. There were small changes in her. Changes only a lover would notice. Her eyes held a wariness now, as if she was no longer so sure of happiness. Her wool cloak was worn along the edge as if it had seen too many winters and at one spot, the hood's lining was beginning to fray. Earlier that afternoon when he had come for her, he had noticed the house needed a coat of paint and that one of the pickets on the fence had come loose at the bottom. Primarily, however, he was concerned over changes in the expression in her eyes and how her face fell into lines of sadness when she didn't know he was watching her.

Gently, Matthew touched her cheek. He wanted to kiss her and to try to make her forget the years they had been apart. She didn't pull away from him, but that look was back in her eyes, that look that said she expected him to hurt her somehow.

Matthew let his hand drop away. "Good night, Angelica."

"Good night," she whispered as she hurried into her house.

All the way back to the Addamses', Matthew puzzled over Angelica. Had he done something to warrant that anxiety in her? Could it be she had loved Phillip so much that she could never consider having another man hold her?

Matthew recalled the days of their courtship, and the all-too-familiar ache began to rise. Her kisses had been as heady and as sweet as mead. She had fit perfectly in his embrace and even though they had gone no farther, her passion had matched his perfectly. Many times in the past years, he had wished they had become lovers in the full sense of the word. Perhaps then he would have been able to get her out of his mind. At the time, he had respected her too much to press her, and he had had no reason to think they wouldn't have years ahead for loving.

On the other hand, if they had made love, Matthew wasn't sure he could have survived the loss of her. He had often told himself that a song was sooner forgotten if the tune were half unplayed. But he could never forget Angelica. Now, more than ever, that was apparent.

Inside the Addamses' house, he found Phoebe sitting by the fire with her children clustered around her while she read to them from a storybook. Geoffrey was sitting opposite her and seemed as enthralled at the view of his family as the children were with the story. When he saw Matthew, however, he smiled and stood, motioning for Matthew to go with him into the drawing room.

"I didn't want to interrupt the story," Geoffrey explained as he shut the drawing room door. "It's one of their favorites."

"They make a beautiful picture," Matthew said with longing. "Any man would be fortunate to have such a family."

Geoffrey smiled as he poured them each a snifter of brandy. "I count my blessings daily. How was the concert?"

"Quite enjoyable. It was a good band."

"And the company? Don't tell me you two quarreled again."

"No, nothing like that. She did give me the impression, however, that she wouldn't encourage me." He took the glass of brandy and let it warm in the palm of his hand.

"Did she?" Geoffrey sounded surprised.

"Evidently, she and Hamilton were so happy together that she isn't interested in anyone else."

Geoffrey sat in the leather wing chair opposite Matthew's. "Angelica told you that?"

"Not in so many words, but it's what she meant."

For a couple of minutes, Geoffrey stared in silence at the fire through his brandy snifter, as if he were trying to decide whether to speak. Finally, he said, "That's not the way it was between them. Angelica and Phillip. Not by a long shot."

"What do you mean?" Matthew watched his friend intently.

"Damn it all, I'm betraying a confidence in telling you this, and Phoebe will have my head if she ever hears I told you, but you have a right to know."

Matthew leaned forward.

"They weren't happy at all. Not that Angelica didn't try to make it work, but there wasn't much to build on. You know what a rounder Phillip was when we were in school."

Matthew nodded. "His brother talked about it all the time."

"Marriage didn't change him. If anything, he became worse. He took to hard drinking and soon was gambling steadily. He wasn't any good at cards and always lost more than he won. That wasn't the worst of it, though. He also started keeping company with loose women."

"He did?" Matthew's voice came out in a growl. His hand tightened on the glass, and he had to restrain himself from breaking it. "Did Angelica know all this?"

"She's not a fool, Matt. Toward the end, he was drunk most of the time. Phoebe and her parents only tolerated him for Angelica's sake. I think Mrs. Baker felt guilty since she had championed him when he was courting Angelica. One night, he gambled away their coach and pair and had to walk home. Of course, Angelica knew. As for the women, she must have at least guessed. If Phillip was stupid enough to brag of his conquests to me, he probably told her, too."

"The blackguard!"

"He was shot, you know. The police called it an accident, but the word down at my club is that a jealous husband pulled the trigger."

"Damn!" Matthew murmured.

"Angelica never complained. She always made excuses about his rudeness and his drunkenness." Geoffrey paused. "Once, and I have to admit I could be wrong about this, he seems to have hurt her. Quite by accident, I saw a bruise on her wrist one day, and from the way she acted when I asked about it, I suspect Phillip put it there."

Red anger was pounding in Matthew's temples, but he forced himself to remain calm externally. "Didn't you try to help her?"

"Of course, I did! What do you take me for? On more than one occasion, I threatened to thrash Hamilton within an inch of his life, but he made it clear that if I did, Angelica would bear the brunt of it. What else could I do? He meant it, and he was her husband."

"That explains a lot," Matthew said slowly. "It explains why she looks at me the way she does."

"She laughs these days. For a while, she had stopped laughing altogether. It might tell you why she isn't encouraging male callers."

"Yes. Yes, it makes everything clear."

"I know it must not be much of a consolation, but Mrs. Baker told Phoebe that she regrets having encouraged Angelica to marry Phillip instead of you. And who knows? If you had tried to patch it up instead of heading to Yorkshire in such a fury, you might have won her back.''

''I was young and foolish,'' Matthew admitted. ''I can see now how stupid I was.''

''We all go through that,'' Geoffrey said tactfully, ''but you're being given a second chance. Not many of us are allowed that privilege. Here you are, a single man, and her a widow, and older and wiser. Don't let this chance slip by, man.''

Matthew managed a crooked smile. ''You've given me a lot to consider. I don't intend to make the same mistake twice. I have a new regret, however.''

''Oh? What's that?''

''I wish I had been the one to put a bullet in Hamilton.''

Geoffrey smiled. ''You aren't the only one in this room who has expressed that sentiment.''

Matthew was filled with determination to win Angelica before his visit was over. Or if not then, to move to London straightaway and court her until he overcame her resistance. He wasn't going to lose her a second time. Not if he could help it.

Chapter Four

"This seems marginally indecent," Angelica repeated. "This is a mourning dress, after all."

"Keep sewing or we'll never finish in time," Phoebe said. "Once we get these ribbons in place, no one will know what it was originally. Besides, if you would let me buy you a new dress, we wouldn't have to do this."

They sat in Angelica's parlor with a basket of pink ribbons between them and a pile of discarded black braid on the floor. Cecilia Neville, who had remained home, sick with a cold, sat wrapped in a lap rug on a chair by the fire. The girl felt too feverish to help sew, but she offered an unending stream of suggestions.

"I have some pink cabbage roses made of silk. Zenobia and I made them to trim hats, but you can have some," Cecilia said.

"Thank you, Cecilia," Phoebe said as Angelica began to shake her head. "Perhaps one at the neck, do you think?"

"It will be too showy," Angelica objected. "I'm a widow, not a girl entering society."

"Nor are you a decrepit old woman," her sister countered. "Even Mother wears silk flowers, and you know how conservative she is."

Miss Lunt came in, her face arranged in what Angelica thought of as her angel-of-mercy expression. She pinned Cecilia to the chair with her gaze. "Where do you think you're off to, miss?"

Cecilia sank back down. "I was going up to get some silk roses for Angelica's dress."

"You'll sit right there by the fire. Wrap that shawl back around you. I'll not have you coming down with pneumonia. I'll fetch the roses. Where are they?"

"In the basket beside my dressing table," Cecilia replied. "Thank you."

As Miss Lunt passed Quinton on the stairs, they nodded warily at each other. Angelica exchanged a wink with Phoebe and Cecilia.

"How are you?" Quinton said as he crossed to check the temperature of Cecilia's forehead. He pursed his lips and shook his head with staccato jerks. "Why do you have that shawl wrapped around you again? You'll never get your fever down at this rate." He whisked the shawl from her and pulled her chair farther from the fire. "You must follow my instructions or you're liable to wind up with consumption. It happened to one of my cousins. I can tell you he regretted to his dying day that he ignored my advice."

Cecilia's eyes widened, and she pushed still farther away from the fire.

"You, there!" Miss Lunt said to Quinton as she came hurrying back down stairs. "What are you doing to that girl!"

"Only what's best for her," Quinton said as he folded his hands like a squirrel over his narrow chest. "I'm only trying to keep her alive."

"By freezing her to death?" Miss Lunt rushed over to Cecilia and tied the shawl around her shoulders.

Angelica and Phoebe exchanged a glance and tried not to smile. This battle over how to doctor Cecilia's cold had been waged all morning.

"I'm feeling better," Cecilia said unconvincingly. "Really I am." But her words had come out sounding like, "Dime feelin' bedder. Really die amb."

Both Quinton and Miss Lunt frowned at her. "Hot water with lemon in it," she said. "Hot cocoa," he said at the same time. They glared at each other.

Phoebe took the silk rose from Miss Lunt and held it to the neck of Angelica's silver-gray dress. "Perfect."

Angelica nodded as she watched the two rivals scurry off toward the kitchen. "I have to admit it's pretty."

"Keep sewing. I want you to wear this dress to the theater tonight."

"Are you sure Matthew wants me to be a part of this? He acts as if he's mad at me half of the time."

"How does he act the other half?"

"I don't know. I never have been able to figure him out."

"You're probably trying too hard," Phoebe replied. "Men aren't as complex as we are. I can read Geoffrey like a book."

Cecilia piped up. "I've heard my mother say the same thing about my father."

"There's nothing simple about Matthew. Every time I expect one thing, he does another." She was still confused about what had happened on her porch after the concert in the park. For a moment, she had been positive he was about to kiss her, then he had said good-night and was gone.

"Matthew specifically asked if you are coming with us, and he seemed pleased to learn you are. Sew faster."

"If I sew faster, my stitches will show."

Miss Lunt reappeared with a glass of hot water cloudy with lemon juice. Quinton was right on her heels with a steaming cup of cocoa. Miss Lunt thrust the glass into Cecilia's hand. "Drink it down."

By the time Cecilia finished the lemon water and then the cocoa Quinton insisted she drink as well, she was pale, but she managed a smile. "Thank you. I feel ever so much better now. I think my fever is breaking."

Miss Lunt put a practiced hand on Cecilia's brow. "You still feel warm."

"Maybe it's the covers and fire," Cecilia suggested.

Quinton felt her cheek. "Of course, that's it. Unbundle, girl. Your health depends on it."

"Could I help you sew since I'm feeling so much better?" Cecilia's eyes pleaded with Angelica.

"Of course, you can. Pull your chair up closer."

Quinton and Miss Lunt headed for the back of the house, each arguing for a different course of action to cure Cecilia.

"How do you really feel?" Angelica whispered.

"Terrible. But if I have to swallow anything else, I'll be sick for sure!"

By the time Phoebe had to leave, the dress trimming was finished, and when Angelica put the dress on that evening, she had to admit it was much improved. Without the heavy black braid, the dress appeared lighter in color. Phoebe had bought bright pink ribbon in a narrow width and paler pink for the wider stripes. The silk rose at her throat made Angelica's cheeks seem pinker and her eyes brighter. Or maybe, Angelica thought, the change in her was brought about by her anticipation of seeing Matthew that night.

The Addamses' carriage arrived promptly, and as Angelica went down to meet it, she was thinking about how much she had been out in public since Matthew's arrival, more than she had been in months. And she was thoroughly enjoying herself.

In the carriage, she sat with Matthew facing Phoebe and Geoffrey. "Stella was pouting when we left," Phoebe said to Angelica. "She thinks she is quite grown-up enough to go see a play."

Geoffrey laughed. "She will lead us a chase when she's a bit older, I'm afraid. She already has more ideas in her head than the twins."

"I'm not so sure about that," Phoebe said. "Tom and Will share adventures between themselves, and Stella has only us to talk to. I imagine they will all turn our hair gray."

"I like children," Matthew said. "Someday, I hope to have a house full of them."

"Speaking of houses, have you found one to buy?" Geoffrey asked.

"Not yet, but there are several I'm considering. It's important to me to find the right one. I don't plan to move again."

"Unless it's to go back to York," Angelica reminded him.

"I'll go there from time to time, of course, but I expect to make this my primary residence." His dark eyes met hers, as if he were asking her an unspoken question.

"I hope you find what you're looking for," she said.

"Oh, I already have. I'm just not sure if it's available."

Angelica looked away. Matthew could be so confusing. She couldn't tell if he was teasing her in fun or if he was trying to irritate her. By Phoebe's smallest of smiles, Angelica knew she assumed Matthew to be flirting. Angelica wished she could tell for certain.

The theater was a popular one and the production starred not only Mrs. Kendall, but Samuel Phelps, as well. Both actors were immensely popular and the theater was already becoming crowded.

"We were lucky to get a box," Geoffrey said as they gave their tickets to an attendant. "I had to reserve it last month."

"You've known that long that Matthew would be here?" Angelica asked. She looked accusingly at Phoebe. She had assumed the visit was more spontaneous than that. Evidently, Phoebe and Geoffrey had planned this matchmaking for quite a while.

The seats in the box were situated so that Angelica was close beside Matthew and had a perfect view of the stage. The red velvet curtains were closed, and the orchestra was playing in the pit.

Geoffrey took the seat behind the women and said to Matthew, "I read Darwin's monkey book. With all the fervor it's causing, I thought I should be informed."

Matthew nodded. "I've read it. I think he presents a good argument for evolution."

With a laugh, Phoebe said, "Don't let Mother and Father hear you say that. Father says—" she lowered her voice in imitation "—'The Bible says everything was created in six days, and there's no mention of ape-men. It's been proven the world was created in 4004 B.C., and that's an end to it.'" To her husband she said, "I think you only read it to irritate my parents."

"You're a fine one to talk," Geoffrey said. "I found your copy of *Ruth* by Mrs. Gaskell."

"You didn't!"

Angelica leaned closer. "When you finish it, can I read it?"

"Yes, but it's terribly scandalous." In a whisper, Phoebe added, "The heroine has an illegitimate child."

"It can't be racier than *Jude the Obscure*," Angelica pointed out. "Mother would die if she knew you gave me that one."

Matthew and Geoffrey exchanged a smile.

"Go ahead, you two," Phoebe said as she tapped her husband's arm. "Laugh at us all you please. Our secrets are out."

"Mother hasn't read anything more recent than *The Mysteries of Udolpho*," Angelica said. "She's out of touch with the times. I loved *Udolpho*, too—who doesn't? But you'd think it was the only novel ever written."

"I remember you were always reading," Matthew said. "You'll be glad to hear I've taken up reading, as well."

"You have? I remember your saying that I read too much."

"I changed my mind."

"It would seem you have a common interest, after all," Geoffrey said. "I suspected you would have. I've never known an intelligent man that didn't eventually turn to books."

"You sound like a graybeard," Phoebe said affectionately. "Doesn't he, Angelica?"

"Look," Angelica said as she leaned forward. "The curtain is going up."

Actually, the curtain had divided in the center and was sweeping into the wings, revealing an elaborately painted backdrop. As soon as the curtain was off-stage, the backdrop rose to reveal the set. Mrs. Kendall sat in one of the parlor chairs, and Samuel Phelps leaned against the mantel. As soon as the audience recognized the stars, there was resounding applause.

The play was the tender story of star-crossed lovers, and soon Phoebe was touching her lace-edged handkerchief to her eyes to stem the flow of tears. Angelica was much too aware of Matthew's nearness in the dark to become absorbed in the play.

Once, Angelica looked at Matthew and, to her surprise, he turned to her and met her gaze. Being in the draped box in the dark gave intimacy to their nearness, and Angelica felt excitement race through her. As the actors spoke of their love, Angelica let herself become lost in Matthew's eyes. He was tall and handsome, and the dimness lent an aura of mystery to him. His lips were sensual without being thick, and showed he was more inclined to laughter than to anger. She wondered what it was about her that provoked him so. It was too dark to read the expression in his eyes, but the reflected limelight touched them as well as illumined the curve of his cheek and jaw.

Angelica tore her eyes away and stared down at the stage. After a few moments, she sensed he had done the same. Although the theater was cool, she felt as if she had come too close to a flame; heat filled her and made her breath come faster.

The play had several parallels with her own broken engagement, and Angelica found herself wondering if Phoebe had known this when the tickets were purchased. She watched Mrs. Kendall fall in love with Samuel Phelps, lose him due to a quirk of fate, and nearly die of a broken heart. Of course, Angelica had never come near dying, though she had been miserable enough to feel as if she might. The heroine endured one trauma after another, but in the end, her pure and gentle nature prevailed. At last, just when hope seemed gone for good, the hero reappeared and saved the day.

Angelica joined in the applause, and Phoebe dabbed her tear-soaked handkerchief at her eyes. Even

Geoffrey's voice sounded gruff as if he, too, were moved to near tears but was determined not to show it.

As they joined the flow of the crowd leaving the theater, Angelica was glad of Matthew's protecting bulk. He kept one hand on her waist and guided her safely to one of the doors. The air outside was crisp and cold. Angelica fastened her cloak securely and drew the hood up over her head before pulling on her gloves.

"Let's walk a bit," Geoffrey suggested. "We won't be able to get the coach out of the traffic for a while."

The two couples strolled down the street and looked in shop windows adorned with Yuletide decorations. Everywhere could be heard the conversation and laughter of the theatergoers, interspersed with the rattle and clop of passing carriages and the rhymes of costermongers selling their wares.

A boy hawking muffins hurried up to them, the bell tinkling on his tray. He gazed at them hopefully as he sang the tune he had devised to bring attention to his wares. Geoffrey reached into his pocket and handed the boy a coin. "How's business this evening?"

The boy grinned. "It ain't bad. Not by half. Folks buys muffins aplenty when it's cold out."

Angelica bit into the muffin the boy handed her from the flannel-wrapped depths of the basket, and she found it was full of currants and still warm.

They wandered past a pieman calling out the traditional, "Toss or buy! Up and win 'em!" Across the street, a tart seller was shouting "Coventrys, Coventrys! Bowlas, bowlas! Chonkeys, chonkeys! Jumbles, jumbles!'' as if he would sell more pastries if he cried the names twice. A man with a brass-fitted urn on a pedestal was extolling, ''Hot elder wine, hot elder.''

Matthew stopped by a man who was roasting chestnuts over a fire in a metal drum and bought a packet for them to eat as they walked.

''Look at this bonnet,'' Phoebe said as she went to a shop window and peered in. ''How adorable.''

Angelica joined her. ''You should go to the milliner shop where the Neville sisters work. To my mind, they do the best work in town. Zenobia was sewing 'cabbages' on a nightcap this evening—you've never seen so many ribbons on a cap. I hope their employer knows what treasures those girls are.''

''Zenobia?'' Matthew asked.

''One of my boarders. She and her sister are such lambs, but their parents ignore them entirely. I really must find them husbands. It's certain their parents won't do anything for them and by the time they come in from the store they are usually too tired or have brought home too much work for them to go out and meet people.''

''And you feel husbands would solve their problems?'' Matthew asked.

''They would certainly be more secure. I can tell they worry about their future. They weren't brought up to ply a trade, and they aren't suited to such long hours as they must work. If they had husbands to support them, they could perhaps go into business for themselves and not ruin their health.''

"They don't actually make the hats themselves, do they?" Phoebe asked. "I've heard that will make a person go mad."

"No, no, the hats are all properly shaped and dried before the sisters touch them."

"You worry more about your boarders than anyone I've ever known," Geoffrey said.

"Of course, I do. We're almost like a family. They have all been abandoned by friends and relatives to some extent and we lean on each other."

"What if someday you should decide to leave Lady Slipper Lane?" Matthew asked. "What then?"

Angelica laughed. "I'll never leave my house. Where on earth would I go? Besides, my people need me. I'm like a mother to the sisters, even if we are almost the same age."

Matthew made no reply, but he regarded her thoughtfully.

After the crowd had thinned, they went to their carriage and drove home over the snow-slushed streets. At the corner of Lady Slipper Lane, Geoffrey knocked on the wall to signal the driver to stop. "Carolers," he said in explanation.

They got out of the carriage and listened to the songs of the group of men, women and children. The tunes were familiar ones, and Angelica found herself humming along with the singers.

"I love Christmas," she said when the carolers finished. "Of all the seasons, it's my favorite." Then she remembered it would also have been her and Matthew's anniversary, and she said, "I should go in. There's no need to drive me any farther. My door is right down there, and it's hard to turn a carriage on this street."

"I'll walk you to the door," Matthew said.

"There's really no need. I'll just—"

Matthew took her elbow before she could finish, and she had no choice but to walk beside him as Phoebe and Geoffrey returned to the carriage.

"Christmas is my favorite season, too," he said as the snow crunched under their boots. "Yet, it can be the saddest of times as well as the happiest."

"I know. How well I know." Angelica was too emotionally confused to evade answering.

"Do you ever think back on what might have been?" he asked.

She was silent for a moment. "Of course. All women do."

"So do men."

"I wish we didn't. Think of the sad times, I mean. We can't change them, and it only makes the pleasant recollections seem bittersweet."

"Geoffrey said something interesting to me the other night. He said there are rare times when we are given second chances, when everything falls into place and we really can change things to the way they were meant to be."

"What did Geoffrey mean by that?" She found she was holding her breath.

"He was talking about us."

Angelica looked up at the house where she had lived as Phillip's wife and a sadness came over her. "He was wrong. No one can ever truly go back. All the things that have happened to us in the interim rise up and shout to be noticed. I'm not the same person I was five years ago, and you aren't the same man.''

''Then you're saying you want me to stop seeing you?'' Matthew asked as he turned to face her. ''Are you telling me that?''

''I don't know!'' she whispered. ''You confuse me. My life may seem dull to you, but it's my life.''

''I wouldn't say anything about you is dull.''

''I have commitments, people who need me!''

''Arrangements could be made.''

She backed away from him. ''I'm afraid.'' Her words came out so softly, she thought he couldn't have heard them, but she couldn't repeat them. They held too much truth.

''You're afraid of me?'' he said at last.

Angelica couldn't answer because she didn't know. Instead, she backed farther away. In the two years of her marriage, she had learned men—husbands in particular—were not to be trusted. Her gentleness had been scorned, her vulnerabilities had been ridiculed and her wishes consistently ignored. All of this by a man who had seemed to be the sweetest of suitors. If Phillip had treated her so badly, what worse would she receive from Matthew? She already knew Matthew had a temper, and he was strong physically as well as emotionally and mentally. She was afraid he, too, might have a dark side, and she had no idea how it might manifest toward her.

Shaking her head again, Angelica turned and ran for her house.

As soon as she was inside, she leaned back against the door as if to block out all her fears. Through the parlor doorway, she heard laughter and strains of conversation.

It was her boarders; they needed her. She might not reach the height of ecstasy in her life now, but she was also safe from the depths of despair. She might not know if she would have a ham for Christmas dinner, but she knew there would be hot food on the table and more than enough to feed everyone. This was the safe road. It was the way she had chosen.

But inside, she ached for Matthew and for the love they had shared.

To keep from thinking, she hurried out of her cloak and into the parlor. Everyone was there, even Peggy. Zenobia was showing the girl how to braid trim to sew around a bonnet, and Peggy looked as seriously contemplative as if she were studying calculus.

Quinton and Miss Lunt were still fussing over Cecilia and driving her to mute distraction. Mr. Hart was telling Blanche and whomever else might be listening of his exploits as a young man. Blanche nodded and laughed as the occasion merited and was sewing diligently on a pillow covering.

When Zenobia saw Angelica, she spoke up. "Did you enjoy the play?"

"Yes. Yes, it was wonderful."

"I had hoped you'd bring your young man in so we could meet him," Blanche said as she worked the needle through the fabric.

"He's only a friend," Angelica replied. "A friend of my sister and brother-in-law."

"A bird told me he's an old flame," Mr. Hart said jovially. "New fire can rise from old ashes."

Angelica didn't answer.

"Mr. Hart, you're not to tease her," Blanche scolded her husband. "If she wants to keep Mr. Thornton a secret, why, she has every right."

"That must have been a very talkative little bird," Angelica said with a frown at Cecilia, who had heard all about Matthew from Phoebe that afternoon.

Cecilia only smiled and made a chirping sound.

"At any rate, Mr. Thornton will be gone soon, and like as not, he will either settle in some other neighborhood or return for good to York. Either way means nothing to me." She went to Blanche's chair. "What are you making?"

Blanche held up the pillowcase to show the appliqué that vaguely resembled a white deer. "It's a white hart. See? It's my name in picture form. Blanche means white."

"She's clever, is Mrs. Blanche," her husband confirmed. "My name has been Hart all my life, and I never thought of it as being a deer."

"It's going to be my insignia," Blanche said. "I'm going to put a white hart on all my pillow slips and use harts in my embroidery work. I've drawn one to needlepoint on my footstool, and I'm going to paint one on the set of teak wood trays where I keep my shell collection."

"We're going to have a whole herd of deer all over our room," Mr. Hart said with a laugh.

Blanche looked at Peggy, who was watching with her eyes wide and solemn. "What about you, girl? What's your last name?"

"O'Mally, ma'am. Peggy O'Mally."

"Hmm," Blanche intoned thoughtfully. "O'Mally. No, I can't do much with that. What about a shamrock, girl, to show you're Irish? I could embroider you one on your Sunday dress."

Peggy favored Blanche with one of her rare smiles. "You'd do that?"

"Surely, I would. I planned to pass all my needle skills down to a daughter, but that wasn't to be. I'll teach them to you."

Peggy glanced quickly at Angelica to see if she would mind.

Angelica smiled and nodded her encouragement. "I could teach you to crochet. Maybe we'll make a needle woman of you."

To their surprise, Peggy's eyes filled with tears. "Thank you!" she exclaimed. "I'll try ever so hard!" She jumped up and ran from the room.

Blanche stared after her. "I never meant to make the girl cry. Why was she crying?"

Angelica found her own eyes were damp. "She was happy, not sad. Peggy has known so little kindness that the least bit overwhelms her. I'll go to her." As Angelica followed the direction Peggy had taken, she knew she was right in her decision not to put herself before the others. No one else would ever try to teach Peggy anything as long as she could scrub and scour. Peggy and the others needed her.

And Angelica needed them.

Chapter Five

"Mrs. Hamilton, I'm going to speak to you as if you were my own daughter."

Angelica looked up at Blanche. "Is something wrong? Quinton and Miss Lunt aren't arguing again, are they?"

"Do they ever leave off? They are at it constantly, I think they have discovered themselves to be kindred spirits." Blanche seated herself in a chair opposite Angelica. "No, it's yourself to whom I'm referring."

"Me? Have I upset you in some way?" Angelica tried to remember where she had left the handkerchief Blanche had embroidered for her. It was a delicate little thing on which Blanche had stitched a spray of angelica, reminiscent of her given name, and Angelica had mislaid it.

"Of course not. I'm concerned about your attitude toward your young man."

"Matthew? I mean, Mr. Thornton?" She returned to the shawl she was crocheting. "I don't know what you mean."

"Yes, you do. Don't you think I see you staring out the window or into the fire as if your mind were far-away?"

"Everyone does those things, Mrs. Blanche."

"Not half the time, they don't. This may make you smile, but I fancy myself to be rather an expert on affairs of the heart. I am a newlywed, you know."

"I know, and I can't tell you how pleased we are to have you here."

"Don't change the subject," Blanche said with a sharp nod that made her gray curls bounce. "I know that because you are a widow woman, you feel your heart is in the grave, but you're still young and have years ahead. Long years," she added.

"I pray so, but Mr. Thornton—"

"Don't pretend and play coy with me, young lady. I know you call him by his Christian name when you don't think about it otherwise."

Angelica began crocheting faster. "There are matters you aren't aware of. Matthew and I weren't merely courting. We were engaged to be married. It was to be a double wedding with my sister and Geoffrey. We quarreled, and the engagement was broken. Matthew has a temper when he's roused and—"

"What man worth his salt does not? I can tell you Mr. Hart and I have had our set-to's. It's the same with any man of passions."

Angelica's crochet hook drifted to a halt as she tried to imagine Mr. Hart as being passionate.

"You have to let bygones be bygones. Five years is long enough to punish any man."

"It's more than that. I even married someone else. I can't act as if nothing has happened but an argument."

"Of course, you can't, and you shouldn't. You're a widow woman, not a blushing virgin. All the more reason to make up with your Matthew."

Before Angelica could object, Blanche leaned forward to depart a confidence.

"I know what I'm talking about." The woman glanced to the corners of the room, as if to be certain they were alone. "The same thing happened to my sister. She and her beau quarreled and she married another man. Four years later, he left her and their three babies for another woman." Her voice dropped to a mere whisper and Angelica had to lean closer to hear. "He *divorced* her. Never saw her or those babies again!"

"What happened to her?" Angelica had never known anyone who had been divorced.

"I may not have told you this before, but my papa was a vicar. Her vicar, to be exact, and he couldn't take her back in. Not with her divorced and all. The church elders had thought her marriage was scandalous in itself, since my sister had married beneath her station."

"If she had been my child, I would have told those elders to—"

"Luckily, her jilted beau heard about her plight. He went to her and married her in spite of everything. He raised her children alongside their own, and you never saw such a happy family."

"I'm happy for your sister, but I'm not in need of rescuing." Angelica began working at the shawl again.

"I never meant that you were. I only say there's no need to throw away your life because of ill-placed pride." Blanche drew herself up. "You must have noticed I'm not in the first blush of youth. I saw what I wanted in Mr. Hart, and I waited for him."

"Why did you wait so long? Why didn't you give up on him and marry someone else?"

"Because I love him." Blanche gave another of her decisive nods. "When you love someone, years don't matter." She stood and patted Angelica on the shoulder. "Think about what I've said and consider my words as if I were your own mother, for that's how I meant them. Give the lad another chance." She went away to give Angelica privacy to meditate on her new insight.

Angelica put the shawl aside and went to the window. Snow was falling outside, and puffs of cold air were hovering near the glass panes. Across the street, some children were playing in the fresh snow, and she could hear their shouts and laughter. As she watched them, her breath fogged the glass.

Blanche had a point. She was letting the main current of life sweep by. In time, she, like Blanche, would be too old to have children, and there would be no one by her side to grow gray along with her. Did she really want her future to be here in her house with boarders who came and went and who died or married or simply moved on? Was she willing to settle for that when she might have Matthew?

Angelica drew away from the window. There was no reason to believe she could have him. Half the time, he acted as if he were barely tolerating her presence. But then the remainder of time, he looked at her in a way that aroused excitement in her such as she had never felt with any other man.

But did she really want any husband at all?

She had been a widow longer than she had been a wife, but her memories were still unfaded. She had grown to detest Phillip long before he died, and there had been nothing about their marriage to recommend another one to her.

Yet with Matthew, she had felt the beginnings of passions that Phillip had never stirred. Even now, she ached for Matthew to hold her and to kiss her. Perhaps with him, the act of lovemaking would be pleasant. Even exciting. Angelica had always suspected it could be that way with the right man. With Matthew.

She had to find out whether there was a chance for them to put their love back together.

She gathered up the shawl and her yarn and put them in the basket she used to carry them. This way, she could take her work to Phoebe's house and look as if she were accustomed to dropping by at this time of day. Besides, the shawl was being made on commission, and she had to finish it in order to buy a ham for Christmas Day.

In no time, she was hurrying through the snowy streets toward her sister's house. Because of soot from coal fires and the burning wastes of factories, London snow soon took on a smudged, grayish layer. The new snow had already brightened the streets to freshness and made every avenue look like the cards that friends sent to each other at Christmas. Children with rosy cheeks and laughing eyes chased each other along the walkways out front of the houses. Angelica saw the same rosy cheeks and laughing eyes in many of the older people she met, just as if age were a circle with youth joining both ends. Every horse seemed to have a bell on its harness and men and women alike had pinned sprigs of holly or mistletoe to their cloaks and capes. Fat turkeys and thick hams hung in shop windows, and in the bakeries, there were breads in loaves or braids and muffins displayed in baskets or on checkered cloth. Angelica felt as if she were singing inside as she hurried past the shops that lined the street nearest Phoebe's house.

She found everyone in the kitchen. Phoebe was supervising the creation of barley-sugar candy, while Mrs. Watson, the cook, made candied orange peel. The spicy aromas filled the kitchen along with laughter.

Matthew and Geoffrey, both in their shirt sleeves, were rubbing cooking oil on the marble slabs used for making cookies and candy and were generally being in the way of those with cooking expertise. When Angelica came in, they were finishing a duet of "Hark the Herald Angels Sing," Matthew's rich baritone carrying the tune while Geoffrey harmonized. When Matthew saw Angelica, he paused.

For a breath, their eyes met and Angelica felt as if time stopped. Then Matthew smiled, and she was a part of the group. She put her needlework basket on a counter where it would be out of the way and took an apron from Mrs. Watson.

Phoebe stood at the stove with the three children a safe distance away. She was stirring a pot of boiling sugar water with one hand while she kept the children away from the stove with the other. "Thank goodness, Angelica! Come test this sugar. I've run out of hands."

Angelica took a wooden spoon and dipped the handle first in the pot, then into cold water. Gingerly, she slipped off the sugar shell that had formed. Holding it close to her ear, she pressed on it and heard a crack. "It's crackling," she confirmed.

"Finally! I put in too much water and I thought my stirring arm would fall off before the sugar was done."

"Here's the lemon juice," Matthew said as he handed Angelica a small bowl.

"Not much, now," Phoebe cautioned. "I still remember the candy you made a few years ago that set all our teeth on edge."

Angelica laughed as she poured a few drops into the pot to keep the sugar from graining. As she stepped aside, Matthew lifted the heavy pot from the stove and set it into a larger bucket of cold water.

At once, Phoebe ladled some of the mixture onto the cold marble. It hardened as it spread and cooled. "Break it into pieces, Geoffrey, and oil the slab again."

"Yes, my lady," her husband said playfully, with a tug to his forelock. "Right away, ma'am."

Phoebe swatted at him with her free hand as he set about doing her bidding.

Angelica and Matthew broke the candy from the second slab and gave pieces to each of the children. The rest they put in the crockery jar Mrs. Watson used to store candy. Matthew surprised Angelica by holding a piece to her lips. As she opened her mouth and took his offering, her lips touched his fingers and the intimacy of the gesture went all through her. He smiled at her and turned away.

Angelica thought it best to turn her attention to something else, as well. Mrs. Watson had soaked orange peels in cold water, changing the water frequently to get rid of the bitterness. Now she was adding the peels to another mixture of bubbling sugar water. Angelica went to her and offered to help.

Mrs. Watson relinquished the spoon, and Angelica took her place. Even as uncomfortably warm as it was beside the stove, this was preferable to having to meet Matthew's eyes. Keeping her thoughts to herself, she ran her tongue over the melting candy in her mouth, making it last as long as possible.

As Mrs. Watson gathered bowls and utensils to be washed, Matthew led the children in another carol. Angelica noticed that Mrs. Watson smiled even though Angelica was sure the woman was more than ready to reclaim her kitchen.

When the orange peels had cooked to transparency, Angelica spooned them out onto a rack over a pan so they could drain. The remaining sugar was to be clarified with an egg white and cold water and used in wine or in other recipes.

"I hope to get a doll for Christmas," Stella was telling Matthew. "Mama says I may, if I've been a good girl."

"I see. And have you been?" Matthew asked as if he were giving this grave consideration.

"Pretty good," Stella said.

"Pretty good for a girl," Tom corrected as he reached for another piece of candy. He broke it in half and gave a piece to Will.

"I want toy soldiers," Will said. "So does Tom. And new sleds."

"A tea party set," Stella said, her blue eyes sparkling.

"And a drummer that will play a tune when I turn a handle," Will added.

"I want a top that hums," Tom said with growing excitement. "And a Jacob's ladder."

"Whoa!" Matthew said with a laugh. "How will old Saint Nicholas remember all that? We must make a list."

Phoebe and Angelica exchanged a smile. All the toys the children had mentioned had already been bought and were stored in a box under Angelica's bed.

"Get your Aunt Angelica and let's make a list," Matthew said.

Stella grabbed Angelica's skirt and leaned back so she could look up at her. "Will you help us? Me and Will and Tom can't write yet."

"Will, Tom and I," Phoebe corrected.

"I ought to help your mother," Angelica said. "We still aren't through in here."

"I'll take care of all of it," Mrs. Watson said hastily. "All of you just get out from under my feet."

"Come along, then," Phoebe said. "We must get out of Mrs. Watson's way."

Angelica picked up her sewing basket as they went toward the parlor. She could hear the cook humming the last carol they'd sung under her breath as she carried the copper pots to the sink.

The twins ran to get paper, and Geoffrey brought in his pens and inkwell from the study. Phoebe cleared a small table and arranged seating so that Angelica and Matthew could share it.

"A doll," Stella said as soon as the paper arrived. "One with hair like me." She pulled on her blond curls so Angelica could see the color and make note of it. She looked thoughtful. "Put my name up here at the top so Saint Nicholas won't leave my doll at the wrong house."

Angelica printed Stella's name where the child had indicated. "How about a blue velvet dress for the doll? One the color of your eyes?"

Stella nodded, her face bright with the possibilities.

One by one, Angelica wrote down the toys Stella wished for, and Matthew did the same for the twins. Phoebe pretended to be engrossed in the Battenberg lace tablecloth she was making for her mother, all the while mentally checking her children's list with that of her purchases.

"I hope Saint Nick has a big bag this year," Matthew said when the lists were finished. "He will need it."

"Do you think we've asked for too much?" Will asked in concern.

"We don't want to be greedy," Tom added.

Matthew had seen Phoebe's smile. "I would say this is just about right. You're not to change your minds, now."

All three children nodded solemnly.

"All right. Fetch me an envelope, Tom, and I'll post this myself."

Tom hurried to get an envelope, Will right on his heels.

"I'm going to go think of a name for my doll," Stella announced. "It's important."

"All right," Geoffrey said. "Think of a good one."

Stella hurried out and soon could be heard climbing the stairs.

"Children grow up so fast," Phoebe said. "It seems as if Stella should still be an infant."

"I was thinking the same thing about the twins," Geoffrey said. "By this time next year, I'll be hiring a tutor for them."

"Don't rush them, Geoffrey. They'll be gone all too soon." Phoebe drew her yellow cashmere shawl closer about her shoulders. She rested her hand briefly on her rounding abdomen as if to reassure herself there was another baby on the way.

Because there was mixed company present, no one mentioned the coming birth, but given how easily Phoebe tired already, Angelica wondered if there might not be twins again. Twins ran on both sides of their family tree.

Angelica looked at Matthew. "Have you decided on a house yet?"

"As a matter of fact, I made an offer on one only this morning."

Geoffrey said, "The one you described to me last night?"

"Exactly. I can't think of one that better suits my needs."

"I never expected you to return to London permanently," Angelica said. "You were always so determined on living in York."

"Times change. So do people. After living there as an adult for a while, I saw it differently than I had as a boy. The old home place is a grand one, and naturally I'll never sell it, but I don't fancy continuing to live in a place where there are drafts strong enough to blow curtains and where most of the chimneys don't draw properly."

"It seems a shame to let it sit idle," Angelica told him.

"Someday, I'll hand it down to one of my children or grandchildren. By then, it may have aged to the point of being picturesque and the inconvenience won't matter so much."

Angelica thoughtfully picked up her crocheting. Most bachelors didn't consider the legacy of unborn children—not unless they were planning to marry. "It requires a wife to have children. Do you have anyone in mind?"

"Yes."

She waited but he didn't elaborate. The idea that he might be interested in someone else gave her a physical twinge of pain. After the theater, he had suggested that she was the one he was interested in, but now that she thought back on it, Matthew had really only been quoting Geoffrey and a conversation they had had. She might have assumed he meant more by his words than he had intended.

"That's a pretty shawl," Phoebe said. "Who is it for?"

"Mr. Dorsey commissioned it for his married daughter. You remember her—she's tall and has black hair? She moved to Kent."

"Of course. That color will be perfect on her."

"Commissioned it?" Matthew asked.

"I sometimes sell my needlework through Mr. Pye's shop on Cricket Lane."

"I see."

"It keeps me busy," Angelica added with an edge to her voice. She was embarrassed to admit having to sell her work. "I hate to sit idle."

"Remember how Grandmother Marsh used to say idle hands were the devil's workshop?" Phoebe laughed. "She was usually looking at me when she said it."

Angelica smiled. "You rarely have time to be idle these days."

"That's true. Without Mrs. Watson and her girl and the children's nanny, I don't think I would have time to sit down from morning until night."

As Phoebe began telling all that had happened since she had started the day, Angelica let her mind stray back to Matthew. Even after two years of marriage— perhaps especially then—Phillip had never fit into this family setting as Matthew did. She couldn't imagine Phillip making a Christmas list for a child. Matthew looked as much at home here as Geoffrey did. She remembered Matthew kneeling on the kitchen floor leading the children in the carol, and she smiled.

"When must you leave?" Geoffrey asked.

"The day after Christmas, I'm afraid. It may take a while to strike a bargain on the house I want, and I have to sort through my home in York and decide what to bring and what should be left behind. If this weather holds, I may not be back in town until spring."

Angelica's crochet hook fairly flew as she listened intently. Spring was months away!

"Well, at least then we will have you again," Phoebe said.

"A great deal depends on how the next week goes."

"Does that mean you may not move here after all?" Phoebe asked. "Surely not. I thought you were already decided."

"There has been a possible complication," Matthew replied. "The matter I returned to resolve isn't going smoothly."

Angelica stared down at the shawl, missed a stitch and had to redo it. What if he decided not to move back to town, after all? Phoebe and Geoffrey could visit him in York, but it certainly wouldn't be proper for her to do so. It might be another five years or longer before she saw him again. Yet she was too uncertain of herself to encourage him to return, especially if he was interested in some other woman.

"I should go," Angelica said. "It's still snowing and the walks are getting deep."

"So soon? You only just arrived," Phoebe objected.

"You're staying for supper, surely," Geoffrey added. "I'll send you home by sleigh if the streets are too deep."

"No, no. I didn't intend to barge in for the duration. I only stopped by to pass the time of day."

"I'll see you home," Matthew said.

"It's much too cold out. I can manage. I'm used to it."

"I want to see you home," he repeated.

"All right." She could see there was no use in arguing. Matthew could be as stubborn as she was.

They wrapped up against the cold, and Phoebe insisted Angelica take home some of the candy they had made. Angelica relented. Peggy rarely got sweets and she loved them so.

Snow was still falling in fat flakes that seemed to whisper as they floated down. Angelica's hood and shoulders were dotted even before Phoebe closed the door behind them. Few carriages were still braving the drifts, and those that were had footmen going alongside, pushing at the wheels when they jammed in the snow. Sleighs full of bundled people skimmed over the new surface, and the horses blew streams of clouds from their nostrils.

"You spend a great deal of time seeing me to my house," Angelica commented wryly. "Once, you even left so hurriedly, you forgot your hat."

"So you did see me then. I wasn't sure. I kept my distance so I wouldn't startle you in the dark."

"Thank you for being so thoughtful, but it wasn't necessary. I've gone between our houses for years, and I've never given it a single thought."

"You always have been independent to a fault."

"Please don't start up on my faults again. I keep a longer list of them than anyone, and I'm all too aware how numerous they are. Why is it we argue so often? Can't we be friends at least for Phoebe and Geoffrey's sake?"

"Is that how you see me? As a family friend?"

"How else should I see you?" She held her breath. Surely now he would give her some hint as to whether he saw her platonically or romantically.

"How else, indeed." He walked in silence for a few paces, then took her sewing basket so he could carry it for her. "Maybe I've been wrong to consider moving to London. I have a life in York—friends and cousins and commitments. Maybe I should go back, repair the chimneys, caulk the windows and be content."

"If you're that easily contented, why did you consider moving in the first place?" She lifted her skirts over a drift and a cold wind wafted up her petticoats. She dropped her hem and let snow clog it.

"At times, I wonder that myself." He took her elbow as he helped her cross a rutted street.

"You said you found a house? Is it near Phoebe's?"

"Near enough. It's a larger house than I considered at first, but it's in an excellent location."

"That's important." Pretending to be no more than casually interested, she asked, "Do you need such a large house if you'll be living there alone? Big houses can seem awfully empty with only servants about."

"I hope it won't be empty long."

"I know it's none of my business, but are you seeing someone in York?"

"I'm not a monk, if that's what you mean. I didn't rush out and marry the first girl I found, but my name isn't entirely unknown in York."

"I see no reason to become defensive. I merely asked a question."

"It's the questions you choose to ask. I don't know how to answer them."

"You'll have to forgive me. They didn't seem like such difficult questions to me. For instance, I know if I'm seeing anyone or not. I don't have to think long and hard to answer that. I marvel that you do."

Matthew lowered his head for a few steps, as if he were thinking. "I may as well be honest with you. I do care about someone, but I can't tell if she cares for me or not."

Angelica felt as if a part of her died. "You were never so lukewarm before. Why not ask her how she feels?"

"I have reason to believe so direct an approach might frighten her away. I can't take that risk."

Angelica didn't know what to say. She knew she should never have broached the subject in the first place, but now that he had confided in her, there was only one decent thing to do. She drew in a deep breath and plunged on. "I suppose I could speak to her for you." She kept her face turned away so he couldn't see the tears in her eyes.

"You?"

"As you said, you're a friend of the family, and believe it or not, I do want you to be happy."

"You would speak to her." He sounded amazed. "About me."

"You needn't keep repeating yourself. I'm not as selfish as that. Who is she? Maybe I already know her, if you met her through Phoebe or Geoffrey."

"No. No, you wouldn't know her. I'm not sure I know her myself." He handed back Angelica's sewing basket and without a word, headed back the way they had come.

Shocked by his abrupt departure, Angelica stared after him until she realized her feet were growing numb. With an angry shake of her head, she hurried toward home.

Chapter Six

Christmas was approaching so quickly, Angelica felt she would scarcely have time to do all she must. The day after Matthew had walked her home, Mr. Pye had send word from his store that five other needlework items had been commissioned, and he had said if she finished them all before Boxing Day, he would give her a bonus.

Not wanting to miss the opportunity to earn the extra money, Angelica began staying up later and rising earlier in order to have enough time to do her regular chores and the extra work, as well. Quinton warned that she was courting disaster by pushing herself so hard, and Miss Lunt forecast her complete and imminent breakdown. Both began plying her with elixirs and herbal potions, most of which Angelica managed to pour down the sink or onto her potted fern.

Not only was the need for extra money justification enough, but the additional activity gave her reason to stay away from Phoebe's house and Matthew. Since the day he walked her home and had left her so abruptly, she had been unable to sleep anyway. She didn't know who he loved, but the fact that he had admitted his love for another had caused her heart to break.

Angelica blamed herself. Matthew had given her no encouragement, and she had fallen back in love with him anyway—if indeed she had ever stopped loving him at all. The things he had said to her in recent days and the small courtesies he had shown her could all be attributed to politeness such as anyone might show a woman alone in the world.

Matthew loved someone else. The words echoed like a litany in her brain whether she was busy or not. She had warned herself not to care about him, but she had been unable to stop herself. She had known she was courting heartbreak to continue seeing him after she realized her love for him was alive and well, but she had seen him anyway. Now the worst had happened and he had admitted that he was in love with someone else. Her only comfort was that she had not let him see how much she cared for him.

All Angelica's household was getting in the Christmas spirit, and in her effort to put Matthew behind her, she tried to join in. Blanche had been true to her word in teaching Peggy to embroider, and the girl showed a surprising talent for the work. Whenever she wasn't cleaning or cooking, Peggy could be found bent over her linen sampler, working with contented determination. For the girl's Christmas gift, Angelica had bought her a number of skeins of embroidery thread in various colors, as well as a hoop and needles.

Zenobia and Cecilia had contributed to the season's gaiety by making a large wreath for the front door of the house and smaller ones for each of the bedroom doors. Blanche had added a small herd of white deerlike creatures to her wreath, then helped Peggy make shamrocks for her own.

Cecilia knew how to play the piano, and Angelica was amazed to find Quinton and Miss Lunt singing a duet to Cecilia's accompaniment on the slightly out of tune piano in the back parlor. Afterward, Quinton complained of a tickle in his throat and, instead of finding a larger discomfort of her own for comparison, Miss Lunt fussed over him and prepared him a concoction of balm, wormwood and yarrow to forestall a fever. This kindness encouraged Quinton to prepare for her a tea of rosemary, skullcap, valerian and balm to prevent her migraines. Within days, they went from being rivals to comrades, comparing recipes for medicinal teas. Cecilia attributed it all to her ability to play "When I Saw Sweet Nellie Home."

The only sadness in the boarders stemmed from the fact that Zenobia and Cecilia's parents had not sent money for them to return home for Christmas. The sisters pretended not to care, but often, they both had watery eyes and pink noses as if they had been crying in secret. Blanche noticed the sisters' plight and announced that something must be done about it, but no one had any ideas on how to arouse parental feelings where none apparently existed.

Angelica did all she could to keep the sisters busy, and as a result, her house became filled with wreaths and evergreen boughs and the scents of baking. Zenobia, who was more skilled at knitting, helped Angelica complete a shawl with an intricate stitch. Cecilia made silk roses to add to the wreaths.

Two days before Christmas, there was another generous snowfall. Angelica, who was in the habit of feeding any stray animals in the neighborhood, collected the breakfast scraps and carried them out to the communal feeding dish in the stable. To provide shelter for the strays, she always left the stable door ajar.

Because of the snow and ice, the stable door was frozen in place, but Angelica had no difficulty slipping her lithe body through the crack. As she entered the darkened interior, two dogs crept toward her as if they expected to be chased away, though their tails were wagging in anticipation. Angelica spoke to them in gentle tones as she scraped half the scraps into the dish. As the dogs hurriedly gobbled up the food, she carried the rest to a workbench where half a dozen cats were mewing and pacing.

As she fed the cats, a sound from the rear of the stable drew her attention. She paused and looked in the direction of the noise, but her eyes had not yet adjusted to the darkness and she couldn't see into the deeper shadows. She pursed her lips and whistled, thinking it must be another dog. There was only silence. Angelica shrugged. Had there been an animal back there, she was sure it would have come forward with the others. The only other explanation was her own imagination.

Idly, she stroked the yellow fur of one of the cats. She had always loved animals, and had she been able to afford their upkeep, she would have owned several pets. She still missed the red mare Phillip had gambled away with the carriage, although she supposed it was a good thing she didn't have another mouth to feed.

Again she heard a noise from the darkness of the stable, and this time, it was accompanied by a half-audible moan. The moan had been so soft, she still wasn't positive it hadn't been her imagination. "Is anyone back there?" she called out. There was no answer.

Angelica turned to go. The wary dogs looked up as she approached and eased to the far side of the plate. She usually found dogs to be more easily befriended than cats, but at the same time, they also showed less confidence. These two had had a difficult time before they had wandered down Lady Slipper Lane and her heart went out to them. As she passed them, she spoke to them gently and made no threatening moves. The dogs wagged their tails again.

"Please. Help me." The words were so faint, Angelica almost missed them.

She turned and peered back into the stable. Her eyes had adjusted enough for her to see the vague outline of two stalls on one side and the open area where the carriage had stood on the other. On the wall at the back hung discarded bits of harness, horse brushes, pails and the like. One corner of the last stall held a jumble of apple crates, straw and a few empty feed sacks. The cats usually slept in this corner because the crates offered a barrier against the dogs. It was from this corner the voice had seemed to come.

"Who is it?" Angelica demanded. "Who's back there?"

Only a broken moan resounded.

She hurried into the deeper shadows and found a man lying on the straw and feed sacks. At first, she was frightened, but when he made no move, she edged closer. "Are you all right? Why are you in my stable?"

"Cold," he whispered. "So cold."

"Who are you? Do I know you?"

"I mean no harm," the man mumbled. "So cold."

Angelica knelt beside him and the last of her trepidation vanished. She touched his arm and felt tremors from the cold. "Why, you're nearly frozen! I'll be right back!"

She ran from the stable and crossed the snowy yard as quickly as possible. "Mr. Hart!" she said as she burst into the kitchen. "Come with me. I need your help."

Mr. Hart paused with the steaming cup of cocoa halfway to his lips. "What's that? Has there been an accident?"

"Please hurry!" Angelica rushed back out. Within seconds, she heard him following her.

By the time she reached the man's side, Mr. Hart had caught up with her. "We've got to get him into the house. Help me lift him."

Together, they hauled the man to his feet, his limp arms draped over either shoulder of his rescuers. The man tried to walk between them, but his strength was gone.

When the three of them entered the kitchen, Peggy closed the door behind them and opened the door that led to the rest of the house. "Let's take him into the back parlor," Angelica said. "The fire is lit in there."

They got him into the parlor and onto the couch by the hearth. Only then did Angelica get a good look at him. He was younger than she had thought, and he had a handsome face in spite of its pallor and the dark circles under his eyes. He wore no top coat, and his clothing wasn't expensive, but neither was it threadbare.

"Peggy, bring me some brandy," Angelica said as she pulled a tasseled pillow under his head. To the man she said, "Are you hurt or sick? Who are you?"

"Keenan," he managed to whisper. "Jerome Keenan. The actor."

"I never heard of him," Mr. Hart said.

Jerome groaned.

"Why were you in my stable, Mr. Keenan?" Angelica asked. She rubbed his hands to warm them.

Peggy came hurrying back with a measure of brandy. Angelica took it and held the glass to Jerome's lips.

He took a swallow, coughed, then took another. "I was thrown out of my lodgings two days ago. I had no money, and no other place was willing to board me on speculation until I could get another part in a play. I was trying to make my way to a friend's place when the snow began."

"A friend?" Mr. Hart asked. "What's his name?"

Jerome took another sip of brandy. "Frank Lamont, but he isn't at home. He's an actor, too, and his troop is performing in Bath. I had hoped to prevail upon his landlady's sympathy and get her to let me into his room."

"You're in no condition to go back out into the cold. It's a wonder you aren't frozen to death." Angelica pulled a lap rug over him and tucked it about him as if he were a child. "Peggy, go get Miss Lunt and Quinton. Tell them what is happening and that Mr. Keenan needs one of their restoratives."

Mr. Hart walked to the other side of the room and motioned for Angelica to come to him. When she did, he leaned toward her and said, "If you ask me, the police should be alerted."

Angelica's eye widened. "The police? Whatever for?"

"We don't know this young man. I fancy myself to be an enthusiast of the arts, and I've never heard of an actor named Jerome Keenan."

"Maybe he's not a very good actor," she whispered back. "Maybe he's from a theater on the Surrey side."

"All the same, we can't be too careful. Not in a house with my bride and four unmarried women."

"Mr. Keenan is hardly in a condition to be a threat to anyone. Why, he's too weak to break a cobweb."

"Could be an act," Mr. Hart said as he cast a suspicious eye toward the young man. "It could be an act to gain entrance to the house. He admits to being an actor."

"Even if he had the sharpest necessity of getting into this particular house, I doubt he would resort to freezing himself to death on the hopes I would discover him and bring him inside. I don't see how he lasted through last night. Even inside the house, the water was frozen in my pitcher. The stable would have been even colder."

"All the same, I urge caution."

Angelica nodded, though she wasn't convinced. "You and I will watch him closely."

Peggy came back with the other boarders hard on her heels. She pointed at the reclining man, and when the others rushed forward, she peered around them to see.

Blanche pressed her hand to her chest as if the sight of the stranger had overcome her. Mr. Hart rushed to her side and fanned her ineffectively with his hand. Quinton and Miss Lunt vacillated as to the best remedy for the man's speedy recovery and whether or not he had some ailment that might prove contagious.

Cecilia knelt by the stranger's side, and Zenobia stayed close behind her. Jerome opened his eyes and his gaze fell on Cecilia's concerned face. She gently took the brandy glass from his fingers and rested her hand for a moment on his brow.

Angelica repeated how she had happened to find Jerome in the stable. Blanche tried to draw a correlation between Jerome and the Christmas season and the more famous stable in Bethlehem, but no one was listening.

"What will we do with him?" Quinton asked as if Jerome were an inanimate object. "We can't leave him here, and there are no other bedrooms."

Angelica said, "This friend of yours, Mr. Keenan, where are his lodgings?"

Jerome gave her the address, and Angelica turned to Peggy. "Bundle up as warmly as you can and go to that address. Ask for Mr. Frank Lamont and if he isn't home, leave a message that when he returns, he's to come here straightaway." As an afterthought, she added, "Take my wool cloak, it's warmer than yours."

Peggy hurried out to do Angelica's bidding.

To Quinton, Angelica said, "Will you and Miss Lunt make a tea for Mr. Keenan? I'll heat some broth. He looks hungry." She looked back at the young man who was staring at Cecilia as if he had found an angel.

When Angelica returned with the broth, Cecilia insisted upon being the one to spoon it down his throat. Jerome made no objection, and even though he was hungry, he continued to show as much interest in the girl as in the food.

In less than an hour, Peggy returned. "Mr. Lamont wasn't at home," she reported. "I gave the message to his landlady. She expects him home by this afternoon, but she says Mr. Keenan can't live there as she has no more beds."

"What are we to do with him?" Quinton asked again.

Angelica bit her lower lip. She couldn't turn him out to freeze. "There's a cot in the attic. We could make him a place to sleep here in the parlor for a day or so—just until he can find other lodging."

"I would be forever grateful," Jerome said. His eyes returned to Cecilia. "I feel as if I've landed in heaven."

"Zenobia and I will take care of him," Cecilia said. "We can take turns reading to him."

"I'm not sick," Jerome said, "only cold. As soon as I warm up, I'll be all right."

"Why were you driven from your last place?" Mr. Hart demanded. "Are you a troublemaker, sirrah?" His use of the derogatory form of address lent additional force to his disapproval.

"No, sir. Not a bit. The play I was in folded, and I ran out of money. I haven't a quid to my name."

"Then you really are an actor?" Cecilia exclaimed. "I've never met one before. What is your theater?"

"I last performed in the Vic, as we call it. The proper name is the Coburg, on Surrey side." He smiled weakly. "I was Mr. Fielding in *The Trials of Miss Dove.*"

"Never heard of it," Mr. Hart said.

"It only played three nights," Jerome said as his smile disappeared. "It was a dismal failure. I've not been cast in another role, and I decided to leave the troupe and try to get in with my friend's group."

Angelica sighed. She had just acquired another nonpaying tenant. "I don't suppose you'd consider finding other employment."

Jerome shook his head. "Once an actor, always an actor. Someday, I plan to be as well known as Samuel Phelps."

Angelica sighed. "Yes. Well, you can stay here for the time being."

Quinton said, "I'll fetch the cot. Will you give me a hand, Mr. Hart?" The two men left the room.

"Zenobia, help me move the table to beneath the window," Angelica said. "The cot will fit into that corner quite nicely."

"I don't know how to thank you..." Jerome said hesitantly, emotion coloring his voice. "To take in a penniless stranger like this... Not many would consider it."

Angelica smiled at him and resigned herself to having one more mouth to feed. "Someday, return the favor to someone and I'll be repaid."

Blanche, who had knowledge of what it cost to run a house of this size, came to Angelica and whispered, "Are you sure you can afford to keep him? I know how much young men can eat, and he looks hungrier than most."

Angelica nodded. "We'll manage. I've come through more difficult times than this, and we'll be fine. I have an angel in my attic." She took note of the manner in which Jerome and Cecilia were looking at each other, and she hoped she hadn't brought a fox into the hen house.

Angelica had just finished eating dinner when she heard a knock on the door. As Peggy was still busy clearing the table, Angelica opened the door, hoping it might be Frank Lamont. Matthew stood there. Behind him was the Addamses' team hitched to a sleigh. "I've come to take you for a ride," he said.

"A ride? We have no engagement for this afternoon."

"I know. You've turned them all down. That's why I came unannounced."

"I have a dozen things I should be doing," Angelica protested as she noticed how Matthew's black coat was only a shade darker than his hair and how the sunlight made the amber flecks in his eyes gleam.

"I intend to stand here until you agree."

"Half of London seems determined to freeze on my doorstep today. All right. Let me get my wrap."

She was determined to keep her feelings in check. Matthew was a friend of the family and as such, she would continue to have contact with him from time to time. She had no choice but to learn to accept that there could never be anything more than friendship between them, and the sooner she did so, the easier things would be. As she swirled the cloak around her, she poked her head around the corner into the back parlor. "Cecilia, I'm going riding with Mr. Thornton. If Mr. Lamont comes, ask him to stay until I return."

Cecilia's face became even brighter. "You're going out with Mr. Thornton? How wonderful!"

"It's only a sleigh ride," Angelica said quickly. "Nothing more. I expect to be back soon." As she reclosed the parlor door, she heard Jerome ask who Mr. Thornton was, and by the tone of Cecilia's voice, Angelica knew she was filling him in on every detail. The Neville sisters and Blanche were determined to match her with Matthew in spite of the fact he didn't want to be matched. Angelica hadn't yet been able to tell the others that Mr. Thornton had confided in her that he had a love interest—and that it wasn't her.

Matthew took her arm and handed her into the sleigh, then got in beside her and took up the reins. "I hope you don't mind, but I left the Adamses' man at home," he said. "I enjoy driving a team such as this."

"I don't mind at all." She knew Matthew shared her love of animals. It was one of the first things she had noticed they had in common. "Geoffrey always keeps good animals."

"That's true." Matthew tapped the reins on the horses' dappled hindquarters and the animals leaned willingly into the harness.

In an effort to keep herself distracted from Matthew, Angelica looked away from him and concentrated on the empty house next door to her as they passed. Footsteps in the snow showed someone had looked at it only that morning. She had been so busy with the newcomer, she hadn't noticed anyone next door. The house was too lovely to waste. She hoped whomever it was would buy the house and move in soon.

To break the silence, which was becoming strained between them, Angelica spoke up as Matthew headed the team toward the edge of town. "I have a new guest," she said. "I don't suppose you could call him anything else since he has no money." Briefly she told Matthew about her discovery of Jerome.

"So you're still taking in strays," he said. "Now you've graduated from cats and dogs to actors."

"You should see the way he and Cecilia were looking at each other," Angelica continued. "I'll swear they fell in love at first sight. I've been hoping to find her a husband, but not one who is an out-of-work actor!"

"They've only known each other a few hours," Matthew replied with a laugh. "Maybe it won't last."

"Both of them look as if they've been struck dumb. And Quinton and Miss Lunt are no better. I even heard him call her Ida the other day. It may be winter in the rest of London, but spring is blooming in my house. Soon Zenobia and I may be the only single women there." Angelica pressed her lips shut. She was nervous sitting on the seat next to Matthew and hadn't expected to admit that she had no marriage prospects at all. She had hoped that Matthew might have assumed otherwise.

"I've decided to move to London after all," he said.

Angelica assumed this change of plans was brought about by a change in the situation between him and his romantic interest. She hoped he wasn't going to tell her about the woman. She asked Matthew no questions and was thankful that he offered nothing else on the subject.

They drove to the fields outside of London where other sleighs full of people were enjoying the crisp air. The horses settled into a quick trot that made their harness bells jingle rhythmically.

"Are you warm enough?" Matthew asked.

"Yes. Yes, I'm fine." Even if she had not had the benefit of the fur-lined lap rug, she was sure she would have been warm beside Matthew. The sleigh seat was narrow and she could feel his thigh pressing against hers through the layers of petticoats and skirts.

She studied his hands. He wore driving gloves, of course, but they molded to his hands like a second skin. By pretending to look at the snowy fields, she caught glimpses of his profile and the breadth of his shoulders. Her pulses were racing, and she knew she had made a mistake in agreeing to ride with him.

Matthew pointed toward a road that curved around a copse of trees. "Remember where that leads?"

"Of course, I do," she answered tartly. "I've lived here all my life." She couldn't believe he would be so crass as to ask if she remembered the road that led to the hill where he had asked her to marry him.

"Let's see if you can still see London from the hill." He reined the team around and headed up the snowy road.

Angelica felt as if her heart were on a treadmill. She wanted to be with him, to hear his voice and see his beloved face, and at the same time, she wanted to be so faraway from him that the memories couldn't touch her.

In an agonizingly short time, they were on the hill's summit, and, as always in winter, London could be seen sprawling beyond the bare trees.

"Remember how it looks at night?" he asked as he drew the horses to a stop. "From here, you can see the lights on the streets and in the houses. You can even see lights on the boats and ships on the Thames, if the air is clear."

"I remember." The night he had proposed to her, he had told her the lights looked like jewels and he had said he wished he could give them to her. Then he had reached into his pocket and brought out a pearl-and-diamond ring and had put it on her finger. She wasn't likely to forget that.

"In two days, we would have been married for five years." He spoke softly as if he were thinking aloud. "We would have a family like Geoffrey and Phoebe. A house of our own. A future and a past."

"Everyone has a future and a past," she retorted, fighting hard against her roiling emotions. "That's a product of living."

"Some futures are more promising than others. I want a family and a home. Don't you?"

"I have a home already. And a family."

"Do you still see Phillip's family?"

"No, not for years now. We were never close, although there aren't hard feelings between us. I see them at church, but we don't visit."

"I sent a wire to my man in York. I told him I've found a place here and will move down after the first of the year." As he spoke, Matthew turned to look at her. "I signed the papers this morning."

"I'm happy for you. Could we go back now? I'm getting cold, after all." She couldn't listen to his plans for the future. Not in the place that had been so special to them. Yet a perverseness in her urged her to ask about the woman in his future. Perhaps if her pain was great enough, she could release him from her heart; but she couldn't allow herself to ask, not when they were alone and he could see her heartbreak. It would be easier to hear about his intended if she had a crowd around her.

Matthew did as Angelica asked and headed back down the hill toward town, but he continued with his reminiscences. In one clearing they passed, he recalled that they had had a picnic and she had worn a pink ribbon in her hair. They crossed the road that led to a Norman ruin, and he reminded her that this was the place where he had first said he loved her. As they passed a large oak whose limbs were heavy with mistletoe, he recalled that this was the place where they had first kissed. Angelica needed no reminders of these events, for the memories of those times crowded about her every time she drove by these places.

At the front of her house, Matthew tied the horses and drew blankets up over their backs. She knew by this action that he expected to be invited in, and she could see no way to gracefully refuse.

As they were hanging their wraps on the hall tree in the foyer, Peggy came hurrying to meet them.

"You've got to come to the back parlor," the girl said. "You've never seen the like of it!"

"What's happening?" Angelica asked. "Is something wrong?"

"Come quick, Mrs. Hamilton," the girl said as she ran away down the hall. "Hurry!"

Angelica and Matthew rushed after the girl and toward the raised voice they could now hear. When they entered the room, Angelica saw her boarders sitting about while Jerome and a strange young man stood in front of the fire. Jerome was still pale, but he glowered convincingly at the other man who was gesturing dramatically as he paced up and down.

"Behold!" the stranger said. "Do you see me as a broken man? Nay, I think not, Sir Reginald. You see before you a man who has made his mark upon the world."

"I see a knave! A knave who would rob me of my only daughter," Jerome exclaimed.

"What on earth is going on here?" Angelica gasped.

The two young men turned to face her, and their frowns vanished. Jerome said, "Mrs. Hamiltion, may I present my friend, Mr. Frank Lamont?"

Lamont bowed deeply. "Charmed, Mrs. Hamilton."

Angelica looked from one to the other in confusion. "Why are you quarreling? What's this about a daughter?"

Frank laughed, and Jerome managed a smile, although he was obviously still weak. "Those are lines from a play we acted in last summer. It went up at Astley's and played the entire season."

Jerome sank into a chair, and Cecilia brought him some tea. "Frank says there's a place for me in his company," he said. "I'm working again. To celebrate, we were performing for our new friends."

Quinton piped up from the back of the room, "Ida...Miss Lunt and I have said we will go to one of their performances."

"But not until warm weather," Miss Lunt amended. "Neither of us is of hardy stock and we must nurture ourselves against the cold."

"Yes, indeed," Quinton confirmed.

Zenobia bounced across the room with a cup of tea for Frank Lamont, and judging by her blushes and his grin, Angelica surmised they had experienced the same transformation as Cecilia and Jerome. Angelica realized she was staring and looked away.

"I showed my needlework to Mr. Lamont," Blanche said, "and he was most complimentary. He suggested I might be called upon to sew some costumes for his friends."

"Mrs. Blanche can sew," Mr. Hart announced. "I've always said it. She takes to it as natural as hair to a sheepdog."

"Thank you, Mr. Hart." Blanche lowered her eyes and blushed as pink as had Zenobia.

Finally remembering her manners, Angelica stepped forward and introduced Matthew to those in the room he had not yet met.

Mr. Hart's eyes narrowed as he observed Matthew. "So you hail from York, do you? Do you recall a Mr. Horace Webber? A small man. Big mustache."

"No, I've never had the pleasure," Matthew replied.

The answer seemed to please Mr. Hart. "Good to meet you, my boy. The wife and I are glad to meet any friend of Mrs. Hamilton's." Blanche nodded eagerly.

Angelica led Matthew to the tea service that had been set up on the table beneath the window. The actors resumed their dialogue where they had left off. As Angelica looked about the room at the collection of people, she had to admit that even to her prejudiced view, the group seemed eccentric if not outright odd. She expected Matthew would say something about them, and she was prepared to defend them.

"So these are your 'commitments,'" he said.

"They may be...unique, but they are all my friends, and—"

"I like them," he said, interrupting. "I can see why you don't want to turn your back on them and start a new life elsewhere."

Angelica handed him a cup and poured another for herself. Matthew never did anything the way she expected. She glanced up to see if he was laughing at them all, but found he was following the actors as attentively as everyone else in the room. Angelica sipped her tea and tried to do the same.

Chapter Seven

"How is Jerome?" Matthew asked Angelica as the sleigh pulled away from her house.

"Who's Jerome?" Phoebe and Geoffrey asked simultaneously.

"He's my newest boarder." As Angelica spread the lap rug over herself and Stella, who had seated herself in her aunt's lap, the little girl snuggled closer. "Or perhaps I should say one of the newest. His friend, Frank Lamont, has also moved in. Mr. Lamont says my rates are more reasonable than the place he had been staying. He has farther to walk to the theater, but my house has the added attraction of one Miss Zenobia Neville." Angelica laughed. "Peggy must be slipping a passion potion in her stews. Everyone in the house seems to be in love."

"Everyone?" Matthew asked.

Angelica realized her mistake. "Nearly everyone," she amended.

"Matthew," Geoffrey teased, "have you been eating Peggy's stew?" He flinched when Phoebe punched him in the ribs.

Angelica pretended to be busy pulling Stella's hood closer about her face. Naturally, Geoffrey would know Matthew was in love with someone, for they had been the closest of friends for years and Angelica was sure they shared their secrets. It was also natural that Phoebe would recall her sister's broken engagement to Matthew and not want her to be uncomfortable at hearing another woman's name linked with Matthew's.

"It seems odd to be going somewhere so late," Tom observed.

"Look how dark it's getting to be," Will said delightedly. "We'll be up way past our bedtimes."

"We're growing so fast," Stella observed in her most grown-up voice. She hugged the stuffed bear she had just received for her birthday and planted a kiss on its soft nose.

The adults laughed, and Angelica hugged her.

"You're all growing up too fast," Phoebe said with a smile. "I wish I could keep you all just as you are now. I wish right now would last forever."

"You have to be careful what you wish on Christmas Eve," Will told her.

"Wishes come true then," Tom agreed.

Phoebe, who held Will, hugged him and patted Tom's knee. Geoffrey pulled Tom closer on his lap, as if he were echoing Phoebe's wish.

"What about you, Angelica?" Matthew asked. "Would you wish to keep everything exactly as it is tonight?"

"I would make one change," she said, but then fell silent. She refused to admit that her wish would be for

Matthew to love her again, and she was thankful no one asked her.

There was to be a fireworks display in Hyde Park, and because it was Stella's birthday as well as Christmas Eve, the children were being allowed to stay up late and see it. Most of London seemed to have the same destination in mind. The streets were crowded even though it was growing dark. In spite of the cold, everyone in the crowd was smiling; no one was visibly upset at being jostled as they clustered together in the park. Because of Phoebe's condition, Angelica held Stella and each of the men lifted a twin for a better view of the night sky.

A whooshing sound signaled the beginning of the show, and with a boom, red sparks showered high up in the air. Stella clapped her hands over her ears against the loud noise, but her eyes were wide with appreciative amazement. She had been too young the year before to see the fireworks.

"Look, Mama, look!" Tom cried out as a blue crackling and sparkling fire soared overhead.

Angelica was having as much fun watching the children as she was in seeing the fireworks. Although Stella was a chubby armful, she enjoyed the weight of the child in her arms. She glanced at Matthew and found he was watching her.

"You're missing the fireworks," she said in a soft voice.

He only smiled.

They were near the edge of the crowd, and soon the children were so excited that they had to be put down on their own feet. Matthew and Angelica edged back from the main body of the crowd so they could keep sight of the children.

"You should have children of your own," Matthew observed. "It's easy to see how you love them."

Angelica nodded. "I was so disappointed when I didn't have a baby. Phillip wanted one, too. A son. He always said he wanted one son, no more. As for myself, I wanted a houseful."

"I remember you used to say that. So did I."

"However, that's no longer possible. Phillip is gone, and I will have Phoebe's children to love."

"Is that enough for you?"

"It has to be," she said with impatience. It wasn't enough for her at all, but there was nothing she could do but accept it. "And this isn't a proper conversation for us to be having, especially not in Hyde Park with all these people around."

"Are you such a stickler for propriety these days? I remember when we intentionally shocked one of your aunts by wading barefoot in a stream."

Angelica smiled despite her attempt to remain reserved. "I remember. Aunt Sophie was in a state! I suppose it was too daring of me—but didn't we enjoy it!"

As the fireworks lit the smoky sky, Matthew said, "I've missed you, Angelica. These last five years have been hell for me."

She jerked her head around and stared at him in disbelief. His lips were turned down, and his eyes were filled with the anguish of which he had spoken. Matthew was telling the truth. After a moment of silence, Angelica said, "I've missed you, too." Then she averted her eyes by turning her face toward the aerial display. "I may have given you the wrong impression about something," she said tentatively. "Phillip and I weren't happy together. As soon as we were married, I realized I had made a mistake. But I was young and headstrong and determined to spite you for breaking our engagement. I never should have married him."

"You called it off, not me."

"Did I? Are you sure?"

"I'm positive."

Angelica frowned. "That makes it even worse, doesn't it? Maybe I deserved Phillip, after all."

"No woman deserves a cruel drunkard for a husband, least of all you."

She looked at Matthew. "How did you know he was cruel and that he drank too much?"

"It doesn't matter. If I had known at the time, however, I would have come back for you, married or not."

Angelica tried to maintain an interest in the fireworks, and quickly reminded herself that Matthew was speaking of how he had felt in the past. His tender feelings for her then had nothing to do with the present.

The display ended with a cacophony of lights, colors and explosions. The children applauded wildly and cheered their appreciation as they danced about in their glee. By the time they all arrived back at the sleigh, however, the children's exuberant excitement had mellowed and they were glad to be carried.

Stella snuggled down in Angelica's lap and said sleepily, "I saw the Christmas star—the one Mama and Papa named me after."

Tom, who was nestled in Matthew's lap, sighed with the impatience of an older brother. "There was only one Christmas star, and it was a long time ago."

"Besides," Will finished for him, "You can't see stars in the city because of all the smoke and gaslights. You're a silly goose."

Phoebe put her hand on Will's knee. "Don't call your sister names."

"Sorry," Will mumbled.

"The children are tired," Geoffrey said as he readjusted his son on his lap. "It's long past their bedtime."

Stella put her rosebud lips near Angelica's ear and whispered, "I did so see my star."

Angelica smiled and held the child close, at one moment wishing she had a child of her own, then the next, chastising herself for hopeless wishing.

By the time they reached the Addamses' house, Stella was sound asleep. Matthew took her from Angelica, and Geoffrey carried a nodding twin on each arm. The men took the children up to the nursery while Phoebe and Angelica went into the parlor.

"I'm so glad Matthew has bought a house and is moving to London," Phoebe said. "We've missed him."

"Where is the house?"

"I'm not sure. Apparently, it's some sort of surprise because he and Geoffrey smiled as though they were hiding something when I asked."

"How odd." Angelica hesitated for a time, then blurted out the question that was burning a hole in her heart. "Who is Matthew seeing?"

Phoebe looked confused. "What do you mean? As far as I know, he has been with us or with you the entire time he's been here."

"You're wrong. He told me himself that he is—" her voice faltered "—in love with someone. I assumed you must know."

"Geoffrey says—"

Whatever Phoebe was about to impart was broken off as the men entered the room. Geoffrey went to the cupboard and poured a brandy for Matthew and himself as the maid came in with hot cocoa for the ladies. "The boys were asleep before we reached the nursery. They had quite a night of it."

"I envy you," Matthew admitted. "You're raising a houseful of angels."

"They aren't always so angelic," Phoebe replied with a laugh. "At times, nothing could be farther from the truth."

Angelica held her mug of cocoa between her palms, warming her hands as she sipped it. "I should be getting back," she said. "It's a shame to keep the horses in harness on such a cold night."

"By now, the horses are in the barn where it's warm. I assumed you would stay and help us decorate the tree," Geoffrey protested.

"Yes, Angelica," Phoebe said. "You can't think of leaving so early on Christmas Eve."

Angelica looked at Matthew. "Please stay," he said softly.

She lowered her eyes. "Perhaps for a while." She knew the longer she was around Matthew, the more difficult it would be to give him up again, but she couldn't leave—not when he had asked her to stay. It was torment being around him, knowing that all too soon, he would be gone, but without this pain, there would be nothing. And the thought of nothing was more difficult to bear. Why he had asked her to stay was a mystery to her. She doubted that he was so insensitive as to be unaware of the strain this was putting on her, yet he had all but insisted she remain. None of this made sense, but then, what sense was there in anything that had ever happened between them?

Geoffrey went out to the carriage house to fetch the tree, and during his absence, Angelica made small talk with Phoebe in an effort to avoid direct conversation with Matthew. She was determined to savor these last few moments with Matthew, but knew she would have to maintain her distance. Almost at once, Geoffrey returned with a beautifully shaped fir. Angelica was almost as amazed seeing a real tree in the parlor as she was sure the children would be. "Whatever will Mother and Father say?" she asked, continuing to steer the conversation away from Matthew and his plans for the future.

"They've already said it," Phoebe said as she took out the boxes of candles. "That's why they didn't go with us to see the fireworks tonight." She smiled impishly and for a minute, she looked like an older replica of Stella. "They aren't so upset, however, as to stay away on Christmas Day. Father has matching hobby horses for the boys, and after dinner tonight, Mother whispered to me that she had a rocking horse for Stella."

"It's only that Christmas trees are new," Geoffrey said. "You know how set in their ways they can be."

Matthew seemed oblivious to Angelica's quandary as he helped Geoffrey stand the tree in front of the large front windows, then knelt and helped spread a sheet on the floor at the base of the tree that they would pretend was snow.

Angelica and Phoebe fit the tiny white candles into the brass bases, and then the men fastened them to the tree's branches. The smell of fir filled the room, and the crackling fire in the hearth made the indoor scene as cozy as the picture on a Christmas card.

Angelica had sent over the box of gifts as well as the snowflakes and garlands of red berries. As she and Matthew draped the garlands around the tree and tied snowflakes in place, Geoffrey and Phoebe went upstairs to get the toys.

"Next year, perhaps I'll put up a tree for my boarders," Angelica said, nervously filling the silence with casual conversation. "The actors may have seen one—who knows what they have experienced—but I doubt many of the others have. Wouldn't it be lovely to decorate a tree on the front lawn for the neighborhood children?"

"I wonder where we will be next year," Matthew said, abruptly returning to the sensitive subject. "A year can bring so many changes." He closed his hand over hers and took the snowflake from her fingers. "Angelica," he murmured in a tone that spoke volumes. Her name had floated off his tongue as if it were a love song.

Transfixed by the resonance of his voice, she gazed up at him, and it was as if all the years they had been apart had rolled away. Outside, there were carolers singing and sleigh bells jingling, but nothing existed in her world but Matthew Thornton and herself.

Slowly, he bent toward her, but paused when his lips were a breath away from hers. Reflexively, she ran her hands up his chest and encircled his neck. As if her response had been the permission he sought, Matthew pressed his warm lips to hers and swept her away with the passion of his kiss.

Angelica often had dreamed of his kisses, but they were nothing compared to the reality of his embrace. His arms were closed around her, strong and protective, and he held her so close, she felt as if she could never bear to be apart from him again. All her doubts and fears fell away as she returned his kiss, and in their place came pure and vibrant love.

She heard a faint sound coming from somewhere beyond the doorway and would have paid it no attention at all, except that Matthew responded by releasing her. As they parted, she could see his eyes were still dark and smoldering with ardor. Although she felt as if she were visibly trembling, she somehow managed to step away from him and turn to the tree.

Geoffrey and Phoebe came into the room and put several boxes containing children's toys on the piano. Phoebe glanced at Angelica and Matthew as if she sensed some change between them, but she wisely said nothing. Angelica's breath came quickly, and she didn't trust herself to look at Matthew.

Angelica could hear Phoebe talking, but could make no sense of her sister's chatter. She forced a smile to her lips and nodded to Phoebe as she took the tumbler clown Phoebe held out to her and with nervous fingers, placed the toy on a branch. In a similar manner, she hid three brightly colored masks among the branches. As she watched, Phoebe balanced a toy horse with a real-hair mane and tail on a cushion of fir needles, then Matthew reached over Angelica's head and positioned three Jacob's ladders on a high branch. The little squares of painted wood on the ladders flapped and clattered over each other. Angelica was so keenly aware of his nearness, she almost dropped the red-and-blue humming top.

"Matthew, look at this." Geoffrey knelt at the edge of the rug and pressed a metal frog onto the wooden floor. He drew back and waited. Several seconds later, the dab of cobbler's wax beneath the frog's tail unstuck from the floor, thrusting the frog into the air.

"Let me try it," Matthew said.

Phoebe and Angelica exchanged a smile, and Phoebe said, "Don't you boys wear out the toys. I'm sure the children will share with you tomorrow."

Finally in control of herself again, Angelica picked up a cardboard man and pulled the string hanging from his coat. At once, the man contorted his arms and legs and his hat raised up on his head. She laughed. "Phoebe, watch!" She pulled the string again to make her sister laugh.

"You're as bad as they are," Phoebe said with amusement.

Geoffrey put the frog on the tree as Matthew took some brightly colored books from the box. He opened one to the letter *A*. "'*A* was an archer and shot at an ant,'" he read aloud. He flipped to the back pages. "'*X* is for Xerxes. *Y* is for yew tree, *Z* is for zebra.' I've read this book. I remember the ending." He carefully put the book on the limbs along with the stories of Robin Hood, the Yellow Dwarf, Red Riding Hood and the Arabian Nights.

"We have a toy theater for the boys and paper characters to act out *The Miller and His Men* and *Elizabeth, or the Exile of Siberia*," Phoebe said. "Stella is getting a doll house with real glass windows and four rooms full of furniture. It even has crockery plates and a turkey dinner glued to a serving dish."

"She will love it. I can't wait to see her face when she opens the box," Angelica said.

"You must be over here tomorrow morning early," Geoffrey said. "I've told the children they can't come into the parlor until you and the grandparents have arrived."

Phoebe smiled. "I think I'm as excited as the children are. Thank goodness the fireworks tired them out, or they might never have gone to sleep."

Geoffrey spoke up. "Tomorrow promises to be an early day. If you'd like, I'll tell my driver to bring a sleigh around for you, Angelica."

Before she could respond, Matthew said, "Don't bother. I'll be walking Angelica home. That is, with her permission."

Angelica found it difficult to mask her amazement. She had thought it too much to even hope that he would see her home. Regaining her voice, she said, "I'd be pleased."

They bundled up against the cold, and Matthew helped her down the snowy steps.

Not many people were still out on the streets. A few hurried past, their arms filled with parcels or huge turkeys for Christmas dinner. At the far corner, the carolers were singing for wassail. In the distance, church bells pealed the hour and were answered by another chime even farther away.

Angelica was hesitant to speak, not because she had nothing to say, for her mind was filled with questions, but because she didn't want to hear the answers. This evening, Matthew had behaved toward her as if he were her suitor, and she had delighted in the fulfillment of her fantasy. She knew the magic was only temporary and that it would have to come to an end, but she was determined to make it last as long as possible. She tried to think of a subject to discuss that was mundane and noncommittal, but talking of the weather at a time like this seemed silly. Then she remembered that the new year was coming. Continuing to look straight ahead of her, she said, "Well, it won't be long until 1861 is here. I'm looking forward to the new year."

"What changes do you expect the new year to bring?" he asked, throwing her off balance.

"I . . . well, I don't know. And you?"

"That depends upon you."

"Me? What do I have to do with it?"

"We kissed not two hours ago. Have you already forgotten?" he demanded.

She was silent for a minute. "No. No, I haven't forgotten. Nor have I forgotten you told me you love another woman."

He frowned at her. "I did no such thing."

"Yes, you did. I offered to speak to her on your behalf."

He sighed. "I never quite know what to expect from you. Why is it you become so literal at such odd moments? I'm not in love with anyone else."

Again she was silent for several steps. "Matthew, I have as much difficulty understanding you as you apparently do in understanding me, so I'm going to ask you outright. Why did you kiss me, and what were you talking about that night if you weren't referring to another woman?"

"I was talking about you, of course. I was trying to see if you would encourage my attentions. I recall your temper all too well, and I wanted to be certain of my reception in courting you."

"Courting me!" She turned to face him. "You were asking to court me? Good heavens, Matthew, but you can certainly be oblique!" Her face softened. "You really want to court me?"

"How can you doubt it? Didn't I freeze us both half to death in a sleigh in order to stir your memories of what we once had? Haven't I done all I could to remind you without coming right out and telling you point-blank?"

"Is that what you were doing? I thought you were trying to torment me."

He made a growling sound and started walking again.

She caught his arm and hurried to keep up. "If you had been that circumspect six years ago, we would never have become engaged at all. How was I to know what you were hinting at?"

"I thought that's one of the things I did wrong, being too direct."

"You didn't do anything wrong at all. At least, nothing but leave me."

"You refused to ever see or speak to me again!"

"I was upset. You shouldn't have been so fainthearted."

Matthew halted abruptly. "Fainthearted? I all but died at having to leave you. For five long years, I've thought of you and dreamed of you and wished like hell I had never let you break our engagement."

"I've been a widow for three years! Why haven't you returned before now?"

"I didn't know until recently that Phillip had died. Geoffrey used to write me about you, but it was so painful for me to hear of you that I told him not to speak of you again. I even made him promise." He looked thoughtful. "I wondered why he has been so insistent about me coming down for a visit."

"When I first saw you, I was upset at them for matchmaking," Angelica said.

"Are you still?"

She smiled. "No."

They walked another block before Matthew said, "When I saw you in that green dress, it was as if the years between had never happened. Your smile, the sound of your voice, the way you tilt your head when you're wondering about something—all the things that have constantly reappeared in my dreams and my thoughts were right there in front of me. I was afraid you hated me.''

"I doubt you were more upset about that than I was when you apparently told me you loved someone else."

"Most of our courtship was a series of misunderstandings, wasn't it?"

"I believe that's an accurate assessment," she replied dryly.

"I see only one solution. In the future, we must be open and forthright with each other."

"How open? How forthright?"

They had turned down Lady Slipper Lane, and he drew her into the shadows of her neighbor's house. "I love you, Angelica. I want you to marry me."

Angelica gazed up at him, and she thought he must hear the thrumming of her heart. "Are there angels singing? I feel there must be angels singing somewhere."

"I don't know yet. What's your answer?"

"I love you, Matthew. I always have. Yes, I want to marry you."

He drew her into his embrace and held her as close as a breath. "Now I hear the angels and, yes, they are singing."

Angelica opened her eyes and saw the lights of her house. A bit sadly, she said, "I want to marry you, but I don't know if I can."

His body stiffened. "What? What did you say?"

She straightened and nodded toward her house. "I still have commitments. I still have people who depend on me. You've bought your new house, but I can't leave mine. Not as long as the Neville sisters have no money and Miss Lunt and Quinton are courting but not yet promised to each other. Then there's Peggy. I feel so sorry for her, and I could never send her back to that dreadful workhouse."

Matthew enclosed both her hands in his and held them to his chest. "Would you like to see my house?"

"Very much so. But—"

He turned her around so she was facing the darkened house beside her own.

"I don't understand," she said, but hope was fluttering to life.

"This is my house. It's paid for, and I have the key in my pocket."

"You bought my neighbor's house? But why? I mean, what if I refused to marry you, or—"

"Angelica, I love you, and I know we're right for each other. If you had refused me, I would have moved in here anyway and courted you until you changed your mind."

"You were taking a terrible risk!" she exclaimed. "I might never have said yes!"

"That's true, but at least I would have been close enough to see you and to speak to you. That's how much I love you."

Angelica threw herself into his arms with such enthusiasm, they both nearly tumbled into a snow drift. "Hold me, Matthew! Hold me tight. Don't ever let me go."

"No," he said, his breath warm against her cheek. "No, I'll never let you go. Not ever again."

As Angelica embraced him, she heard the bells chime in her neighborhood church, and it was, in-deed, as if all the Christmas angels were singing—and her heart sang right along with them.

* * * * *

A Note from Lynda Trent

When our four children were small, I knitted a Christmas stocking for each of them. The stockings, with respective names embroidered on them, were hung over the fireplace when all the rest of the decorations went up; then on Christmas morning, the children would find their stockings stuffed with fruit, nuts, candy and small toys. Dan and I assumed that as they grew older, our kids would tire of the stocking-stuffing tradition and the stockings would become decorations and delightful reminders of Christmases past. However, it didn't happen that way. Every time we suggested it might be time to alter the tradition, our children were appalled. All too soon, they were grown, but the tradition was continued by popular request.

When our son married, I knitted a matching stocking for his wife. Again, we tried to relegate the stockings to the status of decorations, but our daughter-in-law said she had never had a Christmas stocking, so we decided Santa would visit the stockings one more year.

Then came our first grandbaby. She got a stocking, too, but on hers I knitted a white stripe to differentiate it from the previous generation of children. Once more, Dan and I suggested that the grandbaby's first Christmas would be a good time to stop stuffing all the other stockings. The lamentations would have deafened Scrooge. Even Dan finally admitted that he had never had a Christmas stocking, either, so I knitted one for him—and one for myself.

At this point, we're resigned to hanging—and stuffing—Christmas stockings forever. Our children did capitulate on one point, though. From now on, their stockings and ours will hang from the high ledge on our mantel above the mirror, while the babies' stockings (and by this Christmas there will be another grandbaby) will hang directly over the hearth.

Lynda Trent

A SEASON OF JOY

Caryn Cameron

GRANDMA MUDGE'S RAISIN-FILLED COOKIES

Filling
1 package raisins
2 cups sugar
2 tbsp flour
1 cup hot water

Grind raisins in a meat grinder or food processor. Do not overprocess. Raisins should *not* become a paste. In a heavy saucepan, combine ground raisins, sugar, flour and water. Cook over medium heat, stirring until mixture thickens. It should not be runny. Set aside to cool.

Cookie dough
2 cups vegetable shortening
2 cups sugar
1 tsp salt
2 eggs
1 tsp vanilla
1 cup milk
3 tsp baking powder
2 tsp baking soda
7 cups flour

Preheat oven to 400° F.

In a large bowl, mix ingredients together in order, blending after each addition. Add more flour if dough is not stiff enough to roll out easily. On a floured pad or board, roll dough to about a ¼" thickness. Cut into pairs of Christmas shapes. Place one shape of each pair on an ungreased cookie sheet. Put one heaping teaspoon of filling in the center of each shape. Top with the matching shape. Seal edges by gently pressing together.

Bake for 8 to 10 minutes. Before removing from oven, touch cookies to see if they are firm but not turning brown.

Enjoy this taste of an old-fashioned Ohio Christmas!

Chapter One

December 16, 1777

This year Elizabeth McGowan was dreading Christmas. It was not the first year she had been widowed and tried to be both parents to her son. Nor was it the first Christmas she had been without her own dear family, with whom she had shared many happy holidays. But it was the first year she had been desperate to keep little Will and the McGowan farm that was his heritage safe from the dangers that threatened all around.

"Those British soldiers won't come back, will they, Mother?" Will asked as she tucked him in bed. "If they do, I'll fight those lobsterbacks just like one of Washington's boys would!"

She covered his clenched fists with her hands. "I hope not, my dearest. I'll keep a good watch out. But you, thank Providence, are too young to be fighting British soldiers. Besides, they daresn't come in the dark, as they'd trip over their own polished boots and dirty those pure white gaiters of theirs!"

Will grinned at her lame attempt at humor before he sobered again. "But what about Lieutenant Colonel Ross? For certain, he's a good soldier on our side. He was real friendly. Will he be back to see us and bring the American Continental Army, too, like he said?"

She rhythmically smoothed the feather-fine, blond hair from the eight-year-old's forehead as she answered. "I—I can't say, though he did promise. But promises in wartime are sometimes difficult for soldiers to keep."

"Like Father promised he'd be back and then got killed anyway," the boy concluded.

She bit her lower lip to stem the tears. Will had said that so matter-of-factly. Though she had finally accepted William's loss, her son's resignation made her want to cry.

"Yes," she managed. "People sometimes make promises to those they love that they want desperately to keep and then—they just can't." She cleared her throat. "But I do promise you we are going to have a wonderful Christmas here, just the two of us."

He half yawned, half smiled up at her. "For certain! And Sheba, too," he added, referring to his pet sheep. "You said if it gets much colder we can both sleep downstairs by the hearth on Christmas Eve, and Sheba can come in with us, just like in the carved manger scene. Only nine more days till Christmas, and I'll have a real fine gift for you...."

His words drifted off as he cuddled deeper into his goose-down pillow. She tugged up the quilt snugly to his chin, snuffed the candlewick and tiptoed out.

With the full moon shining on the new snow outside, the interior of the house seemed softly silvered, so she did not need a candle. Besides, she knew every step of this home and farm. And most of all, the darkness suited her mood.

She sighed and hugged herself harder through her knitted shawl and quilted dressing gown as she walked along the narrow upstairs hall. In her bedroom, cold seeped through the windowpanes. Still, she had no desire to slide the warming pan between the sheets and climb in the big canopied bed. And she didn't want to build a fire on the hearth that would eat away at their supply of winter fuel. These past few weeks, she had made herself a pallet downstairs and slept there to keep a closer eye on things.

Beth, as her family had always called her, had been only seventeen when she wed William McGowan, twenty years her senior and a friend of her father. She knew now she had been coddled all her life by both men. Those eight years she was married before the war began, she had enjoyed a kindly, doting husband and this big farmhouse staffed with servants. It had been a calm, contented life. William had not wanted her to soil her hands with farm work. But when the hired men enlisted after William left, she had learned to fight her own little war for independence to keep the place going. Now, at age twenty-seven, it was all hers to command—and to salvage as best she could for young Will's future while the big War of Independence raged nearby.

Suddenly exhausted, Beth clasped the bedpost and leaned her cheek against her hands. Tree branches scratched against the window, and she squinted out through the thick, frost-framed windowpanes. Casting a huge, gray moon shadow, the stout stone-and-timber barn sat at the other end of the yard beyond the now denuded chicken coop. The rich apple orchards and fields of winter wheat stretched to the fishing pond and Berwyn-Haverford Road. It was so deep and dark and silent between here and the Pembroke farm, where her nearest neighbors lived. The two Pembroke boys and their hired men had also gone to war, which had made Beth and Charity Pembroke even closer friends, even though they seldom had time to call upon each other now.

Beth sank down on her high straw tick mattress. Both in her childhood home and then later in this house, Christmas coming had always meant friends calling, laughter, warmth and trading gifts of the heart as well as the hands or purse. But no one was in a giving mood as this Christmas approached. War meant lives were taken as well as everything else.

In September, the British had captured Philadelphia, the young nation's new capital. Soon after, the hated Hessian troops that the British had hired had looted the rich apron of land outside the city, just missing the McGowan farm, and in October the British had beaten the Americans at Germantown near Philadelphia. Afterward, the Americans had encamped at several sites some distance away, but an American brigade had visited Beth's hometown of Berwyn, asking for donations of warm clothing to get Washington's troops through the winter.

Amid her sad thoughts, Beth smiled at the memory of donating clothing to the Americans. That was when she had met Lieutenant Colonel Jerrod Ross. Her recollection of his intense eyes, sunny smile and deep voice warmed her yet. He was the only man who had ever really been her suitor, albeit only for a few brief, golden days. Her marriage had been so hastily arranged to a man she had thought of only as a family friend that she had never enjoyed a courtship. But last October, for one precious week, Jerrod Ross's attentions had kept the war at bay. Jerrod made her feel solid ground had collapsed from under her feet when all he did was gaze at her.

He had looked so fine, doffing his bicorne hat to her; his hair was so dark it shone like polished ebony in the sun. She always noted people's hair, because her father had made and sold wigs. Jerrod wore his hair pulled straight back and tied by a leather thong, as if to emphasize his high forehead and broad, black brows that framed deep-set, brown eyes. He came calling on her and strolled with her and Will through their apple-laden orchards, the pride of the McGowan farm. Another day he rode by again and stayed for supper. Each day after that, he visited for several hours. His farewell kiss had shaken her to her toes. He had promised to return someday, but she knew better than to trust a man's vows in wartime. Where he was now she had no way of knowing, but she still kept thoughts of him tucked away in the treasure chest of her memory.

Then, after he had ridden away with her fondest wishes for his safe and soon return, the worst had happened here.

Just three weeks ago, with no American troops in the immediate area, the British had widened their foraging net. Marauding soldiers had taken all the McGowan horses but the two Will managed to let loose in the woodlot in time. They had stolen all but one cow and every pig the neighbors had not butchered for her. They had taken all the chickens, stuffing the squawking birds in her clean pillowcases, which she had left drying on the bushes. And they had taken with them the tattered remnants of her sense of security, which Jerrod had helped to build for the first time since William's death with his promise of protection from the American army.

Now, neighborhood gossip said the British would be back for more, so she had to keep watch. And she felt a slow anger burn within her. The Americans she had helped and her husband had died for should have protected upstanding citizens when the British came to rob and terrorize them. How could General Washington's armies hope to free these United States if they could not even stop the enemy from taking a widow's farm animals? The next time the British came through pillaging her son's inheritance, she just might get her father-in-law's old flintlock and order them off her property at gunpoint!

Restive again—lately she slept but a few hours near dawn for watching and worrying—Beth went downstairs, her hand skimming the familiar banister in the dark. Even in the kitchen, she did not light a candle nor stir the crimson ashes on the hearth to flame. The darkness kept her from having to gaze in the convex hearth mirror, which showed the entire room from one glance anywhere.

She knew she looked tired and tousled, haunted and older than she was. She was thinner and ruddier than she should be, too, for her bonnets hardly kept the sun and wind away when she did chores outside with Will. And her hair, which her father used to insist be properly piled and powdered even when she did not wear a wig, had gone back to its unruly, natural honey blond shade. Even now it was escaping in flyaway strands from its single thick braid. She loosened and combed it free to her shoulder blades while she paced. Who would believe now she had been reared in Berwyn by the town's well-to-do wig maker and she had had her own maidservant once, too?

In her dressing gown, stockings and slippers, she lay down on the pallet beside the hearth. She settled in, punching her pillow, pulling the sheet and blankets up like a cocoon. But soon she flopped over the other way. She knew that once again she would not sleep. After thrashing a while longer, she got up. Nervously, she lifted the lid from the big iron kettle and stirred the breakfast porridge. With the stores she had in the cellar and several smoked hams and slabs of bacon hanging in the attic, they would get through the winter all right, she comforted herself. She'd dried and sulfured apples, too, and had two barrels of pickled meat and another of minced—

She froze at the sudden sound outside. A horse neighing nearby? But surely it was just the wind, a creak of old wood in the cold. She replaced the lid of the kettle and lifted the old flintlock leaning by the hearth. She kept it loaded and could refill the pan and ram a new ball "quicker than greased lightning," as her father-in-law would have said if he had ever seen her do it. Since the American army would not return William's musket, she had taught herself to clean and use this old gun, though it kicked hard and bellowed a big blast. Now, its barrel felt cold and its stock heavy between her trembling upper arm and breast.

She moved the muslin curtain aside and squinted out the window toward the barnyard. Nothing disturbed the cold calm. Surely the British would not return at night. But then she gasped. Plain to see in the moonlight, one of the front doors of the barn stood open a crack. As she watched, it slowly closed. Yes! Someone had gone in. Had the horse she had thought she heard been from that rider?

Her heart thudded in her chest like cart wheels over cobbles. She could watch until morning and then, when the intruder appeared, hold him at gunpoint. And maybe he wasn't dangerous. Sometimes American army deserters or other travelers just passed through. But what if he stole her two precious remaining horses or Will's dear Sheba, the sheep? Maybe if she waited a while, then went out, she could surprise and order the person away.

She jumped when a wan light flared in the single first-floor window of the barn. What if the marauder had come to burn her barn? She had seen what could happen with fire—destruction, devastation of the past and future.

Furious now, she unbolted and yanked open her back door. She moved the hammer of the flintlock to half cock. Despite her nighttime garb, she did not even feel the chill as she strode out into the shallow snow. If this person had come to burn her out, he'd pay dearly! She'd peek in the back door and get the drop on him by the very light he intended to use to burn her barn. She'd shoot first and inquire later!

The horrid memories of the great conflagration of her girlhood hurried her steps. She recalled again the sound of flames crackling into the night like the raving fury of some seething beast, devouring furniture, floors, walls and roofs. It had all glowed crimson like a thousand demon eyes and then had crashed to the cellar amid the awestruck screams of those who stood by to watch. She would not just stand by now, not if some enemy soldier had come to steal or burn her out!

She moved stealthily to the back door of the barn, her anger and energy making her feel flushed and feverish. She ignored the wind that knifed up the sleeves and skirts of her dressing gown and tugged at her loosened hair. She lifted the heavy wooden bar on the back door.

She crept in and let the door swing slowly, silently shut behind her. The familiar animal warmth comforted her. She halted. A small lantern burned on the stone floor near the front entrance of the barn. At least it had been placed away from strewed straw and stored corn shocks that could catch fire. She squinted into the gray-black shadows of the barn. Wind wailed through the empty loft. A horse stamped and snorted.

When she moved the hammer to full cock, the noise seemed incredibly loud.

Her knees bent, she swung the gun barrel in a slow circle. Where was the intruder? Then she sensed movement nearby. Behind the door?

She turned and saw he was too close for her to shoot him. The dark figure spoke, but in her terror she'd missed what he said. He grabbed the barrel and pushed it away, yanking her finger off the trigger. She cried out and tried to swing the stock, but he pulled it away from her, then grasped her in hard arms.

"Mistress McGowan! Beth, it's Jerrod!" a deep voice cried. She collapsed against him, and they sank to the floor with a thud.

"Oh!" was all she managed at first.

"I wanted to be sure it was you."

"Why didn't you come to the house?"

"I would have in the morning. I didn't want to scare you."

"But you did! And it's so cold!"

"I'm used to worse. The house looked dark. I thought you'd be asleep. I had no notion you'd be on late night watch. And with a blasted gun! I'm sorry, Beth. This wasn't the reunion I had planned."

Though she surely would not have greeted him this way in broad daylight, she clung to him. His arms came like iron bands around her waist and back; he cradled her on his lap. His leather boot felt cold and sleek against her bare calf where her gown had opened to her knees. Her nostrils flared at the outdoors scent of damp hair, wool cloak and uniform. She could feel his pulse throbbing where her fingers clasped his neck just above his cravat, and his breath coming fast as his chest moved against her arm and ribs, thudding his rapid heartbeats through her. She must have frightened him, too! Suddenly her good sense returned, though he had swamped her body's senses. Being in his arms felt so good, but it was entirely improper.

"Come inside," she said and struggled to get up. "You must need a bed— Food, too," she added quickly at the thought of inviting Jerrod Ross to sleep under her roof. Leaning together, bumping knees and shoulders, they helped each other up.

"The British came through," she blurted, "and that's why I was watching with my gun."

"I heard they did. That's partly why I'm here, to check up on what they did and took. And to scout a winter campsite in the area for our army, though that's best kept in confidence for now."

She clapped her hands like an excited child. "That means we'll have the protection of the army in this area! You don't know how much having you near will mean to my neighbors—to me."

"And to me, Beth."

His huge smile flashed white in the dimness as he handed her the gun. He went over to retrieve his small lamp. Holding Beth's elbow, he led her out the back door and dropped the bar in place.

When the wind blew out his lantern, she stared at his profile in moonlight, amazed he was real. As exhausted as she felt, it seemed she had conjured him up from her dreams. She had been wishing for some sort of giving spirit as Christmas approached, and the December night had bestowed Jerrod upon her!

His mere nearness made her limbs go even weaker than they already were. Toting his musket, haversack and lantern, he took her arm and escorted her to the house. The snow crunched underfoot. They bent together into the wind, but he sheltered her by keeping as close as he could.

She did not protest that he seemed to have taken over. He was used to commanding men in war, and she felt so safe with him. Strange, she thought, this feeling they had known each other much longer than they had. She recalled that first day they'd met. Their eyes had spoken their mutual interest that day in Berwyn, though their words had been so proper. But that day the sun was warm and a carpet of crisp leaves, not snow, crackled underfoot....

"Some cambric shirts and work breeches for our fine, fighting boys. I hope they will be able to use them," had been Beth's first words to him as she donated some of William's winter things she could not see saving for little Will. "And two stout pairs of work shoes, though they're a bit worn." As she extended the pile of clothing to him, the tall, handsome officer's hands touched hers to send a little jolt of lightning through her.

"Much obliged for your patriotism and generosity, mistress," he replied with a nod and a smile. Without breaking their shared gaze, he handed the pile of clothing to the soldier behind him, then doffed his hat to her with an elegant bow and a click of booted heels. His sword glinted as brightly in the sun as his loam brown eyes and his flashing smile.

Even before they so much as exchanged names, she felt drawn to him. He was everything an American soldier should be, she decided instantly: not braver perhaps, but much younger and stronger looking than her husband. Even with one hand resting on a pile of blankets, this officer with broad shoulders stood ramrod straight, topping her by a head.

"I didn't realize you could use blankets," she said quickly when she realized she was staring back as boldly as he examined her.

She felt the slightest flush of embarrassment—or was it sheer pleasure?—prickle the swell of her breasts above her modesty piece and heat her skin, throat to ear tips. Though she always took more care with her appearance when she came back to Berwyn, she wished she had worn a newer gown. But they'd brought apples in the cart to sell today, and she'd been lifting and toting all morning. She probably looked every bit like a field hand or carter.

"You have some blankets you could spare, too?" he was saying. "The army would really appreciate anything you could find it in your heart to give."

"If you'll be here again Tuesday next, I could bring them in on market day."

"Alas, we'll be gone by then," he said.

It thrilled her that his face fell, but of course, he was just disappointed about missing the donation of her blankets.

"As you've probably heard, the main army is camped north by Pawling's Mill on Perkiomen Creek," he explained. "That's just close enough to keep an eye on the British in Philadelphia. I don't know how long we'll be there, but I'll be heading back soon with the donations we've gathered.''

Then she saw a light flare in his brown eyes. His expression was warm and friendly, but there was something more.

''But, you know, ma'am, I reckon I could send someone to fetch your blankets before we leave if you just tell me where.''

''Yes, of course,'' she agreed quickly. ''The McGowan farm just east of town, the one with the apple orchard along the road.'' She noted he had big, capable-looking hands, one of which perched itself almost jauntily on the shiny hilt of his sword. ''My son and I live there.''

''A fine boy. I saw him when I noticed you across the street,'' he told her, making her pulse dance even faster.

She tried to scold herself for her foolishness. She had things to do, responsibilities to return to, yet she dawdled on the town green, chatting with a stranger. A stranger, who had noticed her even when she stood across the street—

And so, after she explained about her husband dying in battle, it had not been one of his men who rode out the next day to fetch the blankets. It had been Lieutenant Colonel Jerrod Ross himself, assistant to the Commissary General of Forage of the Continental Army.

During the next week, they talked of so many things, though never much about the past. Mostly they conversed about the tenuous present or the hopeful future of their infant nation. He was totally dedicated

to the American cause. But he also asked her many
questions about the farm and this area.

They shared some sweet hours together, walking the
land, enjoying a meal as if the three of them were a
family. Will took to him immediately, as if the man
and the boy had an unspoken bond between them.
Jerrod removed his coat and worked up a sweat chopping wood with the eager Will at his side. Although
Jerrod was city-bred and knew little about farms, he
helped them mend the pump handle. He showed the
boy how to fence with an old rusty blade while Beth
hurrahed from her perch on the ladder-back chair
Jerrod had carried outside for her. And always they
exchanged deep, long glances over the boy's head, as
if to vow what went unspoken for now: "We feel more
between us than we're saying."

When it was time for him to leave that last time, she
realized she faced the pain of separation and fear of
losing *him*. It was not simply a reaction to losing her
husband. She had finally laid to rest the loving respect and gratitude she felt for William McGowan.
Saying farewell to this man brought a special agony of
its own.

It was dark when Jerrod shook Will's hand and gave
the boy one of his mock military orders to go back inside while he bade farewell to his mother. With a re-
gretful look back over his shoulder, Will saluted and
ran off. Jerrod led Beth around to the far side of his
waiting horse.

"I'm not real good at words when I'm not giving
orders," he confessed. "But these few, fast days—

well, the hours we've shared have bucked me up again to face this war.''

He spoke in a rush, his voice almost gruff. He did not just doff his bicorne nor clasp her hand as he had the other times he'd ridden off. He grasped her upper arms in his big hands and gently pulled her to him.

''I'll always treasure—'' she began.

''But I'll be back. I *will* be back to see you and the boy.''

He tilted her against him as his mouth covered hers.

The impact on her was stunning. She felt like some featherbrained girl who had never been kissed before. She had wondered about his touch; even these last few days, she had hankered for his kiss. Now it was real and sweetly demanding and at first she almost wilted at the sweet rapture of it. Then she gave herself up to him and the feelings he evoked in her. For one moment she forgot the pain and hardships and fears awaiting both of them. Her senses swirled and she could have soared. She grasped his epauletted shoulders, letting him deepen the kiss. And when she thought it was over, he only settled himself closer and grasped her to him full-length to angle his mouth and delve deeper.

It was pure heaven. She returned his embrace, moving her arms around his neck to press herself to his hard chest and flat stomach. His thighs cradled hers as he tipped them back. Her toes dangled. But his sword belt and hilt pressed against her hip to remind her of reality. Her lips and body tingled for days after he loosed her and mounted quickly, only to bend back down to seize her hand in a crushing grip.

"I have no family anymore," he told her, his voice breaking. "You and Will have given me that—and I *will* be back!"

With that he had gone, leaving her with a hundred questions about his past that she wished she had asked. All she had gleaned was that he was a second son in the family of a Boston merchant, but they had had Tory leanings and had gone to live in Canada. Though he was twenty-eight years old, he had assured her he was a bachelor. The way he had said that but not wanted to explain made her believe that perhaps he had loved and lost and looked no further—until now.

And, after all, on this December night as they walked through the snow, she realized he had kept his promise to come back. Right this moment, he put his hand to open the door of her kitchen to make all the things about him she had remembered real and possible again.

Around the muslin towel with which he was drying his face, Jerrod watched Beth stir the glowing ashes of the hearth to flame. Despite how ready he felt for food, he wanted to hold her again. She looked thinner, but with a healthy color, not that paste-pale look women often had. Living out in all sorts of weather this past year, he was used to seeing folks with both sun- and windburn making their faces bloom. With that gun, she had looked almost like a wild female soldier, one he would like to both conquer and surrender to—if she would ever allow such in these hard, hit-and-miss times. In that blue dressing gown with her hair loose, she seemed fresh out of a warm bed, and that lured him and disturbed him in ways that rattled him to his boot soles. Seeing her like this was a husband's privilege, and he valued it as much as he did the very warmth of the room and the aroma of good, solid food.

He watched her ladle out a big bowl of porridge for him while slices of bacon sizzled and coffee heated like his blood. Each time she bent over the hearth, his eyes drank in her shapely curves, unobscured by the barrier of hoops and padding. Meanwhile, he asked her about how Will was and questioned her carefully about what the British had taken from her and the neighbors. He understood the bitterness and fear in her voice, yet she still emanated sweetness and strength.

When she put the food on the table, he was so hungry he could have lunged at it—and her. But he sat properly across the width of oak table as she spread two thick slices of pumpkin bread with butter and honey and they bowed their heads for a quick blessing. She sat there, hands grasping her saucer of coffee, staring at him with those huge, blue eyes. She had a certain classic beauty with her oval face and prominent nose. He studied her full, lush mouth. Her lower lip trembled; she darted out the tip of her tongue to wet it. He shifted on the hard bench, and forced his attention back to his food. Soon, she was jumping up again to fetch him a hot apple tart she pulled from a short-legged, iron oven on the hearth.

"That hot wash water was heaven," he told her. "Everything here is. It's like, well, coming home. You just don't know."

"It's been bad, I'm sure. When things get bad here, we tend to forget how much worse it must be for all of you out there."

Their eyes met and held. She could not, of course, know how bad it really was, he thought. Men who were supposed to be the pride of the new nation and the barrier against the British were gaunt and ragged. The hospital tents were full of amputees and feverish boys with infected wounds from the defeats of Brandywine and Germantown. But Beth had lost her husband to this war, and he would not make things worse for her by sharing his griefs and fears. Instead, he would give her something—he hoped and prayed—to further light that pretty face of hers. He would not tell her he had been sent to decide what provisions the Americans could take from this area when they wintered here, but he would tell her the happier tidings.

"Now here's some good news," he told her. "As I said, I've been sent ahead to help scout a possible site for winter camp. The one that will probably be chosen is quite near here, though I can't announce the place to civilians yet."

He held his breath for her reaction. He could almost see her nimble brain working again behind that lively face. Doubt, worry, interest. Hope?

"That means you can visit Will and me sometimes, the way you did before," she said.

A huge weight lifted from his shoulders. "Yes! Yes, I'd like to." He reached to take her hand, but she wasn't some sort of dunce not to realize the dangers involved.

"But, Jerrod, folks hereabouts will be sitting ducks between two armies, both of which need fuel and food to last the winter! Worse, if the British come rampaging out of Philadelphia to take the Americans on, this area—this farm—could become a battlefield!"

"We won't let that happen. The American camp will provide a buffer for the area around here. There will be no more surprise raids from enemy soldiers demanding food and provender, so I hope you'll be willing to sell some things to our army."

"Whatever I can do and still preserve this farm for Will's future, I am certainly eager to do."

He released her hand, but only long enough to move around the table and lift her to her feet. He hoped it would only come to that—purchases and not forced donations. He put one arm around her shoulders and tipped up her chin, though he did not crush her to him as he wanted.

"Please, Beth, try to trust me when I say that the American army, and I, will do all we can to protect you and this farm. And I was hoping, if I can get away, we could share Christmas here together somehow—the three of us. In these terrible days, we have to seize what time we can together, seize any joys we can for the Christmas season, seize—"

She threw her arms around him and whooped for joy. The hope of a happy Christmas—Christmas together—thrilled her. She forgot that she and Will could be crushed by two hostile armies. Terrors about keeping the farm intact and food on the table temporarily waned. The sad past diminished; the once frightening future now gleamed with promise. Christmas here, the three of them!

"Yes, oh, yes!" she cried and clung to him.

He lifted her off her feet and swung her around, just missing andirons and the table before he set her down. Dizzy, they collapsed side by side on the wooden settle, sitting sideways to the fire.

Grasping for sanity again, she pulled the skirt of her dressing gown closed across her knees, so aware he watched her every move. There was a hunger in his dark eyes that fed the ache she felt deep inside, but she was uncertain what she felt. It was all a tumble of feelings, like a big snowball rolling down a hill and picking up more snow, just spinning over and over down toward— Toward what? Just across the warm hearth, her pallet of disturbed sheets and blankets beckoned. Her hair prickled along the nape of her neck, and little butterflies beat their wings madly in the pit of her belly.

She tried to keep her head, no matter what this man did to her heart and body. She would offer him this pallet and sleep in her own room—as soon as she could bear to leave him.

Silence stretched between them, but it was companionable and not at all uncomfortable. They held hands, resting them on her knee. Their shoulders leaned together; his hard thigh pressed to her soft one. They spoke of the recent defeat at Germantown and of the army trying to choose a secure campsite for the winter. He told her what he'd heard about conditions in Philadelphia, where her sister and her family lived.

They spoke of what she and Will had done lately to keep up the place and prepare for winter. Sitting beside the flaming hearth, they spoke of many things, of everything but their own feelings.

"Times seem so bad and yet we have these moments," he told her sometime very late at night, his voice a rough whisper. It was the last thing she remembered before a screech awoke both of them to blinding daylight.

"Oh, Mother! Lieutenant Colonel Ross is here sleeping with you!"

For one swift moment, Beth was aware of a heavy, warm head cradled by her thighs and a big, limp arm thrown around her hips. Her head was resting on the wooden wing of the settle and Jerrod had slumped over until his mussed head lay in her lap.

She jerked to her feet. Jerrod had sprung to a crouched stance.

"He came back last night for a visit," Beth muttered, trying to still her son's happy cavortings. "Will, stop that noise!"

Jerrod had relaxed. He grinned and rubbed sleep from his eyes. Beth had the oddest feeling that Will's blurted remark about their sleeping together had caused that devilish grin. Quickly, she rewrapped her robe and shoved her wild hair back over her shoulders. In the light of day, she realized what a sight they must be and what deductions a person might draw. Jerrod's beard shadow and wrinkled clothes, the mussed sleeping pallet by the hearth, her own blush that she could feel spreading even now. And the wrinkles across her lap and thighs where his head had been!

She would certainly have to have a talk with Will to be sure he understood this was all completely innocent before he chattered to the neighbors!

"I'll gown myself and be down directly to fix breakfast," she shouted as she fled upstairs. Behind her, she heard the two of them chattering like squirrels as if nothing were amiss.

An hour after breakfast, they shared another parting, but this one was not so bad. "In a few days, when the army's situated," he said, gazing down at her from the height of his saddle, "I'll be back. I'll try to find a goose or pheasant for the table. And you get out those Christmas decorations you mentioned and have this place ready for a celebration."

Beth smiled up at him. She wore her burgundy, flower-sprigged gown and had piled her hair up on her head—no more just knocking about in work garments!

"I will," she vowed. She had to admit it seemed wonderful to have someone else making decisions instead of her. She would never go back to having a man control her life, but she appreciated his strength and concern. "You've given me the best gift of all already."

Before Jerrod could say more, Will came running around his mount so fast the horse almost shied.

"Here's the muffler Mother knitted me, but I've got another," Will said and tossed the red wool scarf up to Jerrod. "Since all the officers' trunks are in storage for a while, hope you can use it. Sorry it's that lobsterback color!"

"But it's one of the colors of the new American national banner, too!" Jerrod assured him, and waved it back and forth as if it were a flag. "I thank you heartily. And the fact your mother knitted this will make it dearer yet."

Beth marveled at the way that Jerrod could turn anything that sounded even remotely dire to good news, and make her go all giddy in the process. She'd been such a downtrodden, choleric fretter of late! In the spirit of the coming Christmas, she decided to trust him and hope for the best. Jerrod made her feel things so intensely—and not only these strange feelings toward him she could not yet define. He made her experience and cherish everything else much more deeply, too: the tingle of the wind on her cheeks; the flash of a blue jay on the red brick chimney; the scent of breeze-swept wood smoke; and Will's warmth as she laid her hand on his shoulder.

With the war, of course, and all she had to do, there could be no thought of serious feelings or any sort of commitment to anyone but Will for years. But perhaps after everything was over, Jerrod would come back to Pennsylvania and court her again. And then, when the farm was safely in Will's control, who knew? If only she didn't long for Jerrod to be here at the farm—and not only for Christmas—so much right now!

"The Americans will soon be able to provide protection in these parts, and I will, too," Jerrod called to them. "Now don't either of you worry. And take good care of your mother, Will!" he ordered, though his eyes were only on Beth again.

"I will for certain!" the boy promised.

"He's only a lad," Beth protested quietly to Jerrod as Will began to run along the lane in the direction Jerrod would ride.

He leaned down so as to squeeze her hand as he had the last time. "But that doesn't mean he needs constant tending," he whispered. "He can be a bigger help and comfort to you, and he should know he is valued for such."

Before she could react to that, he backed his mount away and wheeled him toward the road. The muffler he'd knotted around his neck flapped merrily. Will cheered and waved and ran a ways along before coming back to stand by his mother. The two of them stood there, waving in the cold until Jerrod disappeared down the lane. Finally, Beth shooed Will back inside.

"Colonel Ross says I can be a bigger help to you around here!" Will boasted. He crossed his arms smugly over his chest, almost as if to defy her. For one moment, she thought Will had overheard Jerrod's parting advice to her, but then she realized he must have told the boy the same thing on the sly.

"Is that so? Then I think filling the wood box would be a good start on that," she declared.

"Oh, Mother. He means other, *bigger* things a man could do," the boy grumbled as he begrudgingly obeyed.

Beth's heated yearning for more time with Jerrod Ross cooled a bit. How dare he, an outsider, suggest she was rearing her boy wrong! And yet the thought of Christmas with him still warmed her heart. Why did her feelings for him have to be so confusing?

While Will refilled the wood bin in the kitchen—whistling "Yankee Doodle" all the while, just as Jarrod had earlier—Beth went straight upstairs and climbed the narrow steps to the attic. Flinging wide the inside shutters to let in light, she surveyed with pride the hanging hams and bacon slabs. Then she opened the humpbacked lid of the old family trunk and lifted out her Christmas treasures.

There were six gray-green bayberry candles. They had gone a bit warped from the summer heat up here, but they would have to do this year. After all, their wonderful scent would remain the same. Perhaps she could melt them all and refashion them into one sturdy candle.

Next she lifted out the carved figures of a manger scene—Mary, Joseph, baby Jesus, angels and a shepherd boy and his sheep. Her father-in-law had loved to carve on long winter evenings, and though Will hardly recalled the old man, he had inherited that skill from him. And beneath all the rest lay the one Christmas item she had salvaged from her own family—the Christmas heirloom quilt her mother had made to celebrate the joy of each holiday season.

The quilt was made of white muslin squares framed in green velvet. Within each was embroidered a family scene from a particular Christmas: the year they were snowed in; the year her younger sister Sarah received a rocking horse; the year her father made enough profit from the boom in stylish Ramillies wigs to buy them a harpsichord.

After her mother died, Beth Richards, as elder daughter, had continued the family tradition with her needlework. Here was a scene from the Christmas when Berwyn had held an illumination, with candles in all the windows of the town. Ironically, that was the year of the fire that had burned their home and wig shop—the fire in which her father had died trying to save some family treasures, while neighbors held his daughters back from running inside to pull him out. The quilt had been saved only because Beth had wrapped it around Sarah when they fled the flames.

She had not embroidered a square the next year, for she and her sister had been living grief-stricken and destitute on a neighbor's charity. But then her father's friend, William McGowan, had come calling. He had seemed the only security in a world of shock and change. He offered marriage and a place for Elizabeth and Sarah to live. He was a rock from the past to cling to and a beacon to light her future. Beth accepted readily and willingly. But her sister, too, became betrothed and moved away to Philadelphia. And so it had been Beth alone who moved to become wife and mistress of the McGowan farm and learned not only to rely on and to respect her husband but to love him, too. And that love had made her able to embroider squares on the Christmas quilt once again.

The next scenes commemorated her years in her own home as Mistress McGowan. This section was from the year Will was born and they had the Pembrokes in to sing Yuletide carols. Next came squares recording holiday events as the boy grew, including three years ago when he received Sheba the sheep to care for on his own.

She smoothed the quilt over her knees to stroke the careful stitches from her mother's and her own hand. Blank squares remained yet to be filled. Last winter, after William was gone, she could not bear to do one. Now, perhaps, someday...

"Mother! You up there?" Will shouted from below. "I want to go out to feed the animals, but you said I wasn't to go out 'less I told you."

"Yes. I'm coming!" she called. Then she remembered Jerrod's last words to her. Perhaps she did worry about Will too much and try to hold him back when he endeavored to take his father's place at chores as best he could. Then too, Jerrod had promised that the Americans would soon make an encampment in the area to protect them from any possible raids.

"Will," she yelled down, "I think you're old enough to get a good start on those man's chores. I'll be out shortly."

"Oh, for certain. Don't worry 'bout me then!" he called, breaking her heart with this evidence of how the war was making him older than his years.

She wrapped the candles and manger items in the quilt and closed the shutters again. Her arms full of Christmas treasures, she felt her way carefully downstairs in the chilly dark. But the warmth of this new day of promise still shone brightly in her heart.

Chapter Two

Four days later, after they had finished their chores, Beth and Will went ice fishing in the pond between McGowan and Pembroke land. Will's father had taught him to fish in all weather. Though Beth did not enjoy it herself, she went along so the boy would not be lonely. Besides, American soldiers had been up and down the road all day, and she was wishing a tall, dark-haired lieutenant colonel would be one of them. With the large string of fish Will had hauled up, she hoped Jerrod would come by and stay for supper. But today nothing got by Will, neither fish nor the fact she'd taken great care lately with her coiffure and clothes.

"You're real fancied up under that cloak just to watch me catch fish," the boy had observed with a tight grin as he hacked a hole in the ice.

By now, everyone in the area knew the Continental Army under General Washington had just settled into permanent winter quarters seven miles away. They had chosen a small, easily fortified area called Valley Forge after the ruins of a smithy there that the British had burned last year. Despite all the dangers of being trapped between two hostile armies, Beth McGowan had been giving more thought of late to being trapped between her desire to have Jerrod here and the fear he might be kept so busy she would never see him again. But he had promised to return, so she kept glancing up each time a quick-riding soldier went by on the windy road.

However, the next rider was their neighbor Charity Pembroke. Wrapped in a snuff-hued, hooded cloak Beth recognized immediately, Charity reined in as Beth and Will walked through the shallow snow to greet her.

"Silas isn't worse?" Beth asked when Charity dismounted. Worry was written plain on her friend's plump, pleasant face. Silas Pembroke suffered from gout so severe it often confined him to his bed. In a way it was a blessing, for if he had been well enough to go to war, Charity, too, might be running her farm by herself.

"He's only sick at heart since we heard the news from town," Charity blurted as she grasped Beth's mittened hands. "As if that horrid British raid wasn't enough, our army has orders from Congress it can take all but one horse from patriotic, upstanding American families like us!"

"Oh, no!" Will cried. "We've only got two left, that nag Nellie and Father's old stallion, and—"

"That can't be true!" Beth cut him off. "The Americans might ask for donations again, but—"

"No, it is true!" Charity insisted.

"But Colonel Ross said he hoped we'd be willing to sell more things to our army. *Willing* to *sell,* Charity—"

"There's more, and it's even worse!" Charity declared, shaking her head so hard her hood bobbed off. "An order that the American army can force any farm within a seventy-mile radius of Valley Forge to cut its winter wheat and sell it real cheap to them. And if we refuse, it's to be seized and paid for as straw! Silas and I want to help, but there will be nothing left of us to free from the British at this rate, even if our army does get through the winter!"

"This cannot be!" Beth cried, gripping her friend's hands. "We won't let it be! We cannot just be coldly commanded like this—as if we were enemies or prisoners instead of patriots!"

She whirled away and began to pace the few steps between Will and Charity, hugging her elbows with her crossed arms as if she were freezing.

Jerrod had deceived her. He had promised protection. He had asked for trust. He knew how the British raids had devastated them already! And if he thought for one moment he could—could do all this to them, and then expect her and Will to share the joyous season of Christmas with him, the man was demented!

"Congress is going to have to find some provender for our boys elsewhere, too," she muttered. "If it's come to this, it won't just be horses and winter wheat. Just because we happen to live in their path doesn't mean we alone should bear the burden! We've got to make a plan to protest, to stand up to our own forces, if need be! Charity, come into the house, and I'll fix us some hot coffee, even if it *is* made from parched rye and chestnuts.''

''I've got to get back, but do you see what I mean?'' her friend demanded. ''We're in dire straits and heading for worse. And Beth, that officer friend of yours is the one in charge in town, the one overseeing this pilfering!''

Beth's insides cartwheeled. Then these things were not happening outside his knowledge and control! At least she knew whom to deal with now to fight this. She struggled to calm herself, but fury fed by fear roiled through her. Her only hope was that since Jerrod knew they had been hard hit by the enemy, he would spare them. Yes, perhaps that was it. Since he cared for her and Will and knew what had happened here, he would still protect her farm and her area. Surely, he would not enact those cruel, unjust orders here!

''I'm certain Colonel Ross will help us, Charity. Perhaps the orders were only aimed at Tories. Or perhaps they will overlook those who were raided by the British before. I can reason with him. He's not one to just take things, not since he understands we're barely holding on this winter,'' she plunged on, trying desperately to convince herself as much as Charity. ''With me a widow and you with Silas the way he is, there is no way we can lose all but one horse and then cut and sell our wheat like that. I know it won't be as bad as it sounds. It cannot be. He—he promised me.''

But Charity just shook her head as Beth helped her remount.

"Will, string some of those fish for Charity and Silas's supper," Beth suggested.

After all, she reasoned, if even the slightest bit of this terrible news were true, the neighbors would have to begin to share even more things after they took their stand against these unjust Americans' orders. And if Jerrod was overseeing townfolk, whom the British had not bothered, in the handing over of their horses, there would probably only be her and Will for supper.

But she was wrong. No sooner had they begun their meal than they heard a single horse. Beth darted to the window with flintlock in hand, but put away the weapon when she the rider was Jerrod. As she opened the door, her heart thudded louder than his hoof-beats. At first when she had heard Charity's dire news, she had planned to make her point by meeting him at the door with her gun. But her mother used to say that honey attracted more flies than vinegar. Not that she was trying to attract Jerrod as a woman would lure a man, of course, she assured herself. But she meant to be fair and friendly until she heard his true intentions.

"Welcome!" she called, but her voice broke. She waved as Will sprinted out to tie his horse. "I hope you're hungry!"

"Suddenly, more than ever!" he told her with a quick squeeze of her shoulder as he entered.

His dark eyes and bright smile told her that he was hungry for the sight of her. She felt better already. Surely he had no intention of enacting those vile orders here.

But after she scurried to set a place for him, foreboding slowed her steps. He stood so silently by the hearth, rotating his bicorne in his big hands. Even the fact he wore the red muffler over the collar of his black cape did not make her feel better. She turned to face him, a pewter plate in her hands, her own stance suddenly so stiff it matched his.

"So, have you returned to ask for more donations for the troops?" she prompted. Every muscle and nerve was coiled tight in her, waiting for some sign he was a traitor to all she had believed and wanted him to be.

He only nodded at first. Then he spoke, his voice jerky and abrupt. "The generous donations you made to me in October and last week—you'll never know how dear they are. But Congress has given General Washington orders to take provisions if he must—and not only rely on folks to give them."

She banged the plate on the table. "I heard tell of this, but I could not believe it! And I certainly could not believe you would be a party to this! You must mean to requisition things only from Tories! If the American army takes things from patriots, they will be stooping as low as the thieving British, and people may turn against our own army!"

Jerrod hated himself for having to tell her this—to do this. He wasn't sure how to handle it. He was too used to giving orders in desperate circumstances where there could be no question of disobedience or rebellion. He knew his voice cracked out cold and hard.

"The army must survive the winter, Beth. We've got to be intact in the spring to fight the bloody bastards again. Sometimes individuals have to sacrifice for the common good."

"I assure you," she said as she drew herself up and lifted her chin, "I know that."

"Yes, I know you do. I didn't mean it that way. Your family has given the ultimate sacrifice. I am grieved to say there may be more. But Continental currency will be offered for whatever goods are appropriated by our troops."

"Pretty words—*appropriated, donated,* even *bought!* But no one trusts that new paper currency compared to good gold guineas, and—"

"I don't give a hang!" he roared and banged his fist on the table. "They have to learn to trust, or there won't *be* united colonies to fight for come spring!"

"The other orders," she said slowly, dreading what was to come. "About our horses and wheat. It means me and my neighbors? It's all true?"

"But you said, Mother," Will began to argue with her instead of Jerrod, "that he was our friend and would take care of us!"

"Will, please! Colonel Ross knows we have only two horses here, and his orders aside—"

"I'm afraid I can't put orders aside, even for you," Jerrod said, his voice quiet and controlled now. "That's one thing we're going to have to deal with in this war, Beth—that what I *have* to do and *want* to do might be separate things. But I had to explain myself without my brigade in tow."

"They're both old horses," she insisted and scooted the chair she had meant for him so hard under the table that the plates shuddered and rattled. "The mare

Nellie wheezes in the cold, and the other was once my husband's favorite stallion and is retired. Your proposed actions are entirely unjust, and I must protest vehemently.''

"You are. And I'm sorry, but we can use the stallion to haul fuel and building material to camp."

She felt so torn. His face was set in hard lines, but his eyes asked for understanding. But he had said he would protect and help them, and he was breaking his word. She feared that soldiers always broke their word; that terrified and grieved as well as angered her.

"As for the wheat," she clipped out, "our field hands helped to plant it before they went off to serve, but I'll never manage to harvest it, especially without that stallion. So one of your 'requests' or the other is quite impossible, let alone unreasonable and unfair."

"I'm sure your neighbors can pitch in, or I'll get some volunteers from camp after they've built themselves huts."

He turned away to stare into the fire on the hearth for a moment. He felt as if his face would crumble; he could not bear to have her see tears in his eyes. He understood her pleas, but knew they must be countermanded. If only she could see the poverty and pain of the boys trying to settle into Valley Forge, he thought. Frostbitten fingers and toes; dysentery that sapped strength and made lads look like old men. Men were dying almost as fast as horses. The troops were building their own crude huts, gathering their own firewood, going without pay all the time, without food most of the time, and without hope—

He bit his lower lip hard and spun back to face her.

"Anyway," he said, his voice controlled and cold, "only half the wheat has to be threshed by the first of February and the rest not till March, so—"

"It's obvious you've never been a farmer!" Beth exploded. "You're even dictating dates for the threshing and, therefore, the cutting? Don't you know weather plays a part? And acts of God, though of course you'll be telling Him what to do next! And maybe I'd rather have my wheat be sold as straw then lose my independence to an army that is supposed to be protecting the same! Maybe I'd rather just have you haul me and Will off to some prison stockade than be led on and lied to. Maybe—"

"Beth, just listen," he interrupted, moving rapidly toward her, almost catching Will between them. "I don't make the rules, but I will obey and defend them. You're only a woman and a boy, and the entire army's got to make it through the winter. I'll see that you are protected, but it's going to have to be my—the army's—way."

"Let me go! I don't believe you anymore!"

The moment she tried to push him away and said those words, she regretted them, but she was frightened again. It was still she and Will against the world. She had thought Jerrod to be a friend and ally, a mainstay. Her dear husband, who had given his life for this evidently lost cause, had been all of those things for her. But in a very real way, Jerrod and his Americans were the enemy, too. Yet he still turned her blood to molten fire when he so much as touched her—even angrily like this.

He let her go and stepped back. A stern look furrowed his high brow and twisted his mouth to a taut, jagged line. He put his bicorne back on and drew himself up to a military stance.

"I'm sorry we've had these—these difficult words when we got off to such a fine beginning, Mistress McGowan. But I tell you," he went on, pointing a finger at her, "I will do anything I can, consistent with my loyalty to the army and its cause, to help you and Will this winter, whether you want my help or not. I understand it's a hard thing for a woman and a boy to try to hold body and soul together, but—" he bit off the next words so low, she had to strain to catch them "—it's just like a woman to turn on one who wants to help her."

He spun away and strode to the door. "When spring comes, *if I can,*" he said without looking back again, "I shall see you get a sturdy horse for planting in return for the one I'm going to take from the barn now. And I do not expect to have an old flintlock poked in my back as I do my duty!"

The door banged closed behind him. Beth ran to the window and sagged against it. Tears stung her eyes as she watched him pull his own horse with him to the barn, then mount and lead away her husband's old, swaybacked stallion, Granger. Will took her hand as if to comfort her, but she heard him sniffle, too.

"But I still like Colonel Ross, and if Father believed in the war enough to die for it, he'd give Granger, too!" Will choked out and ran from the kitchen. She heard his footsteps on the stairs and the door of his room bang behind him.

Beth stood there as Jerrod and the two horses disappeared around the bend in the lane past the orchard. How had their beautiful beginning gone so wrong? she agonized. Jerrod was not the enemy, yet she had treated him like one, and it had taken her son's bold words to make her realize it. Indeed, Jerrod was right in saying that the boy was trying to be a man, even if he was probably sobbing his heart out in his room right now. But how quickly Jerrod's face had gone hard as flint toward her. With the insult he had muttered about women, she surmised again that some woman he had loved had let him down. Drat, but she couldn't help the man's past, and now, after this, there was no future with him, either!

She turned away from the window and started up the stairs to comfort Will. Her heart was as heavy as her steps. Her emotions toward Jerrod churned and clashed in her. She was furious with him for his role in seizing supplies, however much he valued his dear duty! But she already grieved for the tarnishing of their shining season of joy that she had been polishing in the depths of her heart.

The next day Beth was making soap in the kitchen, stirring the boiling lard and lye with a stick, when she heard Will's cries. "Mother, Mother, down by the road!" he shouted as he rushed in breathless. "Ragged soldiers took down our rail fence, and now they're chopping down the apple trees!"

She grunted as she lifted the heavy kettle off the hearth hook so it would not boil over and start a fire while she went to see. Those blasted, brazen British must be back! Another promise of protection from the Americans broken! But as she whirled her cloak around her shoulders and reached for her flintlock and ammunition, she realized what Will had said. Suddenly, she knew the marauders were American foragers this time, and not the British.

"You mean Americans?" she asked the panting, wide-eyed Will as she made for the door.

"Dressed too much like scarecrows to be German George's fancy boys," he told her. "But there's six of them and— What do you think you're going to do with Grandfather's gun? I could get on old Nellie and ride to town for Colonel Ross!"

"No! The illustrious Colonel Ross probably sent these men here to take our wood," she said, waspishly, though, somehow, she knew better. "Drat, I wish I had your father's good rifle now."

They walked down the lane almost to the pond, far enough to see that, indeed, six men had taken down their fence rails and had even loaded a few onto two long wagons. They had now taken axes to the trees at the edge of the apple orchard along the road. One venerable old tree creaked, then crashed as Beth and Will watched, crouched behind a juniper bush.

Beth's blood boiled. That orchard was the future fortune of this farm—especially if war took everything else. She squinted at the scene while her mind raced. The two horses harnessed to each of the wagons looked nervous and feisty. The soldiers' muskets and haversacks, no doubt stuffed with powder and shot, lay nearby them on the ground within their easy reach. There was really no way she could force them off at gunpoint, but perhaps ...

"Will, stay here."

"Aw, mother! I want to help. I can sneak from tree to tree and grab their guns and then—"

"Shh! I just want them off our property before they ruin the orchard. Ragamuffins like that are welcome to the fence rails. Please, Will, just wait here."

Boldy, she sauntered out from behind the bush and around to the road near where two men were hacking madly at the next tree while the four others delimbed the downed one. She called to them, "Excuse me, men!"

The chopping stopped. Backs unbent; heads turned. She moved a few steps closer to the four horses harnessed to the wagons.

"I just wanted to say," she began, her voice shaky "that wood is green and will smoke you out if you use it for fuel. Take the fence rails and go, please. You know, I feared you were British at first, so I brought an old gun I really don't know much about—"

She pulled the trigger, exploding the gun straight up into the air. Its kick slammed the stock into her hip. As always, it banged louder than ten modern muskets. She tried to look surprised. Just as she had hoped, the horses panicked. Evidently they were spirited ones not used to harnesses and wagon traces, probably ones the Americans had recently taken from folks nearby. The wagons, still light with only a few fence rails, jerked and moved. The soldiers ran up toward the road, slipping and sliding in their attempt to get to the wagons before the horses ran off. Beth fought to keep from cheering. She tried to look as distressed as these men, but it served the army right, taking pilfered horses to haul purloined wood!

Two men managed to start after the wagons, but the rutted roads caused them to stumble and they soon stopped. They all looked blistering mad and she braced herself for their reaction.

"Look what you done, mistress!" one soldier bellowed. "It's gonna take us miles in this cold to run them down! Keep that old gun for the likes of the plaguey Brits and Hessians if you don't know more 'bout it than that!"

"And Colonel Ross said to be back with two wagon loads by nightfall," one groused to another with a disgusted glance her way. "I'll be ding-danged if we don't tell him why we're not!"

"Please inform your Colonel Ross," she said, backing away steadily, step by step, "that the fence rails are one thing, but the apple treees are another. And tell him he'll not be strolling through the Mc-Gowan orchards again!"

She spun away and strode up the lane toward the house. She was grateful they did not pursue her, but gathered their things and hurried as best they could after their runaway wagons. When she got back to the bug-eyed, grinning Will, she was feeling she had just won a great victory to save the farm from utter destruction.

"You know," she told the boy, "as long as they've taken our fence apart, let's get one of the rails for you to chop into a Yule log. I have a feeling it will be just you and me for Christmas after all, but we'll still have the best time!''

At her own words, her exultation waned. She'd never have the best time now, not without Jerrod here too, not after he heard what she'd done. But even in wartime, people had to stand up for their own rights. She had told the men they could have the fence rails, but if they wanted live trees to cut, next time she'd direct them to the back woodlot and tell them to leave her and her son's livelihood alone!

Between the two of them, she and Will lugged a fence rail back up to the house. They chattered on with great bravado all the way, but her thoughts were hardly so bold. What would Jerrod do when those men told him what she had done? She had a good notion to use this rail for a big bar to keep him out of her house! And yet, she wanted him to come again. She felt ripped apart by concern for him, which warred with her fury at the way things were going. But if he'd actually sent those louts to cut down the orchard that she'd shared with him, both with her apple tarts and their autumn strolls, that was the end of anything that ever could have been between them!

Before Will could see the tears in her eyes, she dropped her end of the rail by the woodpile and hurried back into the warmth of the kitchen.

It was after dark that night when she heard hoofbeats. Even they sounded angry. She was glad she had made Will turn in, though he had wanted to spend the night with her downstairs, arguing like a lawyer that it was only five days before Christmas. She had checked a while ago, and the boy slept the sleep of the innocent. She envied him that. She felt only ready to do battle.

She glanced out carefully through a crack in the curtains; she had let the fire burn down to one big, glowing log so she could see out better. Yes, the rider was Jerrod. She unbolted the door and, cradling the flintlock in her arms, waited. Even though she was expecting it, his firm knock jolted her. She opened the door and stepped out on the porch with only her gown, shawl and gun between her and the bite of wind—and his dark-eyed glare she could feel but not see.

"Back for the rest of the orchard?" she challenged.

"Hardly. How was I to know they would end up here or chopping trees? We're desperate in camp for fuel and logs to build huts, and I did tell them to do what was necessary. Your orchards won't be touched again, unless it's unavoidable later. But what's this about your stampeding our wagons? And then letting on you didn't have a notion about how to shoot that old gun? You and Will both told me you could pick off an apple at twenty paces. Are you trying to get even with me? You're not dealing with some naive farm boy here, you know!"

"Oh, I do know. I'm dealing with a whole army of men who are supposed to be bright enough to realize they can't take all the good horses and then have the wheat cut and delivered, too! Men who are supposed to know that they need the nearby civilians on their side, not hostile—"

"I see you're hostile to me now. Whose side are you on in this war anyway, Mistress McGowan? And it's danged cold out here, and I need to talk to you."

"You are talking."

"Inside, blast it! Now! And I've had enough of that dangerous old gun!"

"Then the army should have sent my husband's musket back when he was killed protecting General Washington's retreat from the Brooklyn Heights!"

She felt so confused. She wanted both to embrace and strangle Jerrod. Terrifying, conflicting emotions roiled through her. But she did not argue when he took the flintlock from her and turned her around to herd her into the house. He had gone all stiff and strong, the commanding officer in charge again, and that both comforted and infuriated her.

Inside, she walked a few steps away from him and turned her back. She crossed her arms over her chest, pulling her shawl tighter. She feared that one look at his face in the glow of the fire might melt her resolve. She heard him close the door and put both guns down and walk closer, not even taking the time to remove his cape. His presence, inches away, almost burned her. She was expecting a barrage of accusations, and it took her unawares when he gently cupped her shoulders with both big hands.

"I'm sorry about the orchard, but you should have talked with my men, suggesting they speak with me."

"They already had. All they cared about was reporting back to Colonel Ross 'with two wagonloads by nightfall,' as you'd ordered. I suppose I should be grateful they did not start to tear down the house from over our heads."

"Don't be absurd! But since I am to oversee the brigade in the Berwyn area, I am responsible for certain quotas of forage."

She spun to face him, mostly to put some space between her and his touch. But when she backed against the wall he stalked after her and placed his hands on either side of her head, hemming her in.

"And just what do you expect to forage from me now?" she demanded. "My son's pet sheep? More apple tarts I made from the trees your men want to destroy? More—"

"Dang it, I want warmth, understanding—I don't know," he interrupted. "Or maybe this is what I want from you!"

He pushed her gently against the wall, and pressed slowly to her, full length, chest to breasts, his hard hips to her soft belly, solid thigh to soft. His lips claimed and challenged hers. As his hands moved to her waist, she responded as if she could not bear to be without his touch.

The man confused her so! He did not offer security and warmth and understanding—those same things he said he sought—as her husband had. He was devious and dangerous, so why did she feel this strongly for him? And how could she admire him for his devotion to his duty when that very duty threatened all she valued?

"Jerrod, Jerrod," she breathed as his lips marauded down her throat. "This is all so confused!" She could not yet think of going farther with such luxurious liberties, and yet she wanted to do so with every fiber of her being.

He lifted his head to gaze raptly into her flushed face. "I know," he whispered. "The war—my coming and going. Things between us... I feel that way, too, but I'll take care of you, I swear it. Please trust me!" He pulled her away from the wall and tilted her back in his arms so they were eye to eye. "The thing is, when I'm in town, things like stray soldiers marauding might happen again. But if I were to make my headquarters here—"

"What? Here?"

"Yes, let's say, myself and maybe four of my men."

He tried to sound nonchalant, as if he had just thought of the possibility. He needed to protect her and be with her. This was the best way, though he hated to invite himself almost as much as he dreaded just to tell her he had gone so far as to obtain official quartering orders for himself and his men here. He leaned her back against the wall again, propping himself close to her with one hand by her head, the other smoothing from her cheek the golden hair he'd tumbled loose.

"We'd have a strategic position here that way, and you'd be better protected," he went on. "I regret my orders about the horses and the wheat, but at least if I was here, others wouldn't come along to bother you. Our work is not in town, anyway, but mostly up and down this road. I and my men would have to be away from here sometimes during the day, but word would surely get around in case the British or their Hessian lackeys dared to come back—"

"And," she said, still looking dazed but ducking under his arm to collapse on the bench at the table, "word would get around to the neighbors, too." She shook her head, tossing back her glorious wreath of hair. He restrained the longing to touch it again. "I can hear it now, 'the widow McGowan and the Master of Forage all cozy this winter!' You're not exactly as beloved as Washington around here, you know," she accused.

He felt himself bristle at that, but he kept his voice in check. "I'm not the Master of Forage, Beth." He sank down on the bench beside her. "Believe me, I take orders, too. I have two superiors between me and Commander in Chief Washington. And I was wondering if what you said before, about your husband's death covering Washington's retreat, means you have mixed feelings toward the general or our cause."

He noted she looked down at her clasped hands before she shrugged. "Not exactly," she replied. "Despite the way I've carried on, I want to do what I can to help the cause of freedom. It's just that it's important to me I have *my* freedom to protect Will and this farm. And I have no intention of going back to letting my life be always controlled by men—however much I loved and respected my father and my husband."

She saw his eyes widen and his nostrils flare, as if he had just taken in something very important. He nodded and stroked her cheek again with the backs of his fingers. That slightest rasp of his skin against hers shot sparks clear down between her thighs.

"All right, I see," he whispered. "But how about my offer? And how about a warm winter truce between you and me?"

She nodded before she realized she should ask for time to think it all over. Only, somehow, thinking went right out the window with this man nearby. Too often this surge of warring emotions ruled her. But she knew his being here would protect her from outsiders. And if he and his men were about the premises, she could more easily convince him that his orders about the winter wheat were unfair. Perhaps he would even take some of her ideas—and protests—to General Washington through his two superior officers.

"Did that nod mean yes?" he probed, his face as eager as a boy's.

"Yes."

He heaved a huge sigh as he led her over to the hearth and they sat on the familiar settle. He untied his cloak and dropped it on the pallet at their feet.

"Then I'll be out tomorrow early with my men to arrange things here," he told her as they stretched out their feet toward the warmth. "Since you and Will use the kitchen so much, we'll stick to the two drawing rooms as best we can. Agreed?"

She nodded again. "I appreciate that you asked me and didn't just command it," she admitted. "That's important to me, especially these days when folks are forced to do things they don't want."

He nodded in return, though she thought he avoided her eyes at her compliment. And here she'd thought she was offering him an olive branch to show she understood his dilemma! She took his square chin in her hand and turned his head so he gazed back at her. She could see her own intense visage reflected in the deep pools of his eyes. She would have liked to lose herself there, to swim in their warmth forever, she thought.

"There is only one problem for you and me," he added as his fingers stroked the slant of her throat. "When we arrive tomorrow, it goes without saying, with the men and Will around—I mean, you and I will be hard-pressed to find . . . some private time."

Hard-pressed. The words echoed in her brain. *Private time,* he had said, *you and I . . .*

They were in each other's arms again, pressing, caressing. She inhaled his masculine essence. It was as if they breathed together while their tongues touched and their hands tangled as they roamed. She came so alive in his arms like this.

But she jumped away from him when the big hearth log shuddered and bumped to shoot out a shower of sparks. Little prickles of silver and scarlet peppered the edges of the pallet blanket and even reached her skirt hems and his cape.

"Oh—fire!" she cried and bolted to stamp and smack out the sparks.

"It's all right now," he protested and reached for her.

"No, I've seen what can happen!" she insisted.

Elbows propped on his knees as he stared into the fire, he heaved a sigh. She scuffed the ashes back toward the grate, then rescued his cape, shook it out and draped it over a chair back. And just as the newly settled log flared to give them more light, a narrow piece of paper fell from his coat.

She bent to retrieve it. She skimmed the paper. She noted the long, dark signature at the bottom of the single page: *General G. Washington!*

She gasped as she read. Jerrod Ross had not planned at all to give her a choice about his being quartered here! In her shaking hand, she held a command!

Mistress Elizabeth McGowan, widow, of the farm at the bend of the Berwyn-Haverford Road, seven miles from Valley Forge, Pennsylvania, will provide bed and board for Lt. Col. Jerrod Ross, assistant to the Commissary General of Forage, and four of his men at said farm until further notice.

All her fervor about being allowed to make her own decisions—about keeping her independence—was so much stuff and nonsense to Jerrod! It was worse than when her father and husband had commanded her life—she was related to them! It was as if Jerrod and his army were not forage masters, but puppet masters jerking her strings! No doubt the kiss was planned to seduce her to his will! It was obvious his loyalty to the army was more valuable to him than anything that might have been between them.

She smacked the document down on the table. His eyes widened at the sight of her angry face.

''I can explain,'' he began, holding up his hands as if to ward her off.

Jerrod cursed himself silently. Things had gone better tonight between them than he could have expected—until now. He had intended to save this formal command he'd obtained from headquarters as a last resort. All he wanted was to do his duty—and look after this woman he cared for and desired so desperately. He tried to explain, but he was exasperated and exhausted, too.

"My first notion was to send you and Will to safety into town or to live with your neighbors, the Pembrokes, while the army used the place, but I knew—"

"That I'd see you for the tricky, deceitful sneak you are!"

"You wouldn't want to leave."

"I won't leave!"

"I asked you first. I didn't just spring this on you!"

"Maybe so, but if I had said no, you would still be quartering yourself here tomorrow, wouldn't you? And you used your buttering-up tactics before you just happened to mention it as a passing thought! Now I see your real intent from the first. The day we met, the minute you heard this farm was located a few miles out on this road and learned it was inhabited only by a *helpless* widow and a boy, you had your foraging heart set on it! Anything for the army, even if Will and I perish here!"

"That's not true!" he roared. He marveled at how easily this woman could make him lose his temper and control, when he'd been through the heat and danger of battle and stayed steely calm. "No-Loss Ross," he knew his men called him behind his back. He was afraid he'd lost Beth now, but still, his blood was up.

"I was only glad to hear you were a widow because when I saw you had a son, I thought you might be married. My only 'real intent from the first' was that I was drawn to you—dang it, desired you!''

"Desired this place to quarter your men in to take things from this area, you mean! Besides, you said you were a second son with no hopes of inheritance, so I suppose this farm looked especially interesting for private reasons!''

"Only the private reason that you appealed to me! As for my loyalty to the army, you bet your life. Because it is our lives that are at stake. If the army fails, where will you and Will be then?''

"At least under British rule we had horses and wheat!''

"That comparison's not fair!''

"Nothing is fair right now—nothing!'' She reached for the paper. Ripping it across once, then twice, she wadded it up in pieces and tossed them in the fire.

"That doesn't change a danged thing,'' he told her between gritted teeth.

"Everything's changed between us!'' She set her hands at her waist. "That so-called winter truce you tried to seduce me to—never! We may both be on the same side in this big war, but we've got our own war here now, and don't you forget it!''

He seized her by her wrists and hauled her close. "If you think I would ever so much as touch a woman I didn't want, you don't know me at all! And if I *am* a second son who has no prospects, it's only because my family are dyed-in-the-wool Tories in voluntary exile and have disowned a son who believes in the colonial independence that will save us all from being British bootlickers! But if you want an armed camp here in this house from which I'm going to run my part of the war because it's best for all of us, you've got it!''

"Mother, Colonel Ross—what's all the shouting?" Will stood at the doorway to the stairs, bleary-eyed. "At first I thought maybe those redcoat soldiers came back."

Beth pulled away from Jerrod and hurried to Will's side. She was touched to tears at the sight of him: he had his carving knife in his hands. He had come down to defend her with a boys' carving knife! She put her arms around him, but felt him stiffen slightly and pull away as if to wordlessly insist, "Aw, Mother!"

"Colonel Ross and I were discussing coming events we don't—don't agree on," she faltered without meeting Jerrod's harsh glare.

"Our Christmas together?" Will asked.

Beth's gaze slammed into Jerrod's. In the heat of the moment she had forgotten that. She tried to form an answer, but all that seemed so sad now, so broken. Had Jerrod, her knight in shining armor, just been using her and Will from the beginning for his own ends?

"I will be here for Christmas, and we'll make of it what we can," Jerrod told the boy when Beth didn't answer. "But it's late now, so I suggest you and your mother go on upstairs to your beds. I'll sleep down here on this pallet until dawn and then be off to town to fetch my men. A few of us are going to move in here for a while to make sure—" here, Beth noted, his authoritative tone wavered "—that this place comes to no harm."

"Really, Mother?" Will asked and hugged her now. "Soldiers here? Colonel Ross, sir, I'll do anything you want to help!"

"Offer accepted, Civilian Volunteer Will Mc-Gowan!"

"Will, I don't want you, or either of us, to get in the men's way—especially Colonel Ross's," Beth insisted. She took a candle from the sideboard and pushed Will ahead of her toward the stairs, without a word or a look back. She left Jerrod just standing there, watching. She could feel his eyes on her as she shooed her protesting son up the stairs. She became suddenly totally aware of her walk, of the slight sway of her hips, of the friction between her thighs as her woolen stockings brushed each other.

She sent Will back to bed and closed herself in her bedroom. She jammed the back of a chair up under the latch of her door. She felt a prisoner in her own home, but not as much as she felt trapped by her own feelings. She was so confused by the idea that Jerrod might have had ulterior motives for courting her. But tomorrow she would show him she was still the owner here—and still in command of her feelings and desires, too!

Fully dressed but for her shoes and petticoat, she shivered as she scooted down between her icy sheets. Yet she felt flushed and warmed from their loving and their fighting tonight. It was only much later as she lay there, unable to sleep, straining for sounds of him below, that she wished she had a warming pan.

A floorboard creaked in the hall. She stiffened and stared into the dark, afraid it would be Jerrod. But there was no further sound except the sweep of the wind and the rattle of a shutter from outside. And as she slipped into slumber, she wished, drat her foolish heart, for Jerrod's warm arms tight around her again.

Chapter Three

When Beth rose the next morning, the sky was gun-metal gray and spitting ice crystals, but Jerrod had ridden off to town already. She hurried to prepare breakfast for her and Will and to get a good start on her chores. She had no intention of even appearing to be in Jerrod's or his men's way. He might think she yearned to be near him, or worse—had set her cap for him. How could she ever have thought he was really interested in her and not just the farm? her inner voice tormented.

And yet she knew she was fighting herself as much as him. She was coming to care for him. She wanted to accept that the expression of his feelings and his touch had been sincere. She wanted to believe that he had planned to quarter himself and his men here, at least partly, to protect and be near her and Will. Surely, despite his fierce dedication to winning the war, she was not just another item of military business to him.

But she would express none of these hopes and desires to Jerrod, not the way things stood between them now. He had treated her as if she were a green private under his command, required to do his bidding without argument, not a patriot or even an ally, as she deserved. He had tricked her about the quartering command. If she was to provide his soldiers with room *and* board, wouldn't that deplete her food reserves in a short time? She had been so pleased and proud to cook for and serve Jerrod here, but not if she was ordered to—not if she was just cook or maidservant to him and his men now. Who knew what else they would demand from her when they arrived? And just in case he had thought she was an easy mark for his passions—which she feared, indeed, she was—she would not give in to these feelings for him that were rampaging through her! She had her pride, war or not!

She almost felt another woman's hands were at her tasks while her mind worked apart. She fed Will and answered his barrage of questions as best she could, but her thoughts kept flitting back to Jerrod.

She tried to convince herself that she didn't care if Jerrod ever rode back in. Still, she kept straining to hear, waiting for the sound of hoofbeats. And when he arrived and introduced his men as politely as if they were all assembled at some fine cotillion, she was well enough pleased by their proper demeanor.

Corporal Marcus Collier was blond and rather brusque; she could tell he admired Jerrod almost as much as Will did. The other three were youthful privates: Adrian Wyatt, Simon Murry and Kit Irwin. They seemed to have boundless energy and obviously appreciated being quartered in a warm house.

After Jerrod supervised taking up the rugs and moving aside the few pieces of upholstered furniture so they would not be soiled, the men quickly established themselves in the two drawing rooms. Into one, they moved the dining table for a massive desk to spread out maps and lists. In the other, they placed their bedrolls and equipment.

Beth had to pull Will away from watching the young, red-haired Private Irwin clean his musket, but at least this had not been as bad a beginning as she had expected. Jerrod was treating her formally and distantly. He had not spoken directly to her except to say, "The men are quite used to preparing their own provisions they've gathered, so if we can just arrange a time to use your kitchen hearth when we won't bother you—I mean to say, I don't expect you to provide and cook for the five of us with your limited supplies and your chores around here."

"That would be fine," she said, staring at his epaulets and not his face. "Only I've plenty of porridge, so I'd be happy to make breakfast for all of you to get you going each day...."

Her voice faded away as their eyes met. He looked as if he might crush her to him as he had more than once before. She almost swayed against him, like a compass needle toward true north.

"That's generous and gracious of you, Mistress McGowan. The men will be grateful."

They left it at that when his corporal hurried in, though Beth longed to say so much more. But it was certainly not her fault things had gone awry between them, she assured herself as she wrapped up against the cold, tied her leather buskins to her knees and went on about her tasks outside. Since Will was chopping wood, she had said she would care for the animals, except for his precious pet sheep Sheba, whom he fed soon after waking each day. It would not take her long since there were only three animals left from the array of stock the farm once boasted.

Compared to the sharp chill outside, the barn seemed warm to her. She even took off her cloak as she entered. She fed and curried old Nellie, the mare she had ridden so much when she first came to be mistress here. _Mistress_ McGowan, Jerrod had called her this morning: the warmth of their shared intimacies was evidently over now by mutual, unspoken agreement.

She sniffed back tears as she patted Sheba. She chatted to the silly thing about her promise to Will that the sheep could spend Christmas Eve with them in the house. When Sheba was a lamb, it had often been allowed in during the winter, especially that time Will almost died from spotted fever.

She moved on to milk their last brown-and-white cow, which had been saved from the British simply because she'd wandered off into the woodlot and they'd overlooked her. Scratch was more used to Will's touch, but Beth had made certain after the field hands had left that she knew how to milk.

''There, my girl, just let me wedge this stool in here beside you. I can't thank you enough for your contributions of milk and butter these days.''

She squirted streams of foam into the pail in a rhythmic swish-swish. She was so intent on agonizing over Jerrod that she did not even look around at Will when she heard the barn door open.

"Done chopping all that wood already?" she asked.

"Beth, it's Jerrod."

Jerrod. Her hands missed the beat before she went on again.

"What is it you want?"

"If I answer that truthfully, you will toss us all out."

She bit her lower lip. She wanted to believe him so badly. She wanted to make everything perfect between them again, but that wasn't quite how the words came out.

"I can't toss you out," she said and stood, wiping her hands on her apron. "You're officially here by order of the almighty General Washington." She lugged the pail out of the stall; he reached to take it from her. She bent back for the stool and faced him outside the cow's stall, holding the three-legged stool before her as if it were a shield.

"You know," he said, "even when it's so cold outside, the barn and the animals create a lot of warmth in here."

Strange, she thought, how they agreed on so many things, even little things. Why couldn't it always be that way between them? But, "Yes," was all she said.

"Don't take this amiss now, but that's what you did for me, Beth. When I was leading a cold, lonely life with nothing to keep me going but dedication to winning the war, you gave me a warm place to be— With you, I mean, not just when I visited the barn. Dang, but when I'm with you I never say what I mean!"

She clutched the stool even more tightly. She had no intention of just falling into his arms and his power again as she had before. But even when she knew how vulnerable she was to this man, the strength of his allure astounded her. Silence stretched between them. Then, fortunately, he broke the spell by reaching over to pat the cow.

"All of your animals seem to have names," he observed. "Granger, Nellie, Sheba. What's this one's?"

"Scratch," she said, grateful for his lighter tone.

"Because she likes to be scratched?"

"No. You see those funny tufts of hair in her ears? I always thought those looked like inexpensive scratch wigs made from the castoffs of good hanks of hair in my father's wig shop."

The mention of her father's shop brought back to her all her other painful losses. In one awful night, it seemed, her childhood had gone up in smoke and flames, but she'd die before she'd let someone consume this life she'd built here for herself and Will! She would protect Will's right to his childhood if it were the last thing she did, and here this man was always urging her to let Will grow up!

"Quite an interesting menagerie you have here," Jerrod observed.

"Only a city boy would put it that way. No wonder you have little background for understanding the workings of this farm or cutting wheat or—"

"But you're hardly a born and bred farm girl," he countered. "I got the notion *you* were reared quite a city girl!"

"I was, but when I came here I learned and changed."

"You said you had house servants and field hands here. You said—"

"I don't care what I said. I know how to farm and care for the orchards, crops and animals—and my son—which you marauding armies in these parts have seen fit to leave me! Will and I don't need any advice or someone taking over this farm from us!"

Even as she raised her voice, she regretted the loss of the warm, quiet moment between them he had tried to build again. But how dare he imply she did not know how to manage this place! Panic over what had been her greatest fear when her husband died spilled from her in a tumble of words.

"I can care for all this now, Colonel Ross. I taught myself about the place and even how to shoot, after the last field hand went off to war. Of course, in the beginning, my husband didn't want me to have to work that way. When he asked me to wed him, he promised he'd keep me in the style to which I'd been accustomed. But I always wanted to be part of his life here. At first, except for riding out to look things over and for overseeing the cook and maid, I felt I had no part. But they went back to their farms to help out when their fathers went away. And I learned to do everything after William died! Little Will even had to teach me things like milking, a mere boy teaching his mother how to preserve everything when we were all alone—"

She wasn't sure when the torrent of emotions became a torrent of tears. She only knew Jerrod tugged the milk stool away from her and pulled her into his arms as he leaned against the stall. Her head pressed into his strong shoulder, she sobbed as she had not done since she heard William was dead and realized she'd have to go on alone to protect for Will a farm she did not know how to manage. And caught between the pincers of two armies like this, she was so afraid, now more than ever, so afraid she'd lose it all!

"You're very brave," he told her, his mouth very close, his breath very warm. "I didn't mean otherwise. I'm not sure I could have done what you have here. I haven't a notion how to milk a cow, but perhaps, sometime, among other things, you and Will could teach me."

"Colonel Ross?" The sharp voice sounded from outside just before the barn door creaked open. Beth and Jerrod leaped apart, and she bent shakily over her milk pail to wipe at her wet cheeks.

"Sir, word of marauding enemy provision parties to the east!"

Jerrod strode toward Corporal Collier. "How far away?"

"The lad who rode in got it secondhand. He's not really sure."

"Then," Jerrod said with a quick doff of his bicorne to Beth before he clapped it back on, "we'd best ride out to see. Mistress McGowan, I'll be leaving one man behind."

The door let in a huge whoosh of cold as the two men hurried out. She heard shouts, then horses' hooves thundering away. She leaned back against the cow's stall, dazed by it all. Not only that the British threatened again, but that her feelings for Jerrod did, too. Strange, how much safer she felt with him here, but how much more in danger of telling him she was coming to care for him so deeply. Still wiping at her cheeks, she donned her cloak and toted the pail out into the wind, grateful for the dusting of ice flakes that hid her tears.

As the morning and afternoon wore on, time hung heavy on Beth's hands. She thought she might put up the Christmas decorations, but something held her back. After her argument with Jerrod last night, she had planned only to decorate upstairs so it would be clear he was to be no part of her and Will's celebration. But after this morning, if they could come to some understanding, perhaps she would place a few of the things in the kitchen.

She could do some Christmas baking, but she was hardly in the mood. Besides, it would not be fair for the men coming in and out to see and smell such when they would be no real part of it. So, right now, Christmas seemed as up in the air as her confusion over Jerrod. Instead, she darned and sewed, though she was so jumpy she pricked her finger enough times to dot the linens with cheery Christmas red.

Occasionally, one of Jerrod's men rode in or out to speak with Private Irwin, whom he had left behind. The young man spent some time in what Will importantly called "the war room," and some time at the bottom of the lane, talking to travelers on the road. She learned from him that an armed party of British looters had been in the Haverford area yesterday. Finally, Private Irwin told her that Colonel Ross was supervising a roadblock to the east by a bridge that spanned a rocky stream. Beth knew the spot exactly. She could ride through McGowan land almost the entire way there. It was after she and Will had eaten a nervous-stomach dinner about two in the afternoon and she had sent Will down the lane with a plate of food for Private Irwin, that the thought came to her.

Jerrod and his men must be cold and hungry out at that roadblock. The least she could do was take them something made from dried apples in the cellar. Maybe they would think twice later about letting anyone chop down her orchards! She immediately got busy making two pans of dumplings. She informed Will that she planned to deliver her goods, but told him not to worry Private Irwin with that knowledge. She did not fret about Will staying at the house, because the soldier was about the premises. Will fussed over not going with her, but it soothed him to hear the farm would be in his and Private Irwin's care during the short time she was gone. Wishing she had a way to take a hot beverage to the men, she finally filled a covered tin cream pail with cold liberty coffee and hoped they could heat it there. With Will's help, she saddled and mounted Nellie.

"I hope when Colonel Ross sees Nellie is in better shape than you told him she was, he doesn't take her, too," Will said, looking up at her.

"He wouldn't dare," she declared and, with her offerings, took the back lane toward Willow Creek.

It seemed just like old times, riding Nellie over the farm, Beth thought as she jogged along parallel to the main road. But in those earlier days, there had been peace in the land. How she longed for it again! Longed for peace on earth for Christmas, peace in her own heart, peace with Jerrod, no matter what problems stood between them. She tried to analyze further her tumbled feelings for him. Surely she could not actually love him. No, she refused to even entertain such thoughts—at least until she could find some way to discover what he really thought of her.

The ground was crunchy underfoot, but the ice flakes had stopped falling hours ago. The lane was beautiful here in a stark way with so many whites and grays. From somewhere drifted the smell of tart wood smoke. The apple dumplings, on which she had squandered the last of her cinnamon, sent their pungent aroma from the baskets strapped on Nellie's flanks. At last Beth came to the stream that led to the road and the bridge, and turned Nellie to the right.

It was only then that she considered possible danger to herself—not from the British, who would never be back off the road this way, but from Jerrod's men. After all, they were on the lookout for marauders, and if she surprised them, someone might panic and shoot. So she backtracked a bit and rode out onto the road itself to approach them.

But her heart fell when she didn't see any sort of roadblock or anyone by the bridge. Something must have happened, and they'd moved on! But then Jerrod strode into the road from the bushes, and his men's heads peeked out.

"What's wrong?" Jerrod called as he ran over and reached up to take her horse's bridle.

"Nothing, except I thought you might be hungry."

"You mean, Private Irwin let you leave for that?"

"I didn't realize I was actually a prisoner," she declared acidly before she calmed herself again. "Now, don't be angry with him, as I came the back way. I thought you'd be pleased to have fresh McGowan apple orchard dumplings and coffee—"

Though Jerrod still looked caught between surprise and a scowl, his three men cheered and relieved her of her burdens. Jerrod lifted her down, his hands lingering on her waist.

"Consider it a holiday gift," she told him. "After all, it is just four days before Christmas."

"It's as if I cannot begin to keep up with you," he told her as he escorted her off the road to their makeshift camp beyond the bushes. "I thought you were angry, then you cried. I thought you were sad, then you were smiling. I thought you didn't want any part of quartering my troops, and then you're offering breakfast and baking to ravish a man's sanity just with the sweet smell of it all—and you."

He loosed her reluctantly as one of his men thrust a small pewter plate with an apple dumpling into his hand. She had brought eating utensils out here? he marveled. But, like the others, he devoured the sweet treat, still warm from her oven, and savored it. Talk about seductions, he thought. The cinnamon-apple-pastry taste exploded in his mouth just as his desire for this woman exploded anew in his heart and mind and spirit. As for his body, even out here in the cold, amid the threat of danger, he could have made hot love to her on the ground right this moment!

His need for her staggered him. But he was certain his desire to protect her went as deep as his desire to possess her. He could never just enjoy her and then desert her, when he rode off to fight again in the spring. He would not be able to bear to leave her and Will behind—and maybe a child of his own loins. And how would she react to his forced departure? He knew from bitter experience that a woman could turn away from him, and then the old horror of distrust and desertion would haunt him again. With military self-control, "No-Loss Ross" would have to force himself to keep his and Beth's relationship from deepening or leading to the lovemaking he wanted desperately to have with her. Facing years of national struggle, they could make no permanent commitment now.

He shuddered despite the heat of his emotions and of the steaming coffee his men had heated over their fire. Cradling his small tin cup in his hands, he walked back and forth in the little clearing. His men took turns watching the road, even as they demolished the dumplings. He returned to Beth and helped her repack her goods, then escorted her to her mount.

"Be sure to cover that fire with soil and snow," Beth called back to Corporal Collier with a wave and a smile. "You never know about flames spreading."

Flames were spreading through him, that was all Jerrod knew! Even things she did and said innocently shook him. Last night—and he knew it would be the same in the nights to come—it had been torment sleeping while she lay upstairs, warm and tousled in her own bed. As for Christmas, which they'd once decided to spend together—he dared not torture himself with thoughts of losing that now.

And when he'd seen her in the warmth of the barn today with those soft piles of straw about, he'd been hard-pressed to keep his head and not just tumble her there in the straw, before they argued once again. These passions that racked him could not have come at a more inopportune time. With the problems and misunderstandings between them, and worse perhaps yet to come if the army needed to take more from her farm, things couldn't have been more volatile. And yet he knew in this moment he not only desired her but admired her more than any woman he had ever known.

"We all thank you for this kindly gesture," he told her as he lifted her up on her horse. He had noted that the old mare was not wheezing one bit in the cold weather, but he'd save voicing that observation for another day.

"I wanted to make a contribution," she said. "Since we're probably going to have Christmas together—your men, too, I mean—we should at least be civil."

"I guess we won't have Christmas quite like a family now, since it's considerably more than just the three of us," he admitted. "And, until we make certain this area is secure, maybe I won't even be about much."

She bit her lower lip, but nodded.

His hopes fell at how stoically she had taken that news. So perhaps she was just being patriotic and not extending a truce to him. Perhaps her kindly gesture was more of a bribe than anything. Maybe it was something she could throw at him later if he had to take some of the orchard. Yes, "McGowan apple orchard dumplings," she'd called them, probably so she could fight back better later. That hurt him, but perhaps it was just as well they stayed potential adversaries.

"Well, lookee way up the road, sir," Private Murry called to Jerrod. "At least twenty Brits on horseback with a coupla big wagons!"

Jerrod ran up to the bridge to look. At least a good country mile away, the flash of red uniforms, black hats and silver guns stood out starkly against the snow. Jerrod made a quick decision, then hurried back to Beth and half pulled, half lifted her off her horse.

"Jerrod, what—"

"I'm going to put you on my horse and send you down the road to tell Private Irwin to ride to Valley Forge for reinforcements for us. That's a big enemy foraging party. It's a blessing you're here, as I don't have a man to spare."

"They'll be here by then, and there are only four of you!"

"With the element of surprise, we can hold this bridge for a good while if the enemy insists on coming farther. And I'm leaving my pistols in the pack on the horse for you and Will to keep at the house—just in case the British should get that far."

"But—"

"Don't argue, but do as I say for once!"

She nodded without another word. She knew she would do anything to help. He helped her mount and arrange her skirts so she could ride astride. She reached down to touch his shoulder. In that instant he covered her hand with his and turned to give her wrist a swift kiss.

"Godspeed, my stubborn sweetheart," he said. He looked surprised, then annoyed he'd blurted out those words. He smacked his horse on the rump to send him off.

She held tightly to the big, strong stallion, but found it was easier to ride sitting astride than sidesaddle. So much roared through her mind in her frenzy of emotions, but one thing kept snagging her thoughts: *Sweetheart!* Amid danger and possible destruction, he had called her *my sweetheart!*

Beth pounded along the short distance back to where the McGowan lane met the road, but Private Irwin was not there. She rode up the lane, assuming he'd be at the house, but Will ran out to meet her. He had her old flintlock in his hands.

"I told you you're not to touch that, Will Mc-Gowan! Where's Private Irwin?"

"There was trouble with some merchants in town, and another soldier fetched him there! He said Colonel Ross told him not to leave unless there was trouble."

"Well, there's trouble now. Our men have spotted British troops, so you get down in the cellar until I come back, and don't you dare shoot that gun even if they come. You could get hurt."

"But you could, too!" the boy protested and shouldered the musket as if he were ready to march out to battle. "And where are you going on Colonel Ross's horse?"

"Just to town to tell Private Irwin," she shouted back over her shoulder. "Jerrod needs help!"

Jerrod needs help, Jerrod needs help. The horse's hooves beat those brave words back to her as she charged the big animal down the rutted, frozen road toward Berwyn. Only Jerrod and three American soldiers against at least twenty British! She had to get him reinforcements fast.

But what if she couldn't quickly locate Private Irwin or some of Jerrod's other men in town? What if their own difficulties had taken them out somewhere? What if she could find only a few of Jerrod's brigade and that was not enough to help? Still, she knew that only a little ways on would be the outer rim of the American encampment itself. There, she would surely find enough soldiers to ride out to head off those marauding lobsterbacks whom German George had sent over here to rob the Americans of their well-deserved freedom!

She rode right past Berwyn and headed for the outskirts of Valley Forge. Her face tingled in the nip of the wind; she began to tremble. It was taking so long! Where were the sentries she could send for help? What if she lost Jerrod in a battle to defend the road, her neighborhood and farm? She should have told him how much she cared for him. What if he and his men had to retreat and he was shot, just as William had been. Oh, no! No! She prayed very, very hard that in this Christmas season Jerrod would not be taken from her.

She had silently cursed the pockmarked and slippery road all the way, but now things suddenly got so much worse she had to nearly walk the horse. Numerous supply wagons had been through here, churning the mud to deeper ruts. Small, scattered iron spikes studded the road, evidently to slow enemy horses. And then she heard a shouted order and reined in.

"You, woman! Halt there!"

Soon, she had explained everything to the three sentries who surrounded her. While she waited with two of them, the third took Jerrod's horse and rode into camp to fetch help. The sentries used an outcrop of rock as their only shelter; they had no fire and looked more raggedy than the men who'd tried to cut down her trees.

"Andrew Stiles is the name, mistress," the older, sunken-cheeked man introduced himself with a stiff smile. "And this here's Johnny Cooper," he added as the younger man mumbled, "How-de-do, mistress."

"It's not far into camp where your friend can get help, is it?" she asked the mismatched duo.

"Not far, but men ready to ride is pretty scarce," old man Stiles told her.

Beth could not help but think Andrew Stiles ought to be home before his own hearthfire, enjoying his grandchildren and the waning years of his life. And Johnny Cooper looked hardly dry behind the ears— what she could see of them swathed in sundry rags wrapped around his head. And then she became calm enough to take in the rest of the scene, and really hear what these two were telling her beyond their polite patter.

She noted that the countryside from here on toward the American camp was a stripped, windswept no-man's-land, studded with the stumps of felled trees. Johnny stood in his hat to keep his feet warm;

she could see slits in the sides of his shoes, which looked entirely too small for him. And old Andrew Stiles had no shoes at all, only layers of bulky stockings he had obviously borrowed anywhere he could.

"See, we're so short of things right now at camp, and with the men all havin' to build their own huts, it might've taken a while to scare up some help—and horses," Andrew Stiles explained, patting her cloaked shoulder comfortingly with his rag-bound hand.

"But men's lives are at stake!" she protested.

"Yes'm, don't we know."

The full impact of reality hit her like a fist to her stomach. Even though she could not see the infant camp from here, she suddenly grasped the import of it all: the American cause hung by a ragged thread. Winter racked the land and the army. Some of the soldiers were elderly men or boys not so many years older than Will. They were ragged and hungry and cold, but they had not yet lost their spirit. Led by their desperate officers like Jerrod, they were all that stood between the British and destruction. And here she still had hams and barrels of apples, minced meat and a supply of wood to burn on the hearth, and the hope of a warm Christmas dinner at home! In her inner eye, she could almost see the crude huts these men must be building with their own hands when they had barely enough to fill their bellies. How foolish, how selfish she had been. But she hadn't known!

"General Washington must be very proud of all of you," was all she managed as tears filled her eyes.

"We be right proud o' him, too!" Johnny Cooper finally said something for himself. "Said he wouldn't move into his house at camp, he did, till all the huts was built. He's sleepin' in a tent, jest like me! Seein' him always bucks me up, like that time at the Brooklyn Heights. He kept rallyin' the men and tellin' those he had to order to protect our rear that they was savin' the day for the army to fight again.''

"At—Brooklyn Heights?" Beth said as a chill that had nothing to do with the weather racked her. "My husband died at Brooklyn Heights, covering the retreat with the Third Pennsylvania!"

Andrew Stiles snatched off his ragged bicorne to doff it to her, and Johnny nodded. "Then your man was a hero, an' I heard the general say so time an' time again," Andrew assured her, "'cause, in the beginnin', our retreats was our only vict'ries."

Something that had been so tightly wound inside Beth ever since she had heard the circumstances of William's death uncoiled and laid itself to rest. But *where* were those soldiers? she thought, just before she heard hoofbeats. Then ten or so men rode by. One man, a corporal, who was riding Jerrod's horse, reined in as she and the sentries ran back out to the road.

"I'll give you a hand up, ma'am, and ride you back!" the corporal called down to her.

"Thank you both—for everything!" she said to Andrew Stiles and Johnny Cooper. She gave the corporal her arm and he swung her up sideways behind him. At the last moment, she untied her cape and threw it back to the two sentries. "I want you to share it. For your help, for Christmas—" was all she got out before the corporal spurred Jerrod's horse and she had to hold on hard. The sentries cheered them on. Though she knew she might never see those two men again, she felt she owed them so much more than she could ever, ever repay.

Back at the farmhouse, Beth was tempted when she heard the rattle of distant shots to take her flintlock and go help. But at least the shooting meant no one was retreating; the Americans were still fighting. She paced and paced and then made a decision.

"Will," she called out the door to the boy, who stood in the early haze of dusk, looking off in the direction of the shots. "I'm going to decorate for Christmas and I need some pine boughs cut."

"Now, Mother? But how can you think of Christmas when Colonel Ross—"

"It's *for* Colonel Ross. We promised him Christmas, and who knows, we might have to have it early for him. When he returns tonight, I want to have a meal on the table for him and the decorations all up!"

"Oh, I see. Well, for certain if it will cheer him!"

"It will cheer him," Beth muttered to herself. "I wish I could invite every last one of General Washington's soldiers!" She turned back into the kitchen. "But I love Jerrod, and we're going to have a joyous Christmas together!"

"What's that?" Will asked as he came in to get his hatchet. "General Washington's coming, too?"

"No, just a family gathering," she told the boy before she realized what she'd said.

She realized then how much Jerrod had come to mean to her, in a different, deeper way than she had cared for her husband. Jerrod was not, as William had been, someone she came to slowly grow to love because he provided sustenance or security—far from it. Yet despite the differing demands on them of duty and danger, of her own free will, she loved, yes *loved*, Jerrod Ross!

As Will banged out the door, she leaned her hands on the mantel and her forehead on her hands. "Please, dear Lord God," she whispered. "I know my prayers about William coming home just couldn't work out, but this time—maybe this time..."

She choked back a sob and lifted her chin defiantly. This was no time to lose courage or resolve! She gazed up into the mirror over the hearth, taking in the sweep of kitchen from sideboard to table to cupboards and door. The woman reflected back looked up at her with tears but hope in her eyes. She realized then what had changed: she heard Will's chopping but no longer the shooting! Soon, soon, she would know what had happened.

Determinedly, she began to clear the mantel for a place to put the pine boughs and the carved manger scene.

Much later, when she heard the hoofbeats of more than one horse, she even lit the single, precious bayberry candle she'd made from the warped remnants of the others. It was the last, perfect touch to the early holiday welcome she had made here for Jerrod. Then, unable to keep up her charade of calm and strength, she tore to the door.

Yes, Jerrod! There was no second rider, but he pulled old Nellie behind him. Cheering, Will hurried out behind her and took the horses. She flew to Jerrod, arms outstretched. Though she didn't mean to, she thumped the breath from him.

"Uh! But—ah, the best welcome I've had yet," he said and kissed her hard.

"You're really all right? And your men?"

"We used the bridge for a barrier. The injuries weren't severe, but the others took the wounded back to the hospital hut at Valley Forge. I'll fetch several of my other men out here from Berwyn in an hour or so. And I, at least, have only a slight wound in the left arm, so—"

"Oh, why didn't you say so? And I could have hurt you!"

He gave her a bemused but pained look that spoke of the fact that she *had* hurt him. But he looked so relieved at the welcome and so exultant to be escorted inside. And when he saw the pine boughs, the manger scene, the candles and the Christmas quilt pinned to the wall for a festive backdrop, she noted that tears gilded his eyes and his lower lip trembled.

"Here, just sit here, and let me tend to your arm!" she told him as she pushed him onto the settle by the hearth and scurried for warm water and a towel.

He leaned back his head with its mussed hair and watched her through slitted eyelids. She helped him shrug out of his coat and waistcoat. Her hands shaking now at the sight of the blood and so much bare skin and curly chest hair, she cut away his ruined shirt. Bare to the waist, he seemed bigger and stronger, despite the blood. And when she grasped his shoulder to wash away the blood, his body heat seemed to leap up her arm and ignite her very woman's core.

"Does it hurt?" she asked as she wrapped the wound and draped a blanket around him.

"Nothing does when you care for me like this. Beth, before Will comes back from tending the horses, I want us to get something clear. I heard you rode all the way to Valley Forge when Kit Irwin wasn't here—I can't thank you enough. But I want to tell you you've saved me—healed me—in another way. Just quit fussing a moment and listen to me!"

She sat on the settle close to him, her hands stilled in her lap, their knees touching.

"I need to explain something to you about my past."

Looking more agonized by his thoughts than he had by his wound, he paused. Silence stretched between them and, but for the look of his countenance of pained concentration, she actually woundered if he slept.

"About the other woman you loved who... let you down?" she prompted in a whisper.

"Yes," he said, and his eyes flew open. They were dark with remembered pain. "But it's not what you think. You see, when I was Will's age, my father took my older brother James and went back to London to arrange things for the family's Boston business. I really took to heart my father's parting words that I should look after my mother."

Beth nodded. William had said much the same to Will when he left. She felt another stab of guilt that she had tried to coddle the boy so, but he'd been all she had left to love. At least now, she understood better why Jerrod had championed Will's independence so strongly.

"I loved my mother very much and tried so hard to please her. I thought we were very close, just as my father was close to James—his heir. But my rearing was all American, whereas Father and James still considered themselves British to the core and loyal to the crown. When the early disagreements began between the Tories and the rebel factions in Boston, I took the side of independence. When Father and James returned and things really got violent, they insisted on my loyalty to them and the king—and that I join them in exile in Canada. I rebelled, and foolishly expected my mother to at least stand up for me, if not side with me. She did neither, and after all I'd done, all I thought we had meant to each other, she said she'd never trust me now and...she disowned me, too. It was a thousand times worse than losing Father or James."

His voice was metallic, matching the harsh set of his features. "*That* was the time a woman let me down, and I've not sought another before you. I joined first the local militia and then Washington's forces when they came to liberate Boston. The army and the cause became my only family—until you."

Beth could see his pain cut so deep she ached for him. "I am very, very sorry," she whispered, but then they just stared deeply, unspeaking, hardly breathing, into each other's eyes. She clasped his hands tightly in hers.

He cleared his throat. "So, here, Elizabeth Mc-Gowan, you see a man in a dangerous profession in terrible times who knows next to nothing about farming and has found himself desperately desiring the company of a woman who lives on a farm she treasures. I am an outcast from my family. I have no prospects but my meager soldier's pay, and that's in the Continental currency you said you don't trust. But...I'd still like you to consider loving me, too, whatever lies ahead."

She was stunned to silence for one moment. But her heart soared so that she could have flown around the room. That was what she had wished for—wasn't it? Not only that she could love him in this season of joy, but that he might love her in return. Yet, what was he declaring here? His love: an affair, an understanding, a commitment—for what? She supposed there could be no serious consideration of any promises fulfilled before the end of this war, not with their different responsibilities.

"And here," she managed, "I thought you were wretched at fine speeches. The king himself could not have done better than that!"

Jerrod's lower lip quivered again. "King George's speech," he said, his voice wavering, "would probably have been in German, just like those danged Hessians—"

She was careful not to bump his bad shoulder as she hugged him, stilling his mouth with a kiss. Despite his injured arm, his other came hard around her, pinning her to him. Somehow, she slid up into his lap.

"Jerrod, this danger today made me realize how deeply I regarded you, too. I've felt such a toss of emotions, but the one that lasted—that matters—is love. And now that I've told you and you have declared much the same, it's even more sobering, isn't it?"

He hugged her to him and bumped the top of her head with his chin when he nodded. "Maybe it's some sort of gift to us this Christmas, one we can treasure, even if we can't really open it all the way now. Until the war is over I cannot possibly talk about commitments."

She lifted her head to stare into his eyes. "I know. It's the same for me. Then our love will be like the Christmas quilt. We can add something to it each year until it's finished!"

In the midst of another searing kiss, she heard the door and opened one eye to see that Will had come in from outside. His mouth formed a little O of surprise as if *he* were going to kiss someone. Then she saw him grin, turn back outside and close the door quietly behind him.

Even after Will went to bed, Beth and Jerrod sat side by side at the table and drank their heated applejack, making holiday plans. Somehow, unless the British came calling again, they would find a way to share both Christmas Eve and Christmas day.

"Who knows where I'll be for the next holiday or the one after?" he mused. "Last Christmas night I was sitting in a cold, rocking rowboat crossing the

Delaware River to give the Hessians at Trenton a little
Christmas surprise."

"And surprise them you did. You've been a surprise to me, too, but the most wonderful kind. I'm
sorry I ever doubted your motives or your intent."

He turned her to him, his right hand cupping her
chin. "My intent, my beloved Beth, is for us to take
the best advantage of our time together. I need you
so!" he vowed as his hands tightened on her back and
waist.

"I need you, too. But I guess I also need a dose of
common sense when you . . . touch me."

"I try to keep my head around you, but it doesn't
work. Beth, you're not afraid of the fire between us,
are you? The other night when I thought we might
become . . . really intimate right there," he said,
pointing at her hearth pallet, "you jumped away, even
before we argued again."

"No, it really was the fire—the fear of real fire," she
explained. "You see, my father's apprentice in his wig
shop drank too much one night and let his candle
catch on some mohair wigs. The fire spread to the
curtain and the beamed roof. The wig shop, our at-
tached house and two adjoining shops were burned to
the ground. The wretched apprentice lived, but I told
you my father died—that's how. It was horrible to
know he was suffering and dying in there, and the
neighbors held us back and said it was too late to help
him."

She looked away. Tears blurred the room, but she
wiped them away when they spilled. He, too, dabbed
at them with the corner of his blanket. "My sister,

Sarah, and I moved in with friends," she went on shakily, "but it felt wrong to be so beholden to those who weren't kin. When Father's friend, William McGowan, came calling with his kind offer of marriage, I took it to save us and—and found later I could love him for himself, too."

"I see."

"But there is more. You see, my father had been making the major decisions in my life for so long, it was natural just to turn all that over to William. But as I matured—especially when Will was born—I wanted to make some of my own choices in life—or at least to make them *with* my husband. But until he left for the war, it wasn't that way. Lately, I've made all the decisions for Will and me, despite feeling so lonely and scared sometimes. Now, I have chosen to love you, Jerrod." She smiled. "Not that I haven't been partly convinced by my wild feelings for you, too. Despite our hard times ahead, I choose to—to wait for you. That is what you want, what we've decided, isn't it?"

"Yes. It has to be the way. It certainly gives me more dedication to ending this danged war sooner. And I didn't mean to force you to relive all that about the fire and your father's death. But I shall always cherish those confessions, especially the one about choosing to love me."

"Yes, but about not making commitments—neither of us is really free to now—I see why. So whatever shall we do about this fire of desire between us? When we touch, Jerrod, the way I react is different, stronger than the way I've ever been before. And I don't know what to make of that sometimes.''

He sighed and smiled as though a great weight had been lifted from his broad shoulders. "Let's make everything of it, my sweetheart. Only, for now it must be out of bed and not in.''

His voice broke and he said no more, cursing the war and circumstances that made them wait. Was he noble or stupid to delay their complete delight in each other? Others didn't wait for the war to end to take their pleasures. They used looming danger as an excuse to grab everything now. But he would not leave her with another child besides Will to fend for! In the long, lonely months away from her, plans for their future would keep him going.

And yet he wanted her right now, blast it. What if he was killed and had never really possessed her? He didn't actually believe he would die. He could not fathom that would happen to him. But what if they never bedded at all because of this dedication to higher virtues?

Though he didn't know it, Beth, too, was agonizing over their dilemma. Joy delayed could be joy denied. She dreamed for one moment that they could wed this year, as soon as they could arrange to have three weeks of the banns read. But, of course, she could not bear to lose a second husband.

He turned her toward him. She lifted her mouth to his again to surrender to the power of his touch. She inhaled the sweet bayberry smell in the room while she savored the very scent and feel of the man she loved—

skin, sinew, strong muscle, but so much more that went deeper than the physical. And she hoped and prayed, war or not, that nothing bad could ever come between them again.

Chapter Four

The morning before Christmas, Beth rose and hurried downstairs to prepare porridge for Jerrod and the three new soldiers he had ridden to fetch from Berwyn last night. Will hung around with the new men and soon made friends with a young private, whom he followed outside. The other two went out to leave Beth and Jerrod sitting at the big table over the saucer of coffee they had long been tending.

"Well," he said, breaking the intense gaze between them, "I'd best be off to make certain the roadblock is reestablished at the bridge. You'd think the lobsterbacks would have enough sense to stay in town so close to Christmas, but who knows?"

"Should I look to your arm again?" she asked as he stood.

"When I return later today. I promise, barring major battles, I shall be here with you and Will tonight for the beginning of our Christmas celebraton."

She nodded and rose on the other side of the table. He could make that specific promise well enough, but beyond Christmas, what promise did she have? If only, she thought, the war would go away so that they could have mornings like this when he would only leave to walk out to the fields or orchards. How she wished General Washington would leave Jerrod here in the spring when the Americans marched away to do battle. But she knew better. Jerrod's place was with his men, and her place was here with her son, fighting any battle she must to keep this farm.

But why should that mean they could not make plans? How much dearer and more secure would be their hours together or apart if there was some sort of real promise for a future together. She needed to find the courage to tell him she hoped they could build a foundation of commitment beneath their declaration of love.

All last night she had been thinking about the prospect of no real plans or future commitment. As she had thought back on her life—especially the all-too-short weeks with Jerrod here—she realized she was ready for promises that went deeper than the vow, "I love you." They had shared their painful pasts, so, even if the future brought loss or pain, couldn't they face that better if they were bound by a plan to bring their love to fruition?

Even when she had explained to Will this morning that she and Jerrod had come to love each other, the first thing the boy blurted was, "Good, but what does that mean? Are you promised to him for after the war or getting wed soon or what?"

Or what? She herself wondered. After all, Jerrod was a man who did not fear to make long-term, loyal commitments, at least to the army. Could he not at least declare his loyalty or duty to her? Even if something happened to him later, she would know she had meant at least as much to him as the cause for independence did! Though she had lost William, she had known the full extent of his dedication to her and Will, and she would always treasure that.

"You know, sweetheart, my father asked my mother to wed him when they'd known each other but a week," Jerrod told her at the door, as if he'd read her mind. "With you and me, it will be a longer path to finally deciding things, that's all."

She nodded, her heart thudding so loud she feared he'd hear. At least he had mentioned the promise of marriage before she did! But was that what he meant by "deciding things"? Deciding to become betrothed or deciding to marry? Could he have been thinking along the same lines she did last night, but like her, was he hesitating to express his thoughts? After all, they had arrived at their admission of mutual love at the same time. Had he meant to give her an opening here? Yet her courage faltered a bit. She did not wish to seem forward. And what if he did not agree?

"I believe you still treasure your times with your family, even though you've lost them now," she began carefully.

"Yes," he admitted. "Losing them hurts, but I still love them very much and treasure many times past."

"Times past, yes, but what about the future? I mean, indeed, I cherish Christmases past, but I want to make future ones happy, too. It could be that way for us, even if something separated us later. And we could better share the time we have, if we were more committed now to be a family!"

His face became very still, then his features hardened, dashing her hopes before he even responded. "Beth, we both know why that's not the best idea. I refuse to chance leaving you with another child to care for. And in war, the future's always cloudy. Blast it, I can't think beyond this Christmas when I have things to do. We'll talk about it later!"

He pecked a kiss on her cheek and was out the door. Although she thought she had proceeded cautiously and steeled herself against his possible refusal, she stared aghast after him. He had been deeply wounded by his mother's turning against him. Perhaps he would never be willing to make a commitment beyond declaring his love and hinting at distant promises. After all, the man was twenty-eight and very handsome. There must have been other women he had attracted and favored once, then left behind with nothing but memories. Yet she didn't intend to accept defeat from the man she loved, not when she wouldn't even accept it from the enemy she detested.

She strode out into the snow as he mounted. "Jerrod Ross, I never took you for a coward!"

He gazed down at her, surprise and confusion plain on his face. "What in tarnation does that mean?"

"Leave me 'with another child to care for'? I believe you're the one who's been telling me—and Will— that he can assist me in manly tasks. The possibility of another child—your child—does not worry me in any way. I only worry, upon serious pondering of our circumstances, that we will part with regrets that we tiptoed around our own emotions and desires. And if you think I'm being brazen, sir, I tell you it is all your fault for choosing to love a woman who has learned to make up and then speak her own mind!''

He looked as if he'd argue, then didn't. She saw him swallow hard. He obviously couldn't even summon up the resolve to give her one of his orders to ''get back in the house.'' He fidgeted in his saddle, then said in a rush, ''I'd be the first to say a spitfire patriot like you ought to have many fine sons for our new nation.''

''Exactly!''

''But Beth, I just— Look, we'll discuss all this when I ride back in tonight.''

''Very well. Negotiations will be in order, even though it is Christmas Eve.''

She realized that neither of them had mentioned anything specific. His mention of a proposal and marriage had come only in his reminiscence of his parents, who had deserted him. She hoped that did not run in the family. And what if he thought she was just offering herself in bed, but expected nothing else? She almost shouted after him that he had obviously misunderstood, but Will or Jerrod's men might hear. So she turned and marched back into the house, as ramrod straight as any soldier.

The morning raced by as Beth baked pies—three apple and three mincemeat. Will had done all his chores and was upstairs working hard on something, which she assumed to be her Christmas surprise. The boy always did things at the last minute, while she'd had her gifts for him made since November. More than once lately in straightening Will's bed, she had found wood shavings both on the floor and among the sheets, so she assumed he was carving her a gift.

She disturbed the boy only once, to have him help her bring down a huge ham from the attic. But, as busy as her hands were, she thought and thought about her exchange with Jerrod this morning. She might have been a bit forward, but knew she had been absolutely right. They were meant to be together, so why was he unable to make any promises? War or not, looming separations or not, such a promise would make the future brighter. Then she and Will would hold the farm for all three of them until Jerrod came home to fulfill his vow—of marriage as well as love.

She found herself humming old Yuletide carols as she worked. She hardly had an angel's voice, but at least Will was used to it. Besides, Jerrod had taken all his soldiers from the farm to man the roadblock this morning, so there was no one to suffer as she warbled away, banging pots and kettles to prepare the Christmas Eve meal.

Sometime later, she heard horses close by. She stood, startled. She'd been making such a din that Jerrod and his men must have ridden all the way up and she'd not heard them. Wiping her floury hands on her apron, she hurried to the door to let them in. But a raggedy band of seven dismounted strangers stood surrounding her door, staring at her.

"Mornin', mistress. Jest good American soldier boys askin' for some Christmas charity," the burly one closest to her said. His small, black eyes skimmed the farmyard.

"I'm relieved to hear you're on the right side," she said, trying to be friendly, though she didn't like the looks of them. Those ragamuffin American soldiers cutting her orchard had looked hungry, but there was something else in these men's eyes she did not trust. How she wished Jerrod would ride down the lane right now. She'd offer them something, but insist they wait outside.

"I'll be glad to pass you out some things—are you some of Colonel Ross's men from town?" she inquired.

"Sure, that's it."

"He's just down the road," she said, "and will be back in a minute. If you'll just wait here, I'll—"

The burly man wrenched the door from her grasp, then shoved her back inside. "She's bluffing! She's got no one here in these times or he would've come," he called to his men. They stampeded into the house.

"Now just wait! Stand back," she insisted, but she did not scream. She did not want Will to come running and get hurt. But if he could only look out to see what was happening, perhaps he could sneak out the other door and ride for help from Jerrod. These men sounded like Americans, but surely—

"Stop it!" she ordered as they elbowed her even farther in and grabbed at the pies cooling on the table. One man seized fistfuls of mincemeat and shoved it in his mouth.

Will came running, and was grabbed and held by one big lout, who even took Will's carving knife. He tossed it to another man, who hacked into the ham

and threw huge chunks to the others. They all devoured the meat like ravenous animals.

"Let my son go!" Beth shouted. "Leave this
house—"

The burly man slapped her face, and she backed
away with her hand pressed to her cheek. She spun and
grabbed for her flintlock, but another man yanked it
from her and smashed its wooden stock against the
stone mantel. The mirror fell to the floor and shat-
tered.

It seemed that that destruction served as a signal for
general mayhem. The ragged crew ransacked her
shelves, stuffing food and pewterware in a huge sack
they made from her tablecloth. The burly man, evidently their leader, held both Beth and Will at gunpoint while the nightmare intensified. Beth and Will
clung to each other while the men ravaged her linen
press and used her ironed damask for more bags to
hold food they looted from both the cellar and the attic.

"Never mind stealing stuff we can't eat or sell!" the
burly man bellowed out. "But get some blankets and
those bedrolls in the other room! Get a move on, will
ya?"

"Being Christmas, Rand, we can peddle that fancy
quilt for plenty," a bearded ruffian said to the burly
man holding the gun on them. He pointed to her family heirloom hanging on the wall. "This other holiday
stuff, too, since the men are as hungry for that."

"Take it all!" Rand ordered as the bearded man
yanked her precious quilt from the wall. Into it went

the carved manger scene, while tears of shock and despair poured down Beth's face at last.

"No, please," she heard herself beg, even though she'd have liked nothing better than to claw at their faces.

But she should have held her tongue. Will pulled away from her embrace. "I'm the man of the house here now, and I—"

Beth wasn't sure what he said after that. She only knew the things Jerrod had been telling Will about being a man went terribly awry. Will ducked and lunged for the gun the man held on them. The burly lout stepped forward and slammed the gun butt into the boy's jaw. Beth screamed. Will crumpled, his head hitting the corner of the iron oven on the hearth. He lay limp and still as, sobbing, she threw herself to her knees over him.

"Let's go," was all she heard as she cradled Will.

There was no blood, but the boy lay quiet among the glittering shards of the mirror and the dusty ashes on the hearth. Beth was so terrified he was dead that she did not even hear the band of looters ride away.

But he was breathing! There was a faint but steady pulse in his throat! He had tried to protect her and their goods. Fury and hatred churned in her. Jerrod had convinced Will he was a man who could protect her and this farm. But he wasn't. He was just a boy. A boy she had to protect. Jerrod had promised her no marauding band would ever come here again. Why had he taken all his men down the road to stop the British, when his own American foragers could come and do this? She cursed her confidence that everything would go well when she and Jerrod declared their love. Jerrod made vows he would never fulfill!

"Will! Will, please wake up. Will! Wi-ill!"

The kitchen and Christmas and her future lay ruined all about her. If she was being unreasonable, she could not help it. But no, the crushing of all her hopes for happiness made perfect sense. She and Will had trusted a charming stranger. A stranger who vowed security and then left them alone to face this destruction, just as he would leave them alone when he rode off in the spring. She felt utterly betrayed. Betrayed by those brutal thieves, by Americans, by Christmas—by Jerrod. Where was he when she desperately needed him?

She carefully moved her son to the pallet by the hearth and sponged his face. She lifted his pale lids to stare into his unseeing blue eyes.

"Will! Will, can you hear Mother? Will?"

She felt fear bite her belly. She wrapped him more warmly, chafed his hands and wrists. She needed help, but she could not leave Will to ride for Jerrod. She had heard of people losing consciousness, people having spells. Of course, a fist to the jaw or a blow to the head could temporarily stun someone. But why didn't he wake up? The devastation of her Christmas dreams, of this room itself and all her plans, began to creep inside her, cold and clammy like lingering catastrophe. But none of that mattered now but Will!

Sometime later, she heard a horse. She reached for her faithful flintlock before she remembered that it, too, was broken and lost. She ran to the door. Jerrod!

She tore outside. Snow was falling thick and heavy, and she hadn't even known it. How long had the men been gone? How long had Will been lying that way?

"The fresh snow makes everything look so peaceful and calm," he called to her. "Beth, I've been thinking, and—" He gasped as he took in her ravaged face and wild appearance.

"Americans came here—your men, I don't know—they took food—but more!" She panted out her words as if she'd run miles. She dragged the horrified Jerrod into the house. He fell to his knees over Will's unmoving form.

"He's alive, Beth!"

"I know, but his head!" she sobbed. Then she managed to choke out what had happened. She saw Jerrod's wide eyes devour the devastation in one glance.

"If it was my men, they'll hang," he vowed. "But right now I'm riding for a camp surgeon, Washington's own, if I have to drag him here."

He squeezed her shoulder and vaulted to his feet. "And I'll send a soldier back from town," he called back to her.

She leaped up and raced to the door after him. The snow suddenly looked so deep as he sprang on his horse. He spurred the stallion away before she could say another word.

But what could she say? That she blamed him for Will's declaring he was a man and trying to save her? That, as far as she could tell, Jerrod was a man who made promises he could not back up? After all, he could not even control his own men, neither those who cut down apple trees nor those who felled young boys. She wanted nothing else in her life but her dedication to her son. Even if Jerrod begged her, she could not commit her life to someone who didn't understand that Will was just a child and needed her protection. Even if she had failed to provide it. It was fortunate she had failed, too, in winning commitment from Jerrod this morning. Now, any sort of happy future seemed entirely impossible.

She ran back inside to Will, her feet crunching glass and the ruins of the Christmas meal. She kept a vigil by his side, shedding silent, lonely tears, sealed from the world by the sweep of snow.

It seemed eternity before Jerrod returned. Darkness threatened outside the house as it did inside Beth. The surgeon bent over the boy and carefully felt his head.

"A huge lump here beside that bruise to his jaw," he informed them. "Blows to the head are strange things. Sometimes the state of consciousness returns quickly, sometimes—forgive the truth, ma'am—it takes months. And, as for memory loss, that's possible, too. I could bleed him, of course, but modern medical science knows so little about blows to the head, I'd best not."

Beth sat beside Will's pallet on the hearth holding his hand. He felt normal to the touch; his face looked serene as if he were asleep, despite that ugly bruise on his chin. How could this be? This war had taken everything from her now, even her chance for happiness, perhaps all her Christmases to come.

Beth thanked the doctor before Jerrod escorted him outside to his horse. She heard Jerrod come back in. He sat down on the floor beside her and covered her hand over Will's. Then, in his other hand, he extended to her the carved baby Jesus and the wooden sheep from the manger scene the brutes had stolen.

"I found these outside in the snow, Beth."

"They must have fallen from the quilt. Will always said that sheep was Sheba when he was younger."

"Beth, Sheba's gone. The bastards took the animals from the barn, too."

She shrugged, feeling so beaten. Her voice came slow and faint. "Strange, but with Will like this, it almost doesn't matter. I would have given the men food, Jarrod. I was singing so loud while getting our Christmas Eve dinner that I didn't hear them come," she choked out. She turned her face away, afraid she'd cry again.

"It's not your fault!" he assured her, grasping her shoulders.

"It is mine, but it's yours, too! If you hadn't convinced Will he was the man here, he wouldn't have tried to fight them! You never should have come and—and promised things you could not make come true!"

"Beth, please, I know you're distraught. It's hard for you, but I want you to describe those men to me. Maybe they weren't really soldiers but deserters or even renegade civilians out thieving since times are bad. Tell me and maybe I can help."

"Not anymore. You can't help anymore. Jerrod, I—it's obvious other plans—between us—are impossible now, not that you meant to make them. With Will like this, maybe there is no future anyway, and—"

He turned her to face him. His hands dropped to her wrists and gripped them. "We'll save that for later—the blame and accusations I see in your eyes, too. But now, tell me what they looked like, Beth, so maybe I can do something to stop them before it's too late."

She feared it was too late already, since the snow would cover all their tracks, but she told him what she could remember from the terror. The burly man, the bearded man, she described as best she could, though it chilled her blood to even recall them. "And—the burly man who was their leader—one of them called him Rand!"

Jerrod knew it wasn't much, but he was grasping at straws here anyway. Fear mingled with fury in him. On Christmas Eve, when he almost held happiness in his hand, some brutal bastards had come to rob Beth and him of their future. And perhaps rob little Will of his future, too. Seeing the innocent, protected boy struck down like this made him realize his certainty he would survive the war intact was pure foolishness and bravado. Now he had so much to live for, but, curse it, he was even more desperate to have Beth *now,* in case disaster struck him, too.

He'd come to terms at last, also, with the fact that his eventually leaving Beth to ride off to war would not be the same as his own father's deserting him and his mother for several years just for the sake of business profit. This morning, when Beth had tried to tell him they should make plans for a future now, he'd been so surprised and frightened that he'd been almost cruel.

But there was no time to set things right now—if she'd ever give him the chance anyway.

Biting back a sob himself, Jerrod rose to his feet. "If you want the guard I brought back from camp for anything, just put a candle in the kitchen window," he told her. "I'll be back as soon as I can."

She nodded, not looking at him. He thought his heart would shatter like the bright pieces of mirror that gritted beneath his feet. But he had things to do before those criminals in the guise of American soldiers escaped justice after this outrage. And he needed to show Beth that he could make good on his promise to catch those men. Maybe then she'd believe his promise to love her and take care of her—and of poor Will.

At the door he turned to look back at her. "I love you, Beth, and Will, too," he told her. Then he hurried out into the cold, black night.

Beth kept a vigil that Christmas Eve and into Christmas morning. Will had been so excited, looking forward to everything. So, too, had she, as she cooked and cleaned—and planned. But all that was over now. Only Will's getting better mattered. If she could just turn back time and have everything ready for him to come downstairs to her again, to smell the pies and give her the gift he had carved for her.

And, if only everything wonderful could be waiting for Jerrod, too! Yes, she still loved Jerrod. She should not have blamed him for this. He was doing what he could to help. She loved Jerrod and he had vowed he loved her and Will. And she was going to be brave. She was going to make that vow enough to build a future on for all of them!

Sometime before dawn, long after the guard Jerrod left behind had told her he would sleep in the barn, she decided to put the room to rights. It would be a first step toward that future for all of them. After all, Will might be alarmed when he woke and saw the destruction. She wanted to have Christmas ready for him. She wanted to please him and protect him and make everything perfect for him. After all, she had promised him he could sleep down here on Christmas Eve, and here he was. Perhaps that and the carvings of baby Jesus and the sheep that Jerrod had rescued were a sign that Will would soon be well.

Resolution and energy poured back into her, and she went to work with a will. She swept debris from the floor. She replaced the pine boughs on the hearth. She straightened cupboards and the table, glancing every few minutes to be certain Will had not awakened. She even left the room for a moment to change her gown and brush her hair. No good looking like a drab if the boy awoke—that is, *when* he awoke, for Christmas day. In determination tinged by desperation and exhaustion, she became very convinced he would soon awake and that the future would be beautiful.

When Will woke, he would be hungry. He would have to eat something to build his strength. She heated thin gruel she hoped to spoon between his lips. She hurried up to the attic. The looters had somehow knocked the smallest of the hams onto the floor and missed it in their hurry. She carried it downstairs, cradling it against her apron. In the cellar, she scooped up handfuls of flour from a sack on the floor that they had sliced open. She ladled a bowl of mincemeat from the bottom of a keg, and fished out sulfured apples from a barrel, because they'd ransacked the ones she'd carefully dried.

In big wooden bowls, she began to make more pies. She ignored the fact that the heirloom quilt was gone, that only two pieces of the manger scene graced the mantel, and that the place where the mirror had hung was empty. Will's poor sheep might become someone's mutton stew, but such losses could be put in perspective if Will would just awaken.

As daylight came, she took four fresh pies from her hearth oven. Still, she worked on, peeling potatoes, slicing ham and bread. She went upstairs and brought down the crewelwork counterpane from the spare bed to serve as a tablecloth. Despite the lack of some pieces of pewter, she began to set places at the table—six of them, since she didn't know whom to expect. Will had so admired Jerrod's soldiers that it would please him to have a few of them to Christmas dinner. They had all been kind to the boy. And Jerrod—of course, Jerrod had been wonderful to him from the first, almost like—a new father. Those villains who had done all this to Will and the house had nothing in common with Jerrod or his fine men. Nothing in common with Jerrod, the man she loved, and had accused of such terrible things.

She had fallen asleep at last, curled up on the hard settle across the hearth from Will, when sounds awoke her. The nightmare leaped back at her. She stumbled to her feet, almost tripping over her skirts. A knock on the door. She saw she had latched it.

"Beth, it's Jerrod!"

She let him in.

"How is he?"

"The same," she admitted as they walked to the hearth to stand over the boy together. "I am fighting so hard not to be bitter." She saw Jerrod's eyes widen as they took in the transformed room, then her blue, flower-sprigged gown and beribboned hair. His nostrils flared at the aromas of dinner. She reached for his hand; they wove their fingers tightly together.

"I know with Will still like this, the news won't be much consolation," he told her, "but I asked around and traced the man named Rand. His commanding officer and I were waiting for him when he rode into Valley Forge a few hours ago with your animals and some other things he still had to sell. He'll be tried for breaking orders and looting, Beth, and be severely punished. The general's been looking for a blatant case to make an example of. Wait a moment. I'll be right back."

She clasped her hands together as he went out to his horse, then toted in his saddle pack. "Sheba's back in the barn, and Scratch and Nellie are on the way. The men had evidently lost or sold the other pieces of the manger scene already, but it may yet turn up. But here's your heirloom quilt," he said as he pulled it from his pack and flapped it open. It was stained and mussed, but it had never looked better to her.

"How can I ever thank you?" she murmured. But she already knew the answer to that, so she began to make amends. "Jerrod, even with Will like this, I don't blame the Americans, because I've seen how fine most of them are. And I don't blame you. I only love you no matter what the future brings. I was so wrong to accuse you or think that Will's accident made a difference to our love, or that you wouldn't keep a promise—"

Evidently, that was all that had held Jerrod back. Now he pulled her hard into his embrace and buried his face in her hair. They pressed the quilt between them, as if they could already brand into it a square of happiness for this Christmas day—if only Will would wake up.

"And once again, danger has only convinced me I need to hold you closer, and I don't just mean like this! Beth, you're right about making a commitment now."

"Not quite now," she told him. "Not when Will's like this. He's going to be better soon, and then we can plan! Jerrod, he just has to be!'

They held to each other for a long while, then she insisted Jerrod sit down to eat. While he washed up, she covered her son with the Christmas quilt and tucked it in snugly around his limp body.

"It's not the day we had planned, but as soon as Will awakes, things will be even better," she assured Jerrod again as she served him hot ham and potatoes. "If I ever used to think I wanted *things* for Christmas, I didn't know what was really important. Even the thought of losing the entire farm suddenly wasn't important when Will got hurt. I realized I was blaming both you and me. That would have ruined all we could have had together.''

"Then to keep your strength up, sit down here and eat something with me," he cajoled.

"I couldn't. I'm just not hungry."

"Well, for certain, I am!"

Beth gasped and Jerrod scraped back his chair. They both stared at Will, wrapped cozily in the quilt. His eyes were open and focused.

"I'm real hungry," Will declared. "And if it's Christmas Eve yet, you said I could have Sheba in here too. But, oh," he added, freeing his arms to rub his fists in his eyes, "it looks like a new day already."

"It is, Will, it is!" Jerrod cried joyously. "And I'll just get Sheba in here right now while your mother feeds you!"

Jerrod made a fast exit to the barn while Beth hugged Will. Relief coursed through her; chills shivered up and down her spine. She shook with stifled sobs.

"Aw, Mother! Don't cry yet, not till you see the great gift I have for you, and Colonel Ross, too," he protested as he sat up and looked around. "Oh, why's that counterpane there instead of the tablecloth?"

"Don't you remember—how you got hurt?" she asked.

He shook his head, then tenderly touched the lump on his head and the bruise on his chin. "I remember hearing loud voices and running downstairs to help you. I was just upstairs carving and—maybe it was just a bad dream about the British coming back. But if it's Christmas, I have to get my present for you." He shoved off the quilt and struggled to kick his feet free. "It's almost done and I can just finish it tomorrow after you see it—"

"Just hold on, young man!" Beth insisted as she pushed him back gently. "Well, since you don't recall, I want to tell you that you got hurt defending me. I cannot thank you enough. Even when Jerrod's gone, I'm going to feel so much safer with you here."

Despite his shaky look, Will beamed. She heard Jerrod open the door. "Now I will go upstairs," she said to Will, "and fetch the gift you've made, but you just lie there and rest while I get you some gruel first before the other food—"

The door banged and a blast of cold and snow came in with Jerrod and the baaing Sheba. But Beth could not stop Will from getting to his knees to hug the sheep.

"When a man's hungry, he doesn't need gruel, Beth," Jerrod said with a meaningful nod toward Will. "And I'll go up and fetch the gift for your mother, Will, if you just tell me where it is."

Will whispered to Jerrod and went back to hugging the protesting Sheba all the harder. Beth was so happy she did not know what to do, though she envied Sheba all those hugs. But if Will never hugged her again as he was growing up, she was eternally grateful that she had him back, both the boy and the man he would always be to her. She dished him up a heaping plate and reheated Jerrod's plate of cold food as he reappeared in the kitchen with a lumpy object wrapped in scraps from a potato sack.

"I've been carving this for months," Will told her proudly, "but when Colonel Ross came along, I had to do him, too. Several nights when you thought I was asleep, I worked on it, Mother, but I was real careful not to catch the covers on fire with my candle near the bed, and the one of Colonel Ross still needs a bit of work on the face." He chattered on as Jerrod gave him the sack and Will thrust it proudly into Beth's hands.

And then, before her eyes, the third miracle of this precious Christmas day occurred. The first had been that, despite the devastation of yesterday, she and Jerrod were even more in love and perhaps ready for commitments. The second was that Will had come back to her, all wrapped in the Christmas quilt. And the third—

"Oh, Will, what an intricate carving! And so perfect!" she cried as she pulled out three wooden figures joined in one. It was a rendition of herself, with her flintlock braced against her skirts, between two other figures. Will—much taller than he really was, almost as tall as the figure of Jerrod on her other side—had his arm around his mother's shoulders and a knife almost as long as a sword in his hand as if ready to protect her. And a partly completed Jerrod stood also with one arm around Beth and with what appeared to be the new striped American banner in his other hand.

For once Beth was too deeply moved to cry. With Sheba butting her head against her legs and Jerrod steadying Will to his feet, the three of them admired Will's work. Really, she thought, they stood now in much the same positions as in this wonderful carving.

"It's so lovely, my son," she told him as she turned and put the piece in a place of honor on the mantel so that the carving of the three of them now stood in the manger scene with the lone sheep before the baby Jesus.

They sat and ate and talked together, the three of them, like a family, that Christmas day. When Jerrod's men came, some returning Scratch and Nellie, they fed them, too. Beth was so delirious with gratitude and joy, she knew she could hardly taste the food or treasure each moment as she should. Whatever the future held for them all, they would have this Christmas to cherish forever. She felt she soared with an ecstasy so rare she might never capture such a day again. She gave both Will and Jerrod the warm wool shirts she had made for them. And when Will finally wore himself out just after sunset and together she and Jerrod put him to bed, the boy asked, "But what did you get Mother, Colonel Ross?"

"Something very special I'll tell you about tomorrow, Will. And, if you would, I'd like one more thing from you."

"Sure, for certain."

"When I wed your mother, I'd like for you to call me Jerrod. And when I'm away, you'll be the man in charge here."

The boy could only nod. His eyes were big as saucers with boyish joy and a man's pride. But Beth, too, felt stunned. It was more than she had dared hope for. But now that Will was himself again, it was *not* more than she could handle.

She was eager to know more, but she hated to leave Will. She was afraid for him to close his eyes, worried that once he fell asleep—

No, she told herself, as she kissed the boy, pinched the candlewick and tiptoed out behind Jerrod. She was not going to fear anymore that promises for the future would not come true. She was just going to live and love in the present as fully as she could, and that would build the future. Still, she could not contain her eagerness to hear what else Jerrod would say.

They were barely into the kitchen when he embraced her. "If you're willing, I'd like us to marry," he told her, his face so eager.

She clapped her hands together like a child and stood on tiptoe to hug him. "Yes, my dearest! As soon as the war is over, if that's what you want."

"Actually, the past few days have made me realize I want more than that—more and sooner. Being wounded for the first time, and then realizing no one was safe when Will was hurt—and you could have been injured, too—has made me do some hard thinking. And that lecture you gave me yesterday morning. What I mean is, I don't want to leave you behind unless you're fully mine. I want the three of us to really be a family. I want to dedicate myself to our future now."

"So, you mean you want us to marry after the three weeks of wedding banns can be read? That way we could have the whole winter together before the army leaves in the spring!"

"I guess now's the time for my Christmas gift to you. Besides the betrothal ring I've sent for from my trunks in storage, here is a little something else. I hope you will take this in the spirit it's offered and not burn it the way you did the last quartering orders."

"What—" she began as he produced a piece of vellum from the inside pocket of his uniform. As once before, she skimmed it for the familiar signature, *General G. Washington*. Still standing in the circle of Jerrod's arms, she read:

> At the special request of Lt. Col. Jerrod Ross, I hereby grant that for the duration of the winter months he continue to be quartered at the home of Elizabeth McGowan, his bride. And, as commander in chief of the American forces, I hereby rescind the period of waiting commonly called the reading of the banns so that they might be wed forthwith by my chaplain upon the time and date of their mutual choice. And I extend my most heartfelt best wishes for a long life of happiness through both difficult times and the many good years yet to come for our nation and our people.

"Oh!" Beth whispered.

"You won't burn it?"

"I shall frame it!"

"You're not angry because I assumed you would consider wedding me so soon? After that dressing down you gave me yesterday morning, I could hardly consider another alternative without being both a bully and a coward," he teased. His face was perfectly straight, but his brown eyes twinkled.

She cradled the paper to her as if it were the rarest, most delicate piece of porcelain. "And when would be a time and date of our mutual choice?" she dared.

"I thought tomorrow, as soon after dawn as I can fetch the chaplain, snow and war and neighbors' talk be danged," he said, and plunged on when she stood speechless at first. "That is, if you would choose to be my bride then. We'll have the wedding right here in the kitchen before the hearth."

"I could use the quilt to decorate the mantel where the mirror used to be," she mused, smiling. Suddenly she was speechless no more, though she felt weak at the knees. She swayed toward him.

"There will be time enough for decking the halls while I ride to camp first thing tomorrow," he told her. "And I'll fetch your friend Mistress Pembroke on the way back. Tonight, I'm going to take you up to your bed and tuck you in. We're both dog-tired."

"But I don't want our first Christmas together to end!"

"There will be many, many more. I don't want a sleepy bride tomorrow night when you're really mine. And," he said, picking her up in his arms as though she were his bride being carried over the threshold of a new life already, "when I put you to bed, I'll be right down here on my cozy hearth pallet. Until tomorrow that is, when I plan never to sleep alone in this house again."

Until tomorrow, he had said. Her hazy future with Jerrod Ross would have to wait only *until tomorrow.* He had vowed to love her and had proved his loyalty to her. She held to him, still with General Washington's orders in her hand. Imagine, the man had as good as ordered them to marry immediately, and she was delighted to toe the line.

"My bed's chilly up here, Jerrod," she pouted as she began to nibble at his ear on their way up the stairs. "I don't like to expend wood for the bedroom hearth these days and I always forget a warming pan."

"Starting tomorrow night, my sweetheart, I promise you will need neither," he boasted and carefully laid her down. "Besides, one more bite of my ear like that, and the honeymoon might come a bit early."

She laughed deep in her throat. She felt all floaty, both in excitement and exhaustion. He removed her shoes and helped her unlace and wriggle out of her petticoats as if he were a lady's maid. Who cared if he didn't know a fig about farming, she thought, if he could undress a woman like that.

"What is that little smile for?" he asked after he covered her up to her chin.

"For today and all our other Christmases together," she told him smugly.

"I think, if we can be together, it could be Christmas every day." He kissed her good-night. She could tell he had to force himself to stop at that. But the devilish streak she so loved in him emerged again as he fondled her breast through the covers and went out, leaving the door ajar.

Elizabeth Richards McGowan felt awash in golden love as she wed Lieutenant Colonel Jerrod Ross the next day at one in the afternoon. A deep inner peace and joy bathed her heart. They stood, holding hands, with Will beside Jerrod and Charity Pembroke beside her, taking their vows before General Washington's personal chaplain. Over the blazing hearth hung the Christmas quilt. On the mantel their own personal family crest of the manger blessed the proceedings. Nearly a dozen of Jerrod's men stood at parade rest in the kitchen until it was all over and the bride and groom kissed. Then cheers and huzzahs boomed like fireworks.

They shared a dinner that reminded Beth of the biblical loaves and fishes. She had thought there would not be much food for such a crowd, but somehow the guests had produced ham, pheasant, fish and rabbit stew, besides the large, two-layered apple cake she herself had made this morning. When people put their hands and hearts together, there was bounty in the land, despite harsh times.

By late afternoon, everyone but the soldier who would sleep in the barn had left. Will was excited, but still tired from his trials, he fell asleep with his head on his arms at the table.

"I'm ready for an early bed, too," Jerrod whispered to Beth with a wink and a grin. He lifted the boy, and Beth banked the hearth ashes carefully, but filled the brass warming pan with embers for the first time in months. She hurried upstairs, but met Jerrod coming back down. "I was going to carry you up, too," he said.

"But I'm here on my own to volunteer, sir!" she told him and stood at attention with the long-handled brass warming pan like a musket over her shoulder.

He swept her into his arms and carried her down the hall and over the threshold of her—their room. "My beautiful Beth, my stubborn sweetheart," he murmured with his face pressed deep in her loose bridal tresses.

"Perhaps stubborn no more, except to seize us as much time together as we can manage," she told him. They lay on the bed together, side by side. Only then did he take the warming pan from her hands and put it on the floor.

"I have a feeling we won't need this," he said. "Our personal future looks not only bright, but warm."

Her eyes widened. In the light of the single lantern, she could see herself in the deep pools of his dark eyes. "I have a feeling too," she whispered, "but it's love for you, the love and passion I've been trying so hard to control—"

Those were the last words that passed between them for a long time. They spoke with their hands and lips, then the rest of their eager bodies. They began to disrobe each other. He pulled her shawl from her shoulders and tossed it away. They stripped off his coat. She untied and unwound his cravat just to touch more of him. In the V of his cambric shirt, so white in the dim light, she snagged her fingers through his curly chest hair. Suddenly, he was kissing the hard nubs of her breasts right through her boned stays and tautly stretched bodice as he tipped her back in his arms.

He unlaced her gown, then scooted the sleeves slowly down her shoulders. He tugged her modesty piece awry. He pleasured her as he slowly, lingeringly removed each piece of clothing, stroking and touching and looking at each stretch and swell of silken skin he uncovered. The heat they generated could have melted the snow outside, which was piling up ever deeper to seal them in together. She, too, became adept at the game of loving waiting, of drawing out the yearning until neither of them could bear more, and he spoke at last in the fast-breathed silence between them.

"I love you so much. I've wanted you from the first, my sweetheart, my—wife."

"And every time we fought, I only wanted to surrender!"

He moved to lie atop her, keeping his weight from her with spread knees next to her naked hips and elbows on either side of her disheveled head. Then his hard thighs intruded between her legs to nudge her open to him. He lavished love with hands and tongue the fervent, trembling length of her. He knelt over her as if to adore her. And then he moved closer to bind them together forever.

The moment of their union shone incandescent for her. A safe haven here, a joining of more than their eager bodies. And the stunning impact of her need for him swirled her outside herself. This was indeed perfection. She embraced him with arms and legs; she would never lose him now, never really be apart from him, even if they were separated. Love had never been like this before, both the promise and the fulfillment, this giving wholeheartedly as equals in the quest for each other. They moved in harmony, spiraling up and outward together, then down to blessed peace.

Only after it was over did they realize it was so cold in the room that frost framed each windowpane and their breath made puffy clouds. They pulled up the counterpane and sheets and snuggled against each other's warmth under them. He drew her to him spoonlike with her bottom bumped back into his hips and his arms around her and one leg over her. She felt toasty and warm, but she did not doze. She was too excited. To think that they belonged to each other now and that they could create love between them all over again in endless variation. And that they could create a child together, one she could love as much as she did Will, and learn to let grow and become an individual, too. Among other things, her beloved Jerrod had taught her that.

"Still awake, sweetheart?"

"Yes. You know, I was dreading Christmas this year, and it turned out to be the most wonderful of my life."

"For me, too," he murmured as his lips meandered through her hair to the side of her throat. "A real season of joy for me, too."

As he turned her toward him and reached for her again, she realized what she would embroider on the square of heirloom quilt for this year: a copy of Will's carving, which she considered to be their wedding portrait. But she knew that the real Christmas heirloom was cherished memories of people sharing precious times together, which families passed down to those who came after them. The real Christmas heirloom was love.

* * * * *

A Note from Caryn Cameron

As I was growing up in Toledo, Ohio, Christmas always meant family. I was fortunate to have all four grandparents, an aunt, an uncle and cousins in town. With my own parents, my two younger brothers and myself, we all shared many wonderful holiday celebrations. We would gather at one grandmother's house or the other. After dinner and gifts, we five kids would put on some sort of talent show for the adults—skits, songs, dances, recitations. That is, until we reached high school age and such things were too far beneath us!

As my grandparents aged, my parents' house became the gathering place for Christmas, first, when I was away at college and later, when I and my brothers married. Slowly, the grandparents left us, but in years of listening to their tales of earlier Christmases, I learned to value the past. Maybe this is one of the reasons I write historical novels today.

Now that my grandparents and my father are gone, Christmas is in my new hometown of Columbus, Ohio, where my husband and I, and Jim—my youngest brother—and his family live. Mother comes down from Toledo, unless she is in Atlanta at brother Tom's house. These third-generation holidays are joyous times, too. Christmas Day focuses on my three lively nephews, whose lives will reach out through many Christmases to come. A few weeks before Christmas, my husband's large family gathers at our house, and Christmas Eve is reserved for celebrating with my three grown stepchildren and a son-in-law.

Yes, family is important, but as I've seen Christmas seasons go by, I've realized, like Beth in *A Season of Joy*, that giving and sharing outside the family can bring memorable blessings, too. One of the most rewarding things I have done is volunteer to play the piano for year-round church services at several nursing homes in the area.

I have found the residents there are so grateful for the

visit. They really appreciate folks coming in to spread a bit of Christmas love, whether it is holiday time or not. So many oldsters—some without their own family visitors—tell beautiful stories of Christmases past. They make me realize this season of the year is a treasure that reaches even beyond our biological families. Christmas is a cherished heirloom we can keep all our lives and yet give away without diminishing its value.

Caryn Cameron

FORTUNE'S GIFT

DeLoras Scott

Swedish Pancakes were a traditional Christmas breakfast when I was a child, and I've carried that tradition forth with my children and grandchildren. The pancakes are very thin, and we had the option of either sprinkling sugar or spreading jelly over them, before we rolled them up. Or we just used good old maple syrup. Oh, what fun, and so good!

SWEDISH PANCAKES

3 eggs
1 cup flour
½ tsp salt
2 cups milk
6 tbsp butter, melted

Beat eggs with ½ cup milk. Add flour and beat mixture until smooth. Add remaining milk, then butter and salt. Blend.

Lightly coat frying pan with vegetable-oil spray. Pour enough batter into pan to just coat bottom evenly. Cook over medium heat. Turn pancake when edges lift. Make sure second side browns but does not burn. Pancakes should be thin and crepelike.

These pancakes can be cooked ahead of time, rolled and then placed in a warm oven until served.

Chapter One

San Diego, 1889

"I quit," Carlton declared as he placed his cards on the table. "You've won all the chips."

April gave her brother a complacent smile, then raised her fan. Fortunately the breeze through the open French doors had kept the salon relatively comfortable most of the evening.

"April's just too good for you, darling," Carlton's wife teased. Standing behind her husband, she placed a loving hand on his shoulder. "You should never have taught her to play poker."

"But you must understand your husband's thinking at the time, Ruth." April collapsed her fan and, leaving the table, glided majestically toward the French doors. "We were living in dusty old Calico when he started teaching me the game. He thought he was too grown-up to attend to menial chores. So," she said, turning back to her audience, "since I was eager to learn, Carlton agreed to teach me. However, there was one stipulation. If I lost, I had to do his chores. Needless to say, he kept me quite busy.''

Ruth looked down at her husband. "Carlton! You didn't.''

"I'm guilty." He chuckled. "And everything was going so well until Mother and Father found out.''

"But now that he knows I can beat him," April continued, "Carlton refuses to place a real wager.''

"But April, what if our friends, or the gentlemen that come courting, discovered—''

"Fah. How would anyone find out, Ruth? Besides, in Paris all the ladies gambled. And as for these so-called men, there isn't a single one in the lot who's worth his weight in silver. At least none that I've met. Where are the men you read about in those penny and dime magazines? The real men of the West?''

"You wouldn't look twice at a man like that." Carlton lifted his glass and took an appreciative drink of aged whiskey. "You want the type that tags behind your skirts and attends to your every wish.''

"Actually, you're quite right. So, Carlton," April said, her chin pertly raised, "after winning so resoundingly, can I assume I'm the best poker player you know?''

"No, I wouldn't say that. I will admit you're as good as most I know. But just because you can beat me certainly doesn't mean you can beat everyone.''

"Don't be so modest, Carlton. You always said you're one of the best.''

"Well . . . I am. But not *the* best.''

"Then who is?" April persisted.

Carlton laughed, then went to the sideboard to pour himself another drink. "Without a doubt, Yancy Medford. Why do you ask?" he inquired as he joined his wife on the sofa. Reaching over, he placed Ruth's hand in his.

"Just curious, I guess."

Carlton couldn't help but wonder what had happened to the happy, vivacious sister he'd loved. Though beautiful, April was now spoiled and arrogant, just like the other wealthy women she associated with. On more than one occasion he had asked himself what he could do to get back that spark she used to have before school and Europe had "civilized" her. She was her father's daughter, so it had to be still embedded somewhere within her. When he'd mentioned there was someone better at cards, the old April would have taken up the challenge!

He suddenly smiled. "Since you've accused me of not wanting to wager, April, how would you like to make a really worthwhile bet?"

"You'll lose, you know."

"Maybe, but you don't always beat me."

"What sort of wager?"

"You've been wanting that black stallion of mine, so if you win, he's yours."

"And if I lose?" April asked suspiciously. She wasn't about to admit how much she wanted the stallion. There wasn't a faster animal in the county.

Carlton thought for a moment. "If I win, you'll get married by Christmas."

Ruth gasped.

April began to fan herself vigorously. "Why would I even consider such a ridiculous wager? You're becoming weak in the head, Carlton."

"Then you admit you're not that good at poker and are actually bluffing about wanting to wager? Apparently your complaints earlier were nothing but words." Carlton watched her eyes turn dark green, always a sign that she was becoming upset. "I'm taking a chance at losing an extremely valuable animal," he added, pressing his point.

"And I would lose my freedom!"

Carlton was quite enjoying himself. He hadn't seen this much fire in his sister since her return three months ago. "You were saying just the other day that your gentlemen callers were boring and you might as well get married and put an end to it."

Ruth glared at her husband. "Surely you're not serious."

"I'm quite serious, my dear. I'm tired of April's superior attitude. She can either accept the wager or keep her mouth closed from now on."

"I don't believe what I'm hearing." Ruth cast aside Carlton's hand and stood. "I'm going to bed. Are you coming?"

"In a moment."

Ruth marched out of the room.

Her mind centered on Carlton's demeaning words, April paid scant attention to what her sister-in-law had said or done. "You seem to have this all worked out in your mind, brother dear," she said angrily. "So, how many games would you suggest we play?"

"As many as it takes for either party to win five hundred dollars. But I won't be involved in the game."

April glowered at Carlton, now comfortably relaxed on the sofa. "And just what does that mean?"

"If we're to make a bet of such magnitude, I'm not going to make it easy. You'll play Yancy Medford."

Some of her friends had mentioned that name, but at the time April had given little consideration to what was said. "Who is this man? A gambler, or one of those cardsharpers who used to play in the saloons at Calico?"

Carlton slowly rose to his feet. "You don't know him. He is a bit of a rake, but not the type you're referring to. He's very wealthy, owns a fleet of ships and has only lived here about a year. He's a member of the Men's Club and I've played poker with him on several occasions. What's wrong, dear sister," Carlton chided, "afraid you're not as good as you think you are?"

Her jaw set, April looked her brother straight in the eye. "You're right. I am bored. When will you set up the game?"

"Oh, no. You'll do that." Carlton had become totally serious. "And, if you do not play or should lose, you will be married by Christmas. Or you can refuse the challenge and admit you are no better or different than any other woman. I am more than a little tired of your haughty attitude, April. Also, I will require an apology to Ruth for what you said about her not handling the servants properly."

"But she doesn't!" April was furious. Had she had somewhere else to go she would have left immediately. How dared he say these things to her? She had gone to finishing school and toured Europe, claims few other local girls could make. She was a polished woman of substance, and he should be boasting about her instead of belittling her. If it took a poker game and the loss of a prized stallion for him to show respect, so be it.

Removing all emotion from her face, she calmly said, "Very well. However, I feel the wager is rather one-sided. When I win, you will also give me that new mare you bought two weeks ago, as well as an apology for your unfair accusations."

"Done."

"One last thing, brother. On the doubtful assumption that I should lose, will I be permitted to select my husband?"

"Of course."

"And what if he refuses to marry me?"

"You needn't worry about that. I'll make damn sure he finds his way to the preacher."

As he climbed the stairs, two at a time, Carlton was surprised by the anger he felt. What had started out as a means of getting his sister to regain some part of her old self had turned into an argument. He hadn't intended to let his feelings get away from him, nor had he originally planned on holding April to a marriage commitment if she lost. Now he wondered if a Christmas marriage wasn't just the answer. On the other hand, damn if it wouldn't be just like April to win, and he'd be out two fine animals plus an apology for simply speaking his mind!

"Now, Ruth," Carlton said as he entered the bedroom, "there is no need to be upset with me."

Ruth ignored him and continued brushing her hair.

Going to her, Carlton leaned down and kissed her neck. "Listen to me, Ruth," he said softly.

The brush stopped.

"My father was the happiest man I've ever known. He enjoyed life and wanted his children to do the same. And we did. April laughed a lot, was game to try most anything and was always in trouble with Mother. I clearly remember one incident. We were living in Calico, and Mother caught April with two boys the same age jumping up and down in the trough behind the house. The problem was, the boys and April were stark naked. Mother grabbed April by the ear and marched her into the house, scolding her and saying that young ladies do not behave in such a manner." Carlton laughed.

"Surely you don't expect April to act that way now? She's a grown woman!"

"Of course not, but hear me out." Carlton stepped away and began unbuttoning his white shirt. "Mother did her best to make April a lady, which was fine while the family was still struggling in Calico. But when Father hit a big silver lode and moved us to San Diego, put us in a big house and sent me to law school, Mother changed. She had more money than she could spend in a lifetime and let everyone know it. Even old friends were suddenly beneath her. From the moment we moved here, she never acknowledged we had ever been poor. My father loved her and agreed to anything she said. I'm not saying I didn't love Mother.

Losing her hurt just as much as losing Father, but Mother was wrong. Don't you see, Ruth? April has become just like Mother, and no matter what she may say or do, I know she's not happy. I'm responsible for her, and I want her to return to the fun-loving, caring woman I know she can be. If for no other reason than that Father won't be turning over in his grave."

"I fail to see how a poker game or that stupid wager is going to accomplish anything."

"I hope she'll get her comeuppance, which is well past due. I doubt that there will even be a game. Yancy is out of town. Besides, why would he even agree to play poker with her?"

"I'm not sure it's a wise move, Carlton. Can't you see that April's only problem is boredom? She's young and just feathering her wings."

"They don't need feathering. They need to be clipped."

April had deliberately chosen Sidney Bishop to escort her on her Sunday outing. Though he was not the most attractive of her suitors, Sidney loved to gossip and knew, or knew of, everyone of importance.

As they drove through the park, Sidney kept the prancing bays at a slow pace. The top of the buggy was folded back, and April held a blue-frilled parasol over her head to protect her face from the sun. Only after they had talked of other things did April broach the subject uppermost in her mind.

"Sidney, have you ever met Yancy Medford?" she asked, feigning disinterest.

"Oh, Miss Simpson! Surely you haven't turned pigeon-eyed over that man like all the other women?"

"Heavens, no." She smiled and nodded at friends passing by.

"I'm certainly glad to hear that. You shouldn't be around the likes of him."

"I've heard," she said confidentially, "that he rather likes to gamble."

By the time Sidney returned April to her home, she knew a great deal about Mr. Medford. Most important, she found out that the questionable gentleman played cards on Wednesday nights, and only at the Men's Club, which Carlton had failed to mention. No wonder he'd added the stipulation that he was the winner if she didn't play. But April had no intention of losing, at least not without a fight. There had to be a way to set up a game—it was simply a matter of sitting down and thinking it out.

As the days passed April did her homework. It was always wise to know as much as possible about one's opponent. She visited many of her female friends, always making a point of mentioning Yancy Medford's name. This time she listened closely to what was said. The comments were unanimous. He was unbelievably handsome, very masculine and notorious with the women. His latest conquest was the young widow Brookmire, who had been bragging of late that she planned on his becoming her second husband. April also found out where the gentleman lived.

On more than one occasion April had her carriage driver pass the notorious man's large home in hopes of "accidentally" meeting him. Her plan was simple.

She would draw him into a conversation, ask his name, feign surprise, then tell him of the bet with her brother. Being a gentleman, naturally he would agree to a private game. But never once did she see anyone except servants leave or enter the house.

Since that course of action was doing nothing but wasting time, April sent a note requesting Mr. Medford to call on her. A week went by and he still hadn't made an appearance. He hadn't even had the courtesy to send a reply!

April was beginning to feel an intense dislike for the unreachable rogue. He snubbed protocol, and he had snubbed her. She resented the latter more.

"Tell me, April," Carlton asked one night at dinner, "how is the proposed game going?"

"You made an unfair bet."

"I admit that, but if you want to gamble, that's a risk you take."

"If friends had not described the man, I would think that you made him up in your head." She took a bite of the rock cod, savoring the flavor.

Carlton found it interesting that apparently none of her friends knew Medford had been out of town. "Oh he's real, all right. In fact, I saw him last night at the club. I don't know how much longer he'll be staying in San Diego. He came here because there was supposed to be a seaport built, but now it looks like it will be in Los Angeles instead."

Carlton's mocking grin made April all the more determined. Time was passing, and she was being forced to more drastic methods.

April wasn't sure when the idea began forming in the back of her mind. It was a perfectly ridiculous plan. That she was even considering it shocked her. If she were caught, her name would be on people's lips for years to come. She'd never live down the embarrassment, but then, getting out of the marriage part of the bet wouldn't be a problem because respectable families would never allow their sons to marry her. She'd probably end up returning to Europe, which at this time didn't seem like a bad idea. Why had she allowed her pride to get her into this fix in the first place? She dismissed the question. Hindsight would get her nowhere. April finally decided to enlist the aid of her longtime friend, Mary Broom.

Dressed in an expensive, sky blue riding suit, April went to the carriage house to locate the groom. After she called several times, he finally ambled in from the outside. She waited impatiently for him to saddle her favorite mare and guide the horse to the mounting block. As soon as she was firmly seated on the sidesaddle, April gathered the reins and rode off.

She enjoyed the warm breeze drifting off the bay as she kept the frisky mare in an easy lope. The sky was azure blue with nary a cloud, and the sun shone brightly. A perfect day for riding, April thought. Unfortunately, there was business to be taken care of. That Mary might not be home didn't so much as enter April's mind. Married, her stomach swollen with child, the woman seldom left home.

After arriving at the two-story house and exchanging small chitchat, April told Mary her plan. Mary was properly appalled.

"I can't believe that you, of all people, would even consider such a thing!" Mary exclaimed. She sipped her tea and avoided looking at her friend.

"Do you have a better idea?" April asked calmly.

"But to dress like a man, enter the Men's Club and then play poker, it's the most absurd thing I've ever heard. I know you're only fooling with me. There's too much at risk." Mary broke out laughing. "Oh, but wouldn't it be a delicious stunt to pull? I've always wondered what it was like inside that stone building." With difficulty, she leaned forward and placed her cup and saucer on the table. "I'll be so glad when this baby arrives. Four weeks more seems like a lifetime."

"I'm quite serious, Mary. Either I go to Mr. Medford's lair, or by this time next year I'll be in the same condition you're in now."

Mary shifted in her chair, trying to get comfortable. "When do you plan on doing it?" she asked, suddenly excited. No one put spice into her life like April did.

"A week from Wednesday."

"That's an ideal time for me. Paul will be out of town. What do you want me to do?"

April frowned. "I've decided to take some of Carlton's clothes, but we'll have to alter them. He has so many, he'll never miss them. I'll need to change and spend the night here."

"What if Carlton arrives at the club?" Mary asked, enjoying the intrigue. This was the most fun she'd had since getting pregnant.

"He won't. He and Ruth will be entertaining that evening. I think I should wear one of Carlton's top hats."

"You'll have to leave it on, and the men will wonder why you don't take it off."

"I'll say it brings me luck."

"Paul mustn't find out about my part in this, April. He'd be furious." Mary giggled softly. "I still remember the trouble you used to get me in."

April smiled. "There will be no need for Paul or anyone else to know. Only Carlton."

Chapter Two

Why would April Simpson have asked me to call upon her? Yancy Medford wondered. He leaned his hips against his desk, continuing to tap the note in the palm of his hand. The message had come as a surprise. Though he'd never met the lady, he'd certainly heard a lot about her. He had been told she was beautiful, poised and quite adept at breaking men's hearts. Yancy naturally assumed conceited, boring and spoiled were a few more of the lady's attributes.

Yancy's friends were mostly bachelors like himself, or ladies older and wiser than young women in search of husbands, so there had been little occasion for him to become acquainted with Miss Simpson. And he was certainly not in the market for a bride, which led him back to the same question. Why would Miss Simpson want to meet him? His reputation? Though probably some of the talk was justly deserved, a good deal had been stretched a bit far. Did she feel he should also be paying homage, like her many other beaux?

Under normal circumstances, he would have tossed the note aside and forgotten it. This wasn't the first such request he'd received from a woman. But he liked

Carlton Simpson, and had no desire to insult the man's family by ignoring a command performance. He placed the missive back on the desk. This afternoon he'd ride over to Carlton's law office. It would take only a few minutes to explain his apparent lack of manners.

It was nearing two when Yancy tied his horse to the hitching post in front of the small frame house. He went inside, and after a few quick words with the male secretary, was led into Carlton's office.

"What a pleasant surprise," Carlton said, rising from behind his desk. "Are you here on a legal matter or just stopping by for a visit?"

"A visit, but I won't take but a moment of your time. As you know, I've been in New Orleans attending to business for two months, and didn't arrive back in town until late yesterday. After visiting the club last night, I returned home and went straight to bed. It wasn't until this morning that I finally got a chance to look at my correspondence." He handed the note to Carlton. "My manservant said this arrived more than two weeks ago. I simply wanted you to know why I didn't reply."

Carlton opened the envelope. After a quick perusal, he broke out laughing. He motioned for Yancy to take a seat before returning to his own chair. "I think I'm the one who should be doing the explaining." Carlton proceeded to tell Yancy about the wager, and the two men agreed that the note was simply a means of setting up a poker game.

An hour later, Yancy mounted his horse, a smile tugging at the corner of his lips. Because he had in-

herited a lot of money at an early age, there was little
he hadn't seen or done during his twenty-nine years.
But never had a woman sought him out for a poker
game. The only games he enjoyed with the fair sex
took place in the bedroom. He had to admit, though,
this entire situation regarding Miss Simpson was so
preposterous, it was almost tempting. Was she really
that good at the game? He nudged the gray stallion
into a gallop. He'd just wait and see what happened
next. If the lady was as determined as her brother
claimed, she'd think of another approach.

Three days after his talk with Carlton, Yancy saw
April for the first time. He was sitting in a secluded
corner of the Horton House dining room with a female companion. Norma Fisher was pretty but unfortunately of a talkative nature. So much so that
Yancy just sat and pretended to listen. When he heard
the name April Simpson, Norma had his full attention.

"I'm sorry, what did you say?" he asked.

"April Simpson. She just entered with another
beau." Norma smirked. "I simply cannot see what it
is about her that attracts men. Probably her money."

Yancy only half listened as he studied the woman
standing just inside the door. A small hat sat atop her
blond coiffed hair, and even from where he sat, Yancy
could see her large eyes fringed with thick lashes, and
her full lips, the type that seemed to beg to be kissed.
The blue-and-gold striped day suit fit her ample
bosom and tiny waist to perfection. Tall and regal, the
lady was indeed a true beauty. But being a man of the
world, Yancy could tell by her carriage that April

Simpson might as well have had a big sign across her chest declaring, Do Not Touch! A most enticing combination.

Their meal was served, and although Yancy tried to return his attention to his companion, his gaze kept drifting to the table on the other side of the room. He knew that one way or another, he would eventually meet the blond beauty seated there.

A week later, April stood studying herself in the tall diamond glass mirror. The white starched shirt, brocade vest and gray trousers were now a perfect fit. "Do you think I'll pass as a man?"

Mary shook her head. "I hope the room isn't too well lit. You simply do not have a man's face."

"I've taken care of that. I remembered a tailor who once designed Carlton's clothes for a costume ball. At the time he told Carlton that a mustache could be pasted on the lip. I went to see him this afternoon. He's waiting at his shop to apply a mustache on me before I go to the Men's Club." April pulled at the watch fob. "I have to go, Mary, or I'll be too late to get in the game."

Mary rose in mock somberness from the edge of the bed. "April, I think it is my duty to try and talk you out of this. I'm worried that someone will discover what you're up to. Heaven knows, the men would never forgive you for entering their domain. It's absolutely unheard of." Mary couldn't suppress a giggle. "And absolutely delicious."

"Very well, Mary, you've done your duty. Now help me on with the coat."

With Mary's help, April slipped on the black frock coat. A black top hat followed.

Mary stepped back, took another look, and laughed. "I must admit, other than your face, you could pass as a young gentleman. Being five foot seven helps. Well, if you're determined, come along. We'll go out the back entrance. I had a horse saddled earlier and he's tied in front of the carriage house. There'll be no one around to recognize you, though I doubt any one would."

It wasn't until April walked into the club that she became nervous. The place seemed gloomy and smelled strongly of tobacco. Several men stood in front of the bar, which stretched across one side of the room. She was fascinated with the large picture of a naked lady on another wall. As with similar paintings she'd seen at the Louvre Museum in Paris, she considered the woman to be plump. She looked away and continued scanning the room. A few other men were seated on the plush chairs and sofas scattered about. Where was the poker game being held? she wondered helplessly.

"Excuse me, sir, but this is a private club."

April turned to the man standing directly behind her. "I'm aware of that," she said in a lowered voice. As she'd practiced, she adopted the same pompous manner she'd seen in most of her suitors. "My brother, Carlton Simpson, suggested that since he would not be playing cards tonight, I might take his place. Having nothing else to do, I decided to accept the offer."

"Oh, I'm sorry, sir," the man said. His entire attitude immediately changed. "I didn't know. Follow me, sir, and I'll lead you to the poker room. Some of the other gentlemen have already arrived."

April took long strides, rather enjoying the freedom the trousers allowed. She had especially liked riding astride instead of using a sidesaddle.

As they entered the small room, April took a deep breath. If she could fool these gentlemen, her plan would work.

Three men were already seated at the table, all of whom looked up questioningly. None fit the description she'd been given of Yancy Medford.

"This is Mr. Carlton Simpson's younger brother, gentlemen," announced the man who had brought her. "He will be filling in as the fifth player. Mr. Medford hasn't arrived as yet, but should be here any time. May I get your drinks?" The other men nodded. "And how about you, Mr. Simpson?"

It took a moment for April to realize he was addressing her. "No, I never mix drink with cards."

Even more nervous than before, April took the empty chair nearest the door. If things didn't go right, she wanted to be able to escape as quickly as possible.

One by one the men leaned over, shook hands and introduced themselves. One was slender, another rather portly. "You a good poker player, boy?" the last man asked. He was well along in years, possessing gray hair and a weathered face.

April gave him a lopsided smile. "I can hold my own." She had already forgotten the men's names. "How much is the buy-in?" she asked, noticing that the chips had already been counted out. She blessed the days she'd watched the men play poker at Lil's Saloon in Calico. She used to borrow clothes from the boy next door, and no one had ever suspected she was a girl. Strange, she hadn't thought about that in years. Maybe that was where the idea for her escapade tonight had come from.

"Hundred dollars," the slender man answered as he shuffled a deck of cards, "and we play only draw poker. I swear, I didn't know Carlton had a brother. Did you boys know that?"

The others shook their heads.

"I've been in Europe. Just arrived back a couple of nights ago." Her false mustache was tickling her lip, but she didn't dare scratch for fear it would fall off.

"Yancy! You're just in time," the portly man said.

At last, April thought, her nerves frazzled from the men's scrutiny. Now maybe the game will begin and they'll pay less attention to me.

When the fifth player took his place across from her, it was all April could do to keep her mouth from dropping open. It was easy to see why all the women were aflutter when they spoke of Yancy Medford. Everything about him exuded masculinity and danger. Never had she seen a more attractive man. His hair was raven black, his eyes sky blue and his shoulders broad.

"I don't believe we've been introduced."

His voice was deep and most pleasing to the ear. Words failed April.

"That there is Carlton's younger brother," the gray-headed man stated. "Never did say your name, boy."

Having had a moment to collect herself, April started to speak. Just in time she remembered to lower her voice. "Adam. Adam Simpson." She watched Yancy Medford's chiseled lip spread into a grin, revealing a line of perfectly even white teeth.

"Call me Yancy. We play a friendly game of poker and don't bother with last names."

"A friendly game, hell!" the portly man with glasses grumbled. "You're gonna have to be on your toes, Adam. Yancy cleans us out most every game. Like fools, we keep returning, hoping to win some of it back."

"Your drinks, gentlemen."

April jumped when the man spoke.

"I took the liberty to bring your favorite whiskey, Mr. Medford."

"Thank you, Bristol. Aren't you drinking, Adam?"

"Says he don't drink when playing cards," the gray-haired man answered.

"I see. For some people I would say that's a wise move. Tell me, Adam, is keeping your hat on some sort of superstition?"

"Yes." Her hands shaking, April pulled out the five-hundred dollars she and Carlton had agreed upon, and placed it on the table. "Here's my hundred," she said, picking up a hundred-dollar bill and tossing it in the center. "Now, gentlemen, are we here to play or gab?"

The slender man spread out the cards. Each player drew to see who would deal first.

It was a long time since Yancy had been so amused. The lady was dressed in perfect male attire and somehow had even managed to flatten her breasts, which seemed almost criminal. Where in the hell had she found that bushy mustache? The fact that she had so easily fooled the others surprised him. Wouldn't they at least notice the delicate hands, long tapered fingers and well-shaped nails? After seeing the trouble she'd taken to track him down, Yancy wasn't about to make the lady's real identity known. She had earned her poker game.

For four hours they played, with April holding her own. Yancy had to admit the lady was good. She smiled occasionally when she raked in a pot, but not a bat of long eyelash or twitch of a finger gave away what cards she held. She even bluffed well.

"That's enough for me," the man with the glasses said. He tossed in his hand but remained to watch the game.

An hour later the slender man dropped out.

Thirty minutes after that the gray-haired gentleman followed suit. He smiled at April. "I have to tell you, Adam, you're even better than your brother, and that's saying something. Well, boys, guess we might as well call it quits for tonight." He raked back his chair and stood.

April didn't want the game to stop, but wasn't sure how to prevent it. The wager with Carlton was that she had to win five hundred from Yancy, and even though she was well ahead, she still didn't have enough money to win the bet. Trying for another game at a later time was impossible. Once Carlton found out what she'd been up to, he'd make sure she never got loose again.

Yancy leaned back in his chair, eyes narrowed. The woman had played well. She had probably won even more than he. But Yancy knew that wasn't the wager her future depended on. For the first time since the game began, her green eyes mirrored confusion. What the hell, he told himself, a woman with this much guts deserves a chance. He leaned forward. "Tell you what, Adam," he said nonchalantly. "We're about even, how would you like to play two last hands? Hundred-dollar minimum bet." He watched her eyes light up and her lips curve into a slight smile.

"Very well," she quickly agreed.

"You deal."

The other men sat back down.

April won the first game with a pair of kings. She had her five hundred, but she had agreed to play two hands. The next hand Yancy dealt her two aces. What with the hundred-dollar ante, she couldn't fold or she'd be short. She bet a hundred. He raised. She called.

Though she remained outwardly calm, her heart practically leaped into her throat when she drew a third ace. Then Yancy bet five hundred, after drawing only one card. Was he bluffing? If he had two pairs, her three of a kind would win. So much was at stake. She called. Yancy laid down a straight.

She had lost.

It was all April could do to smile and extend her hand for a shake. "My congratulations," she said, trying to sound sincere. She turned to the others. "Gentlemen, it has indeed been an experience." With head high and shoulders back, she left the room.

April was woebegone as she rode back to Mary's house. Had it not been for that confounded bet with Carlton, she would have enjoyed tonight's game. But damn it—she silently admonished herself for using such language—she had lost!

She could handle the apology to Ruth, even though she still felt her sister-in-law was too lax with the servants. It was the thought of Carlton's smugness when he discovered she'd lost that really vexed her. And last, but certainly not least, there was the little matter of having to select a husband. There was no possible way she could lie to Carlton. He'd hear of tonight's incident at the club and know exactly who the so-called brother was.

When April returned to the house, Mary immediately escorted her to the guest bedroom. After a few questions, she was well-informed as to what had happened.

"You'd been gone so long I was becoming worried." Mary helped April undress. "At least you had the wisdom to tell Carlton you would be spending the night here." She turned back the covers on the large four-poster bed.

"Oh, April, what are you going to do now?" Mary collapsed onto the rocking chair while April slipped into a white nightdress.

"I guess I'm going to have to pick a husband."

"You could lie."

"How? Besides, that wouldn't be ethical."

"You're not a man, April. Who said you have to be ethical?"

April had to laugh at her friend's reasoning. Yet Mary did have a point. "Have you ever met Yancy Medford?" April asked in an attempt to change the subject.

"Once. He's very handsome and charming. What did you think of him?"

"Nothing. Why should I? He's just like any other man. It's late, Mary, and I think we could both use some sleep."

"You're right. I'm exhausted." Mary struggled out of the chair. "I'll see you in the morning."

Mary closed the door behind her, then headed down the hall toward her own room. Why had April lied? No woman could say Mr. Medford was just another man. Mary giggled. Wouldn't that be an interesting combination? Granite and stiff starch.

After turning off the oil lamp, April climbed upon the high bed. As exhausted as she was, she couldn't go to sleep. Whom should she consider marrying? She gave due consideration to each suitor, then dismissed them one by one. She didn't even want one of them to kiss her, let alone to take her to his bed. In her opinion, when it came to wooing a lady, American men could learn a lot from the Europeans. She even thought about the men she'd already discarded, and dismissed them as quickly as she had when she told them not to come calling again.

April sat up, fluffed her pillow and flopped back down. She still had more than a month to decide, and perhaps someone new would enter her life. Yancy Medford came to mind. He was a handsome devil, but good looks didn't make a man. Besides, he wasn't her type. She wanted a husband she could lead around by the ear, and he was definitely not that sort of man. He would probably want some little thing constantly worshiping at his feet.

Before finally falling asleep, April decided that in order to forestall further misery, she would not say a thing to Carlton about tonight. He'd started this whole mess, and could find out about it the hard way.

Chapter Three

By the time April returned home the next day, she had decided on a different approach. Though it went against the grain, she would confess all. Then, after Carlton had recovered from his outrage at her having invaded the sanctity of his hallowed club, she would apologize appropriately to Ruth and swear that from this time on she would be more agreeable. Maintaining a harmonious attitude over a period of time would surely help to persuade her brother to release her from the rest of the wager.

April had just started up the stairs to her bedroom when she heard, "Excuse, Señorita Simpson."

April turned and saw the chubby Mexican housekeeper rushing toward her.

"A message was delivered by a manservant earlier this morning. He said it was important."

"I doubt that." Realizing she was being snippy, April smiled and quickly added, "But thank you, *señora,* for making sure I received it."

"You're most welcome."

April accepted the envelope, then continued on, eager for a bath and change of clothing. As she en-

tered her room, her thoughts were still centered on
what she was going to say to Carlton. She started to
toss the note on the bed, then changed her mind. Better to be done with it. She tore open the envelope and
read the scrawled handwriting.

Dear Miss Simpson,
First let me explain that I know you are the supposed Adam Simpson, and I am also aware of the
wager between you and your brother. It has occurred to me that you would probably prefer
Carlton not know about last night's game. This
note is to assure you I will play innocent as to who
the boy was, and if you do the same, Carlton will
have nothing to prove his suspicion.

Yours truly,
Yancy Medford

P.S. I suggest you destroy this note.

In a state of shock, April moved to a chair and
plopped down in a most unladylike manner. The note
slipped from her fingers onto the floor. How did
Yancy know? She'd never met the man until last night!
Were the other players also aware of her real identity?
She'd be the laughingstock of San Diego! She had
known all along Carlton would eventually find out,
but she'd felt sure that, since she'd gotten away with
it, his anger would at least be somewhat tempered.
Carlton would never admit to his friends who his so-
called brother actually was, and she had been positive
no one would ever find out.

Finally her mind began to function. Reaching over the arm of the chair, she retrieved the note. Yes! He did say he knew about the wager, and there was only one person who could have told him. Carlton. The only thing that didn't fit was the poker game. Had Carlton actually incorporated Yancy's help? The game could have gone either way, unless Yancy was a sleight-of-hand artist. It hurt to know that Carlton could possibly have gone to such lengths to get her married off. Well, there was one way to find out the answers.

Yancy laughed. The note contained one sentence:

Would you care to say we played poker and I won?

He scribbled out a reply.

I'll arrive at your house at eight this evening. We can discuss the matter over supper at Maison Riche.

April shook her head, trying to decide what she should do. If only she knew what had transpired between Yancy and Carlton. If her brother hadn't as yet heard about the game, she could ill afford to have Yancy come to the house. She went to her small secretary and pulled out paper and pen.

Carlton would become suspicious if you came to the house. I'll meet you at the restaurant at eight.

April went out back to give the message to the stable hand. She smiled sympathetically at the boy busily oiling the tack. When he looked up, she handed him a coin. "I know you have work to do, Julio, but maybe this will help."

His brown eyes lit up when he saw the money.

"This will be the last time you'll have to go to Mr. Medford's house. You haven't told anyone about this, have you?"

He looked at her adoringly. "No, *señorita*. You asked me not to."

Yancy sat in the French restaurant tapping his fingers on the table. Again he pulled his gold watch from his vest pocket to check the time. The woman was already thirty minutes late. He was not accustomed to waiting for any woman. Had she changed her mind? Another fifteen minutes passed and he was about to have his food brought to the table when he saw George Vigneron leading Miss April Simpson toward him.

As before, she was cool and regal, appearing to have nary a care in the world. Her green silk dress and emerald earrings matched the color of her eyes. Her hair was a masterpiece, and Yancy wondered what it would look like flying free in the wind. He stood and waited.

"You're a bit late," he said when the proprietor had seated her and left. Yancy sat back down.

"Really?" April picked up the menu and studied it.

"I've taken the liberty of ordering."

"How nice," she said sarcastically. "But how do you know what I want?" She gave him a cold smile.

"It saves having to explain what the words mean."

"I'm quite fluent in French, Mr. Medford. I have also toured Europe."

"Last night it was Yancy. How quickly things change."

The waiter arrived with a bottle of wine. "Compliments of the house, Mr. Medford." He poured some in a crystal wineglass and awaited Yancy's approval.

"Excellent," Yancy said after tasting it. "My compliments to George for the selection."

The waiter filled April's glass.

"Please tell the chef we're ready to eat."

"Yes, Mr. Medford."

"I'm not here to be entertained," April said as soon as the waiter left.

"Actually, my dear, I'm surprised you're here at all. Was it a lost slipper or something of equal importance that made you forty-five minutes late?"

"Gentlemen never complain if I'm late," she replied flippantly.

"And ladies never want to keep me waiting."

April gave him a sharp look. "That's as conceited a remark as I've ever heard."

"And yours was as vain a remark as I've ever heard."

"You have quite a reputation with the women, Mr. Medford, but frankly, I for one find you repugnant. I'm leaving." She stood.

"Sit down, April. I'm not above making a scene."

April paused. Though his voice was soft, it was definitely commanding. "You wouldn't," she whispered, quickly glancing about to be sure there wasn't anyone she knew nearby.

"I'm not one of your namby-pamby suitors. Now sit down!"

April was furious at being ordered about but nevertheless did as she was told. "I'm here for only one reason, Mr. Medford." She kept her voice low so that their conversation couldn't be overheard. "Are you and my brother working together to get me married off?"

The question took Yancy completely by surprise. "Try your wine. It's really quite good."

April gave him a hard kick under the table. To her pleasure, she saw him flinch. "Are you going to answer my question?"

Yancy rested his arms on the table and leaned forward. "Like it or not, we will discuss business after dinner. And if you try something like that again, it will be my pleasure to carry you out of here and give you the spanking I suspect you should have had years ago. And that is no idle threat. I asked you to dine with me and that's exactly what you're going to do. Furthermore, you will eat every damn bite!" He leaned back in his chair, his blue eyes daring her to do otherwise.

April was smoldering, but she believed him to be just the type who would carry out his threat. If ever there was a rogue, she was sitting directly across from him! When the meal was served, it took a supreme effort for her not to throw it in Mr. Medford's face.

Yancy continued to study April throughout the meal. Why did he even bother with her? She was so different from last night. She reminded him of a chameleon, changing colors as befitted the circumstance. He'd liked the woman who dared to defy society to enter the Men's Club, but the woman tonight was a spoiled brat who thought she ruled the world. As they ate the lemon soufflé dessert, he finally understood why he remained interested. Admittedly, his pride was at stake, since it was apparent she liked nothing about him. But April Simpson was a challenge. And he had never been able to refuse a challenge.

April had also been giving thought to the situation. Though she refused to look at Yancy, she'd felt his gaze on her throughout the evening. Was he attracted to her? If so, perhaps she could use the fact to her advantage. Getting upset about his rudeness would solve nothing, nor would making him angry. It would be far better if she could make him her ally instead of her enemy.

April blotted her lips with the linen napkin and placed it by the plate. "I must admit, Yancy, that was an excellent dinner." She gave him her best smile.

So, Yancy thought, the chameleon is changing color again.

"I want to apologize for the way I've acted. My only excuse is that I'm worried about the wager with my brother. Can we start over and at least try to be friends?"

If Yancy had never seen honey drip from a woman's mouth, he was surely seeing it now. "I'd like that," he said with equal insincerity.

"We've finished our meal. Can we talk now?" April asked sweetly.

"Absolutely."

"How did you know about the wager with my brother?"

He explained.

"That's a relief. I was beginning to think you were a cardsharper and the two of you had made an arrangement to make sure I lost. Did the other men at the game know my real identity?"

"No, and you do not do justice to your brother. I don't believe Carlton's the type to cheat on a bet."

April suddenly felt guilty for misjudging Carlton.

The conversation ceased until the waiter had finished clearing the table.

April knew the only safe way out of her mess would be to coax Yancy into saying they had played cards and he'd lost. She didn't want to get married! Of course she'd act magnanimous and refuse to take Carlton's horses. She could say she really didn't want them and was simply proving a point. However, it would be heavenly to hear him apologize for the things he'd said.

"Yancy, I want to thank you for being a gentleman and not disclosing my identity. Even to Carlton. But you see, I still have a bit of a problem."

"Oh? What's that?" he asked innocently.

"There is still the matter of a poker game."

"What about the poker game?"

"How do I explain we played, and where?"

"Yes, I imagine that would be a bit of a problem. I guess we could say the game took place at my home."

"You can't be serious!"

"My boat?"

"Of course not."

"My carriage."

"I don't think you are taking this with the right attitude."

"On the contrary. I'm taking it quite seriously. I just don't seem to be able to come up with a solution."

She finished her wine and Yancy refilled the glass. In her anger, she'd eaten little, but he made no comment. She did, however, drink most of the contents of the bottle. He was curious to see how long it would be before the wine took effect.

"Do you have any ideas?" He watched her reach for the glass, noting that it took a bit of effort for her to raise it to her lips.

"No. It's something I'll have to think on." She set the glass on the table, spilling some of the contents.

Yancy laughed.

"I don't happen to think my problems are the least bit funny, Mr. Medford!"

Yancy knew she was unaware of what he was laughing at, which made it all the more amusing.

"But then you're not in my shoes, are you?" Having a degree of difficulty speaking, April lifted her chin and looked him in the eye. "I wonder how you would feel if the circumstances were reversed?"

"Any time I make a bet, my dear, I'm always prepared to pay up. That's part of the game."

"Are you saying I'm not?" She had tried to hold her temper in check, but it was starting to get away from her.

"It would appear that way, wouldn't it?"

"I'm leaving, and don't try to stop me." April propped an unladylike elbow on the table to steady her weaving torso and met Yancy's amused grin with an unyielding stare. "But before I go, I want to say that you are an extremely handsome man."

He nodded. "Thank you. And you are a very beautiful woman."

"Oh, but let me finish. I also think you are a side-winder. In case you don't know, that's a rattlesnake, Mr. Medford. And I don't like rattlesnakes. I never want to see you again. I can handle my own problems."

"And you, my dear, are a cobra, but I will see you again. Probably sooner than you think. You see, I know that before too long you will be happily sharing my bed."

"Of all the nerve!" April jumped up. The quick movement made her dizzy. She didn't even realize she'd knocked over her chair. She staggered, and then there was the blurry realization that she was being carried somewhere.

As Yancy approached the door, he smiled and told George to put the bill on his tab. Without any explanation, he went out the door with April in his arms.

"Is something wrong with Miss Simpson?" her concerned coachman asked.

"No, she's fine. You go on back and I'll see that she gets home."

The coachman hesitated.

Yancy gave him an ingratiating smile. "She's had a little too much to drink and needs some fresh air. I'll see she gets home," he repeated.

"Yes, sir." Relieved, the coachman climbed onto the seat of the carriage and a moment later drove off.

"Where am I?" April muttered.

"On your way home, my dear."

Yancy entered his coach and set April on the seat beside him. Before closing the door he ordered Thomas to head for home. April snuggled up to him, then felt warm lips on hers. Wonderful lips that were kissing her as she'd never been kissed before. She didn't want it to stop. Then everything went black.

When April awoke, her mouth tasted awful. She sat up, her head pounding unmercifully. Groaning, she slowly opened her eyes. Her physical condition was forgotten when she discovered she wasn't in her own bedroom. She remembered the dinner, the wine, the dizziness and someone carrying her. And last, but certainly not least, Yancy's kiss. She placed her hands on her throbbing head. "Oh no," she muttered, distinctly recalling kissing him back. Quite thoroughly, too.

To make matter worse, she had slept in a strange bed with only her underclothing on. Quickly glancing around the bedroom, she finally spied her dress and petticoats lying across a chair.

April jumped out of bed, but had to stand still a moment to stop the dizziness. Head still pounding, but feeling steadier on her feet, she slowly placed one foot in front of the other until she reached her clothes.

Without the services of a maid, dressing proved to be no easy task. After finally managing to get her clothes on in some degree of orderliness, she opened the door and peeked up and down the long hallway. There was no one in sight. Quickly she made her way to the stairs, then began tiptoeing down. She had a sneaky suspicion whose house she was in.

"Good morning."

April stopped and looked down at Yancy, standing at the bottom of the stairs, completely dressed and looking as fit as a fiddle. "What am I doing here?" she demanded.

"Sleeping off your tipsy. Breakfast has been awaiting your pleasure."

Lifting her long skirts a fraction, she continued down the stairs. "I do not want any breakfast. I want to go home. Immediately!"

"I wouldn't be a proper host if I didn't see that you were fed before leaving."

"A host, indeed!" She started toward the front door, then stopped. "Is it locked?" she asked without turning.

Yancy grinned. "You do have a vivid imagination. What kind of a man do you think I am?"

"I don't think you want to hear my answer." She turned and faced the enemy. "How did I get undressed?"

"A maid performed the honor."

April didn't like the way his smile stretched from earlobe to earlobe. "And did I sleep alone?"

"I don't sleep with women who aren't well aware of my lovemaking. It takes away the pleasure."

She sneered. "Pleasure? Do try to be serious."

"You enjoyed my kiss last night, but I realize you've yet to share a man's bed. Therefore, I can believe your lack of understanding in such matters. I would be more than willing to change your unfortunate condition and teach you what you've missed."

The blood drained from April's face. "If I had a gun, I'd shoot you for making such a statement to a lady. Mr. Medford, you are despicable!"

"But honest."

She continued toward the door.

"How do you plan on getting home?" he asked casually.

"If need be, I'll walk."

Before she could place her hand on the doorknob, Yancy stepped forward and turned it for her. "Walking won't be necessary. My carriage is already waiting. You see, I knew you wouldn't tarry. After you, my dear."

April hiked up her skirt and stormed out, still fuming.

Silence prevailed as the coach headed toward April's home. She could see no reason why Yancy had to insist on accompanying her. How could Carlton have dared refer to this man as a gentleman?

"Have you thought about what you're going to say to Carlton?" Yancy asked.

"I . . . I'll think of something. I'm more interested in what reason you could have had for not taking me home last night."

"You're the one who said you didn't want your brother to see us together. Isn't that why you met me at Maison Riche? And how would it have looked when I had to carry you inside?"

April hated his amusement in the face of such a deplorable situation. "You don't give a damn about my reputation, do you?"

"To be perfectly frank, no. But I did care about the reputation of the woman I played poker with."

"What do you mean by that?"

"I believe that woman was the real April Simpson. Not the one I see now. In some strange way, you remind me of Ebenezer Scrooge, in Dickens's *Christmas Carol*. Have you ever read the story?"

"No, and I don't care to."

"Keep on the way you're going and you'll end up an unhappy old woman. Let yourself go, April, and you might see an entirely different world around you."

April was surprised at how serious he'd become. "Oh, you'd like that, wouldn't you! You of all people have no room to talk. You're—"

"But I don't pretend to be something I'm not. You'll have to admit, I've made no secret of my intentions. Stop here, Hartford," he called to the coachman.

April couldn't understand why he would stop. This wasn't her house.

"I thought you might want to walk the short distance home."

"You're right."

He reached over and opened the door for her.

April started to climb out but was suddenly pulled against the hateful man. "What are you doing?" she demanded. As he drew her closer, April knew she was about to be kissed. She tried to escape, but he was holding her too tight. Then his lips were on hers, soft at first, then becoming more demanding.

He finally allowed her to pull away, and laughed. "When a lady spends the night in my home, I think it only proper we kiss goodbye."

"It is my sincere hope, Yancy Medford, that I never set eyes on you again." Again April started to climb out of the carriage.

"But you will."

She stopped and sat back down. "What do you mean by that?"

"I hold the key to your future, my dear. I would be more than willing to remain silent about last night, and even to say we played a poker game and you won. But for a price. Are you really willing to pay that price?"

"Are you trying to blackmail me?"

"I think the question is, how far will you go to keep your brother from knowing the game was played and lost. You should be busily searching for a husband. However, as I said, I'm willing to remain silent."

"That's the most ungentlemanly thing I have ever heard!"

"My dear April, you should know by now that being a gentleman is merely a convenience that money allows. Nothing more, nothing less."

"Gentleman? What would you know about being a gentleman? And just what is your price for remaining silent and saying I won the game?"

"I don't have to answer that. You already know."

"You are a bastard. I would rather marry the first man who came along than submit to such underhandedness! And don't think I'm not going to inform my brother about this." She stepped out of the carriage, and almost fell. Throwing her shoulders back and brushing her loose hair from her face, she marched down the street toward home. Never once did she look back.

Yancy broke out laughing. He would have been sorely disappointed had she said anything different. Now the huffy miss would have to face up to her wager. He would have given anything to witness the confrontation. He motioned his coachman to drive on.

Chapter Four

Ruth was walking through the upstairs hallway when she saw her sister-in-law heading toward her room. Seeing April's condition, Ruth clapped her hand over her mouth in horror. "Oh, my dear, what has happened to you? Your hair and clothing look a mess! Here, let me help you to your room."

"Ruth, if I can walk up the stairs, I can certainly make it to my room." Ruth meant well, and the hurt look on her face made April want to bite off her tongue for speaking so sharply. "Really, Ruth, I'm just fine," she assured the woman. Though Ruth was only three years her senior, April often felt that the quiet beauty was a good twenty years beyond her in maturity.

"I'll see that a bath is prepared immediately and send Nita to assist you," Ruth said, having collected her wits. "April, I'm a good listener. If you need someone to talk to later, I'll be in the sitting room."

Not having had to account for her whereabouts since she was a schoolgirl, April resented Ruth's inquisitiveness, even though it was laced with good intentions. Still, if she did talk to her, maybe Ruth could buffer Carlton's anger. Ruth could also be the one to tell Carlton what a cad Yancy Medford was, and how shabbily he had treated her.

Feeling refreshed after her toilet, and wearing a pale yellow dress with appliquéd daisies that bolstered her morale, April headed downstairs. Though she wasn't about to allow Yancy to blackmail her, neither did she want to face the consequences of the lost wager. There had to be a way of avoiding this entire mess. She needed time. How long would Yancy wait before telling all?

When April entered the sitting room she wasn't expecting to see Carlton. He stood in front of the French doors, hands locked behind his back and a thunderous scowl cemented on his handsome face. Ruth sat near him, nervously twisting a lace handkerchief in her hands.

"So, my brother Adam has deigned to give us the pleasure of his company!" Carlton's words were biting. "Please be seated, sir. I believe we have much to discuss."

Feigning calmness, April glided across the room and gracefully sat on a chair.

"Tell me, *brother,*" Carlton said sarcastically, "are you going to admit you were at the Men's Club two nights ago, or do you intend to play innocent?"

"What are you talking about, Carlton?" Ruth asked. "You know women are not allowed there."

"I'm talking to April. Well?"

"No, I'm not going to deny it."

"Why did they let you enter?" Ruth asked in shocked wonder.

"They didn't," Carlton answered. "They did, however, allow my brother in. You see, April dressed as a man."

Ruth looked at April, stunned. "Is that true?"

"How did you know it was me?" April asked.

"I really didn't figure it out until I heard my friends commenting on what a good poker player you were. May I be so bold as to ask what right you had to enter an establishment that is restricted to men only?"

April's back stiffened. "Was I going to contaminate it? I have been to places in Paris that would turn—"

"Oh, my." Ruth blushed.

"This is not my fault, Carlton! How else was I to play cards with Yancy Medford? You forced the issue, knowing that was the only place I could play a game with him. And there are a few other matters that I think you should be aware of in regard to the man you call a gentleman."

"You lost your wager," Carlton persisted. "You can start paying off by apologizing to Ruth."

"But don't you want to know—"

"Your apology."

April clenched her teeth and lifted her chin. "Ruth, I apologize for what I said about the way you run your household, and I promise to make an effort to be more agreeable." All of a sudden, April knew how to get out of the marriage agreement. She wondered why she hadn't thought of it sooner. She looked at Carlton and smiled. "There is another matter I believe also needs to be settled. You said I could choose my husband-to-be. I have made my decision."

"Fine," Carlton said, still angry. "What poor devil have you selected?"

"Yancy Medford." April was delighted to see her brother's face turn ashen. He stood there, quite obviously at a loss for words.

"And he's agreed to this?" Carlton finally managed to ask.

"Not at all." April made a pretense of smoothing out her skirt. "I recall your saying that whoever I picked, you would personally make sure the gentleman made it to the preacher. As I see it, if you can't do that, the wager is off. After all, I've kept my end of the bargain."

"He would never agree to such an arrangement!"

"I know. In fact, I'm counting on it. As I look at it, there are two options. Either concede that there will be no marriage come Christmas, or tie the man up and keep him a captive until he says 'I do.' But I would think that having Mr. Medford for a brother-in-law would not be to your liking." She proceeded to tell them about the dinner, her being taken to his house, as well as his efforts to blackmail her.

Seeing how red her brother's face had become, April then realized this was one time she might have been wiser to keep her lips closed. She knew she needed to temper the situation before Carlton faced Yancy. "There is really nothing to be upset about. I'm fine, and at least we've all come to realize the type of man he is. I feel we'd be better off just forgetting the whole episode. Now, if you will excuse me, I have an engagement at Elizabeth Holter's house. She's planning a grand ball for Thanksgiving, and has asked me to assist in arranging the details.''

When April had left the room, Ruth broke out laughing. She couldn't even stop when Carlton glared at her.

"May I ask just what's so funny?"

Ruth only laughed harder.

"I find no humor in this, Ruth!"

"Did—" Tears were rolling down her cheeks. "Did she really go in dressed as a man? Don't you see, Carlton? She did the very thing you admired when she was a child. The spark is still there."

"How can you find humor in this mess? Look at what Yancy did to her. Doesn't that bother you in the least?"

Ruth managed to become somewhat sober. "Stop and think a minute, Carlton. You know how your sister is. She said nothing happened, and I believe her, but I'm not too sure about the rest of her story. You've always spoken highly of the man. Does it follow that he would say such things?"

"He has a notorious reputation with women, my dear."

"Therefore, there is no reason for him to blackmail April. Either drop the matter or find out his side of the story." Ruth rose and went to her husband. Placing her arms around his neck, she smiled. "Other than being angry about the way she was treated, April didn't seem the least concerned. I think she's playing a different game of poker with you, my dear, and by choosing Mr. Medford, she's won. Telling us about what he supposedly pulled was what you call...an ace in the hole."

"You could very well be right." He leaned over and kissed his wife. "I don't think my sister has the least idea how perceptive you are."

When Carlton entered the Men's Club that evening, he saw Yancy standing at the bar talking to another member. Carlton had given a lot of thought to what Ruth said, especially when April acted quite smug during supper. He still hadn't decided whether or not to confront Yancy with April's accusations. Yancy was a man one didn't confront unless one was prepared to back it up. And if April had lied, or stretched the truth, things would probably be better left alone. On the other hand, if what she said was true, it was Carlton's obligation to stand up for his family. He was about to turn around and leave when he saw Yancy headed in his direction. He expelled a silent groan.

Yancy was grinning when he said, "Carlton. Just the man I was hoping to see. Let's go sit down and have a drink."

Knowing no way of begging off gracefully, Carlton headed toward one of the small tables.

"How is the wager with your sister going?" Yancy asked after their drinks had been served.

Carlton settled in his seat and took a hard look at the man. "It is my understanding you knew before I did."

"How did you find out?"

"Let's not mince words, Yancy. April told me everything."

Yancy laughed. "So she finally confessed. She probably figured she had no choice when I threatened to blackmail her. Your sister, my friend, is a wily woman. I figured she could use a little nudge."

"So you admit you threatened her. And did she spend the night at your house as well?"

"Now don't go getting yourself all riled. I didn't do a thing. She just became upset because I didn't fall on my knees and kiss her feet."

"She was a complete mess when she returned home. How do you explain that?"

"I think I would be more interested in her explanation. However, she was a mess as a result of a hangover, a bad night's sleep and not having the luxury of a servant to help her with her toilet. Believe me, Carlton, it isn't necessary for me to force women into doing anything against their will. And there is no need to think you have to uphold the family honor. April just received a dose of her own medicine, and she didn't like it one damn bit."

Carlton relaxed. "My wife said it was probably something like that."

"So are you still going to insist on a Christmas wedding?" He motioned for two more drinks.

"Probably not, but I should just to teach her a lesson."

The two drinks were placed in front of them.

"Right now she thinks she has the upper hand." Carlton took a healthy drink before continuing. "You see, she told me she has selected her husband. The problem is, I gave her that choice.''

"Well, since she committed herself, it sounds like your problems are solved. Which one of her followers did she select?''

"You."

Yancy began coughing on the drink he'd just taken. He had to stand to finally catch his breath. "Me?" he exploded. Realizing how loud he'd spoken, he sat down again and asked in a hushed tone, "Why in hell would she pick me?''

"Because she knows she's safe. As I told you before, it was all to teach her a lesson, but instead, I think she's taught me one.''

"So it's a stalemate.''

"You could say that. At least for a short time she was the April I once knew.''

"You're talking about her dressing as a man?''

Carlton laughed. "I have to admit that at first I was sore as hell, but the more I've thought about it the funnier it's become. I wish there was a way I could have watched.''

Yancy rolled the glass in his hands, thinking. "Sounds to me like you need to find a man who is not only willing to marry her, but is also capable of handling her. I don't envy you, my friend. She'll probably end up marrying some namby-pamby and make his life hell. But at least she'll be off your hands.''

Carlton glanced at Yancy. Who better to do the job than the man sitting beside him? In fact, he was the only man Carlton knew who hadn't bowed to April's every wish. "I understand you have a horse you've entered in the race Sunday."

Yancy grinned. "You should place a bet on him. There isn't a horse around that can beat him."

"I disagree. I think I have the fastest steed in the county."

"Care to place a wager?"

Carlton shrugged noncommittally. "What kind of wager?"

"You name the price."

"You're that sure of a victory?"

"I'm that sure."

"Very well, if I lose, my stallion is yours. If you lose, you court April."

"What the hell kind of a bet is that?"

"If by Christmas you have decided you don't want to marry her, we'll consider the wager finalized."

"That doesn't make sense. Of course I won't want to marry her, so you'll have gained nothing. I may indeed marry someday, but certainly not her."

Carlton hoped the same approach that had worked on April would work on Yancy. "Are you saying you don't have that much confidence?"

"It's a ridiculous bet."

"Then you're saying my horse can beat yours."

"I'm saying no such thing." Yancy smiled confidently. "Very well, if you're so anxious to lose your horse, the bet's on. And don't say I didn't give you a chance to back out."

"Good. Oh, there is one other thing. Should you lose, I would prefer April not to know what we've agreed to."

Yancy's smile broadened. "Have it any way you like, my friend. We'll see on Sunday who's the bigger fool."

By the time Carlton returned home, he was so pleased he felt sure his feet weren't even touching the ground. Yancy had the strong hand April needed, and if things turned out the way he hoped, she would settle down and make a most delightful wife.

Carlton was humming as he entered the salon. Ruth sat quietly working on some mending. "My dear," Carlton said proudly, "I think I have found just the husband for April."

"Who?"

"Yancy Medford."

Ruth's face went blank.

Early Sunday morning, the race was run. It was close all the way to the finish line, where Carlton's horse surged forward just in time. Yancy had lost.

When April entered the salon prior to Sunday dinner, she was more than a little surprised to see Yancy quietly talking to Ruth and Carlton. "What are you doing here?" she demanded. As Yancy moved forward, she definitely did not like the twinkle in his blue eyes.

He lifted her hand and kissed the back of it. "Why, my dear," he said smoothly, "since we are to be married, I felt it only proper that there be a period of courting. I intend to be at your side every day so we can become better acquainted."

"But this can't be!" She glanced at her brother. "You know what kind of a cad he is. How can you even consider such a union?"

"It was your choice, April."

"No! I won't have it. I've changed my mind. There is another I wish to marry. Sidney Bishop."

Carlton looked at her sympathetically. "I'm sorry, my dear, but you have already made your choice. As your guardian, I shall hold you to your commitment. Now how do you think Yancy must feel having to listen to us carry on so?"

"I don't care what Yancy thinks."

"I'm sure you'll feel differently by the time we wed," Yancy said confidently. "Other women have found me to be most charming."

"Oh!"

April started to leave the room, but Yancy grabbed her arm and placed it in the crook of his elbow, effectively detaining her. "I do believe supper is ready." He headed for the dining room. When they reached the table, Yancy seated April then took the chair beside her.

Seething, April refused to partake in any of the conversation and hardly ate a thing. Watching Yancy charm Carlton and Ruth didn't improve her mood one bit. They were thoroughly enjoying his company. How could they be so blind? The man might be handsome enough to steal a woman's breath away, but she considered him dishonest and shifty.

As April began to recover from her shock at discovering Yancy was agreeable to the marriage, she started thinking of ways to get out of it. The solution was actually quite simple. She'd make him miserable and he'd withdraw from the agreement. Unthinkingly, she smiled.

Everyone at the table saw the smile and knew April had devised another plan of attack. Carlton looked at Yancy and shrugged his shoulders.

Yancy had already accepted his fate. If he was to court April, he was going to do it in proper fashion. He also knew April would pull every stunt she could think of to make him back off. But it wasn't going to work, at least not until he decided he'd fulfilled his debt. Wouldn't the beautiful vixen change her colors if she knew he had no intention of marrying her?

"My dear," Yancy said evenly, "since we are now betrothed, I shall be accompanying you to the Holter ball tomorrow night. Do try to look your most charming. I have a reputation to uphold."

"And I would appreciate it, *my dear,* if you would make an effort to act like a gentleman, something you seem to have difficulty with."

"You are absolutely right. Something you would do well to remember." He gave her a friendly smile.

Seeing the glint in Yancy's eyes, it was all Ruth could do to keep from laughing. Carlton was right. Yancy and April would make the perfect couple. "You will be having Thanksgiving dinner with us, won't you, Yancy?" she asked.

"It would be my pleasure."

Yancy told April what time he would arrive at the house the next night, but other than that, they exchanged no further words.

When Yancy finally left, April turned her full attention on her brother. "How can you even consider my marrying such a man?" she demanded. "I would think you'd be more apt to shoot him after the way he treated me!" She rubbed her temples. "I guess I never realized how desperate you were to get me out of the house."

Carlton was ready to capitulate. He'd come to believe nothing could penetrate April's thick hide, but seeing hurt in her eyes was more than he could handle. "April..."

"It's not that we want you out of the house," Ruth spoke up. She went over and hugged her sister-in-law's shoulders. "We want to see you happily settled with a life of your own. Contrary to what you may be thinking, we both love you dearly. You will always be welcome here."

April stormed out of the room, not wanting anyone to see the tears forming in her eyes.

The following evening, April stood in front of the mirror, checking her appearance one last time. Her dress was created from pale blue silk crepe, with a neckline scooped low in the front and back and with straps over her shoulders, leaving her arms bare. The skirt was full and sweeping, the train just the right length. Her hair had been pulled to the back, and small cloth flowers were pinned among the curls that cascaded down. Her only other adornments were long diamond and pearl earrings and a matching bracelet. Pleased with her appearance, she picked her gloves off the bed and pulled them on.

April had recovered from last night, her composure and self-esteem intact. There was really no doubt in her mind that her family loved her and truly thought the plans being made were for her own good. She'd come to accept that she had gotten herself into this fix, and it was up to her to get herself out.

Her problems now stemmed from something entirely different. She'd always had control over her adoring suitors, and felt comfortable in this dominant role. But such was not the case with Yancy Medford. Though she would never admit it to a soul, he frightened her. She had no control, nor did she seem to be able to manipulate or intimidate him. She didn't even understand the man. Why would he agree to be her husband? It didn't make sense. She'd certainly never seen any indication that he wanted to marry, and if he did it would certainly not be to her. They didn't even know each other!

April picked up her chinchilla cloak and placed it over her arm. She silently vowed that tonight she wasn't going to worry about such things. This was the first ball she'd been to since her return from Europe, and she had every intention of enjoying herself.

When April entered the parlor to join the others, she had to admit that Yancy was a most handsome man in his formal attire. But then, he wore all his clothes well. Certainly no one could accuse him of being prissy. His broad shoulders tapered to narrow hips, and even his sculptured face left no doubt that he was totally male.

"I do believe you have surpassed yourself this evening," Yancy complimented as he took April's cloak and placed it around her shoulders. "It was almost worth the wait." He glanced toward Carlton and Ruth. "If everyone is ready, my carriage is out front."

All the windows were alight and the ball was in full progress when the carriage stopped in front of the elegant mansion. When the two couples entered, Elizabeth and Jason Holter came forward to welcome them. The women acknowledged one another, and the men shook hands.

"I was beginning to think you weren't coming," Elizabeth said. "But you're always late, April, and I should have known better. I don't believe I've met your handsome escort." She offered her hand to Yancy.

"Yancy Medford," Yancy said, brushing a kiss across the back of her hand.

No one missed the surprise on Elizabeth's face. "I've heard a great deal about you, Mr. Medford. You should be ashamed of yourself for taking so long to get acquainted."

"My sincere apologies."

Elizabeth was in the height of her glory. All her friends had tried more than once to invite the elusive man to their gatherings, but as far as she knew, this was the first social event of its kind he had attended. Her ball would now be a raging success, and quite the talk of the town. "I hope your evening is most enjoyable," she cooed.

"With such a charming hostess, how could it not be?"

"Oh my," Elizabeth said, obviously pleased with the compliment. "He *is* a charmer."

No one heard April's disgusted grunt.

A butler took their wraps, and the two couples moved on to the ballroom. When they entered the large room, a full orchestra was playing a waltz, and the beautifully gowned women swirling around the floor with their partners made the room a blaze of color. It seemed to April that all those not dancing turned their heads upon seeing her on the arm of such a talked-about personality. She could even hear people whisper. Remembering how all the women had become aflutter when she had been inquiring about Yancy, April smiled. She knew there wasn't a woman in the place who wasn't pea green with envy and dying to know how she had managed to capture the notorious Yancy Medford as her escort.

Before anyone could ply her with questions, Yancy led her into the dance and April quickly discovered that for a man his size, he was very light of foot. Too bad his personality wasn't as agreeable as his dancing.

April's dance card was quickly filled, as all the eligible young blades vied for her attention. But every time she danced around the long room, she saw Yancy with yet another woman in his arms. April thought it disgusting that the ladies laughed and smiled up at him as if he were a Greek god.

Following through with her resolution to be rid of the man, on several occasions she sought him out. At such times she would order him to bring her a drink of punch or anything else she could think of. To her aggravation he never balked or complained. This wasn't what she'd expected, although it did please her vanity to have him waiting on her.

Seeing her plan wasn't working, April decided to try a different tactic. When women approached her with questions concerning her relationship to the handsome gentleman, April replied that he was just like a puppy dog she kept around for amusement. Wait until he hears that bit of news, she thought to herself.

It wasn't until later that April received her first shock of the evening. Clarence French informed her that according to Yancy, he had escorted April to the party only because he felt sorry for her.

"He also said you had asked your brother to arrange a marriage between you," Clarence added.

April's eyes grew as wide as wagon wheels. "How dare that insolent man make such a statement!" she exploded. "Did anyone else hear him?"

Clarence's cheeks turned red. "Well, there were a few men standing close by who had gone outside to enjoy a smoke," he said apologetically. "Of course I'm not knowledgeable in fisticuffs, but someone should have given him a good beating for saying such an ungentlemanly thing about you."

By now everyone has heard about it, April thought angrily. The women are probably whispering and laughing behind their fans at this very moment. The nerve of the man!

"I want you to know I didn't believe a word of it."

"Thank you, Clarence." April glanced around the room. "Do you know where Mr. Medford is now? I would like to have a word with him."

The music suddenly stopped, and Elizabeth Holter rushed to the middle of the floor and clapped her hands. "May I have everyone's attention?" she asked excitedly. After she made the request several times, the room quieted. "I feel so privileged to announce the engagement of Yancy Medford to our lovely April Simpson."

The room hummed with voices as everyone began talking at once. April wanted to find a chair and crawl under it. Instead, she smiled as one person after another came to offer their congratulations. "There will be no wedding!" she mumbled under her breath. She felt an arm placed around her shoulders and, turning, discovered Yancy standing by her side. "I want to talk to you," she demanded.

Yancy raised an eyebrow. "Puppy dog?"

"Thank you...thank you," April said as more congratulations were given.

"Will the wedding be soon?" a plain-looking woman asked.

"Christmas," Yancy replied. "I consider it the perfect time, since I will be marrying an angel." He hugged April's shoulder and grinned.

"Oh, that's so romantic. You make a beautiful couple."

"If you'll excuse us," April said not too kindly, "I would like to have a private word with my... betrothed."

"Oh, but of course."

The couple left.

"Would you be so kind as to step out to the courtyard with me?" April asked Yancy. "At this moment

I can think of nothing I would enjoy more than to scratch your eyes out! But my, my. Whatever would people think?" she said sarcastically.

Yancy laughed. "You lead, I'll follow."

By the time they made it through the maze of people and outside, April's temper had grown by leaps and bounds. Convinced they were alone, she turned to face her nemesis. The light silhouetted his large frame, but though she couldn't see his face, she aimed her hand in the right direction. He caught her wrist, preventing the slap she'd intended.

April jerked her arm free. "By all that is holy, what right did you have to make such an announcement or to say I asked Carlton to arrange a marriage? Was it to humiliate me?"

"What's wrong, Duchess, you can give but can't take? You brought it on yourself. Whatever you try to pull, I have every intention of retaliating. At least my comment bore some semblance of truth. Saying I'm your puppy dog was an out-and-out lie."

"You're insufferable!"

"I don't think you can afford to cast stones, my sweet. As for the announcement, Carlton made it, not I. Now, is there anything else you care to discuss?"

"I will not marry you. I'd slit my throat first."

Yancy let out a deep laugh.

"I mean it!"

"Not in a thousand years. You might try slitting mine, though."

"Why are you doing this, Yancy? I can't believe you want to marry me any more than I want to marry you. We'd end up killing each other within a month."

"I don't think so."

"You haven't answered my question!"

"I don't have to answer your question. However, should you ask nicely..."

April inhaled deeply in an effort to regain her composure. "No, Mr. Medford," she said, "I won't."

Yancy chuckled.

"Nor will I grovel at your feet," she added.

"Likewise, my dear. Now that we've settled that, are we finished with our little conversation?"

"Tomorrow I want to go shopping. As my betrothed, I will expect you to be at my house at eleven in the morning to escort me. Then the following day Ruth and I will be at your house to inspect the servants and see that I'm moving into a properly run place. Naturally I'll want a suite of rooms of my own. I'll start attending to those arrangements once I see how your house is laid out. Another wing may have to be built. And—"

"I'm so fortunate to have such a capable fiancée."

"Yes. You are."

"Then from what you've said, I shall assume you have accepted the marriage agreement and the wedding will take place on Christmas Day."

April lifted her skirts and slowly strolled away, but not out of hearing distance. "Unless you change your mind," she said, keeping her back turned.

Yancy moved behind her and circled her tiny waist with his hands. She struggled but he had no trouble holding her still.

"You are taking liberties!" April practically spit out the words. "Release me at once!"

He leaned down and kissed the base of her neck, then trailed his tongue upward until he could nibble her earlobe. "Since we are to be married," he whispered, "I should have the right to taste some of the pleasures you'll be offering."

April stiffened. "There... there will be no pleasures." She *would not* allow him to have any effect on her. "I have no intention of sharing your bed." Suddenly she was spun around, and before she could resist he pulled her into his arms and his lips were on hers. April steeled herself not to react, even though his kiss was coaxing and admittedly most pleasurable. When he sucked on her bottom lip she squeezed her eyes shut, fighting the excitement that ran up her spine.

"Should we marry," he said, "I guarantee you will share my bed."

April's eyes flew open. "Is that a threat?"

"Uh-huh."

April struggled to free herself, then stopped when he clamped her hands behind her, easily holding them with just one of his own. She couldn't prevent the quiver that ran through her body as he trailed a finger down the rise of her breast, stopping where the low-cut bodice began.

"You're full of fire, April my love, and you're just waiting for someone with the right match to light it."

His smile and bearing made it clear to April that what had just taken place had had absolutely no effect on the impudent man. Probably something he did quite frequently, according to his reputation! "If you're finished, Mr. Medford, you can remove your finger and release me. I would like to return to more pleasant company."

"As your fiancé, I claim the rest of your dances."

"I refuse."

His finger moved inside the bodice. "Do you want me to light the fire?"

April knew it would take little to lower the material and expose her swollen breasts. For a fraction of a moment, she almost wished he would. "There is no fire, Mr. Medford, only loathing."

Yancy broke out laughing, removed his finger and released her. "As I noted before, you do a good bluff." Still grinning, he took hold of her elbow and led her back toward the house. "I meant what I said about claiming the rest of your dances. Also, I suggest you say only nice things about me from now on, or I shall retaliate. You have but one thing to remember, my dear. As ye give, so shall ye receive."

When they entered the ballroom, the first person April saw was Ruth, heading toward her.

Yancy leaned down and said quietly, "Remember, every single dance."

"You were gone so long, people were starting to talk," Ruth said, but she was smiling.

"If you will excuse me, I shall fetch April some punch. I'm sure she needs it."

"Is something wrong?" Ruth asked as soon as Yancy left. "Your face is flushed."

"I cannot marry that man! I am quite willing to abide by Carlton's decree that I marry. But surely he could allow me to make another choice."

"You're just nervous. I've seen other women go through the same thing. I didn't. I was too in love with your brother."

"You don't understand, Ruth. I'm desperate to be rid of the man."

Ruth's heart went out to her lovely sister-in-law. But Ruth saw something in April's green eyes she'd never seen before. Could it be April was starting to have feelings for the handsome Mr. Medford? "Just give it time, dear, and see what happens."

"I don't have time! Christmas is only a month away!"

"Excuse me, Miss Simpson, but I believe this next dance is ours."

April turned and looked at the short dandy with a wide mustache and long sideburns. Out of pure hatefulness she started to take his offered hand, but suddenly thought better of it. She had no idea how Yancy would retaliate if she accepted, but there was no doubt in her mind that he would indeed retaliate. "I'm sorry," she said kindly, "but I have promised the rest of my dances to my fiancé."

Ruth was completely taken aback. How in heaven's name had Yancy managed that? Ruth found herself becoming more and more impressed with the gentleman.

For April, the rest of the evening seemed almost unreal, with Yancy constantly at her side. Well-wishers continued to come forth to bid them future happiness, and Yancy always acted the perfect gentleman.

When they left the ball, April was convinced there wasn't a single soul who didn't think Yancy Medford was the most marvelous man God had ever created.

Chapter Five

Ruth sat watching April pace the floor. "Are you sure you told him to be here at eleven?" she asked.

"Yes, and I even repeated it before leaving the coach last night. I refuse to wait a moment longer. How dare he keep me waiting for almost an hour! When and if he decides to make an appearance, tell him I've changed my mind about going shopping."

They heard footsteps, and a moment later Yancy entered the room. He went directly to Ruth. "Carlton is very fortunate to have such a lovely wife." He brushed a kiss on her offered hand. "I hope my delay hasn't inconvenienced you in any way."

"Not at all. I'm afraid I can't say the same for April, however. Shame on you for being so late."

April watched with her mouth open. Yancy hadn't even acknowledged her presence!

"Will you be joining us today?" Yancy asked Ruth.

"No, I've already done most of my Christmas buying. You two go on and enjoy yourselves."

Yancy finally turned and looked at April. As usual, she was quite stunning in her apricot town suit. "Are you ready, April?" he asked nonchalantly.

"Do you have any idea how late you are?"

"It would be my guess that it is approximately the same length of time you kept me waiting at the restaurant the other night." He cocked a dark eyebrow. "Shall we go? I also have shopping to do. Unlike Ruth, I've purchased very little for Christmas."

April squared her shoulders and headed for the doorway. If she hadn't planned on making Yancy's day miserable, she would have flatly refused to go anywhere with the man.

"Oh, Yancy," Ruth said as she stood, "you're still planning on having Thanksgiving dinner with us tomorrow, aren't you?"

"I'm looking forward to it. Will that be before or after you've inspected my house?"

"I beg your pardon?"

"Hasn't April informed you of her plans to remodel my house?"

April flinched, but her steps didn't falter as she left the room. Out of sight, she halted to hear what else was said.

Ruth gave Yancy a blank look. "What are you talking about? Why would she want to do that?"

Yancy laughed. "I'll let her explain. What time..."

Satisfied, April continued toward the front door. The only reason she'd said anything about redoing Yancy's house was to vex him. She wasn't surprised it hadn't worked. In fact, nothing she'd tried so far seemed to deter the man. She smiled as she considered placing nitroglycerin in his bedroom.

The butler opened the door and April stepped outside. To her surprise, there was no carriage waiting.

She looked up and down the wide, circular drive. There wasn't even one in sight. Hearing the door open and close behind her, she asked, "How do you propose we get to town?" She could feel Yancy's presence by her side.

"How else?" he replied. "We walk." He took hold of her elbow to lead her down the steps.

April balked. "I have no intention of walking!"

"You plan on traipsing me from one store to another in hopes of wearing me out, so I figured a stroll to town would be of little consequence. It's only a short distance."

April wasn't going to admit his assumption was correct.

"Or would you rather I carry you?"

April snickered viciously. "You couldn't possibly carry me that far."

"Would you care to find out?"

"No, I wouldn't. I am just as capable of walking as you are." She proceeded down the stairs without his help.

By the fifth block, April's breathing was labored. "Must we walk so fast?" she snapped at Yancy.

"Not at all. You're the one who set the pace."

She hated him. He wasn't even panting.

April blessed her good fortune that the first shop they came to was a milliner's. Though she had never frequented the place, she went straight inside, knowing she would finally be able to sit down.

"Please have a seat, madam," the milliner said enthusiastically. "Are you looking for anything in particular? We have a wide selection."

Yancy sat on another chair and relaxed. He thoroughly enjoyed watching April try on one awful hat after another while at the same time telling the milliner how lovely they were. He knew April had gotten her second wind when she stood and said, "I'm afraid none is suitable. Perhaps another time." Yancy followed her out the door.

For two hours, April marched from one store to another. In each one she stopped and looked at practically every item for sale. The only thing she purchased was a diamond brooch for Ruth's Christmas present. Through it all, it aggravated her that Yancy expressed not a single complaint. The effort had done nothing but wear her out. Though the thought of having to walk back was almost more than she could bear, she told Yancy she was ready to return to the house.

"Does that mean you're through shopping?"

"Of course that's what it means!"

"Then why don't we have lunch?"

April was ready for any excuse to delay the inevitable.

It wasn't until they had finished their meal that Yancy said, "Now we can do my shopping."

April's eyes became two sizes larger. "Surely you're teasing?"

"Why not? I went shopping with you."

April smiled wryly. His words spoken last night about giving and receiving rang in her head. Yancy was not a man to be fooled with. One way or another he paid her back for everything she tried. So why did she even bother? Invariably she ended up on the wrong end of the stick.

Yancy studied the beautiful woman sitting across from him. Her suit wasn't nearly as crisp as when they had started out, and her hair was beginning to droop. Her cheeks were a bit flushed, but other than that, her face showed no sign of what she'd been through today. She still carried herself regally. Had she learned her lesson yet? He doubted it. Come tomorrow she'd try a different line of attack. He had to admire her gumption. In fact, there were quite a few things he was beginning to admire about her.

April had had enough for today. He pulled his watch out and checked the time. "On second thought, it's getting too late. I have a dinner engagement. If I don't return you home, I'll be pushed for time."

April knew he was just giving her an excuse, and oddly she was grateful. She suddenly wondered why he didn't ask her to go to the engagement as well. Another woman? "Who will you be dining with?" April asked suspiciously. "Anyone I know?"

"Hazel Brookmire asked me to her house for supper."

April's temper flared. "I see." She had difficulty maintaining an outward calmness. "I've heard rumors that the widow has every intention of making you her second husband."

Yancy grinned. "Now that would be rather difficult, since I'm supposed to be marrying you."

"It would seem to me that your attitude is a bit one-sided."

"Why do you say that?" Yancy knew exactly what she meant. She was referring to last night when he had refused to allow her to dance with other men.

"Nothing," April replied. She drank the last of her coffee and set the empty cup on the table. "Are you ready to leave?"

Yancy wasn't even sure why he'd lied, much less why he'd included Hazel Brookmire in his fabrication. Maybe his pride was stinging again and he wanted to see if he could make April jealous, knowing she would have heard the preposterous rumors about his relationship with the lovely widow.

By the time April reached her bedroom, she was drained and her feet were killing her. She had been tempted to let Yancy carry her the last few blocks, but of course she didn't. She refused to give him the satisfaction of knowing he had worn her out.

April was standing in the middle of her bedroom when the maid entered carrying the bucket of hot water April had requested the moment she stepped inside the front door.

"You'll have to take my shoes off, Maria. I don't think I can even bend over."

It seemed to take forever for Maria to get her undressed, but finally April was able to sit on the lounge. She expelled a deep sigh when her feet were submerged in the hot water. "Maria, bring...please bring me writing material, and I'll want someone to deliver a note for me."

"*Sí, señorita.*" The maid hurried out of the room.

By the time the note was on its way and she'd had a foot massage, April was ready to take a short nap. She smiled as she closed her eyes. Yancy Medford was going to learn all about an eye for an eye.

April smiled and spoke to everyone she knew dining at the Horton House restaurant. She wanted to be very sure Yancy heard of her dinner engagement. Her escort was Larry Crisp, the most handsome of her beaux. Admittedly he wasn't as attractive as Yancy, but she deemed it a pleasure to be with someone witty for a change.

As the evening progressed, however, April became bored. Even her laugh sounded forced. While they ate delicious steaks, Larry plied her with all sorts of compliments. For the first time they sounded like nothing more than well-rehearsed words.

Though she tried not to, April found herself comparing Larry with Yancy. Larry didn't exude that masculine virility that seemed inherent in Yancy's very being, nor did Larry have the self-assuredness and quiet strength that was also part of Yancy's character. April shifted uncomfortably in her chair. As a matter of fact, Larry didn't even have as good a sense of humor as Yancy did.

Why am I thinking these things? April chastised herself. Yancy is nothing more than an abrasive man that I need out of my life once and for all!

April glared at her partially eaten dessert. At least Larry hadn't asked why she wanted to go out with him when she was supposed to be engaged. He probably considers himself irresistible, she thought.

"Larry," she said to her dinner partner, "I'm afraid I have a terrible headache. Would you be upset if I asked you to take me home?"

"Not in the least. Perhaps you're coming down with something."

"I think you're right."

Because Christmas was always such a big affair, only the family and very close friends were invited to Thanksgiving dinner at the Simpson household. Yancy arrived at three in the afternoon and easily blended in. April kept waiting for him to make some comment about her going out with another man last night, but none was forthcoming. As usual, he exemplified the charming partner. Had he not heard the news yet?

When Yancy returned home that night, he was grinning. He'd watched April fidget during his entire visit and was well aware of the reason for her discomfort. This morning, so-called friends had made a bee-line to his house to inform him that April had dined out with another man. He'd managed to avoid a scandal by saying she had his permission. Then he'd made up his mind to remain silent about the matter and let her fret over it for a while. She knew he'd get even.

With Thanksgiving out of the way, the Christmas season began in earnest. Store windows were gaily decorated, and people were busy shopping and planning balls and parties. For a week Yancy wined and dined April, always acting the perfect gentleman. She found it hard to believe that he never once so much as tried to kiss her. When he returned her to her house he would thank her for the pleasant evening and leave. If she tried to have a serious conversation with him, he managed to change the subject. April was beginning to view his new gentlemanly behavior as most unflattering. Had he lost interest? This was something she'd never had to deal with before and her pride smarted. At the same time, Christmas was just around the corner and Yancy showed no inclination to call off the wedding. April was becoming desperate.

They had been to the theater and were awaiting Yancy's carriage when April decided it was time to have it out with him. "I know it's late, but could we drive around for a while? I want to talk to you."

"Very well." Yancy told his driver to head for the park before they climbed inside. "What is it you want to talk about?" he asked as the carriage moved forward. "What I'm going to buy you for Christmas?"

"The greatest gift you could give me would be to call off the marriage. I demand to know if you plan to continue with this farce."

"Yep. Fight it all you like, but come Christmas, we'll be married."

"Why, for God's sake? We don't even like each other. You've been around me enough to know I have a most disagreeable disposition."

"I've been around you enough to know you're a woman who craves fulfillment."

"That's the most absurd thing I've ever heard. And how would you know? You don't even try to... Well, that's of little importance." April looked out the carriage window, unable to see anything because of the cloudy night. "I warn you, Yancy, if you don't break off this engagement, I'll run away."

"You don't know what you want," he said in a hushed voice.

"Now you're beginning to sound like Carlton. How could I ever have been so stupid as to make that foolish bet with him?"

Yancy had asked himself the same question on more than one occasion. Carlton had cleverly trapped him, in more ways than one. "Tell me, my dear, why did you go out with Larry Crisp?"

"I've been wondering how long it would take you to bring up that subject. If you could enjoy the evening with your lady friend I saw no reason why I shouldn't enjoy the company of a very handsome gentleman."

"Did he kiss you good-night?"

"I don't believe you have the right to ask that question. I certainly haven't inquired about your activities. However, I don't mind answering it. Yes, he did," she lied, "and it was most pleasurable."

"But not as enjoyable as mine."

"Better. He didn't have to force himself on me."

"If you're so free with your kisses, why don't you kiss me? At least it would give you a better means of comparison."

It surprised April that the thought of kissing him made her heart pump faster. "You're changing the subject again. I want to know why you are so insistent about this wedding."

Yancy laughed. "You know, April, for a week I have tried acting the gentlemen, thinking that just perhaps we could settle this situation in an amicable manner. But as I suspected, you have too wild a spirit. I guess I'm just going to have to handle things differently."

"Are you going to answer my question?" April persisted.

"I'll answer your question, but not now. I'll do it when I'm good and ready."

"Then take me home! You had your chance, Yancy Medford, and you won't get another one."

"I wouldn't count on it. Now if I remember correctly, we were talking about comparing kisses. The least I can do is to help with your education. And since you apparently experiment on all your escorts, I'm waiting for my kiss."

It galled April to hear humor in his voice. "Very well, but it's the man's place to kiss the woman."

"It depends on the man. I personally like it when a woman comes to me."

"You mean women."

"Perhaps."

The inside of the carriage became so quiet April felt almost smothered by it. Still, she refused to turn in his direction.

"You are indeed a proud woman, April Simpson, but pride can also destroy a person." Yancy reached out and drew her to him.

April was confused. She wanted to push him away, while at the same time her body tingled with anticipation. When his lips touched hers, it was but a brush of a kiss. "Afraid?" she heard him ask. Yes, her mind screamed, I'm scared as hell! Then his lips returned to hers, coaxing, demanding. All thoughts left her mind except the glorious need to have him continue. He pulled her across his lap and her arms went around his neck.

"Am I giving you a good comparison?" he asked between tiny kisses.

His mouth was so close she could feel his breath. "Yes," she whispered, her voice husky.

Yancy kissed the base of her neck. "Did he do something I should know about that would make this more pleasurable for you?"

"Oh, no. You're doing just fine."

He pushed back her cloak and trailed his tongue down the rise of her breast. "Are you sure?"

"Absolutely," she said breathlessly. It was all April could do to even manage a reply. To her surprise, she felt herself being lifted and placed back on her side of the seat.

"Good," Yancy said, "then I guess there is no need to carry this any further."

April was mortified. She couldn't even come up with a tart reply.

Yancy rapped on the top of the carriage and directed the driver to head for April's house. He settled back in his seat. "I don't want to ever hear so much as a whisper of your seeing another man, or next time you won't leave my arms a maiden. Do I make myself clear?"

April noted that there was not even a trace of humor in Yancy's voice this time. "I believe I have the right to make the same request of you," she bit out at him.

"That sounds fair to me."

When Yancy walked her to her door, April wasn't about to let him kiss her after the way he'd acted in the coach. But when the butler opened the door and Yancy turned to leave, April was furious. "Shut the door, Juanito," she ordered before lifting her skirts and taking off after Yancy. "Just one minute!"

Yancy had already reached the coach. He turned and waited for her to catch up with him.

"I am tired of this game of cat and mouse!" April dropped her skirts and looked up at him. "First you ply me with wine, take me to your house, say you intend to bed me, force your kisses on me, then you turn around and appear not to be interested. I have never been treated as despicably by anyone as I have by you!"

"If you wanted me to kiss you good-night, why didn't you just say so?" He reached for her, but she darted out of reach.

"Don't you dare touch me," April warned. "Let me try to make it clear to you what I'm saying. I not only don't want to marry you, I don't ever want to see you again!"

"I don't make idle threats, so let me make things clear to you. We will marry and I will have you in my bed. Like it or not, you are already starting to have feelings for me. You derive pleasure from my kisses, and you're more than a little curious as to what it would be like to lie naked beside me and discover the secret pleasures you know I can show you."

April slapped him so hard, the sound echoed through the night air. She spun on her heel and headed back up the stairs to the door. By the time the butler opened it, April heard the carriage driving away.

In her room, April was flooded with anger and panic. There wasn't a thing Yancy had said that wasn't true. She'd tried ignoring then fighting her feelings, but now that the truth had been spoken aloud, she could no longer deny it. She had no idea how or why it had happened, but she was falling in love. At the same time, it frightened her to know that Yancy could control her mind and body so easily. Never once had he shown affection or expressed any feeling of love. She had to get away while she could still force herself to leave. Tomorrow she'd talk to Ruth and plead with her sister-in-law to help her escape.

Chapter Six

The next morning Ruth collapsed onto the chair in her husband's office. "I can't believe it! Yancy really wants to go through with the wedding?"

Carlton grinned. "That's what he told me less than an hour ago."

"Does he love April?"

"I didn't ask, and he didn't say."

"But Carlton," Ruth said worriedly, "if they don't love each other they'll be unhappy for the rest of their lives. You can't do that to April."

"Yancy assured me that if April hasn't declared her love by Christmas Eve, he'll back off. He has a plan."

When Ruth returned home, she found April waiting in the salon. It took but one glance to see how distraught the younger woman was.

"My dear," Ruth said as she set her packages down, "what's the matter?"

April rushed to her sister-in-law. "Ruth, you have to let me have some money. I'll receive my inheritance in three months and I promise to pay you back."

"But you have money, and if you need anything Carlton will pay your bills."

"Please try to understand. I have to leave. I can't stay and marry Yancy. Oh Ruth, you have to help me. You're the only one I can trust. I want to return to Europe."

"Sit down, April. This isn't something that has to be done this very moment." Ruth guided April to the sofa. "Do you hate Yancy so much?" she asked when they were seated.

"I detest him."

The look on April's face and the way she said it made Ruth question the validity of the statement. Still, she tried to soothe her sister-in-law. "Well, if you truly feel you won't be happy with Yancy, I'll try talking with Carlton. Believe me, dear, he usually listens to what I say."

"You don't understand. Yancy will force me to marry him!"

"Now how can he do that?"

"He . . . well, he . . . he just could."

"April, is there something you're not telling me? Has he—?"

"Yes." April glanced down, unable to look Ruth in the eye. She said a silent prayer asking God to forgive her. "I'm not in the family way, but if this continues I will be. Then Carlton will insist I marry him." She looked up and said honestly, "Ruth, when Yancy's around I seem to have no control over anything. I've never known such a man and it scares me."

Ruth was thoroughly upset. "I didn't know . . . I would never have thought he . . . Of course I'll help you

get away, at least for a week or two, or until I can
make Carlton see what a mistake he's made. Besides,
you need time to yourself. Carlton isn't going to like
this one bit, but he'll change his mind when I explain.
We'll have to start getting you packed right away. You
can leave early in the morning.''

"Where can I go?"

"To the summer house in the mountains."

"Yes. That's perfect! Ruth, I'd rather Carlton not
know about what we discussed. I know he would be
disappointed in me, and I couldn't stand that." Besides, April thought, I don't want him to get into a
fight with Yancy, "And you won't tell Carlton until
after I've left, will you?"

Though she couldn't tell April, Ruth knew that the
only way to get Carlton to put an end to all this would
be to tell him everything. "He won't know you've left
until late tomorrow night. You need to send a note to
Yancy saying you're feeling ill and will be staying
home tonight."

"You have to promise that under no circumstance
will you tell Yancy where I am."

"I promise. Now don't you worry about another
thing. You just wait and see. Everything will turn out
fine."

When Yancy read April's quickly penned note, he
had a gut feeling that she was up to something, but he
decided to give her the benefit of the doubt. Besides,
he'd enjoy a quiet night at home, especially since in a
couple of days he would be doing a lot of riding. As
he'd explained to Carlton, he was going to take April
back to Calico. Oh, she'd fight and scream like a cor-

nered cat, but it wouldn't do her any good. It was time she realized how proud she should be of just what her father had accomplished, and remembered the happier days of the past.

As soon as Carlton left for his office the next morning, April came out of her room. In the kitchen, a plate of eggs, gravy and biscuits was on the table waiting for her.

When Ruth was satisfied with the supplies on the packhorse, she waited patiently for her sister-in-law to finish her breakfast. Wearing a divided skirt, flannel shirt, boots and a wide-brimmed hat with a chin strap, April looked very different from her usual, fashionable self. Her beautiful blond hair hung down her back, contained only by a scarf at the base of her neck. Ruth suddenly realized that this was the young woman Carlton had talked about. The girl who had ridden horses since childhood, the girl Carlton had taught to shoot as soon as she was big enough to hold a rifle. Ruth had to smile. Whether it was the wager, Carlton or Yancy, the real April Simpson was starting to emerge. This morning there was even an air of serenity about her that Ruth had never seen. However the engagement turned out, Ruth was now confident that April would be all right.

She wasn't at all pleased when April refused to let one of the servants go with her, but Ruth ended up letting the younger woman have her way. Carlton had often told her that in matters such as this, April was more than capable of taking care of herself. Ruth hoped Carlton hadn't exaggerated.

April mounted the big gelding and took the reins of the packhorse that Julio handed her. She smiled down at Ruth. "Thank you," she said sincerely. "And don't worry, I'll be fine." She nudged the horse with her knees.

Not until April was well out of town and riding through the hills did she finally relax. She began to realize how much she'd missed the hunting trips she and Carlton used to take.

Ruth didn't tell her husband that April had left until that night. Carlton was absolutely furious. It took a lot of talking on Ruth's part to finally calm him down. He flared up again when he found out that Yancy had taken advantage of his sister, and he stormed out of the house before Ruth could stop him.

Because it wasn't Yancy's usual night for playing poker, the Men's Club was the last place Carlton looked.

Carlton barged into the room and said, "Medford, I want to see you outside. Now!"

"Deal me out, fellows." Yancy stood and followed Carlton out of the club. "Is something wrong?" he asked when Carlton came to an abrupt stop. Yancy had no trouble dodging Carlton's fist. "I don't know what you're so damn mad about, but calm down and let's talk it over 'cause the next time you swing at me I'm going to knock the hell out of you!"

Carlton's shoulders slumped. "Why did you do it? Was it the gentlemanly side of you that said you should marry her now?"

"I don't have the vaguest idea what you're talking about, but obviously it has to do with April. What's she done now?"

"She said you've been bedding her, damn it! That wasn't part of our bet!"

Yancy rubbed the back of his neck. "It's not true, Carlton."

"Are you calling my sister a liar?"

"You're damn right I am. And don't think it's been easy keeping my hands off her. Let's go to your house and I'll make her tell the truth."

Carlton straightened the front of his frock coat. "You won't be seeing her again. The wedding's off."

"So you're going to let her outfox you? Don't do it, Carlton. Don't allow her to talk herself out of this."

"It's too late. She's left."

"Where is she?" Yancy's words were soft but deadly.

"Ruth promised she'd keep it from you, and I'm not convinced you're telling the truth."

Yancy combed his fingers through his thick black hair. "Damn it, Ruth's not telling me, you are. Can't you see April loves me and is running scared? Now I don't want to do it, Carlton, but so help me, you're not leaving until I find out where April is."

"Do you love her?"

"I would never have agreed to marry her if I didn't!"

Carlton told Yancy where April was and how to get there.

"Just out of curiosity," Carlton called as Yancy started back into the club, "what happened? Frankly, the way she's been acting since her return from Europe I can't picture any man loving her."

Yancy slowly turned, a devilish grin spread across his face. "I like her spirit." He went inside to collect his money.

Carlton scratched the back of his head. "Damn," he muttered. "Ruth's going to be mad as hell."

"You know what a charmer Yancy can be," Ruth said, still angry at her husband. "He could convince anyone a black table is white. If April was telling the truth, you will regret your decision until your dying day."

Carlton climbed into bed and pulled his wife close to him. "You're right, of course, but there was a look on Yancy's face I've never seen before. I believed him."

It was late afternoon when April put on her fleece-lined coat and went outside to collect firewood. She inhaled deeply, enjoying the sweet smell of pine. When her arms were full of chopped wood, she gazed out over the small lake glistening in the waning sunlight. Seeing a raccoon swim to shore, she stood very still. The fat animal shook his body and rivulets of water danced in the air. Taking his time, he proceeded on his way.

April felt saddened. Why couldn't she be like the raccoon and have no worries? In a little more than a week it would be Christmas. It had always been her favorite time of the year and she'd looked forward to spending this one with her family. She'd even forgotten to tell Ruth about the wrapped presents under her bed.

April looked back toward the house. Though she'd always loved it here, the log house was too big for one person. It only served to increase her loneliness.

A horse's whinny suddenly broke the silence. Startled, April jerked around. No more than fifty feet away, Yancy sat atop his mount, watching her. The thunderous look on his face spoke volumes. April dropped her armload of wood and bolted toward the house.

Yancy kicked the stallion in the ribs and the animal leaped forward, successfully blocking April's path. With the ease of a man who had spent years in the saddle, Yancy slowly dismounted.

Seeing she could no longer get to the house, April changed direction. I can make it to the boat, she told herself as she ran for the dock.

Yancy took off after her. April was nearing the end of the short dock when he made a flying tackle, sending them both plunging into the water.

The icy water wasn't deep, and once April managed to get her footing, she attacked Yancy with a fervor that took him completely off guard. She beat, clawed and bit. He kept trying to grab hold of her, but she was wet and slippery. Finally he managed to get behind her. Placing his hand on her chin he pulled her backward, making her immobile. April attempted to twist free, but his hand placed on her back kept her afloat. When they'd drifted into deep water, he turned her loose.

Satisfied she could swim, Yancy headed back for the bank. Long, powerful strokes easily carried him to shore well ahead of April. He stood on dry land, angry and waiting, puddles quickly forming around his feet.

Because of her coat, skirts and boots, April was exhausted when she finally managed to pull herself out of the water and collapse on the ground. Gasping for breath, she had no way of preventing Yancy from picking her up in his arms and heading for the house.

By the time they were inside, April's teeth were chattering. None too gently Yancy placed her on the floor in front of the fireplace. He left and a moment later returned with a blanket and tossed it at her. "Get out of those wet clothes," he ordered.

After starting a fire, he went outside for more wood. When he returned, April was still where he'd left her. The blanket was around her shoulders and she'd removed her coat, but nothing else. "I told you to get those wet clothes off." He dropped the wood in the bin.

"I'll not take a stitch off as long as you remain in this house!" April had a hard time getting the words out, but she knew they were clear enough for him to understand.

Yancy stood over her like an avenging devil. "Then if I have to, I'll remove them for you." He leaned down and pulled off her boots, the water from inside spilling onto the braided rug. "Believe me, I am in no mood for an argument. Which is it going to be?"

"You . . . you can't expect me to undress in front of you!"

"I'm going back outside to get my gear and put my horse up. When I return, I want to see you dry."

April was shivering and her body was covered with goose bumps, but the moment Yancy left the house she jumped to her feet. Her heavy, wet clothes slowed her progress as she tried to hurry toward the door. Finally reaching it, she shoved the bar across so he couldn't come back in. "There," she said through chattering teeth. "That will teach you you're not welcome!"

When Yancy discovered he couldn't open the heavy door, he was furious. The air was already crisp and a breeze was now coming off the lake. He went back to the barn, stripped and dried off with a blanket. Then he pulled a change of clothes from his saddlebag. With dry clothes on, he felt considerably warmer, but still angry as hell. So help him God, one way or another this was going to be settled tonight!

He headed back to the house, and without missing a step, raised his foot and jammed it hard against the door. He heard wood splinter on the other side.

April was still dressing by the warm fireplace when she heard the hard thud. She grabbed the blanket from the floor and held it up to her, her eyes growing larger with each additional thump. In a state of disbelief, she watched the wooden catch give way. The door flew open, and Yancy's big frame filled the doorway. Panic consumed her. Too late, she thought of the rifle in her bedroom. He was already headed in her direction.

Yancy yanked the blanket from April's grasp. "You've got a hell of a lot of explaining to do, lady!"

April glanced at the bedroom door.

"Don't try it. You're not fast enough." Yancy jerked her to him.

Dressed only in her chemise and pantalettes, April could feel her breasts being crushed against his hard chest. She struggled, but when his hand twisted in her wet hair, she was forced to be still.

"I told you I would have you in my bed, and the time has come to settle up."

April gasped. "No! You can't do this!"

"The hell I can't."

His lips came down on hers, hard and punishing. April couldn't breathe. At last he released her hair, ending the cruel kiss.

Yancy kept a strong arm wrapped around April, preventing her from going anywhere. With a quick yank, he ripped her chemise, freeing a firm, ripe breast. He cupped it in his hand, his fingers toying with the taut nipple.

"Please, Yancy, don't do this," April begged. She was frightened, but at the same time her body was reacting with shivers of delight.

"Why not?" he growled, still manipulating the sensitive area. "According to your brother, I've already spent hours indulging my carnal lust. I might as well enjoy what I've been accused of. Did you also say you're pregnant to get more sympathy?"

"I—"

"Why did you run away? Afraid of what you were starting to feel for me?"

"I warned you I would if you didn't call off the wedding." She tried removing his hand. He grabbed her wrist and pulled it behind her.

"What if I said I was in love with you?"

"I wouldn't believe you. You've never shown the least affection."

"If it's affection you want..." He leaned down and suckled her breast. Hearing April moan with pleasure, he trailed his tongue back up to her lips. "Do you have any idea how difficult it has been for me to keep my hands off you?" he asked, his lips practically touching hers. "Or how many times I've thought about carrying you off on one of my ships and spending weeks doing nothing but making love?"

"No...no, I had no idea." Just the thought of it made April's knees weak.

Yancy leaned down and picked her up in his arms.

"Don't make me do this," April whispered, hating her own words.

"Give me one good reason why not? And don't say you don't want me, because I know better."

"Because I don't love you."

"The hell you don't. You're just too damn stubborn to admit it to yourself!" He entered the bedroom, then dropped her on the bed. "All right, April, this one time I'm going to let you have your way. But mark my words, you'll come to regret your decision. Get dressed." He turned and left the room.

April slowly climbed off the bed, already sorry she had stopped Yancy. Why hadn't she just admitted she wanted him? She started getting dressed. In all fairness, she couldn't say she didn't deserve the treatment she'd received. Yancy had proved too many times that what she gave she would receive, so she had known what was coming. That was one of the reasons she'd made Ruth promise not to tell him her whereabouts.

Dressed, April left the bedroom. She was going to have to be very careful of what she said, because if there was a recurrence of what had just happened, she would lose her maidenhood. Yancy wouldn't stop the second time.

April found Yancy standing by the fireplace. She could tell he was studying her as she moved forward. For the first time she noticed the stubble of a beard. "Would you like something to eat?" she asked meekly.

"I believe I've come up with a reasonable solution to our problem," he stated flatly. "I think it's important we at least get to know each other. With people around most of the time, we haven't had the opportunity. You say you don't want to marry me, and I need to decide if I really want to marry you."

"What?" April sputtered. "You make it sound as though I'm not good enough for you."

"You have to admit you're a bit of a shrew."

"I'm no such thing! It's just you who makes me that way."

"Not according to Carlton." He moved toward the kitchen. "As a matter of fact, I would like something to eat. I'm always hungry after a swim."

April followed. "Just a minute. You can't make a statement like that and walk away."

He stopped and turned. "I'll tell you what. Why don't we make a pact? I'll stay for one week. During that time there will be no lies, no tricks, and we'll treat each other with honest consideration. After that time, you're free to do as you please.''

"You'll leave me alone after that?''

"I had already decided to move back to New Orleans, so you'll never have to worry about seeing me again.''

"You're not trying to trick me?'' she asked suspiciously.

Yancy shook his head.

"It's a deal.''

"Good. I'll repair the door while you get us some supper.''

At first April wasn't sure about their arrangement, but as the evening progressed, she began to feel more comfortable. After supper they sat by the fire and Yancy told her about some of the trouble he'd gotten into as a child. April laughed at his escapades, and in turn told him about some of her childhood. She was sorry when Yancy wanted to call it a night, saying he'd put in a hard two-day ride.

She grinned and teasingly said, "And a swim as well.''

Yancy laughed. "And that, too. Which bedroom should I take?''

"The one to the left.''

"Good night, April.''

"Good night, Yancy.''

April felt almost giddy when she went to her own room. In a week, she'd be free again. Surprisingly, she'd actually enjoyed Yancy's company tonight. It also felt good to have someone else in the house.

She might have felt differently had she seen the smile on Yancy's face as he closed his bedroom door behind him.

Chapter Seven

The delicious aroma of coffee woke April. She stretched lazily, then hopped out of bed. Last night she'd had such a wonderful dream about Yancy making love to her. Her skin became sensitive just from the remembering. "Foolish woman," she scolded herself. She hurried with her toilet.

April didn't see Yancy in the house. She poured herself a cup of coffee while looking at his open bedroom door. She was deliberating whether he was in there when she heard the sound of wood being chopped. She strolled to the front door and opened it. What she saw caused her to stop breathing. The man wielding the ax was stripped to the waist. April knew Yancy was strong, but she'd had no idea just how magnificent his body was. Hard, powerful muscles rippled as he brought down the ax on a log, splitting it perfectly. The mat of hair on his chest tapered down to a flat stomach and disappeared beneath the waist of his jeans. He'd even shaved. She'd noticed last night how different he looked in jeans and a shirt with the sleeves rolled up, exposing strong forearms. He'd brought his gun and holster into the house to dry, and in many ways April was reminded of the books she'd read about men of the West. Regaining her composure, she headed in his direction.

"Good morning," she greeted. Now that she was closer she could see the perspiration on his broad chest.

"Good morning," he replied, resting the ax on the ground.

"I think you can stop now. There's more than enough firewood."

"I'm enjoying the exercise." He gave her an ornery grin. "Excuse my lack of dress."

"Carlton always took his shirt off when he chopped wood." But he never looked anything like you, she thought. She sat on one of the tipped logs and sipped her coffee. "I wouldn't have thought you'd know how to chop wood." Yancy's deep laugh caused her to smile.

"I can assure you, there's little I haven't done at one time or another."

"Yancy, if we're going to do this right, I want to offer my apology for the lies I told to Ruth."

Yancy found it hard to believe what he'd just heard. "Does that mean you're not fixing to have a baby?" he teased.

Relieved, April laughed. "I didn't tell her that."

As the days passed, April and Yancy took long rides, hunted for game, fished and talked a great deal. At other times they just sat in comfortable silence. Though she hated to admit it, April deeply regretted that Yancy now kept his distance. He didn't even try to kiss her. The nights were the worst, especially when she would lie in bed and remember quite vividly how excited she'd felt when he placed his hands on her body. Her woman's intuition was telling her he'd be a marvelous lover.

Yancy wasn't the least displeased with the way things were going. When April didn't think he was looking, he could see the desire on her face, and when she talked and laughed with him, he saw love growing. But damn if she wasn't a stubborn minx.

On the fifth day, snowflakes began to fall. April ran outside and whirled happily. "Isn't this wonderful?" she said to Yancy, who was standing in the doorway. "Aren't you going to join me?"

He disappeared, then returned with two coats. "Put this on," he said with a big grin, handing her a coat. "You'll catch your death."

"Do you think it will snow enough to make a snowman?" Yancy kept walking toward the barn. "Yancy? Where are you going?"

"It's a surprise," he called. When he came back out, he was on his horse.

April sobered. "Are you leaving?" she asked.

"I'll be back shortly. How about having some hot coffee ready."

April watched him ride off, not sure what to think. Starting to get cold, she went back inside.

The coffee was long since ready. In order to pass the time, April tidied up her bedroom. When she heard the door open and close, she hurried to the front room.

Yancy held out a small, perfectly shaped pine tree. "Since it's almost Christmas, it doesn't seem right not to have a tree."

April clapped her hands in glee. "I have ribbons I can tie on it." Without thinking, she ran to him and hugged his waist. "What a wonderful idea." She looked up and saw how dark his eyes had become. She was sure he would at last kiss her. To her disappointment he just smiled and said, "Do you have that coffee ready?"

"Ah...yes. I do." She took her arms away, suddenly feeling uncomfortable. "Where shall we put the tree?"

"How about on the table by the sofa? I'll get something to stand it on. It's turning cold as hell."

"I'll pour your coffee."

By the time Yancy returned, April had collected herself. But there was now a tension between them that couldn't be denied.

April brought out her ribbons, and to her delight, Yancy's coat pockets were filled with round red berries he'd found, as well as some small pinecones. The atmosphere relaxed somewhat when they began working diligently on their creation. April gave Yancy a needle and thread she'd found in one of the cupboards, and while he strung berries, she tied bows on the branches. They laughed and teased, and April accused him of throwing more berries at her than he was stringing.

When they were finished, they stood back and admired their handiwork.

"It has to be the most beautiful tree I've ever seen," April said softly. "Thank you, Yancy."

"I thought you would like it. Christmas has always been my favorite time of the year."

"You know—" She turned to look at him and the tension returned.

"You're making it hard as hell for me, April Simpson," he said, his voice husky.

April swallowed hard. "Well, surely one kiss wouldn't do any harm."

"You're wrong. One kiss is all I need to carry you to the bedroom. Is that what you want?"

April lowered her head. "Yes," she muttered.

"I didn't hear what you said."

She raised her head, chin tilted. "I said no."

"We agreed, no lies." He placed his large hands on her cheeks and gently brushed his thumb across her full lips. "Why do you fight me, April?"

"Yancy, the one thing I have to offer the man I marry is my virginity. It's something I feel very strongly about."

Yancy laughed. "Then you won't deny you want me."

"Oh! You are impossible." She jerked away, the spell broken. "I'm going to fix supper."

He grabbed her arm and spun her back around. "Marry me, and then there'll be no problem."

"Have you decided now that I'm good enough for you?" April challenged angrily.

"You are absolutely the only woman I know who gets mad when a man asks her to marry him. Hell, forget I even mentioned it."

"In two days I will!"

"You should have taken me up on the offer. Somewhere deep inside your head you know you want a man, not some namby-pamby. You're a strong woman, and you need a strong man by your side. A man who can keep that fire in you alive."

"And you expect me to believe I could be happy with you? Am I also supposed to believe that after all the stories I've heard about your reputation, you would be faithful? Don't take me for that big a fool. And what about love, Yancy?"

"Damn it, haven't you realized by now that I love you?"

"You'll do anything to get what you want, won't you? How many women have you told that to? No, Yancy, I don't believe you." She turned and went to her room, slamming the door behind her.

Yancy ended up fixing his own supper. April never came out of her room.

For a long time, Yancy sat thinking, staring at April's closed door. He knew that if he made love to her she'd be his forever, and it took all his strength to keep from going over and breaking the damn door down. But her statement about wanting to save herself for her husband had had a strong effect on him. "You haven't won the last round, April Simpson," he muttered. "I don't give up that easy."

The next day April could practically hear the air between them crackle. Their happy coexistence had ended. She said little to him, and he said little to her. Yancy will be leaving tomorrow, she told herself, and good riddance.

To her, the day seemed to crawl by. Yancy spent a good deal of the time outside in the cold, which should have helped, but didn't. She could only assume he was taking care of the horses or getting his gear ready to head back to San Diego. April found herself glancing toward the Christmas tree quite often. No matter how she felt toward Yancy, she still thought their tree was beautiful.

That night they sat by the fireplace with nothing left to say. Yancy went to bed first.

Having had little rest, April was up early. Even so, Yancy had already risen, and his horse stood saddled out front.

"I'll cook you something," she said when he came out of his room. He carried a bedroll under one arm and his saddlebags over his shoulder. "You can't travel on an empty stomach."

"I'd appreciate that."

While Yancy went out to tie down his gear, April tossed kindling in the stove and started a fire. By the time Yancy returned she was already cooking flapjacks and had meat sizzling in a pan.

Yancy sat at the table and stretched his long legs. "I've been meaning to ask. Where did you learn to cook?"

"My mother taught me, then when I was in France I liked the food so much I decided to go to a cooking school."

"A woman of many accomplishments."

"None of which are of much use," she said honestly.

You've changed, April Simpson, Yancy thought. You've grown into a full-fledged woman. Or maybe the clothes she wore and being in the middle of nowhere brought out the best in her. No, he decided, the haughty woman of old was gone forever.

April set the plate of food in front of him, then handed him a knife and fork. She filled her plate and joined him.

Yancy smiled. "You know, we should have given that bastard son of ours a proper name."

At first April didn't know what he was talking about. She broke out laughing. "Yes, I guess we should have."

When Yancy had finished his food, he stood. "Guess I'd better be on my way."

"I'll go out with you."

April walked with him to his horse.

Yancy untied the reins and stood looking down at April. "Do I get a final kiss goodbye?"

April could see a twinkle in his eyes. "Is it safe?" she asked.

Yancy grinned. "It's safe."

April went to him, and he placed his arms around her. The kiss was long and tender. "April," he said when he pulled away, "I want you to do me a favor."

April was having a hard time regaining her composure. From the very beginning, Yancy's kisses had had that effect on her. "What?" she finally said.

"I don't want you to say a word, I just want you to listen. Then after I've left, I want you to think about what I've said."

"All right."

"I once said I'd tell you why I wanted to marry you. The answer is very simple. I've fallen hopelessly in love with you. I've shown that love in many different ways, all of which you've chosen to ignore. Everything in me says you love me, too, so I want you to consider a few things. I won't deny that I've known a lot of women over the years, and I could have easily married a good many of them.

"Taking all that to be the truth, why would I spend so much time trying to get you to the altar? Certainly not for lack of women. And why would I ride all the way up here so you could have time to get to know me? Because you said I slept with you? Hardly. And last but not least, why didn't I make love to you when I knew of your desire? Just think about it. You're free of me, April. Forever. And I keep my word." He gently pushed her back, and mounted. Turning his horse around, he rode off.

Two days later, April headed back to town. There was no longer any reason to stay. Besides, she found the place to be unbearably lonesome since Yancy's departure. Why wasn't she happy? She'd tried not to think about what Yancy had said, but his words kept haunting her. Everything he'd said bore truth.

It was turning dark by the time April reached home. Ruth was so relieved to see her sister-in-law, she was sure she would faint.

"Oh, my dear," Ruth asked worriedly when they were in April's room, "are you all right?"

"I'm fine," April replied kindly.

"I can't tell you how sorry I am that Carlton told Yancy where to find you."

"It's nothing to worry about. You shouldn't be apologizing. I should be the one doing that. Ruth, I lied about Yancy making love to me."

"Oh thank heavens! Then he didn't—"

"No."

"Carlton told me Yancy is back in town, and that the wedding is off. I've heard he's selling his house."

April felt as though a knife had just pierced her heart. In order to hide her emotions, she began removing her dirty clothes. "Has he left town yet?" April tried sounding unconcerned. She really hadn't believed Yancy would leave. She had been so sure it was all a ruse.

"Not that I know of. Carlton did say something about him returning to New Orleans."

"If you don't mind, Ruth, I would really like to take a bath and clean up."

"Of course you would. How thoughtless of me. I'll have water sent up immediately." She started to leave, then stopped. "April, are you sure you're all right?"

"Yes. Why do you ask?"

"I don't know, you seem different. It must be my imagination."

Dressed in crisp, clean clothes, April felt considerably better. Still, she couldn't seem to shake the heavy cloud that hung over her. She collected some of her Christmas gifts and went downstairs.

The tree in the salon reached the ceiling and was covered with beautiful decorations. There were already many presents beneath it, all in gaily wrapped packages. April added hers, and as she stood, her gaze fell on one decoration in particular. It was silver, and she recognized it immediately. Her father had given it to her years ago. They had had little money then, but he'd bought it for her because it was shiny and she liked it. Then he'd hung it on the sagebrush that had served as their Christmas tree.

The memory made April think of the tree in the mountains that she and Yancy had decorated. She'd left it there, not having the heart to take it down.

"April?"

Seeing Carlton, she ran into his arms.

"It's so good to have you back with us."

"It's good to be back."

"Are you hungry? Supper's ready."

"Not really, but I'll join you."

They walked to the dining room, arm in arm.

April spent the next day delivering Christmas gifts to friends. Her last stop was at Mary Broom's house. To April's delight, Mary had finally delivered her baby. It was a beautiful strapping boy, and Paul Broom was the perfect proud papa. April held the baby and couldn't stop playing with his tiny hands. He started fussing and she had to hand him back to Mary. Paul left the room and Mary breast-fed her son.

"April," Mary said, "I've heard so many rumors floating around. First that you and Yancy were to be married, then just today I was told he's leaving town. Does that mean the wedding is off?"

"Yes . . . I mean no."

"Well, it has to be one or the other."

April looked at the baby now sleeping peacefully in Mary's arms. "I haven't made up my mind."

"Do you love him?"

April stood. "I'm sorry, Mary, but I really must go. I still have so many presents to deliver. I'll come back in a few days and we can talk." She hurried out of the house.

April went straight home. She found Ruth in the kitchen supervising the desserts for tomorrow's Christmas dinner. The day that April was to have been married.

"Ruth, have I received any messages or anything from Yancy?"

"No, not that I'm aware of. Oh yes. He gave Carlton a Christmas gift for you."

"Where is it?" April asked anxiously.

"Under the tree somewhere. But we're not supposed to open our gifts until tonight."

"Please, Ruth, come help me find it."

It took some searching before Ruth handed over the package. "I'm glad I remembered the wrapping."

April tore off the paper and discovered a round glass ball. Inside was a tiny cabin, and a man stood in the snow with his hand raised as if saying goodbye. When April shook it, snow fell all about. Tears came to her eyes.

"April. What's the matter?"

April sank down on a chair. "Damn it, Ruth, I love him!"

Ruth started to say something about April's cursing, but thought better of it. She smiled instead. "Being in love is supposed to make a woman happy, not sad."

"I've made such a mess of everything," April sobbed. "Now I may have lost him. He knew! He knew all along, but I was too addle-brained to see it."

"Come, come. It can't be all that bad. Does he love you?"

"I think so."

"You think so?" Ruth handed her a handkerchief.

April wiped her eyes, remembering what Yancy had told her. "Yes." She laughed. "I know he does. Ruth, I have to find him before he leaves town."

"Well, I know for a fact he hasn't left yet. I'll have Carlton look for him tomorrow."

"But I have to see him now! Don't you see? I have to tell him I love him!"

"You've waited this long, you can wait until tomorrow."

The evening was spent opening presents and April tried to appear cheerful. As lovely as her gifts were, she thought only of the one Yancy had given her.

April fretted all night. What if Yancy had left? She'd never be able to find him. And what if he'd changed his mind about marrying her? She kept telling herself over and over again what a fool she had been. She'd turned up her nose at the only man who could ever make her happy.

The next morning, Carlton and Ruth talked her into going to church with them. Ruth even insisted she put on the new dress they'd given her for Christmas. It was a beautiful white gown, and April normally would have been overjoyed to have such a lovely garment, but today she couldn't muster any enthusiasm. Carlton should be looking for Yancy, not going to church—even if it was Christmas Day!

"My dear," Ruth said when she saw April descending the stairs, "you look absolutely beautiful. There's another gift for you. Yancy gave it to me before he left to join you in the mountains. He said I wasn't to give it to you until today."

April removed the paper and opened the small box. Nestled inside was the most beautiful emerald and diamond ring she'd ever seen in her entire life. She knew it had to have cost a fortune. Apparently he had expected her to marry him before he left. She was surprised he hadn't taken it back when he returned to San Diego from the country.

When they stepped out of the carriage, April paid little attention to her surroundings. The church bell was ringing and happy people greeted them. Everyone seemed in a Christmas spirit, except her. Suddenly April heard a familiar voice call out, "I understand there is to be a wedding here today."

April looked up and saw Yancy standing a short distance away, a wide grin spread across his handsome face. Her heart stopped beating as she stared in disbelief.

"What do you say we give our son an honest name?" Yancy asked.

People standing around looked at him in shock.

"You mean you're going to let me make you an honest man?" April called back, not caring what anyone thought.

Yancy laughed. "You can try."

Laughing, April picked up her gown and ran to him.

"Thank heavens she never found out about that bet between you and Yancy," Ruth told her husband.

"She will, but not until after they're married. I'll let Yancy tell her."

"When are you going to give them their wedding present?"

"This afternoon. I really hate to part with that stallion and mare, but they're the ones who should own them."

Watching the happy couple kissing, Ruth smiled. "I never really thought it would end this way. Did you?"

"Absolutely."

Ruth knew better.

"Oh Yancy," April said, tears streaming down her cheeks, "I was afraid you had left for New Orleans."

"I plan to, but with my wife at my side. We'll build a grand home. Naturally I expect you to help design it the way you want, but we shall sleep in the same bed. Shall we go in the church? The preacher's waiting."

April was shocked. "You mean you planned all this?"

"I told you, I'm a man of my word."

"I have half a notion to just turn around and leave."

Yancy could clearly see love in her beautiful green eyes. "Tell me you love me, April."

"I'll love you until my dying day."

He leaned down and kissed her. "Merry Christmas, my love." He offered her his arm.

* * * * *

A Note from DeLoras Scott

It was freezing cold outside, the ground icy, but the sky was as clear as a summer's day. Having come all the way by train from Southern California with my mother to spend Christmas in Oklahoma with my grandmother, aunts and uncles, I knew my dreams of a white Christmas were surely doomed. I was seven years old, and what I had looked forward to just wasn't going to happen.

When I awoke Christmas morning, I was convinced that the good Lord had performed a miracle just for me, because a blanket of snow covered the ground and big, light snowflakes were still falling. Presents were opened, breakfast eaten, but all I could think about was getting outside. Finally the time came and, after my uncle put his foot down about me going out in my bathing suit, I was properly bundled in warm clothing.

John, my uncle, brought the car out, and a long sled was tied on with rope to the back. My mother, two aunts and an uncle climbed onto the sled, but I was relegated to sitting in the car beside John. Nevertheless, I could look out the back window, as there were no seat belts then. The country road we pulled out onto was narrow and snow-packed. John soon had the car moving at what I considered a fast speed, much to the delight of the people he was towing. When he turned curves, the sled veered off to the side and up the snowbanks on more than one occasion, leaving its passengers behind. I squealed with laughter at seeing them covered from head to toe with snow and watching them again settle onto the sled as John put the car into gear. It was a marvelous outing, which ended with everyone pitching in to make a snowman.

All the playing in the crisp air had given me a ferocious appetite. When we went back inside, the smells of the food being cooked for our Christmas dinner wafted through the house. I asked how much longer it would be before we ate, and I received the usual, "Shortly," and was handed a carrot. But I hadn't failed to see the three mincemeat pies sitting off to the side.

I don't remember eating any of the Christmas dinner, and when dessert came around only two mincemeat pies were found. I had devoured the third one earlier, and to this day, I can't stand mincemeat. But the memories are sweet of a Christmas day long past.

TAKE A LESSON FROM RUTH LANGAN, BRONWYN WILLIAMS, LYNDA TRENT AND MARIANNE WILLMAN...

A *history* lesson! These and many more of your favorite authors are waiting to sweep you into the world of conquistadors and countesses, pioneers and pirates. In Harlequin Historicals, you'll rediscover the romance of the past, from the Great Crusades to the days of the Gibson girls, with four exciting, sensuous stories each month.

So pick up a Harlequin Historical and travel back in time with some of the best writers in romance.... Don't let history pass you by!

HG92

HARLEQUIN
Season's Greetings

Christmas cards from relatives and friends wishing you love and happiness. Twinkling lights in the nighttime sky. Christmas—the time for magic, dreams... and possibly destiny?

Harlequin American Romance brings you SEASON'S GREETINGS. When a magical, red-cheeked, white-haired postman delivers long-lost letters, the lives of four unsuspecting couples will change forever.

Don't miss the chance to experience the magic of Christmas with these special books, coming to you from American Romance in December.

#417 UNDER THE MISTLETOE
by Rebecca Flanders
#418 CHRISTMAS IN TOYLAND
by Julie Kistler
#419 AN ANGEL IN TIME
by Stella Cameron
#420 FOR AULD LANG SYNE
by Pamela Browning

Christmas—the season when wishes *do* come true....

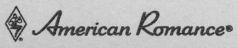
American Romance®

HARLEQUIN
Romance

A Christmas tradition...

Imagine spending Christmas in New
Orleans with a blind stranger and his aged
guide dog—when you're supposed to be
there on your honeymoon!
#3163 Every Kind of Heaven
by Bethany Campbell

Imagine spending Christmas with a man
you once "married"—in a mock ceremony
at the age of eight!
#3166 The Forgetful Bride
by Debbie Macomber

*Available in December 1991, wherever
Harlequin books are sold.*

RXM